With Best Wishes
The Author - Ian

THE PETT LEVEL LANDINGS

PAUL DAYRELL

PUBLISHED BY PAUL DAYRELL
FAIRLIGHT COVE ENGLAND
pauldayrell@sky.com

PUBLISHED BY PAUL DAYRELL
Fairlight Cove England

Copyright © Paul Dayrell 2014

Paul Dayrell asserts the moral right to be identified as the author of this Work, in accordance with the Copyright, Designs and Patents act 1988.

All rights reserved.
No part of this publication may be reproduced, stored in or introduced into a retrieval system, or transmitted, in any form or by any means
(electronic, mechanical, photocopying, recording or otherwise),
without the prior permission of the publisher. Any person who does any unauthorised act in relation to this publication may be liable to criminal prosecution and civil claims for damages.

Printed in Great Britain by:
Berforts Information Press.

23-25, Gunnels Wood Park,
Gunnels Wood Road,
Stevenage, Hertfordshire.
Tel. 01483 312777

ISBN 978-0-9928254-0-9

THE PETT LEVEL LANDINGS

Preface.

Have you ever wondered about the large number of commando raids that British forces undertook during the Second World War? There are many well documented sorties on strategic targets, all aimed at either disrupting or confusing the enemy, or at possibly shortening the war.

How strange then, that there were no 'officially recorded' commando raids by the Germans, onto British soil. If there were, they are still the subject of government secrecy, and may stay that way forever. One thing is true. Any such raids would have been completely 'whitewashed', on the orders of Winston Churchill, for fear that their recognition and acknowledgement would evoke widespread panic.

This story however, tells of two such raids, launched in the build up to Adolf Hitler's planned invasion of Britain, codenamed 'Operation Sealion.' Did these raids take place?

Here are some interesting true facts.

There are people still living in Pett Level, who recall a German submarine emerging from the channel and shelling a house on the cliff top, half way between Fairlight and Pett Level. Tongs House stands defiantly on the cliff top to this day. Thankfully, the swaying motion of the waves caused the deck gun of the submarine to be less than accurate. There is no official recognition that this event ever happened, *but it did.*

There is a pond still visible from the cliff path, some twenty feet below the cliff top. This is an extremely unusual feature for the side of a cliff. Some say that this is a crater formed by one of the stray shells. The targeted house was allegedly used to operate Bombe, the Enigma decoding machine, invented by Alan Turing. This was having a devastating effect on the German submarine fleet, because most of their communications were being intercepted and deciphered.

At the time of writing, there are still a few surviving local members of the '203rd battalion'. They will never tell you who they are and they will take their secrets to the grave. These men were the south's secret defensive army, and one of three 'non existent' auxiliary battalions across the country. These men were all recruited on Churchill's orders. Some were already members of the Home Guard and were often approached without the knowledge of their commanding officers. Others were recruited because they had reason to be out and about at night, such as doctors, farmers, gamekeepers etc. Each local unit consisted of up to seven men.

These men were also chosen for their standing in society, or their knowledge of the local countryside. They were all made to sign the official secrets act and even their close families were not aware of their role. They were trained secretly in all the skills of guerrilla warfare. Informally, they were known as 'The Ministry of un-gentlemanly Warfare'. Should an invasion have taken place, assisted by the home guard, they would collect their hidden weaponry, and harass the enemy from behind, thus slowing their advance inland. They were capable of destroying railway tunnels, river banks, bridges and anything that would have otherwise afforded the enemy an easy passage. They were also charged with the killing of as many German officers as possible.

These men were the keepers of large arsenals of weapons, hidden deep in the countryside. Old mineshafts, caves, cellars or hand built hideouts, were utilised. Although many were destroyed, there are still some long forgotten caches of rusting weapons hidden deep beneath the countryside of East Sussex, and indeed the whole of Britain. There are no maps or written directions available, just the fading memories of the few men left.

The cellar of a local house has a hidden passageway where arms were stored. There are also steel bunks there for six men, who would simply disappear and wait, should a successful invasion have occurred.

I personally knew a man, an officer in the RAF, who was ordered to drive a London bus down from Whitehall. His mission was to collect the bodies of 'about ten' badly burnt German soldiers, found in the sea in the Rye Bay area. The bodies were laid on the lower floor of the bus and driven back to RAF Northolt. Why a bus and not a military vehicle, he didn't know. He also never knew why he had to do this, or what happened to the bodies. There was never any official announcement regarding this incident. To this day there has never been any government recognition of these events although it appears that this was not an isolated case.

There were many fake gun emplacements, sited all along the South Coast. Usually these consisted of a section of telegraph pole, cut to the length of a gun, resting on a semi circle of sand bags, to give the impression from the air, of an area heavily fortified. German spotter planes reported back that there were gun emplacements every couple of hundred metres, defending the entire English coast line.

Pett Level's fields were mined, as well as having deep trenches cut into them, and then flooded, by breaching the sea wall. Millions of gallons of water ran across the level as far inland as the natural hill line, which then formed a containing bank. For the purposes of enhancing this story, I have indulged in a spot of poetic licence, and slightly exaggerated the degree of flooding, beyond the marsh land.

Even without my straying slightly from the original geographical limits of this man made lake, it would have been very difficult terrain to cross and would have slowed up any advance even when the round concrete tank traps which lined the beaches had been breached. Behind the level is a range of hills that would have formed an ideal natural emplacement for a British defending force to operate from. These hills formed the original shoreline, in the days when Winchelsea and Rye were sea ports.

During the war, there were approximately three hundred soldiers, including many Canadians, stationed at the two storey coastal battery and observation post, sitting on top of Toot Rock. The structures have deteriorated over the years, but everything is still accessible, with the exception of the two large Bofors guns, and the shell storage facility set to the East of the observation post. This is now a private dwelling, but evidence of another gun's mountings, is still visible on the house's seaward facing patio. This, according to the owner, was a six inch gun, brought back from Turkey, and set up there. The walls of this house are about a metre thick in places, indicating that the original fortifications would have been almost impenetrable.

Although all now privately owned, the Coastguard cottages were requisitioned by the military as accommodation for the defending troops stationed at Toot Rock. The last house, at the bottom of the lane, was where the officers were billeted. It is today still known as 'The Officer's House', and has an interesting look-out over Pett Level on the top floor.

There was one 'pillbox' style gun emplacement, on the beach at Pett Level, to the side of Cliff End. This has long since been undermined and eroded by the sea, although parts of it are incorporated into the current sea defences starting at Cliff End, along with fragments of the old anti-tank pillars. Another one however, is still standing and fairly accessible, at the far end of the lane leading up to the old coastguard cottages at Toot Rock, just the other side of the royal Military Canal. These two fortified buildings would have formed the initial outer defences against a land attack. Nearby to the lower pillbox, is a bunker that has been concealed by undergrowth and bracken for many years. This particular bunker was for the protection of the officers, in the event of an air attack.

All of the above are true facts. *

The following points add substance to the tale……….

The story of the Pett Level landings, demonstrates the inability of Hastings Police to observe basic evidence, coupled with the Army's failure to properly investigate the breached security at Tongs house. These failings allowed the first and second wave of German troops to settle undiscovered in Beckley Woods. Also, the coroner's report on the murdered Corporal Jenkins was a work of incompetence, having missed the actual cause of death.

Subsequently the British defending forces had fortune on their side, but not without some further horrific events, including the murder of a little boy and his dog. Initially the Rye police were baffled, but their forensic team dug deep and the real cause of death was uncovered. There were also the tragic and cruel killings of a farmer and his wife, and a young home guard. These deaths were followed by the brutal killing and rape of a local housewife. In total, six British people and a dog met their deaths, as a result of the brutality and ruthlessness of the invading force.

Is it possible that some three hundred British and Canadian troops could be made to sign 'The Official Secrets Act', retrospectively? What was the legality of the situation? Whatever it was, nobody ever disclosed the goings on at Toot Rock. Many locals suspected and talked about a cover up, but there was never any substantial evidence to be found.

The conclusion to the story sees the whole incident 'whitewashed' on Winston Churchill's orders, coupled with a gruesome propaganda coup, aimed as a direct warning, to Adolf Hitler.

On a summer's evening, stand on the roof of the sunken barrack room and look back towards the line of hills. Now take a 45 degree walk from the left hand corner about a dozen paces forward and stand on this spot. Look down at the large mound of earth, in front of you. I guarantee you will feel a shiver running down your spine. Well, the thirty four German soldiers had to be buried somewhere!

- *As mentioned above, I have been slightly imaginative regarding the extent of the flooding, as there are no maps or indications as to where the new banks were formed. Also it is worth mentioning here that during 1940, there were another few houses on the cliff top, in front of Tongs House, and the existing cliff path. They have long since fallen prey to cliff erosion, so for the story, I have chosen not to mention these. It does however appear that none of these were damaged by the shelling from the German submarine, either. We can only conclude that the majority of shells hit the cliff face, or flew over the top of the houses, falling into the fields nearby.*

Summary

I have lived in Fairlight Cove for the past thirty years. I have known the Pett Level area, since 1948. At the tender age of two my parents brought us down here from Wimbledon, on our first family holiday. We stayed in an old horse drawn bus, converted into a caravan, and named Thalassa. It has been renamed, but is still there along Chick Hill Brook, (as we knew it then). Sorry, for the local purists, I mean 'Marsham Sewer'.

I remember the long gone pillbox, on the beach at Cliff End. We used to change into our swimming trunks there. I remember the huge round anti tank traps. Out of the thousands, originally lining the entire beach, sadly only one of these is left intact, and a few fragments of the old pillbox, as mentioned earlier. These now form part of the sea defences at Cliff End.

If you live in the area of the landings, you may well be aware of some facts that my research, and personal memories, have missed. I would still be interested to hear them anyway. There could be another story. Please read this with an open mind.

I hope you enjoy it and at the end of the book, you can make your own decision as to whether these landings took place. Failing that, you can wait for the government to release the information in the year 2040. On the other hand, maybe they *never* will.

Sincerely   **Paul Dayrell**

STATEMENTS

1.
The characters in this story are completely fictional,* and any resemblance to persons living or dead, would be purely coincidental. The locations though, are all very real and may be explored by anybody wishing to learn more about the Pett Level Landings.

With the exception of Lou Parsons, who appears as himself aged 10 in this story. In my humble opinion, Lou is 'Mr. Pett Level'. As a child, Lou recalls dodging the guards posted next to The Market Stores, and salvaging many items from the beach, washed overboard from the huge amount of shipping that was sunk by the enemy. Thank you, Lou for your help and friendship. Also, for sharing your extensive local knowledge and contributing to this story. It seems that if I sell some copies of this book, I will owe you a few pale ales! The pleasure will be entirely mine.

2.
I have not made the German soldiers speak in mock Germanic tones. Everything is in English, although having personally spent many years working in the company of Germans, I have used their inflections, and tried to structure sentences in the way that they do.

3.
For the purists, I am aware that there are some anomalies in the text. For example, I am well aware that the German word for 'Devil,' is 'Teufel', and does not rhyme with 'Level'. This and others that you may spot are there for the sake of continuity. You are of course welcome to translate back into German and remake the text. Personally, I wouldn't bother, just enjoy the story!

4.
One final point, if I may. The cliff in front of Tongs House is, as far as I am concerned, virtually impossible to clime. It is composed of soft sandstone. Please do not attempt it. I do not want to be held responsible for injuries to anybody trying to emulate the feat that the Germans accomplished in 1940. They had the help of a professional mountaineer.

The local Coastguard cliff team, along with the crew of the Pett Level Rescue Boat, are kept busy enough, without having to retrieve the bodies of dead climbers from the beach.

Chapter 1

'Your train will be here in half an hour, you'd better get dressed.'
'I know love,' replied her husband, 'I don't want to go, though.'

Soon to be Private Hawkins, of the British army, reluctantly got out of bed. He knew full well that he couldn't miss his train. His call up papers had come through, 'requesting' that he report to Pirbright Barracks in Surrey, by 1600 hours, on Friday 26th April. The year is 1940.

Doleham Halt is a tiny hamlet in Sussex, not far from Guestling and Hastings. It is a couple of miles inland from Rye bay. Peter and his wife Faye had lived here for the last two years since their marriage. There is just one road running through Doleham, and their home is one of a small group of a dozen cottages, just up the hill from the railway station.

Peter Hawkins was a carpenter by trade, so there was no escaping the 'request' that their postman had thrust into his hand, four weeks earlier.

'Looks like you've been called up then,' said George cheerily, as Peter emerged bleary eyed from his door, tool bag and sandwiches in hand.

'Bugger it,' said Peter, 'Are you sure?'
'No mistaking this one,' replied George. 'I've delivered enough of these by now to know that's what it is. One bloke opened his and burst into tears when I gave it to him, big hard looking sod as well. You wouldn't have thought he was the type.'

'I sort of know how he feels,' replied Peter, 'I'm not a fighting man.'
'Well you'd better not let Adolf know that,' laughed George. 'Perhaps we can have a pint or two together before you leave?'

'You remembered to pack your razor?' asked Faye, now fussing around her husband. 'Course I have, love.'

'Then you'd best be on your way, I think I can hear the train coming.' One last kiss, then Peter sprinted down the hill to the station, clutching his brown case, leaving his wife with tears in her eyes. The four coach train rumbled into the station and Peter jumped in. He hadn't yet had time to think about the implications of leaving his home, his wife, his job. The four weeks had gone in a flash. He had informed his employer, Sid Carter from Icklesham that he had been called up. 'Carter's Carpentry won't be the same without you lad,' moaned Sid. 'Suppose I'll have to employ a youngster and train him up all over again.'

'Hopefully I won't be gone that long,' replied Peter. 'This war can't go on for ever, can it? Faye and I were talking about starting a family soon.'

Peter and Faye had visited relatives in Battle and Sedlescombe, to say goodbye. He had enjoyed a night of Worthington's best bitter and friendly banter, with George the postman, and a couple of work mates, down at the local inn. He was quite drunk when he got home.

Faye's parents had come for Sunday lunch last weekend, and her father, Ted had given Peter some helpful advice. He had been a soldier in the First World War, so had a bit of experience, having been gassed, as well as suffering a very nasty case of trench foot. He walked with a bit of a limp and Faye said that she had never seen her Father's bare feet. Her Mother May, told her that he had lost four toes, and didn't like people to see them, including her. Despite his experiences, he was a fit man.

'Never volunteer for anything, son.' Ted advised. 'Keep your head down under fire, and don't ever be too proud to surrender. Lastly son, always remember that in a war, the best seats are at the back.'

Taking on a more serious tone, he said, 'The main thing is to try and keep dry at all times. Oh and if you can keep your back warm, even if the rest of you is freezing, you should always stay fit and healthy.'

Peter had listened to this friendly advice and thanked Ted for his concern. He didn't take it too seriously, after all things were very different these days. With modern weapons, and with Winston Churchill running the war, we would soon get the better of 'Jerry.' We had beaten the Germans before, and we would do it again.

Sitting in the little compartment of the train, a terrible emptiness and feeling of insecurity overtook Peter. He had never been away from home before. He had lived with his parents in Three Oaks, until he met Faye White at the local village dance. They were engaged within six weeks, and married the next spring.

Sid had found them the little cottage at Doleham. He had heard that the previous occupants were going to rent a farm at Fairlight, and that it was becoming available at a very reasonable rent. He had been doing a small job for them, repairing a window frame, when they mentioned it. They told him to do a cheap repair to avoid the landlord, slapping a penalty on them for damage caused during their tenancy. They needed every penny if they were to make a go of things at Fairlight.

Peter and Faye could afford to pay the rent and the other bills, and eat well, and still have nearly ten shillings left over at the end of each week. Most of the time, they were able to save this, with the intention of having quite a nice little nest egg by the time their first baby came along.

'Thank God we haven't got any kids yet,' thought Peter as he sat moodily on the bumpy, jolting train. 'It isn't right to expect a woman to bring up kids by herself. Oh my God, what if I've made her pregnant in the last couple of weeks? We've been at it like rabbits ever since I got my call up papers.'

With this thought in mind, Peter's resolve hardened. 'If I've got to go and fight this bloody war, then I'm going to give it everything I've got. I will do my best to get it over with as quickly as possible so I can get back to normal life once again.'

The train rumbled on. 'Got to remember to change at Ashford, and then on into London,' he thought. 'God knows how I will find my way to Pirbright Barracks by four o'clock this afternoon though. The army is supposed to meet us at Brookwood station, so I must get my correct connection from Waterloo. Maybe there will be others like me, there.'

Back home, Faye had dried her eyes, and started busying around the cottage in an attempt to distract herself. She had similar thoughts about pregnancy. 'Mind you,' she thought, 'I haven't managed to fall during the last two years, so it would be unlikely that I have fallen now.'

With that comforting thought she carried on with her housework. She would make sure that the cottage was kept clean and tidy for when Peter came home again. She would busy herself with her sewing, which she did to make a little extra money, and by the time her husband returned, maybe they would have enough money for a deposit on a house of their own. They had a savings account with the Portman Building Society, which had been building up quite nicely over the last couple of years. 'Maybe I'll get another two or three hens and start selling the eggs as well,' she mused. 'All in all, once this blasted war is over, we are going to be quite nicely placed.'
Neither could have known it, but by a terrible twist of fate, Peter and Faye would never see each other in this life, again.

3

Chapter 2

'Heil Hitler!' shouted the Gruppenfuhrer at the seven smartly dressed 'SS' soldiers sitting in front of him. 'Heil Hitler,' they retorted as they jumped instinctively to their feet.

The men were startled. It was clear from his uniform, that they were being addressed by a Gruppenfuhrer, the Waffen SS equivalent of a Major General. They had been talking between themselves when the officer silently appeared in the room. The effect of his raised voice actually unsettled them.

'Good afternoon Gentlemen.' He now spoke quietly by contrast. 'My name is Gruppenfuhrer Zimmermann.'
'Good afternoon sir.' They replied. The officer standing before them was very striking. He stood about 1.9 metres tall. He removed his military cap and they saw that he was completely bald and had no eyebrows or lashes. There was a scar to his left cheek. He was probably about 35 years old.

'I will get straight to the point. You have all been chosen for a mission, which is of utmost importance to the Fuhrer, personally. Yesterday, I had a meeting with Heinrich Himmler, Von Rundstedt and The Fuhrer. Operation Sealion is imminent so, I don't need to remind you about security, you are all aware of the importance of keeping what we are about to discuss, absolutely top secret.'

He continued 'You do not even discuss with your wives, girlfriends, or close family, is that understood?'
'Yes Gruppenfuhrer,' was the collective response.

'I am here to take control of this mission, following the tragic accident that befell my predecessor during preparation training. You are not yet familiar with me or my methods, so I will explain first about what I require from my men at all times. I cannot stand dirt. You will always need to be pristine. There is never an excuse to be filthy, and I will personally punish any man who disobeys this order.' One man tried to conceal a slight smile. 'Please tell me what you find so amusing, soldier.'

'Sorry Gruppenfuhrer, but I was thinking about the times that we have to crawl through mud in order to surprise the enemy.'
'As a member of the Waffen SS you are aware that you must look like a professional, German soldier at all times. This unit is made up of men with different skills, but one skill must always be cleanliness. When we

have to crawl, we crawl. When the crawling is over there is always soap and water. Your boots will always be cleaned, mud or no mud. Is that clearly understood?'
'Yes Gruppenfuhrer.'
'Your fingernails will always be clean. Is that clearly understood?'
'Yes Gruppenfuhrer.'
'A dirty soldier is an undisciplined soldier. Please remember this, at all times Gentlemen. We cannot run the risk of any infections in the field.'
'Yes Gruppenfuhrer.'

'Now we come to what else I expect of you under my command. You may perhaps already be aware of my reputation. I require total and unconditional obedience at all times.'

The Gruppenfuhrer's eyes burned, as he continued. 'If I have to command you to run directly at an enemy machine gun post, then that is exactly what you will do. If I have to command you to dive into a raging torrent with all your equipment, then I expect you to come out on the other side, still in possession of your equipment. If you lose anything, then you go without it from then on. A soldier fighting without his killing knife or his rifle is not a pretty sight in the field of battle! In short Gentlemen, I expect absolute obedience and cleanliness at all times, whether we are in enemy territory or here in the barrack room.'

One or two of the group squirmed in their seats at the prospect of having Gruppenfuhrer Zimmermann as their commanding officer. Some had heard of him and that he was a disciplinarian of the old school, but hadn't realised that he had an unreasonable obsession with cleanliness as well.

'Now, if you are all happy, I will proceed. You all know the importance that the Fuhrer has placed on defeating Britain, and that swaggering cigar smoking bastard, Winston Churchill. For weeks, the Luftwaffe has been softening up the airfields and defences along the South Coast of England.

Before the mass landings can take place, we will be one of the expeditionary forces, required to prepare the area that we will be focussing our planned assault on. Other units will be operating similar strategies to ours.' The Gruppenfuhrer unfurled a large scale map depicting a small area of the South Coast of England, and clipped it to an easel at the side of the room. 'This area is known as Pett Level. For our purposes, this is the only area that we need to think about. Our tasks will be as follows. We have to assess the fortifications that sit here.' Zimmermann pointed with a well polished stick to an area of cliff just inland from the sea. 'Then we have to totally eliminate the fire power from these guns. It will not be easy, there are probably some three hundred soldiers stationed here, and pictures taken by our reconnaissance aircraft, show these fortifications,' again he pointed to the map, 'to be very well guarded on all sides. Also, the entire coast here is lined with solid concrete anti-tank traps, and it will be our job to create a large enough gap for Von Rundstedt's forces to advance through. In addition, the land has been deliberately flooded behind the sea wall, but we know that a road runs parallel to it which will enable our tanks to travel both Easterly direction, and West and eventually inland.

He stared hard at the group. 'Any questions so far?' The men stared back at their new commander but no-one spoke. They knew the mechanics of what they had to do. God knows they had trained hard enough for this mission. It was during this training that their old commander had been accidently killed. They had been on a training climb and a piton had pulled out of the soft sandstone rock face they were scaling, and two men fell to their deaths.

Generalleutnant Peschel was a more reasonable officer. His attitude was that if everybody did their job well, they could relax a little in his company. The men under his command really looked up to him and genuinely liked him. He was not the type of officer to ask his men to do anything that he would not be prepared to do himself.

Maybe Zimmermann read something in the faces of the men, or maybe it was just instinct. 'Your old commanding officer is dead. He died because he was sloppy in his command and he died because he was sloppy in the execution of his duty.'

'Excuse me, Gruppenfuhrer.' One soldier stood up, his face like thunder. 'In my opinion, Generalleutnant Peschel was a very fine officer, who gave his life trying to protect a fellow soldier.'

'To whom do I have the pleasure of speaking?' Zimmermann asked quite deliberately and coldly, his eyes like steel.
'Schmidt, Sir.'
'And what is your particular skill, Schmidt?' enquired the senior officer.
'Explosives, Sir.'
'Well Schmidt, It seems that you are no longer required for this mission. Guards!! Take this man away and leave him to rot in the cooler until well after our successful invasion of England.'

'Heil Hitler. Outside, wanker! Left right, left right, left right.' The guards marched Schmidt out of the room. All too late he was regretting his outburst. Everyone agreed with him, but no-one else dared speak out.

As if nothing had happened, Zimmermann continued his address. 'Thirdly, we have to find an area of land preferably around here,' again he pointed at an area on the map that was densely wooded, 'where a pre invasion force can be assembled without being detected. This area is known as Beckley Woods. It is the only wood large enough in the area to hide around forty men. It is about two and a half hours march across country from here.'

He continued, 'In short Gentlemen, we have to be able to bring ashore some additional thirty men, undetected. We then have to hide with them in the woods until the main invasion force arrives. It will be our job, along with these soldiers, to attack the enemy from the rear, while they will be desperately pre-occupied, trying to defend their shoreline.'

'These troops have been hand picked, like you, and are only from our regiment. They, like us, will be brought across the Channel, aboard u-boats, and finish the last mile or two in inflatables. We all must survive in our hideout without fires, and all of our food will be eaten cold. We will not carry torches. No-one will be able to smoke, however I don't believe that is an issue. We cannot risk being spotted during these few days, because it would totally compromise the whole of the operation.'

The Gruppenfuhrer took a deep breath. 'We have one final task, Gentlemen. We have received reports that a British decoding machine, known as Bombe, is operating from one of the houses here on the cliff top.' Zimmermann again pointed at the map with his highly polished stick.

'This machine appears to have been able to decode the Enigma coded messages between our submarines and has compromised many of our operations. Our signals team have pin-pointed this property, known as 'Tongs House', and we must either destroy the machine and kill the guards and operatives, or we will leave the task to the submarine commander, who will blast the house from the cliff top. Either way, it is essential that it is destroyed, to alleviate the risk to our invasion forces.'

'Any questions men?' demanded the Gruppenfuhrer.
'Just one sir,' said a soldier. 'Schmidt was our explosive expert and now it looks as if we will need a replacement.'

'I am also an expert with the explosives,' retorted Zimmermann. 'Before I joined the army, I was working at my Father's mining company. What we have to do here is extremely basic compared to the complexities of the commercial mining techniques.'

A tall, fair haired young man stood up and declared, 'Neumann sir, sniper. You mentioned that we must wait with the pre-invasion force in Beckley Woods. How long will we need to wait there with them before the main forces have arrived? I ask this because the longer we are in enemy territory, the greater our chances of being compromised.'

'Good question, Neumann. As I have said, we will be brought in by submarine beneath the shadow of the cliffs, about here.' Once again the well polished stick was bought into play. 'Our team of seven men will use two inflatable boats to come ashore from two miles out, bringing in all our personal equipment, including weapons, explosives, rations and radios. Unusually, the boats will be kept, as I mentioned, this area behind the sea wall has been completely flooded, and they will be needed to attack the inland cliff.'

Once we, or the submarine, have dealt with the cliff top house, we will reconnoitre the troop emplacements to establish the fire power and strategy required to neutralise these guns, believed to be Bofors, as well as the troops guarding them. We will focus on laying the explosive charges on the beach, along here. We will have to wait for the heat to die down once the cliff top house has been dealt with, especially if the submarine has to attack it. The forces there will immediately be put on a greatly heightened alert status.'

'We will be in enemy territory for perhaps three days, once we have completed our first duties, before our comrades from the Waffen SS are landed. From then on, we will wait with them in the designated area, for perhaps two or three more days, before the Fuhrer launches his main invasion forces of Operation Sealion. Of course we are aware that the longer we are on enemy soil, the greater the chances of our mission being compromised, but that is why we are using only the best and most highly trained soldiers of the Waffen SS. We do not expect to be discovered. Does this answer your question, Neumann?'

'Thank you, Sir' responded Neumann.

The Gruppenfuhrer continued. 'Von Rundstedt and I will assume joint overall command of the entire force at this time.'

'Because of the known strength of the British Navy, we have to divide our efforts in order to land all of our forces. Other attacks, identical to ours, will be taking place further along the coast to the East, as far along as Deal here.' Again the stick was used to point to a larger map, showing the entire area that Operation Sealion would encompass. 'We have put out propaganda that suggests the attacks will be much wider spread.'

'These attacks will be staggered, possibly by several hours, in order to force the enemy to focus on one area at a time. The difference is however gentlemen, we shall be the first therefore we cannot afford to fail. Once we have shown our hand it will be impossible to turn back the tide of fury that we will unleash on Britain. A couple of hours before the landing times, we will launch our attack on the garrison at Pett Level and destroy their fire power and kill the troops stationed there. Once accomplished, the initial landing force will be free to advance rapidly inland to the first holding point.'

'I should perhaps have already mentioned, Gentlemen, that our intelligence reports that this Pett Level region is thought by the British to be impenetrable, which is why we are the specialist team charged with neutralising its threat and ensuring the first successful landing. We believe that our action will take the enemy completely by surprise, thus they will be thrown into total disarray.'

'Any more questions, gentlemen?' Gruppenfuhrer Zimmermann enquired.

'Wagner sir, mountaineer. Do we have the composition of these cliffs at this stage, and also the height at the point where we will be ascending them, sir?'

'Again, good questions, Wagner. There will be two separate ascents. The main cliff, where we hope to reach the decoding machine, stands about 40 metres high. The second escarpment, just beneath this fortified observation post, is not so high, at about only 10 metres. Also it is not so steep. It is certainly climbable without equipment, other than our inflatable boats, to reach the base. Our reconnaissance tells us that the composition is sandstone in both cases. Is this a problem, soldier?'

'No sir, it just means that we have to employ different techniques'. 'By different techniques, I assume you mean different to the ones that you employed recently during the tragic training accident?'

'I was bought in after that incident, sir. I am not sure what equipment was being used at that time, but I have the correct tools and skills to get this job done effectively.'

'That is good, soldier. I like your attitude.'
'Thank you Gruppenfuhrer,' Wagner replied, proudly snapping a salute in the air before returning to his seat.

'Gentlemen, I need the rest of you now to introduce yourselves to me and let me know about your special skills.' The assembled men stood up from their seats to attention. One by one, they spoke their names, and coldly stated their area of expertise.

'Fuchs, Sir. I am a specialist with the bayonet and the killing knife. I like to perform the close up, silent kill.'

'Jung, Sir. I am the expert in radio operations. I am also quite good with the knife, as well as being an excellent shot with the pistol, sir.'

'Schultz, Sir. Top sniper. Regular ninety plus hits from one hundred shots on the moving targets. One hundred hits usually on the statics.'

'Klein, Sir. Quite simply, I enjoy killing. I seem to be able to do it instinctively. I love using the knife, especially throwing the blade. Also the cheesewire, the crossbow, my hands, a rock or cosh………..'

'Thank you Klein, I understand.' Zimmermann was an officer who happened to believe there should be some etiquette to war. This man Klein was someone from a different, almost sub-human class. Fuchs was the same. He knew that he needed men like this to achieve his goals but it didn't mean that he had to like them. Also there was a strange look upon the face of Klein as he mentioned each of the tools of his trade. There was a sinister inflection that he put on the word, "*Cheesewire.*"

'So, in total we are seven men. We will now begin our disciplined acclimatisation training, during which time you will have plenty of opportunity to demonstrate your skills to me, and vice versa.'

'Can I ask when we will be leaving, sir?' Wagner enquired.

'You can ask soldier, but I can not give you the answer.' The whole troop wondered whether the Gruppenfuhrer knew and wasn't prepared to tell them, or whether he was awaiting orders from Himmler, the commander in chief of the Waffen SS.

Now that the men knew what their objectives were, they were all eager to get on with the job. In many of their minds they had completed their training, already proved themselves and were ready to do their duty. True, that until now they had not known what the final objective would be. Now that they knew, they just wanted to get going.

Now it seemed that they needed to 'bond' all over again with this rather strange leader of men. Also the majority of the team were loners. They had their own skills but were not the easiest of people to understand, unless you were working alongside them on a mission. Only at that time, did it appear that they were all totally co-ordinated.

'I will leave you now, the guards here will show you to your special quarters which you will occupy from now until our departure date. I will join you at 0500 hours when we will get a feel for the life that we will be sharing from now on.' Suddenly Gruppenfuhrer Zimmermann was gone and the six men stood for a few moments before the two guards returned. 'This way, gentlemen,' one of them called. 'Please collect your kit from the barracks and meet us in the courtyard in five minutes time.'

All six were assembled with their kit within three minutes in the courtyard. They exchanged brief comments about their new commanding officer, and where they thought they were going now. A small, Volkswagen armoured personnel carrier drew up and the driver indicated that they should all get in the back. As soon as they were seated, the driver set off, quickly passing through the guarded gates of the compound and onto the minor roads that he appeared to know very well.

The barracks were in Bavaria, just outside an ancient walled town, but soon they were heading into increasingly heavily wooded terrain. The stink of the exhaust fumes, coupled with the uncomfortable ride did nothing to improve their comfort. It was September 1940, and the early afternoon sun was still very warm. One or two of the men took off their military blouses, whilst others loosened their top buttons.

'Is this that creepy bald bastard's idea of hardening us up?' asked Schultz, to no-one in particular.
'Where the fuck, are we going?' queried Klein.
'We will, no doubt, soon find out,' said Neumann.
'Let's hope so,' agreed Wagner.

They had been on the road for about two hours when suddenly the driver veered off the country road into what appeared to be nothing more than a wide cart track, running deep into the forest. They were aware that the canopy of trees prevented the sun from entering at many places now.

'We are arriving at our destination, gentlemen.' The driver shouted back at them. They were approaching what seemed to be a low, concrete roofed building, hidden deep within the forest. The driver slowed and pulled up two vehicles lengths from the solid wooden door.

'Please disembark,' said their driver, who was already out of the cab. The six of them, by now quite dishevelled, climbed wearily from the rear of the vehicle. They had just laid their kit on the forest floor when Fuchs exclaimed, 'Shit.'

Each one of them looked up to see the driver, holding a sub machine gun which was squarely pointed at all of them. 'I am so sorry gentlemen, but my task was to bring you here to kill you! You already know too much and the Gruppenfuhrer has already decided that he doesn't want any of you in his team. It would be too risky to let you live, the outcome of the war depends on your silence.' The driver's eyes were cold and steady and they were fixed directly on the group.

Not one man appeared to move, but already Klein's hand was upon the well balanced throwing knife that was always within reach in his belt. Instinctively the group spread slightly, almost imperceptibly. Klein whispered to Neumann next to him, 'Diversion.' Without warning, Neumann through himself to his knees, screaming at the driver and pleading for his life. 'Please not me, I have young children.' Klein tensed and prepared to lift his knife arm, he had a perfect throw at the driver's throat. It wouldn't kill him, but he had to count on these other bastards to move in and finish him, before the driver could fire.

The screaming continued and the driver became more distracted. 'Now,' thought Klein. At that same moment he was aware of something pushing hard into his back. 'Put it down slowly, soldier,' said the whispered voice from behind. The knife fell to the floor and Klein turned slightly to see the half smile on the bare face of Gruppenfuhrer Zimmermann.

'Jung, you may also drop the pistol,' said the calm voice of their new commanding officer. The pistol was behind Jung's back but would have been able to fire in a split second. It fell to the ground and the whole group realised they had been tricked.

'You are clearly in need of more training, gentlemen,' laughed the Gruppenfuhrer. 'Only two of you were ready for the kill, and you all walked straight into my little trap. Lesson one, Gentlemen, trust no-one!'

'How the hell did he get here before us?' whispered Neumann to Wagner, as he got back to his feet. They all looked shocked.

'Thank you driver, you are now dismissed.' said Zimmermann coldly. The driver saluted and shouted 'Heil Hitler,' and climbed back into the cab of the Volkswagen then reversed out of the clearing. 'He is a good man,' remarked Zimmermann. 'He trusts me implicitly. That is the ninth time we have performed that little charade. This was probably the closest he has actually come to being killed, though. Do you really believe though, that you could have taken him out before he fired, Gentlemen?'

Almost before the question was completed, there was a steely flash in the air, followed by a thud, and the handle of the throwing knife was quivering in the wooden door, exactly where the driver's head had been. 'There is no doubt about it sir,' replied Klein, who was now in his own comfort zone.

'You are no doubt an accomplished killer, but you must never be so distracted that you are not aware of all the other factors around you. Now gentlemen, we will get settled in together after all. Tomorrow we will start at 0500hours, but tonight, we have some time to get to know each other better. Just to show that I have a human side, I have arranged for some fine food and drinks to be delivered here.'

They all trudged in through the stout wooden door and Klein, still muttering under his breath, retrieved his knife along the way. The building itself was quite light inside as a group of windows were set along the entire back wall of the main section. This main room had the appearance of a small, gentleman's club restaurant.

There were comfortable long seats on the side of the room, and several cosy looking tables with four chairs set at each one. These tables were set with red cloths and proper silver cutlery, the type of which was not normally seen in German army barracks.

To both sides of this room were doors leading off to individual bedrooms. There were four bedrooms to each side. 'Gentlemen, you each have a room,' declared Zimmermann. 'They are all identical, so you don't need to fight over which one you want. May I suggest that we meet back here at 1800 hours, for a pre dinner drink? You may dress casually, but smart. Oh and just one more thing. The shower room on this side will be mine. You can share the ones on that wing, they are more than adequate.'

The men filed left and right and settled in to their rooms. By now, they had a distinct feeling of mistrust for their commanding officer and not one of them felt particularly comfortable in these surroundings.

Both wings had a shower and toilet block, which the four rooms on each side shared. Fuchs was next door to Neumann and he suggested they had all better clean up properly, bearing in mind the fussy bastard that they now had commanding them.

This suggestion was passed along the six rooms that the men occupied. The closest room to the restaurant section on the left hand wing was the room that the Gruppenfuhrer occupied.

One or two of the men chose to sleep for an hour, before getting ready. The men's shower block burst into life at around 1700 hours and the usual men's talk started to flow.

'Better wash your bollocks properly,' laughed Fuchs to Schultz. 'Our new commanding officer will probably smell them at dinner, otherwise.'

'Did he mention no farting?' queried Neumann. At this point he let go a real rip snorter and the others each pretended to develop a coughing fit. 'You dirty bastard!' declared Wagner. 'You had better hope that you never get an underpants inspection.'

Schultz, despite his rank of sargeant, was the joker of the group and he suddenly started to sing, as the water ran down his face, deliberately blowing bubbles as he looked upwards. The effect was a warbled gargle that sounded quite amusing. He then assumed the role of submarine commander and sang out. 'You buggers can all get out of my sub, you have all got to go to Pett Level. I'll shoot you out from my torpedo tubes, and you will swim like the fucking devil.'

Again roars of laughter from the rest. 'What kind of a name is that anyway?' retorted Neumann. 'What kind of half breeds could live in a place called Pett Level?'
'Don't worry about that, my friend,' said Schultz. 'We will find out soon enough now.

'Do you think the women there will like the ever willing, German soldier?' asked Fuchs, as he stood in the shower proudly holding his erect penis in his hand while stabbing it into his own navel.

'Yes, probably,' replied Wagner. 'The men there like their sheep, and I hear that the women prefer a donkey, like you.'

'Well that's you out of the hunt, my friend!' declared Klein to Schultz. 'Don't worry' responded Schultz. 'You would not want this as a boil on the end of your nose, when it is angry!' He squeezed and tried to make bigger his more modest 'handful' as he continued to shower.

Everyone finished their ablutions and disappeared back into the bedrooms to complete their grooming. Suddenly it was 1800 hours and almost as one, they left their rooms and headed for the central section.

Gruppenfuhrer Zimmermann was already standing at the bar with a large glass of white wine in his hand. Behind the bar was a smartly dressed, effeminate looking young man, who appeared to be serving the drinks.

'Just tell Helga here what you want to drink and she will serve you,' said Zimmermann to the men.
'Can we have anything, sir?' asked Schultz.
'We have beer, red and white wine, whisky and schnapps. Oh, and also champagne,' declared the young man behind the bar, in a very girlish voice. He was probably twenty years of age but it was easy to see why he wasn't actively serving in the forces. One by one the men ordered their drinks and their commanding officer addressed them in a less formal way.
'Gentlemen, tonight we can relax. We can have what we like to eat and drink. The next time we will be able to raise a glass together will be on enemy soil.'

'I doubt however that the English inns will have such good beer and wines as these though. Still it will be free of charge!' Some of the men chuckled at the thought of just helping themselves in a foreign country.

The Gruppenfuhrer continued, 'I have to apologise for my little prank earlier, I just wanted to make a point about vigilance at all times. I have every confidence in your abilities, your training has been monitored all the way along and I know that you are all very highly capable of carrying out our little mission. I also wanted to show you that I am also very able to look after myself in combat situations. You needed to have some confidence in me as well.'

The men had absolutely no doubt in their minds that this man could be extremely ruthless. The demonstration earlier had quite clearly shown that he was willing to risk the lives of people who were deemed to be dispensable, or of little consequence.

The driver may have played out the same charade several times before, however they had witnessed many times the speed that Klein could produce and throw his favourite knife, and the deadly accuracy involved. Also there was Jung's pistol. He could have turned and fired in a split second and again his accuracy had proved stunning under all conditions of training. The men gradually became a little more relaxed as the beer and wine began to take hold. They all felt that this was their lot in life and they must become resigned to the fact that Zimmermann was now their commanding officer. At the end of the day, he could not have got to the position of Gruppenfuhrer without being an outstanding soldier in the Waffen SS.

Unlike other divisions of the army, all of these officers and men were of outstanding ability and calibre, hand picked to become Adolf Hitler's elite fighting force. Their leader was one of The Fuhrer's most trusted allies, Heinrich Himmler. His very name evoked fear amongst the lower ranks. He was not the sort of man you wanted to get the wrong side of. If Zimmermann had this man's ear, then he was a soldier of extremely high standing.

'Dinner is about to be served,' sang out the girly voiced young man, and the men made their way to the tables. Zimmermann invited Neumann, Wagner and Schultz to join him. Jung, Fuchs and Klein made their way to an adjoining table and the scene was set.

Two men appeared, pushing a trolley through the stout wooden door and immediately the smell of fine food wafted around the room. 'This is our little surprise, gentlemen,' said the Gruppenfuhrer pleasantly. 'The food is prepared at the sister block just a short walk away.'

Most of the men were not used to being served at table. Some felt a little uncomfortable with it. Others were not sure about the correct cutlery to use. All of them waited for their commanding officer to start and then they simply copied him.

'So this is what these strange shaped knives are for,' thought Jung, as he

got stuck into the fish starter that had been placed in front of him. He had to admit, that this was the best food he had ever tasted. 'How is your fish?' he enquired of the other two soldiers at his table.
'I have to say that this is superb,' replied Schultz.
'Lovely, said Klein,' his mouth so full he could not say more.

The two men who served the food, each came to a table and enquired which wine the gentlemen would prefer. Zimmermann suggested to his table that they try one of their finest German wines, a Riesling.
At the other table, the men felt awkward and did not know what to order. Their 'waiter' suggested that they might like to try the Riesling too.

The conversation slowed, as the men ate heartily. Hardly a word was spoken as the first course was demolished with great enthusiasm.
The 'waiters' cleared the plates and soiled cutlery and disappeared with the trolley. The conversation restarted and soon the room was buzzing with relaxed chatter. Zimmermann started to question the men on his table about their backgrounds.

Neumann was the first to open up. He was perhaps the most confident of the group, in the company of a senior officer. He was quite tall, with light brown hair. He was tanned and good looking and had the look of the outdoors about him.

'I joined the army at the age of seventeen, sir. My Father suggested it would make a man of me, as I had always been quite a sickly child. At first, I hated it. Gradually though, I began to enjoy the challenges that were given to us each day, and also I discovered that I was a very good shot with the rifle. I applied for the Waffen SS once the war had started, and found that I was able to hone my marksmanship skills.'

'So, what is your average score?' enquired Zimmermann.
'On the moving targets I am always in the mid eighties, sir. I am not quite as sharp as Sergeant Schultz, though sir. But then he is exceptional.'
'Yes, I have heard this of you, Schultz.' Zimmermann now turned his attention to the other sniper in the group. 'So what is your secret?'

Schultz was a wiry, blond haired man who had been promoted early. Despite this, he did not feel as comfortable as his fellow sniper when addressing an officer, but he was extremely confident in his ability with the rifle. He covered his embarrassment with his brash sense of humour.
'I do not really take aim sir. When I see the target, I instinctively pull the trigger. It doesn't seem to matter whether it is day or night. My scores

are very high under all conditions. I sometimes believe that I could do it with my eyes closed, sir.'

'Remind me once again of your averages.' Zimmermann sounded quite interested.
'Usually, well over ninety percent for the moving targets and higher of course for the static firing sir,' responded Schultz.

'And the mountaineer of our group. What brought you here?'
Zimmermann turned his attention to the athletic looking, muscular frame of Wagner. This man had already become quite famous in the Fatherland following his ascent of what was at the time, a mountain that was considered to be totally un-climbable. That mountain was the Eiger.

He had been part of the team that had first conquered the North Face of the mountain in 1938. The sheer rock wall has since been responsible for a number of deaths, and as such, has become known in Germany as 'The Murder Wall.' There was no questioning the skills of this man.

'I was shall we say sir, 'approached' by a member of the German aristocracy, who is very close to The Fuhrer.' Wagner chose his words carefully. 'I was told that I was going to be essential to the war effort, so I was promoted directly into this unit. I have to say that at no time was I promised an easy ride or any special treatment, nor would I expect any.'

'Good, good,' responded Zimmermann. 'So, now let's hear from our comrades on the other table.' He looked directly at Fuchs, who shuffled around on his seat and quickly said, 'I have to tell you sir, that I am most comfortable in the killing fields. It is what I do best.'

Fuchs was by any description, an ugly man. He was short, stocky and had very hard features. He looked like a killer and Zimmermann did not question him further. He knew that this man had been saved a lengthy prison sentence for severely injuring another soldier during a fight over a whore in Dusseldorf. He had been 'volunteered' to do what he did best. After the war, his sentence may be reduced or he could even receive a pardon, depending on how he handled himself during this mission.

Zimmermann looked at Fuch's counterpart and thought that they could be brothers. 'So Klein, you also have a flair for the kill?'
'Some say that if the war hadn't come, then I could have become a murderer, sir. I seem to get so much enjoyment from the kill. I have always fantasised about the power involved in taking someone's life.

During this war I have had many opportunities to indulge my fantasies, the more varied the killing, the more exciting it seems to become. I once cut off the head of a Polish soldier as a trophy. I lost it before I could take it home to mount it. I believe that another soldier stole it from me. Hopefully I will bring home the head of a Tommy after this mission.'

'Quite so,' responded Zimmermann, who wondered what the hell this man would do once this war was over.

Finally the officer looked at Jung. 'You are our radio man then?'
'Yes sir,' replied the small, dark haired, intelligent looking, young man. 'I was employed before the war by Siemens in Berlin, in their communications development department. We made some significant advances with communications range, and wavelengths. I can build a radio from nothing. It is essential to keep communications on the battlefield or in enemy territory, and I won't let you down, sir. I helped to develop a clarity enhancing speaker unit, which is now used in all the radio sets produced. I can also shoot very well with the pistol.'

Zimmermann seemed genuinely interested. 'So, should we drop a radio transmitter, or one gets damaged by enemy fire?' he asked.
'Then I will be able to rebuild it, sir. I always carry enough spares to start from scratch, if I have to. I will maintain communications, whatever.'
'Excellent, communication is going to be a vital part of our mission,' replied the Gruppenfuhrer.

The door banged open and once again the two 'waiters' appeared with the trolley. Again the smell of food filled the air and the men sat in anticipation of a superb main course. Zimmermann asked the men what this was. 'Wild duck sir, with sauce, and local vegetables,' was the reply.

The 'waiters' served the meal and the vegetables were left on the table for the men to help themselves. More wine was brought to the table and once again the room fell into relative silence as the men concentrated on the meal in front of them.

During the meal, the effeminate young man came to refill their glasses. 'Thank you Helga,' smiled Zimmermann, and the men began to wonder whether this was actually the young man's name. He certainly did not seem to take any offence at being addressed this way.

'If you fancy a shag before we go to war,' whispered Klein to Fuchs, 'you should take a knob of best butter from the table and for a few reichsmarks I will hold Helga down for you later!'

'I don't think he would need much holding down, I believe he would be eternally grateful!' laughed Fuchs in Klein's direction. At the end of the meal, there was nothing left on any of the tables. All of these men were extremely fit, and required a high food intake each day. Once again, the two 'waiters' removed the dirty plates and cutlery, and disappeared.

The conversation resumed. By now, a few of the men who had been listening to the conversation coming from Zimmermann, began to feel slightly more relaxed about him. 'Maybe he felt that he needed to impress us at the beginning,' thought Neumann, who sat opposite the Gruppenfuhrer at dinner.

Neumann had noticed one thing about him though. At all times, any crumbs that landed on the table were instantly cleaned up, almost instinctively. The Gruppenfuhrer seemed to be unable to help himself. Even whilst talking, his hands would be busy, subconsciously brushing any debris to the floor. He also had a habit of wiping his knife and fork clean on his napkin, many times during the meal. Neumann wondered whether Zimmermann even knew he was doing it.

'So, gentlemen, I believe that we have some very fine Bavarian cheese, to complete the meal,' declared their leader. Most of the men had not eaten food of this quality for a long time. The food served at their training barracks, was adequate and served in good quantities, but this meal, had been very special indeed. They all wondered why they were being treated this way.

Again, as if by instinct, the Gruppenfuhrer seemed to sense their thoughts. 'You may be wondering Gentlemen, why we are enjoying these special things, here on this night. We all know why we are here, and what lies ahead of us. The Fuhrer himself wanted you to realise what our lives will be like once our mission is completed. He sends to all of you personally, this message.'

The Gruppenfuhrer stood to his feet and produced a sheet of notepaper from his jacket, from which he read:
'You men are the spearhead of my operation to neutralise the threat posed by Britain. Once you have achieved my objectives, you will receive special privileges upon returning to The Fatherland. You will have money and houses. In short Gentlemen, you will have security for life.'

'This last night of pleasure is my gift to you, to remind you of the lifestyle that you can look forward to, once the fighting is ended. I know that the training you have undergone will ensure that you succeed, and I thank all of you for the hard work and dedication that you have put in.'

'Finally Gentlemen, please enjoy the rest of the evening and the other little surprises that I have arranged for you. I wish I could be with you all this evening, but the running of the war prevents this. Good luck, God speed, I promise to congratulate all of you personally, once our work is done.'

The men were genuinely surprised. The Fuhrer had taken the trouble to write this letter directly to them. They all seemed to be quite shocked, and the Gruppenfuhrer smiled as he put the note down on the table. 'This was hand written by The Fuhrer, two days ago. He asked that I read it to you over dinner here, this evening.'

At this point the two 'waiters' returned once more through the heavy wooden door with the food trolley. They came straight away to the two tables and served a selection of cheeses, along with fresh butter, grapes and some dry biscuits. 'Helga' came over to the tables and offered the men whisky, or schnapps, to accompany the cheeseboard.

'You had better get used to the whisky,' said Zimmermann. 'When we have taken control in Britain, we will own the finest whisky distilleries, which are based in Scotland. This will be the genuine article and not like that American rubbish!'

By now it was about half past eight in the evening. The men noticed that 'Helga' and the other two men were carrying bottles of champagne from behind the bar and out to the bedroom corridors. They each carried two bottles and they made a couple of trips. Lastly they took through a tray of champagne glasses.

'What's going on here,' asked Jung of the other two men at his table.
'I don't understand this one,' replied Fuchs.
'Nor me,' said Klein.

Zimmermann seemed to appear puzzled too. 'What could this be, gentlemen?' he asked. 'Perhaps we have to go to our rooms and drink alone, for the rest of the evening?' he enquired, almost mischievously. The problem is, that champagne is no fun when drunk alone.' He was almost pushing the men to question him, but no one spoke. 'The letter from the Fuhrer, mentioned some other little surprises. Gentlemen, one of these surprises are the bottles of champagne that you see have already been delivered to your rooms. They were recently 'liberated' from the French. I am assured that the champagne is of the finest quality.'

Almost theatrically now, the Gruppenfuhrer stood up and clapped his hands. At that moment, the wooden door was opened by the young man known as Helga, and in walked a dozen smiling, well dressed women. The look of shock on the men's faces was clear to see. They had not seen any women for months, let alone any as attractive as these.

'Ladies,' said Zimmermann. 'How lovely to see you all again! Helga, champagne for the ladies please. Gentlemen, may I suggest that we spread out a bit onto the other tables so that the ladies may join us?'

The men nervously shuffled around, looking at each other for some reassurance. Fuchs and Klein decided to take over a table together and they were immediately joined by a couple of the girls. Zimmermann waved his dinner companions away and gestured at the empty chairs to three of the girls, calling for them to join him. Wagner and Neumann opted for one table together and they were straight away joined by a couple of girls. This left Jung and Schultz standing and they immediately went to an empty table, and settled together.

Once again they were joined by two girls, who started to chat quite naturally to them. The three remaining girls made themselves comfortable at another table, and soon everyone was chatting and drinking as if this were a perfectly normal occurrence.

One of the two girls seated with Fuchs and Klein, said 'Hello boys. My name is Birgit and this is my friend, Ingrid. We are here to spend the rest of the night with you, if you know what I mean.' They certainly did know what Birgit meant, but already Fuchs was looking past her to the other table with the three girls sitting alone. One of these girls was slightly bigger built than the rest, exactly the sort that he would normally go for.

'By the way boys, don't be shy. If any of you would prefer one of the other girls, just tell me which one and I will get her for you,' said Birgit, cheerfully. Fuchs looked back at her slightly embarrassed, and said, 'Do you mind if I go for that girl there? It's not that you are not beautiful, but she has the larger breasts and bottom, which I really like.
'Of course not sweetie,' said Birgit, who immediately called to the other table, 'Simone, this boy likes you!' Without another word the two girls

had smilingly changed places and the conversation continued. 'Is it all right if I keep you?' enquired Klein nervously to Ingrid.
'Of course it is darling, but only for tonight!' she joked. 'By the way, if any of you fancy a change later on, we can accommodate that as well. We are here to please you, on the orders of our Fuhrer.'

During the next few minutes there was some shuffling between tables while the men settled with their chosen partners. Conversation now turned towards the rest of the evening's expectations. Some of the men looked around nervously, as if to see who was going to be the first to take a girl to his room.

Eventually, a well rehearsed Helga announced. 'We have run out of champagne here, but you each have a couple of bottles in your room.' Almost as one, the men stood up and their chosen partners took their arms. Zimmermann addressed the men for the final time that night.

'One final point. The ladies' transport will be here to collect them at 0400hours, so you have plenty of time for fun. Please remember that we will be leaving here at 0500hours with our kit, we will not be returning. Gentlemen, enjoy!' With this, the Gruppenfuhrer swept away, with a woman on each arm. The trio disappeared into the left hand corridor.

Very soon all of the bedroom doors had shut, leaving four girls in the main restaurant area. As soon as the last door was heard to close, Helga grabbed hold of a bottle and came over to the girls and pulled up a chair. Birgit, Steffi, Heidi and Anna, made him welcome. They had a bottle of whisky to share, and soon they were chattering away as all girls do.

Helga was very keen to know what lipstick they used, and the best way to apply false eyelashes. When the war was over, he was going to get into the entertainment industry. There was a demand for female impersonators, and he was determined to learn as much as he could.

He had failed the medical when he had been called up for the army. The kindly army doctor, realised that Werner Muller, could never be a fighting man, so he signed him off as a severe asthmatic, despite the fact that he now only occasionally suffered an attack.

Hence, he had been sidelined into army catering. He had a flair for this type of work and had been sent out to this special compound a few times now. He knew the score. He got the chance to talk to the girls and drink free army whisky with them. Also he would get a lift back to the main barracks when their transport came in the early hours. He had received the nickname 'Helga' from one of the officers, and rather liked it. In his mind it was a lot better than Werner, anyway.

At first, he couldn't understand why there were always spare girls. Now he knew exactly how it worked. It would not be long until one of the men fancied a change and then another girl would just take over. Sometimes a particular girl would be requested and sometimes the men would just ask for a surprise.

He and the girls would always place bets on who would be the first one out. On this night though, they were all agreed. They felt sure it would be Fuchs who called for 'second helpings,' first. Just after midnight, his chosen girl, Simone, came back into the restaurant with a scowl on her face. 'Zoo Prick!' She hissed. 'That man is an animal, and he doesn't seem to be able to stop!' The girls laughed and Helga pushed a glass towards her and half filled it with whisky. 'Looks like you could do with a large one,' he giggled mischievously.

'That's exactly what I've had for the last three hours,' she moaned. 'Now it is my sad duty to send you in, Anna.'
'Oh God,' Anna replied, 'I was hoping for a quiet night tonight. Why did he choose me?'
'He saw both of us and couldn't make up his mind, so went for me first.'
'Wish me luck!' Anna called over her shoulder, as she headed for the right hand corridor. 'I suppose I can always bite the pillow!'
A couple of other 'exchanges' happened shortly afterwards, surprisingly the radio man Jung, always considered to be the quiet one of the group had called for 'second helpings' in the form of Steffi, a petite blonde.

At exactly 0400hours, the girls' transport arrived and they quickly disappeared into the night. Some of the girls kissed the men goodbye at the door of their room, while other girls just scurried from the rooms and away. The sound of the old bus grinding its way out of the forest slowly faded into the night air. All the men knew that a new day was beginning.

Chapter 3

Zimmermann stared at his face in the mirror. He wiped the steam from the glass and listened to the sound of the men in the other shower block. 'This is the day,' he thought. The date was Wednesday the 11th of September 1940.

He was a tallish man, quite well built and physically very agile and strong. He did not need to shave as he had suffered an attack of total alopecia during his teens. The effects of this condition had left him with a very individual appearance, his head was also completely bald and he had no eyebrows or eyelashes either.

He had a small duelling scar on his left cheek, something that the young aristocratic men of the new Germany, strived to achieve during their early manhood. It was regarded as a sign of manliness and prestige. He had risen through the ranks, partly because he felt at ease with the top men in the Nazi Party, and partly because he was an exceptional soldier.
He was soon recognised by Heinrich Himmler as a loyal and totally reliable officer.

The task ahead though was not an ordinary one. It was his personal responsibility to take this team of men and change the outcome of the war in the Fatherland's favour. Whatever doubts he may have had were immediately pushed to the back of his mind.

'I am very good at what I do,' he told himself. 'This group of men are also the very best, with all the skills required to carry out this mission. There can be only one outcome. When the war is over we will all be rewarded well by The Fuhrer.'

As he towelled himself dry, he focussed on what now lay ahead and the final task that he would put this team of men through before they left for England, tonight! There was no way that he could have told them that their departure was this imminent. It was too risky. They all knew that their training was at its peak and were more than ready to go and do their Fuhrer's bidding.

He inspected his scar in the mirror and half smiled at the memory of how he received it. He was an excellent swordsman and yet during that particular duel, he had almost willed himself to be wounded. Maybe he hadn't defended the blow as well as he might. He had only felt a sharp sting, and then the warmth of the blood running down his face. He was pleased with the end result. It was not a disfigurement, actually an enhancement. He was now quite comfortable with his appearance. There was nothing that his doctors could do about it he just had to live with it. They could not explain why he had suddenly lost all of his hair. It may have been brought on by stress while he studied for his examinations.

He suddenly became aware of his responsibilities for this final day in his home country. Tonight he and his men would be on their way to England. He would not inform them until they had completed this final day's work. 'So, now I have to put these bastards through their final paces, with one last piece of deception,' he mused.

Without thinking, he wiped the mirror totally clean with the towel which he then folded neatly and hung over the radiator in his room. He also made the bed, he couldn't help himself. He knew full well that the room would be stripped and prepared for tonight's new 'guests'.

The men were already assembled outside when the Gruppenfuhrer came out of the stout wooden door. 'Heil Hitler,' they shouted and simultaneously saluted him. 'Heil Hitler,' responded Zimmermann.

'So, Gentlemen. Did anybody score three last night?' He questioned. Nobody responded, so the Gruppenfuhrer enquired, 'Two?'

Several of the men held a hand aloft at this point. The men all looked quite refreshed, despite the obvious lack of sleep. These men were used to grabbing sleep at odd hours, so last night's little treat would not have worried them. They were trained to stay awake for long periods when they had to, and could cat nap at any opportunity as well.

Wagner stepped forward and asked for permission to speak. 'Gruppenfuhrer, on behalf of all the men, I would like to thank you for last night. None of us has seen any of that type of action for a very long time. Also the food and wine were excellent. Thank you, sir.'

'My pleasure,' responded Zimmermann. 'So, now we have to pay for it.' At that point, the Volkswagen carrier suddenly appeared at the end of the clearing and the men prepared to put their kit into the back of it. The man driving it was not the same one who brought them here. They guessed that he was used just for the little charade that they had been subjected to. They all climbed in, and the Gruppenfuhrer joined them in the back.

'From now on, we will do everything together,' he declared. The vehicle chugged away through the darkened areas of the forest, and had been going for about fifteen minutes, when a motorcycle and sidecar came towards them at speed. The rider in uniform waved the driver down and left his machine with the engine running. He removed his goggles and ran to the back of the vehicle.

'Gruppenfuhrer, sir.'
'What is it?' enquired Zimmermann.
The man spoke quickly. 'Sir, I have been ordered to make contact with you and your men, who we knew would be departing from 'The Shack' this morning.'

The rider held a buff coloured envelope in the air and passed it up to the senior officer. 'These orders come from Herr Himmler, who says that you and your men will be able to deal with this situation.' The Gruppenfuhrer scanned the document now in his hand and quickly began to interpret the contents to the men. 'About ten kilometres from here, deep in the forest, there is an interrogation camp, from which four British prisoners have escaped overnight.'

He continued, 'They have managed to overcome the guards and steal their weapons. The three guards are all dead. The escapees were part of a captured British bomber crew. It is essential that these men are located and killed. Herr Himmler cannot allow any of these locations to become known to the enemy. Many other top secret facilities are based here, and we cannot allow the possibility of any attention being brought to this area, with perhaps even the risk of bombing raids.'

'The four were going to be executed this morning, and they will be desperate to get away. The despatch rider here can lead us to the facility and then we must track them down. Gentlemen, it looks as though our planned training for today is to be put on hold.'

'Rider, can our vehicle follow you all the way to this camp?' enquired the Gruppenfuhrer.
'Most of the way sir, but then you will have to walk,' responded the rider. 'I can still ride through and you can follow me on foot for the last couple of kilometres through the more dense part of the forest.'
'Then ride, man now!' barked the Gruppenfuhrer.

The motorcyclist saluted, shouted 'Heil Hitler,' and sprinted back to his machine. Within a few minutes the Volkswagen was bouncing around on the narrow track between the trees. The despatch rider clearly knew these tracks well and was riding as fast as he could. Sometimes the sidecar pitched up perilously into the air as he took a right handed curve. At times the driver fell back from the motorcycle by fifty or sixty metres as he struggled with the terrain, and the cumbersome nature of his vehicle. 'Keep up man,' barked Zimmermann, and the driver did his best.

During this pitching ride, Zimmermann started to agree a plan with the rest of the men. 'This happened about two hours ago, so the bastards will have about three hours on us by the time we pick up a trail. Ideas from you all, please?'
'With respect sir, I don't think that we should separate, because they are bound to have stayed together at least until they get out of the forest. As a group, we can push ourselves harder than if we are on our own.'

'I agree with you, Schultz,' replied Zimmermann. 'But how do we close the gap, Gentlemen?'
'Do you think they might have any more motorcycles at this interrogation facility, sir?' asked Klein. 'I sincerely hope not, otherwise the prisoners will have already taken them!' Klein regretted asking the question. He was a man of action, not a great thinker.

'Could we commandeer the despatch rider's motorcycle to try and locate these men?' asked Wagner. 'At a pinch, we could probably get four of us on the machine while the other three follow in a wider sweep of the area in case the prisoners have dug in until the heat dies down.'

'That is a good idea Wagner, very good. One thing though, I think that three men on the motorcycle would give it more speed, and four men forming a wider sweep of the forest would ensure better coverage.'

'So Gentlemen, who can ride a motorcycle, well?'
'I have a motorcycle at home which I used to ride daily to work, and to the pistol club, before I joined the army sir,' responded Jung.
'Very well, you will take the machine with Fuchs and Klein. You men know what you have to do.' Zimmermann's eyes bored into the heads of the two chosen men.
'Yes Sir, Heil Hitler,' the two killers answered simultaneously.
Zimmermann once again thought how alike these two were and how they could have been brothers.

'The rest of us will fan out to the left and right of the tracks. Wagner, you and I will take one side, while you two,' the same piercing stare was aimed at Neumann and Schultz, 'will take the other.'

'Ride for just over one and a half hours, you will certainly have overtaken them or even found them by then,' Zimmermann addressed Jung. 'At that point, leave Fuchs and Klein as our rear guard, and make your way back for me and Wagner. Then you will repeat the operation with Schultz and Neumann until we are all positioned ahead of the escapees. We will then spread out to form an impenetrable wall.'

The path became rougher and rougher and suddenly the driver was braking and it appeared to the men that there was no longer a track ahead of them. The forest was very dense and the motorcycle and sidecar had stopped on a small path running on from the track.

'This is it, men,' yelled the Gruppenfuhrer. He was out of the wagon in a flash, carrying his small rucksack and rifle and told the despatch rider to stay with the others. The rider knew there was no point in him objecting to the order so he got off of his machine and walked back to the others.

'How far now is the interrogation camp?' said Zimmermann to the rider. 'It's 2 kilometres straight ahead, sir.' The rider fiddled with a compass in his hand and added, 'Approx 220 degrees sir, south westerly direction.' Zimmermann grabbed the compass and ordered the men. 'Jung, get on the motorcycle, and Klein, jump on the back. I will sit on the side chair. The rest of you follow as fast as you can on foot.'

Jung took a little while to adjust to the handling of the NSU motorcycle, it was much heavier than his own BMW that he had at home. Also he had never ridden a combination motorcycle before, and the feel was completely different. The terrain had become more rugged, and it was not always possible to steer a straight course. Every so often, Zimmermann would shout a new direction to him to keep on the compass bearing they had been given.

Meanwhile, Klein perched precariously on the rear of the machine's mudguard and held on tightly to the waist of Jung. He was already preparing his brain for the kill. They picked their way through some fallen trees, each one with their eyes peeled for a building or camp of some description. Suddenly Zimmermann yelled, 'Over there.'

Jung looked across to his right and saw a very similar building to 'the shack,' but with no clearing around it at all. It was almost as if it had been built, and then trees allowed to grow all around it for fifty years.

'Get off the motorcycle and switch off the motor,' instructed Zimmermann. 'We must tread carefully so as not to disturb any trail, or clues that the prisoners may have left for us.' The three men approached the open doorway with extreme caution. They had naturally fanned out and their rifles were pointing directly at the opening. At the same time they were scanning the ground for any indication of what may have happened. Zimmermann went through the doorway first and the other two covered him. No words were spoken.

Once inside, the story started to unfold. The design of the interior was almost identical in appearance to 'the shack,' as the despatch rider had named it, where they had spent last night. The only difference was that this building was cold and hard with just a table and four chairs in the centre part. The windows were barred from top to bottom, and where the bedrooms had been were two corridors containing cells.

A guard with his throat cut sat propped against the wall in the back corner of the central room, his jacket stained almost black with the blood that had run down his chest and over his groin, and was already drying into a large stain on the stone floor. There were flies landing on the open wound and buzzing around his face.

Still gripped in his hand down by his side, was a microphone and cable attached to a Telefunken radio transmitter. A set of headphones had fallen down his neck so that the leather earpieces rested under his chin. His eyes were open and he stared straight ahead.

'Do you think he was the one who reported the escape before he died?' asked Jung, quietly. 'Possibly, replied Zimmermann, under his breath. 'There is a trail of blood across the floor from over there.' He waved towards the left hand corridor. 'How many guards were there?' whispered Klein to Zimmermann. 'Three,' replied the Gruppenfuhrer softly, and then waved towards one of the corridors. They went to the left hand corridor first and found nothing, just four empty cells with the doors open and keys in the locks on the outside. The trail of blood came from the first cell area, where blood was spattered up the walls and across the floor. 'Maybe he tried to lock himself in,' suggested Klein quietly.

They now came back into the main room silently and crossed over into the other corridor. As they entered this section they heard a slight scratching sound. The first three cell doors were open, the same as the others had been, but the last one was closed. Again Zimmermann indicated silently for the other two to cover him.

He quietly grasped the iron handle and began to turn it. The door was locked. Klein took a key from the next door and noticed that it had the legend 'Cell 7', engraved on the metal tag. Zimmermann tried the key in the lock but it would not open.

'It is pointless trying the other keys, they will all be different,' he whispered. He waved the other two back and took aim at the lock with his pistol. Two shots were fired and he whipped the door open as the other two leapt into the cell.

Two rats scurried past the three men and up the corridor. The two dead guards lying on the floor of the cell had been providing a meal for the rodents. The wounds on their throats were clean, and not like the other guard's had been. The appearance was like a half eaten blood orange. There was hardly any blood visible around the area of the wounds, just two large fleshy holes where the men's throats used to be.

Jung was sickened at the sight of these soldiers who had met their deaths in such a horrific way. He started to heave. Zimmermann told him to go outside and throw his guts up. They were talking at normal levels again now. Jung just made it to the outside of the building when he exploded. Last night's meal and drinks were now spread across the forest floor.

The others joined him outside and he immediately apologised to his commanding officer for what must have appeared to be a weakness. Surprisingly, Zimmermann just shrugged his shoulders and said, 'Don't worry soldier, you will become more used to it.' Klein just smiled.
'So think now,' said Zimmermann. 'You have just escaped from here, which direction would you take?'
'South sir, the Swiss border is only about 40 kilometres from here and they could work out their direction from the stars. It would be their only hope of escape,' volunteered Jung, in an effort to make amends for his lack of self control. 'What do you think, Klein,' asked Zimmermann again. Klein was already searching the ground fanning out from the front door of the building. 'It seems to me sir that they ran in this direction.' He moved further away, still staring at the ground and suddenly he called back to the others. 'Over here, sir. I believe I have found something.'

Klein was now on his knees as the other two ran over to where he was gently moving aside some twigs on the ground. The average person would not have spotted what Klein had found. He held up a small copper coin in his hand and passed it to his commanding officer.

'Well, well,' said Zimmermann as he held the coin up to the light. 'We have here the English half penny coin. It is dated 1938 and it has King George 6th of England on the face. There is a ship on the other side, look. It is certain that this was not dropped by one of our men.' Zimmermann put the coin carefully into his tunic pocket. Behind them came a rustling sound and they simultaneously raised their rifles in that direction. The four other men came running into view, and the weapons were lowered.

Zimmermann got busy with the compass again, while the others went inside to witness the scenes of butchery that their comrades had already been subjected to. Not one of them seemed to be affected by the sights that they had seen and once again, Jung, felt even more self conscious.

Klein had moved away quite a distance now, and again exclaimed that he had more signs to go on. Zimmermann and the others all joined him and he pointed to a broken twig between two trees. 'This wasn't done by a deer or wild boar,' exclaimed Klein triumphantly. 'The weight needed to break a twig this size could only be that of a man.'

'So, now we have our direction, it seems your theory was right, Jung. These bastards are heading for Switzerland. They will of course, not make it. Let us put our plan into action immediately, now that we are all here. These men will be desperate, but carrying guns, and having to run on this terrain, I think they will not have covered more than 25 kilometres in the time since their escape. Jung, did you happen to notice what speed you were making when we were all three riding on the motorcycle earlier?'
'Yes sir, it was about 30 kilometres an hour,' replied the young radio operator.

'So, we know that if you maintain the same speed approximately, then you should be ahead of the prisoners in about one and a half hours, to allow a safe margin. Any questions, or are we all clear on what we have to do?' All the men knew what was expected of them. Zimmermann handed the compass to Fuchs, and once again, Jung set off on the motorcycle, with Fuchs and Klein for company. The rest of the men had started to run behind them. Fuchs every so often made waved corrections to the course they were taking and they progressed quite well.

Klein was watching everywhere. If the prisoners were within vision, he would spot them. He could detect cigarette smoke, or the smell of a fire, from an incredible distance, and every distant movement caught his attention. At one point, he made Jung take a detour when he thought he had seen something. As the motorbike got closer to the spot, a deer suddenly leapt out of the trees and ran off at a tangent. They got back on to their set route.

Jung kept watch on the time and he noticed it was now just after 07.30 hours. It had already been a long day. He decided to ride for another 10 minutes and then drop the other two off. This would make absolutely certain that they had not missed their quarry, even though he had made better time than the previous ride. By now, he was feeling a lot more comfortable with the control of the machine, and was averaging better times over the ground.

Klein and Fuchs got off the machine and immediately Jung set off back in the direction of the others. He now had the compass and it should be easy enough to find his way back. At least the others could shout once they heard the motor, so he only had to be within half a kilometre or so.

On the way back, he was very much more alert than he had been on the way out. Fuchs and Klein may be animals, but he felt totally safe with them. Now he was alone, he needed to be much more vigilant.

Meanwhile, the other two decided that they would also start to move back in the direction from which they had come. Not too far, and only about 300 metres apart, where they could still see each other most of the time. They had agreed that they would signal each other every half minute or so to indicate that all was well. If one of them were to spot something then the pre-arranged raised hand signal, would be replaced by arms crossed over the chest. This would immediately signal to the other that he must join his comrade straight away. One thing was certain, if the prisoners were to be found, then they would find them.

Every couple of minutes they stopped to listen. They would listen for several seconds, distinguishing the different sounds of the forest. Occasionally there would be bird song, but not much. This deep in the forest you tended to get more nocturnal hunting birds. They pushed on until they felt that they should stop, they had no desire to get on the wrong side of Zimmermann, by missing their quarry.

Meanwhile, Jung motored on. He had been travelling for about 45 minutes and he re-entered a very thick section of the forest. It was in this area that on the way out took quite a long time to negotiate, as the trees grew very close together. He began to feel a little uneasy with the enforced slower speed, along with the lack of visibility at this point. He checked the compass bearing again and pressed on.

He came to a steep downhill section, followed by another steep uphill climb. On the trip out, he had opened the motor up going down, in order to gain enough speed for the ascent on the other side. He did the same now. The motorcycle hurtled down the slope and his backside hit the saddle hard as the direction changed to uphill. At the top of the climb was a thick clump of trees that he had to pass through the middle of. As he began to gain speed through the first trees, he felt a terrible thud against his chest.

Jung was lying on the ground, winded. At first, he wasn't quite sure what had happened. He sat up in pain and looked up at the two trees he had just tried to negotiate. A branch was solidly jammed between them and he was aware of his motorcycle coming to a halt against a tree a few metres on. In a flash, he realised that he had hit a booby trap. He tried to get his pistol from its holster, and stand up at the same time.

He heard a foreign voice and was instantly aware of two men standing over him pointing machine guns directly at his face. He heard a noise above him and looked up to see two more men shinning down the two trees. He now noticed the rope made from their belts, which was attached to either end of the branch he had hit. As he approached, they had simply dropped the branch down in front of the trees to his chest height. The men were all dressed in British Royal Air Force uniform, he now feared for his life. It occurred to him though, that they could have already killed him while he was lying winded on the ground. The leader of the group prodded him with the sub machine gun, a German Sturmgewehr 44, and indicated for him to get up. He was searched, and relieved of his dagger and Luger pistol. His rifle, lying nearby, was thrown into the trees.

The four men started conversing and gesticulating, while putting their belts back on, and one of them went over to the motorcycle and attempted to restart it. Eventually the NSU coughed into life and the leader again prodded Jung towards it. Jung spoke a little English because his radio engineering career with Siemens required it.

He was however, having great difficulty understanding anything that these men said. He did understand though, when the leader indicated to him to remount the machine and then they all climbed aboard. Jung kept asking himself why they wanted him to drive it, when surely one of them would be capable. Also there was the additional weight factor. The motor had struggled at times with the three of them on it, so asking it to carry five men seemed ludicrous.

One of the four had found the compass on the ground where Jung fell and indicated that he would act as navigator. He sat astride the sidecar right on the nose. One sat in the seat holding the belt of the man in front, while the other straddled the back of the sidecar with his arms firmly on the shoulders of his colleague. The last man and apparent leader of the group, climbed up on the mudguard behind Jung, and clung round his waist. The man in the centre of the sidecar pointed his machine gun upwards towards the rider's head and nodded for him to go forward.

He continually controlled the speed by waving his hand alongside Jung in a slowing motion, or pulling the air in front of him to indicate that he should go faster. They had to negotiate the steep hill in the opposite direction once more, but this time the speed was kept down on the downhill section and the two men on the back jumped off in order to assist the drive uphill on the other side. They pushed quite hard to get the other men and the machine to the top of the slope.

Jung tried to calculate, how far behind the Gruppenfuhrer would be, with the rest of the men. Also he wondered what would happen, once he had got close to Klein and Fuchs again. There was no way that these two killers would allow the escapees to pass them. Suddenly it dawned on him that he was going to be used as a human shield. The thought of this filled him with even more dread. Would Klein and Fuchs care whether he died or not, he wondered. Their only orders were to kill this group of men come what may. A dead radio operator would be an inconvenience to the SS group, but he could be easily replaced.

He started to wonder whether he would be able to grab one of the weapons and throw himself off the motorcycle in an attempt to overcome them. He was not an instinctive killer like the others, merely a good shot with a pistol, but he felt that any effort would be better than just giving up and being killed anyway.

The nearer he got to the area where he had left the other two, the more determined he became to attempt something. He would wait for the next downhill section, and grab the machine gun from the seated man in the sidecar. There was no restraining strap over his shoulder the weapon was simply resting in his lap. At the same time he would open the throttle, giving himself the maximum opportunity to throw himself clear and put a little bit of distance between them.

At least, if he timed it correctly, he would have the higher ground which is always an advantage. He suddenly realised that he wasn't afraid any more, the plan simply had to work, and he was totally focussed on it. He negotiated a clump of tightly knit trees and suddenly saw ahead of him, another downhill section. 'This is it,' he thought calmly. He was almost in a dream state, when suddenly the motor of the NSU stuttered, coughed and died. The machine stopped a few metres from the brow of the hill. Immediately the four men leapt from the machine, suspecting that he was attempting to pull some sort of trick on them. Instantly Jung's brain kicked back to the reality of the situation, and he held up his open hands in a gesture of ignorance.

The men all started to talk quickly, and again the leader gestured towards Jung to restart the machine. He jumped up and down on the kick-start, but although the motor turned over, there was no hint of it firing back up. One of the four came round and pushed Jung out of the way. He looked scornfully at Jung and jumped up and down over and over again on the kick-starter, but the motor still refused to cooperate.

One of the men shouted at Jung, but he had no idea what was said to him. Again he wondered why he could not understand just some of the things that this group were saying. This particular man went up to the machine and grabbed the gasoline filler cap. He twisted it off of the tank and looked inside. His expression said it all. It was obvious that the tank had run dry.

Jung for a moment wondered why his group of crack SS troops had not checked this before they set off. Then he reasoned, 'What difference would it have made?' They didn't have access to any more fuel, the only chance would have been the Volkswagen carrier, but then they would have lost too much time going back for it. Also, the driver would almost certainly have driven off by then, taking the despatch rider with him. They didn't have any orders to stay around.

Again, he had another nagging thought. Why hadn't the Gruppenfuhrer instructed the driver and the despatch rider to go back to barracks for some additional support? Perhaps a team of men on solo motorcycles could have been utilised to catch up with the main party. Had he just left it that they would use their initiatives and do what they thought was best?

36

These questions were running around in Jung's brain, when he looked up to see one of the men pissing in the motorcycle's tank. He felt pretty sure that the men knew that the motor would not run on anybody's piss, so he assumed that they were just making sure that it couldn't be used by anyone else who may have been carrying back up fuel.

The thought process now had to begin all over again. If they bumped in to Klein and Fuchs, the same situation could occur. The fact that there was not a motorcycle now made little difference. His own life would still be in danger. He had to try to formulate another plan.

Only a couple of kilometres ahead, Klein and Fuchs had settled down in the undergrowth, just alongside the path that the motorcycle had taken earlier. They were taking it in turns to talk about their experiences the previous evening. 'That Simone,' declared Fuchs. 'She could not get enough of me, and I had her gasping the whole time. Then I asked for Anna to come in and she was just the same. She whimpered constantly with genuine lust, and she knew everything that I wanted her to do.'

'Are you sure that you are not mistaking the gasping and whimpering for the cries of pain?' enquired Klein, amusingly. 'After all, you are not the normal sized man down there! You could put a donkey to shame.'
'Nonsense, they couldn't get enough of me,' responded Fuchs. 'So now, tell me about your little girlie, then?'

'Ah, Ingrid," smiled Klein. 'You know, that she is just the kind of woman that I would like to marry eventually. She was enough for me for the whole night, and I genuinely felt some affection for her.'

'I hope to meet her again after this war has been won. She is only on the game to help to keep her poor sick Mother comfortable while she is still alive. She explained that the medical bills were very expensive each month and that once her Mother had passed away, she would give it up and settle down. I gave her my Mother's eternity ring and we have arranged to get back in touch as soon as I am back in the Fatherland.'
'What a fucking idiot,' thought Fuchs, but didn't have the heart to tell his mate that he'd been suckered.

They agreed that they would take it in turns to cat nap and alternately watch the area. One of the great skills of these men is the ability to doze for a few minutes, or a couple of hours, and wake up completely refreshed. Fuchs decided to sleep first. He had burnt a lot of energy the previous night and now was his opportunity to catch up on his lost sleep.

Twenty minutes in to the first 'shift', Klein nudged his partner gently and Fuchs was instantly awake. Klein's voice was a whisper. 'Some men are approaching on foot, about 500 metres away.' They both listened intently and were both agreed that this was the case.

This scenario was second nature to them. They had done it so many times in training. They spread apart by about 50 metres through the trees and waited for the approaching people to get closer. Simultaneously they watched as their colleague Jung walked into view, marching ahead of four other men. They instantly understood the situation. Somehow Jung had become captured, and obviously this had happened on his journey back for the others, or there would have been more captives.

A couple of hand signals passed between the two, and they agreed what had to happen. As the men got to within about 30 metres, a shot rang out and the back marker of the group fell to the ground. Instantly the escaping party hit the ground and three machine guns blasted off in the direction of the shot. There was no return of fire. Not a sound. No sign of any movement could be detected by the group.

Klein was already behind them, and Fuchs had moved a long way from where he had fired the single shot. Suddenly the first man behind Jung, stood up and grabbed the young radio operator around the neck, forcing him to stand in front of him. He was pointing a pistol at Jung's head and shouting. Neither Fuchs, nor Klein could understand what was said, but they both got the message, 'Back off or your mate is dead!'

Another shot rang out and the lead man also fell to the ground. At the same time Klein was silently pulling his knife from the still standing, but now lifeless body of the third man in the group. Jung seized his chance and grabbed the pistol that had fallen alongside him in the undergrowth. He spun around as the last living man turned his attention to Klein, whom he had now realised was there. Another shot rang out, this time from the Luger handgun, and the final man was down.

'Well done my friend, I didn't think you had it in you,' declared Klein to his shaking comrade. He put his arm around his shoulders and said quietly, 'You did it instinctively to save my life, and I will not forget.'

Very shortly, Fuchs was up with them and he now pointed his rifle at the head of each of the prisoners in turn. The first was still alive and squinted through one dying eye and mumbled something that sounded like

'Prussian year,' to Jung. 'Never take chances,' said Fuchs calmly, as he put a bullet through the brain of each of the four RAF men.

'We can now rest until the Gruppenfuhrer and the men get here. I don't know how far off they still are but they will have certainly heard the shooting. They will now know that this mission is completed.'
'How did you know that you could hit the one who was holding me?' asked Jung of Fuchs.
'I just knew that I had to hit him and miss you, I also had a good angle on him as I had moved over by some 20 or 30 meters by the time I made the second shot. It opened him up a little, while he was still watching the point that I originally fired from.'

Jung was as white as a sheet, but again he realised that these men were probably the best friends that he could have in this war, God help him. He half smiled at Fuchs and managed to joke, 'Schultz will be proud of you, he is supposed to be the sharpshooter of our group.'

The three men settled down and Klein again agreed to keep watch, while the other two slept. Jung was still shaking as he quickly drifted off to sleep and even the hard nosed Fuchs couldn't help thinking what a shame it was that this intelligent young man had to be involved in the butchery of war. It was fine for him and Klein they were born to this kind of life. This man however was sensitive, and with that thought, Fuchs made up his mind that he would personally ensure that Jung was kept safe during the forthcoming mission. Jung had after all, also shown great courage and resourcefulness in protecting Klein.

Fuchs slept like a baby. On the other hand, Jung's sleep was very restless. He started to dream about bullets missing his head by millimetres. He could feel the draught of them passing by and then feel the spray of blood from the man who was holding him. He was covered in the other man's blood and it just kept spurting over him.

He dreamt of men with their whole skull being eaten by rats. He dreamt of a soldier lying dead on the ground and then jumping up and shouting 'Prussian year,' over and over again, before his head exploded.

Within half an hour or so, the rest of the team arrived. Zimmermann and the rest were hardly out of breath as they settled down around the three, who were now all fully awake. 'Give me the details, gentlemen,' the Gruppenfuhrer enquired quite calmly. The three recounted the whole tale and occasionally, Zimmermann interjected with questions.

At the end, he congratulated the team for their efforts. He then said, 'By the way Jung, you must not feel guilty about getting caught in their clever ambush. Especially as it was you who made the final kill. 'Are any of your ribs broken?' He seemed genuinely concerned for the young radio operator. 'I don't think so, sir. I am just badly bruised,' replied Jung. 'I will be fine.' The group moved a little distance from the airmen's bodies.

'We will rest here for a while and then we will head on out to the South side of the forest,' declared Zimmermann. 'We will be met by transport to take us directly to an airfield, and then we will be flown to the submarine base on the French coast! All of our specialist kit for the mission will be waiting for us at the docks. You see how I manage to think of everything, gentlemen.'

The whole group were completely shocked. Neumann was the first to speak. 'I thought that we were here to continue our training, sir,' he said. 'I thought that you wanted to see all of us in action.'
'I believe that I have seen enough action from you all today. I have one more confession to make, gentlemen. I was already fully confident with each one of your abilities. However, Herr Himmler insists that this final role play is necessary to sharpen you up, ready for the mission ahead. You have all just participated in a live action role play, and performed exceptionally well. Other teams have let the 'prisoners' escape, while others have not had the total success that you have had.'

'Excuse me, sir,' said Neumann. 'If, the exercise we have just participated in was role play, then who are the dead guards? And who are these four bodies here?'

'Yes gentlemen. This is another one of Herr Himmler's little ideas. I think that he would rather call it, 'The sporting chance.' We are using Polish prisoners of war, many of whom would be executed anyway.'

'We first make the ones playing the prisoners, dress in the uniforms of British servicemen. At this stage, none of them know what their participation will be. The servicemen are told first that they can go and are told that there are machine guns, waiting for them, about a kilometre along the path. They are told that there will be a hunt for them, but if they run, they will have a good head start, with a chance for freedom.'

'Once they have gone, the ones who play the German guards are dressed in uniform and given one knife between them, and then two of our specialist team go in and carve them up. The strange thing is gentlemen, not once in any of these role plays, have the first team picked up their machine guns and run back to the camp to see if their comrades need help. True, they are given the impression that the second group will be given the same chances, but wouldn't we automatically want to check on the safety of our comrades?'

Zimmermann looked at his men, and commented, 'Some of the escapees have made it to the edge of the forest, but they are tracked all the time. Once it is clear that they are not going to be caught by the SS team allocated to kill them, they are killed by the 'Catchers' at the point of exit. Gentlemen, I am proud to announce that our 'kill' has been the quickest so far, and also the most thorough. You can all be extremely pleased with yourselves. By the way, I shall keep the half penny coin that was planted on the ground by the preparation team. It might buy us all a beer in England! If it isn't enough to buy a round of drinks, then we will help ourselves anyway.'

Chapter 4

The village hall in Pett, is where the local defence volunteers or Home Guard, meet most evenings. There are seventeen members of the platoon in total. Some are ex servicemen from World War 1. There is also a doctor, two or three farmers, a butcher and a train driver.

They all take their role extremely seriously. A heightened state of alert has existed since the start of 1940, and although everyone in this country had faith in the Royal Navy and Royal Air Force to protect these shores from invasion, the possibility was always there. If, and when it came, the Pett platoon would be ready.

There was talk of an invasion force being towed in on barges behind enemy ships. If this were the case, the Royal Navy would sink them, and if they couldn't get there in time, the RAF would do the job. Either way, there would be an awful lot of German bodies floating in the Channel.

If there was another plan, then Britain would deal with it, as and when it happened. The men of the Pett platoon would be there, alongside their comrades in the surrounding villages, and all the other villages and towns across the nation.

Each evening the members would go out on their designated patrols, sometimes alone, sometimes in pairs. Nothing remarkable had happened, but that didn't dampen their enthusiasm. When they were called upon to do their duty for their country, they could be relied on. They were not well armed, but they had fashioned some very innovative weapons.

The village hall served many purposes. The local Women's Institute, would hold its meetings there, each Monday evening. The Home Guard used it for lectures and training on Wednesday evenings, and most weekends there would be some kind of village activity aimed at keeping the morale of the local community high.

It also served as the out of town, doctor's surgery. Surgeries were held on Tuesday and Thursday mornings. Dr. Adrian Hart was on duty this particular Thursday morning in June, and had worked his way through a variety of cases. There was an unwanted pregnancy from a lady, whose husband had been away at war for more months than she had been expecting. There was an unfortunate farmer with the most severe case of piles that he had ever seen. There were also the usual time wasters, but

Adrian was one Doctor who didn't mince his words, especially when he suspected that someone may be 'swinging the lead'.

'Mrs. Cooper,' the last patient in the waiting room heard him say, in a very firm voice. 'All the time you keep imagining there is something wrong with you, there will be. You will actually make yourself ill in the end, now go home and start enjoying your life, there is nothing ailing you.' The poor hypochondriacally inclined woman left the village hall even more determined to find 'symptoms' that would prove to this rude doctor that she was indeed, quite seriously ill.

Adrian Hart saw the last man sitting in the waiting area, apologised for the outburst, told Maureen, his nurse, to close the door then called him in to the tiny 'surgery'. This was not much more than a large cupboard off of the main hall. 'I don't believe we have met before,' he addressed the man politely. 'Are you new to the area? How can I help you?'

The man sat down on the patient's chair, and looked Adrian Hart directly in the eye. 'I am not here on medical business Doctor Hart, although I must insist that the 'Hippocratic oath' be observed when it comes to our discussion,' he declared. 'Let me introduce myself and all will become clear. My name is Major Gordon Roberts, of the British army. The section that I belong to is all a bit, 'hush hush.' He had Adrian's attention.

'Look Old Boy, I'll come straight to the point. You are already a member of the Home Guard, but I have been asked to approach you as an upright member of the local community, somebody who is beyond reproach. If for example, you are seen out and about at night, you will always have good reason for it.'

'Why the fuck would I need a reason?' responded the Doctor, curiously. Adrian Hart was not the stereotypical general practitioner, and was not averse to using strong language when the need arose. 'Because Old Boy, I am going to invite you to join a very special unit, which will be vital to the outcome of this war, should the threatened invasion actually come.'

'Hold on a moment,' said the Doctor, curtly. He got up and opened the door and told Maureen that she could go home now, there were no more patients to deal with. He thanked her and told her that he would see her tomorrow morning at the main surgery in Hastings. He closed the door, and said to the Major, 'Right, do you want a whisky?'
'Rather,' said the Major, somewhat surprised. The Doctor opened the medical bag which had been sitting on the small leather topped desk.

Adrian reached in and pulled out a half full bottle of Bells Whisky. He slipped off his stethoscope and stuffed it into the bag and produced a couple of cups from the shelf above the desk. He poured two very generous measures and pushed one cup towards the Major. 'Well, bloody hell,' the Major quipped, 'a bloody medic that is human!' Cheers, good health to you.'

They both took a long slow sip, savouring the warm, peaty taste as it trickled down the back of their throats. The Major then said, in quite a matter of fact way, 'Can I call you Adrian? If you are interested, then I can let you know a bit more.'

'Of course I'm fucking interested,' replied the doctor. 'I may be in the business of saving lives, but when it comes to those Nazi bastards, I would happily kill every last one of them. There is no way, while I still have breath in my body, that I will allow this country to be handed over to that bastard, Adolf Hitler.'

'That's rather what I was hoping you would say,' replied the Major. 'By the way, off the record, you can call me Gordon. If we are on official business, it must be military titles only.'
'Okay, so what do you want of me?' asked the Doctor.
'Basically,' replied the Major, 'I have been asked to set up an organisation that will be able to attack and harass the enemy from the rear, should they ever gain a foothold on these shores.'

"I have not approached your Captain Evans, in the home guard, it won't be necessary for him to know. I am setting up groups of six or seven men in each area, here in the south East. You will be in charge of five other men already recruited for this venture. Most of these men you will already know. The point is that all of you have special skills, not necessarily military, but nevertheless vital to the whole operation.'

Adrian replied, 'You must know that I don't have any military training other than the lectures and field events that we do with the home guard?'

The Major replied, 'Not necessary, my friend, you have the leadership skills, you know how to keep your mouth shut, and you also have the ability to deal with the obviously high casualty numbers that we can expect to have inflicted on us. As for the fighting skills, we can get you away for a week's intensive training, and when you come back, you will be just as well equipped to slice open a Nazi's throat as you would be to stitch the wounds of a British soldier. Do I take it that you are on board then?' asked the Major, with a wry smile.

Without hesitation, Adrian Hart replied, 'Fucking right I am.' The tea cups were topped up again and a date was agreed for the intensive guerrilla style training. When the week arrived, Adrian's wife Helen, waved him off, and watched the Alvis open top tourer, disappear down their lane and away towards Hastings. He had told her that he was off on a full week's medical conference in Brighton.

Helen knew he would return full of enthusiasm for the latest techniques and treatments to have evolved in the medical arena. She knew not to call him at the hotel, because he always worked late and needed to spend time debating medical issues with his colleagues. This 'debating' seemed to involve spending a lot of time at the hotel bar, but then again, that was the medical profession. Apparently, alcohol helped them to concentrate.

One week later a very different Doctor Adrian Hart, drove back to his cottage, on the outskirts of Pett Village. He had not had a drink for a week, but also his conscience was troubling him. He was a doctor, committed to saving lives and yet he had just been introduced to some of the most savage and brutal methods of dispatching a human being. His medical knowledge had helped him appreciate and learn these techniques.

This newly formed unit, was known by several unofficial names, one of which was 'The Baker Street Irregulars', after its London headquarters. The training officers at special training school number 5 had called it 'The Ministry of un-gentlemanly warfare'. The official title was the SOE, (Special Operations Executive). Should it be discussed within public hearing, it should be referred to as the 'Joint Technical Board'.

On the drive back, he tried to forget the very sudden changes that had happened in his life. It was a warm Saturday and the top was down on the 1938 Alvis that he loved to drive. He had developed a driving style that suited the car. The large bird of prey mascot, on the end of the long bonnet, served as an indicator for turning in to bends on the Sussex lanes.

He would normally be totally consumed with the pleasure of driving the Alvis, which was his favourite car to date. He had not bought it brand new, although it was only a year old. The long drive back from Coleshill, Buckinghamshire, where he had just undergone his specialist training, would normally have been total enjoyment. The car was reliable and had never let him down, even on some of the coldest nights when he was called out to very sick patients. There were also, of course moments, when he thought about the evening, and getting home to his wonderful wife, Helen. They would talk briefly about his 'Medical Conference', and then they would go out for a meal in one of the Old Town restaurants in Hastings. He was not back on duty until Monday morning and he would be able to consume a fair quantity of food and alcohol during the course of this evening and Sunday.

One evening next week, he was to receive a phone call from the 'Joint Technical Board.' This covert name was good because it covered a wide variety of situations. Should Helen answer the phone, it would seem to her like something associated with the medical profession. Once the message was received, the team would meet up with Major Roberts at Icklesham. They would then drive across to Beckley Wood to jointly inspect the arms cache that had been created for him and his fellow operatives, in a bunker deep inside the forest.

So as not to arouse suspicion, the Major had suggested that those team members, who owned a dog, should bring it along. This way, if anyone spotted them, they would appear quite normal, walking separately or in pairs, out for a stroll with their pets. Four of the six had an animal, including Adrian.

He had met the other five members of his team on the course. One was a patient of his, a former soldier who served in World War One. Although he was in his early fifties, and had been subjected to mustard gas in the trenches, he was still physically fit, apart from a limp. This was caused by the loss of some toes, caused by trench foot, but it did not hinder him, and he coped exceptionally well with the training at Coleshill. He worked in Hastings as an electrician and radio repair man, and was the type of man you could totally rely on. His name was Edward 'Ted' White.

Another man, also known to Adrian as a patient, was reputedly a local poacher, but his knowledge of the countryside was phenomenal. During training he had managed to conceal himself in the most unlikely hiding places. Even the training officers failed to find him on one occasion when they practiced the 'Man hunt'. He had managed to hide himself just beneath the water in a small pond, amongst the reeds.

He was breathing through the neck of a milk bottle that he had broken the bottom off, and even to the trained eye, it simply appeared to be a broken bottle thrown into the water. He was wiry and physically strong and was known to everybody as 'Badger'. His proper name was John Higgins.

He had watched from below the water as training officer Bailey walked past him, and then he silently sat up out of the water and shouted 'Bang'. 'You bastard Badger, that was the best concealment we have ever had,' laughed the officer, full of praise.

The other three men were William 'Bill' Jacobs, a local coal merchant of huge physical strength, George Dobson, a builder, and also a very strong man. Finally, Harry East, who although not so well built as the other two, was very fit and wiry. He ran a local car repair garage, and was very good with all things mechanical. Although Bill, George and Harry were not patients of Adrian's, he knew them all quite well, and indeed had some dealings with all of them over the years. He felt that they were all trustworthy and could be counted on 100% when the need arose.

His mind had been wandering for some time, and he suddenly felt more at ease with the situation. Yes, he was a doctor. Yes, he was dedicated to saving lives. He was also a stalwart patriot, and the thought of his country being overrun by Nazis, with the obvious consequences, was not acceptable. He was an intelligent man. He knew that if the country was successfully invaded, then all men of fighting age would be eliminated one way or another. If that meant that they would be killed, then they might just as well have put up a bloody good fight and died that way. If it meant that they would be deported to labour camps, the same argument applied.

He double declutched down into third gear to take Robertsbridge hill on the A21. This car was a dream to drive and for a moment he dismissed the thoughts of things past and present, and became totally focussed on the pleasure of driving it. As he approached the bottom of the hill, he double declutched again down to second gear as he rounded the bend into the village. The warm breeze blew directly into his grey bearded face as he glided through the narrow little Sussex village. He enjoyed the feeling of the warm breeze in his tousled hair.

As he cleared the last few houses, he accelerated away up the hill and changed up into third as he built up speed for the uphill section towards the village of Johns Cross. He was now only half an hour from his beloved village of Pett, and he mentally started to concoct a story of medical matters, that he knew he would need, in order to keep Helen happy.

The weekend was enjoyable, including a very loving reunion with his wife. They had dined together, at 'The Smithy', a restaurant in the Old

Town area of Hastings. As usual, one diner declared, 'I am so glad I've bumped into you Doc, I've been meaning to come and see you for ages.' As usual, Helen patiently replied, 'Then I will make you an appointment at the surgery. Which suits you best, Monday or Tuesday?'
This occurrence was perfectly normal, and one which Helen and Adrian took in their stride. They often wondered why the hell anybody would want to discuss their piles over the dinner table or at the bar, but it always happened. The Sunday came and went, with a long lunchtime visit to 'The Two Sawyers' in Pett village.

Surgery on Monday also came and went with the usual array of complaints, coughs, colds, and an old boy with a suspected broken rib from a fall at home. Adrian's mind was half on the job in hand, and half of it was buzzing with the thought of his new role in the community. He couldn't wait for the call which would signal the visit to the bunker.

The phone call finally came on Tuesday evening at home. Helen had answered the call to the gentleman on the other end, who stated politely that he was 'Gordon, from the Joint Technical Board.' Adrian took the telephone from his wife and tried to appear nonchalant as he spoke into the receiver.

'Got to pop out Dear,' he said breezily as he grabbed the dog's lead and shouted, 'Rufus'. As he grabbed his medical bag, he muttered something about an ambulance crew that were not sure whether to move a patient who had fallen from a rooftop near the seafront. The Joint Technical Board, whose people came to speak at the conference, now had him listed as the most local GP to Hastings, so he had to assist. 'While I'm out, I might as well walk the dog, as it's so close to the beach.'

The meeting with the Major and the others was at the pre-arranged lay-by on the A259. They all climbed in along with the four dogs, into Adrian and Georges' cars, to travel to Beckley. The Major handed Adrian a large key on the journey. Everyone was filled with anticipation and few words were spoken. They parked both cars at one of several entrances to the woodlands, and proceeded to walk in, whilst allowing the four animals off their leads. Adrian's dog Rufus, was a black and white Border collie. The other three were a Labrador cross named Jess, a big black mongrel called Ziggy, who belonged to Badger, and an Alsatian named Rex.

They walked North Easterly from the top of Ludley Hill, in three groups so as not to look like a group. They allowed the dogs to run around freely and follow their path up through the woods. After about half an hour, the

Major checked his compass and quickly looked at the map. He called to the others, 'Right chaps, let's close up. There isn't anybody else about.' Within twenty seconds they were all gathered together and the Major pointed to some dense woodland to their right hand side.
The dogs were put back on their leads and quickly the whole group moved off the pathway and into the thick layer of fir trees. The Major led the way. There was no path, just an almost impenetrable forest of trees. Everyone was hushed, even the four dogs sensed that they needed to be on guard and after a couple of hundred paces, it was impossible to see daylight anymore, either from where they had penetrated, or in front.
It was about eight o'clock in the evening now and a little light still came in from above them. They had reached a small clearing with a couple of tree stumps, one of which appeared to be that of a very old oak.

The Major stopped, looked around and said, almost theatrically, 'Gentlemen, here is your bunker. Please make a note of this map reference, it must not be written down for obvious reasons. The number is, TQ 865222.' The men spent some time committing this vital number to memory, and gradually once they were all happy that they had retained it, they started to look around.

'Well boys, what do you think?' asked the Major. The men all seemed surprised, and Harry asked, 'Do we have an arms cache to be left here that will be covered with a tarpaulin, Sir?' The Major seemed amused by this question. 'No Harry, the arms are here already,' he exclaimed. 'Well I'm fucked if I can spot them,' said Adrian, as he stared upwards to see whether there was anything hidden in the branches of the firs.

'I promised you a proper bunker and that's what you have got,' the Major announced as he asked Adrian to give him the key. 'It appears to have done the trick as far as concealment is concerned, so I think it's about time I revealed it to you.' With that the Major walked over to the broad oak stump and knelt down. He brushed away a few dead pine needles and cones and inserted the key just below ground level. Suddenly he lifted the stump from the key side and the whole thing tipped over, revealing a large round hole in the ground.

The whole group was amazed and immediately came over to inspect the hole. It was totally ingenious. The tree stump had been fixed to a hinged manhole type cover. The dimensions of the stump were slightly larger than the cover itself, so the surrounding ground was completely covered. In the locked position, it was immovable and as the Major had already proven, could not be detected at all. From just below the cover, a steel ladder ran down into the hole. 'Bloody ingenious, these MOD boys,' said the Major. 'Let me have the dogs, while you go down and inspect your new home. The light switch is just down the ladder.' Adrian was the first to climb down and as his head came level with the top rung of the steel ladder, he spotted the switch in front of him. He switched it downwards and immediately the area below lit up to reveal a cave which appeared to be half sandstone and half concrete. He got to the bottom of the ladder and stepped onto the sandstone floor. From this point, the room ran in a wide corridor approximately twenty feet long, by ten feet wide. On the left side, there were three two tier bunk beds, steel framed with a mattress and blankets placed on each bed. These appeared to be actually built into the wall of the bunker. A very large cupboard occupied the space at the far end. On the right hand side, there was a single row of steel and concrete shelving, about four feet from the ground stuffed with all kinds of armaments. The curved roof was of corrugated steel. The men said nothing, they were completely enthralled.

'Look at this fucking lot,' said Adrian, as he opened the lid of an oblong green wooden box on the floor under the shelves. The boxes all had dirty grey rope handles. The lids were fitted with two green painted hinges and a latch, and upon opening, the boxes were stuffed full with sticks of dynamite, covered in waxed brown paper. There must have been at least thirty boxes, as they were packed three layers deep for almost the length of this wall. On the shelving itself, was laid a stack of maybe forty or fifty rifles, none of which looked familiar to the men. Next to these were stacked green wooden boxes full of ammunition, and Adrian estimated that there could be something like twenty thousand rounds here. The boxes all had strange black sign writing and markings.

'Russian, old boy,' called the Major, down through the entrance tunnel. 'Don't ask how or why, just be grateful.' George, gasped as he opened one of the steel crates stacked next to the ammunition boxes. These were clearly marked 'Property of the Ministry of Defence', and laid inside each crate were probably fifty or more hand grenades, each wrapped in the regulation waxed brown paper. There were four crates. A large box contained fuses, detonators and timers. There were also two flame throwers, identical to the ones at Coleshill.

Towards the end of the shelf were stacked half a dozen five gallon, dark green fuel cans, all full. Several steel crates of empty milk bottles, sat next to the fuel cans and finally there were several sacks of rags, tied up at the neck with coarse string. 'By the way chaps, I should have already

Mentioned, that there must be no smoking here, either in the bunker, or anywhere else where a stray dog end might give our game away.'

'All understood Major,' responded Adrian from down in the bunker. His attention had now been taken up by the large wardrobe style cupboard at the end of the bunker. He opened the doors, to find that it was half cupboard and half doorway through to a smaller lobby. On the left hand side were stacked all kinds of foodstuffs, including cans of corned beef, tinned carrots, peas, and potatoes. There were also lots of tins marked, 'Irish Stew'. There were a couple of large round blue and white tins, with removable lids, marked 'National Dried Milk'.

Set at the top shelf was a large steel drum with a tap, marked 'Drinking Water'. Next to this was an array of enamelled plates and mugs, and army issue knifes, forks and spoons. Most importantly, there were a couple of tin openers.

Ted was the first to walk through into the small lobby, beyond the "Wardrobe". 'This is bloody marvellous,' he called back to the others. 'You will have to come in one at a time to see it, but there's a latrine in here as well as a periscope, and a radio.' One by one they entered the little lobby and looked around in wonder. A round steel chemical toilet sat on one side, and the smell of Jeyes fluid was quite strong around it. The chaps who built the bunker had even taken the trouble to put up a small wooden shelf, which held a dozen boxes of Jeyes toilet paper.

On the other side, which was behind the food storage area, was a tall wooden stool, in front of two more shelves. On the lower shelf stood a Murphy WS 8, field radio unit, with a set of leather headphones, and above it, the top shelf was stacked with dark blue Ever Ready batteries. Some had brown, cotton covered wires fitted to them and some were just standing on the shelf. The two shelves did not take up the whole of the wall, because what appeared to be the periscope from a submarine was fitted through the corrugated iron ceiling. There was just enough room to get behind it next to the shelves, to give a 360 degree view.

They all took it in turns to use this piece of equipment, and they all seemed to be mesmerised by it. As they stood facing the wall, the view was of the clearing where the bunker entrance was located. The Major was clearly visible standing patiently holding the four dog's leads. Next to him was the large, upturned oak stump. As they changed position by slowly walking around and gripping the tube, until their backs were tight against the wall, the view changed to one of pine trees, planted closely together.

Ted had already fiddled with the radio. It was a type that he was fully familiar with. Adrian noted that there was no whisky in the larder. A couple of the others had picked up the Russian rifles and started to get the feel of them. Bullets had been loaded and the actions checked. They all seemed to be very serviceable, they would be as good for killing 'filthy Nazis', as any other weapon, they were all agreed.

'If you've seen enough chaps, I want to point out a couple of other things back out here.' One by one, they climbed the galvanised steel ladder out of the bunker and stood once again with the Major on the forest floor. 'Right chaps,' he said. 'Over here, just inside the trees is where your periscope comes out.' There was a broken stump of fir tree sticking out of the ground by about a foot, and standing one row of trees back from the clearing. The concealment was amazing. The dog owners took charge of their animals again, while the Major shinned down the steel ladder and disappeared.

Suddenly, and slowly, the small fir stump began to move up out of the ground and a glint of glass could be detected below it. The stump made a slow 360 degree turn, and then slowly pulled back down again.

Quickly, the Major was out of the bunker and pointing skyward to the top of the trees. 'One of those carries the aerial for the radio transmitter, the chaps spent a long time prizing away the bark and then re-fixing it once the cable was installed behind it. Even if you look carefully you will not be able to detect which tree it is in. I couldn't even tell you which one it is now, and I watched the buggers do it! Damned clever, eh?'

The entire team were extremely impressed. The Major also informed them that the construction of the bunker had taken just over a week from start to finish. The woods had been 'closed, for military manoeuvres' during that time. George Dobson, as a builder, was very complimentary. 'I wouldn't mind having a couple of these guys on my books, if that's the speed they can work at,' he joked.

The major pointed out a couple of other things to them. 'The power supply down there is battery only, so you may wish to conserve energy by bringing in your own torches. It is estimated, with the batteries you have, that you could get perhaps up to three days lighting, but not with continuous usage.' He continued, 'Also the radio, as you will know, Ted,

is short wave with a range of around five miles. This will be ample to make contact with the other local units around you.'
'All messages concerning co-ordinated attacks will simply be relayed on. There are ten boxes of Swan Vestas matches wrapped inside a rag, in the food store. Needless to say, these must not be opened in the bunker. We want to blow up Jerry, not ourselves. All food will be eaten cold there are no cooking facilities down there. We can't risk the smell of cooked food wafting out of the ventilation system, nor can we risk a naked flame with all that fuel around. Is everybody clear?'

The training they had undergone had covered all of these points, so nobody asked anything regarding the living conditions and the way that they would operate whilst underground. Ted asked a question regarding ventilation. 'How do we get rid of the stale air down there, Major?'

'Good point Ted. There are two clay pipes running through the ground and into the bunker. One of these is situated behind the latrine, which is inclined to make it a bit draughty when you go for a crap. The other one is at the bottom of the steel ladder. Both of these are laid in the direction of the lower ground towards Eggshole Brook, due South of here.' The Major pointed to his map as the men gathered round.

'They just appear out of the ground there, like any other drainage channels heading for the stream. This system works well, as a natural draught is created. If you needed to increase the airflow at any time, there is also a hand bellows pump at the bottom of the ladder, which you only need lift and then allow it to fall again. After a few pumps the air will freshen up quite nicely. One thing I have to tell you though, is that this bunker has no escape tunnel. Most of the others do, but the landscape here doesn't really allow for this. The upside is that it is probably one of the best concealments of any that I have seen.'

'Speaking for myself,' said Adrian, 'This is not an issue.' Almost as one, the others agreed. 'Right Doc, I also believe that an escape tunnel provides one more chance of being discovered,' responded Badger. 'I think that this has got to be better than the bunkers at Coleshill. Let's face it, if the Germans ever find this, we are all fucked anyway.'

A couple more details were discussed, the lights were switched off, and the bunker closed down again. The fir cones and dead wood were then spread back around the large oak stump, and they set off back to the cars.

'Was the patient alright?' enquired Helen, as Adrian settled down in his favourite armchair with a large scotch in his hand. Rufus looked up lovingly at his master, who had just taken him on one of the best walks he had done for a long time. 'Suspected pelvic fracture, plus a bit of concussion, and multiple contusions, which was quite lucky when you see the height that he fell from,' responded her husband.
'Does this new 'Board', mean that you are going to be called out, more frequently than you are at the moment?' asked Helen, resignedly.
'Oh I don't think so, Darling. My guess is that they were just testing out my response time. To be honest, I think that the ambulance crew were perfectly capable of dealing with this, but the man from 'The Board' was in attendance. It should all settle down now.'

'Well, what with your night time call outs, together with your Home Guard duties, and now this, we don't seem to be able to spend any complete evenings together,' complained his wife.
'I know Darling, but it won't be forever,' replied Adrian.

Helen made a cup of cocoa for herself and topped up her husband's whisky glass, and suggested with a glint in her eye, that they have an early night.

Chapter 5

Gruppenfuhrer Zimmermann had pushed his men hard. They had made good time to the Southern edges of the Black Forest, where a 'clean up' squad, together with an army lorry, was awaiting their arrival.

They were close to a small town, named Buchenbach.

Once the co-ordinates were given to the 'clean up squad', for the Polish soldiers' bodies, the team were aboard the Army lorry, which was soon rumbling in the direction of the French border.

Jung, who had been sleeping again as soon as they had settled down in the lorry, suddenly called out, 'What did that Polish guy mean?' and immediately felt totally embarrassed by his accidentally spoken thoughts. The Gruppenfuhrer, in an almost fatherly way, went over to his side of the lorry, and asked quietly what he meant.

Somehow, Jung seemed the most vulnerable of the group, but his radio skills were unrivalled, and it was vital that he be part of this operation. The whole team was aware that he may need some help, and Zimmermann was keen to reassure the young man.

'What did it sound like?' asked Zimmermann, kindly.
'I am sorry Gruppenfuhrer, but I can't get it out of my head. It sounded like "Prussian Year."'
'That would be "Prosze Nie,'' or "Please No", in German. Did he say this just before he was shot?' enquired the Gruppenfuhrer.
'Yes sir,' replied Jung. 'He was dying anyway, but we just put him out of his misery.'

'You have nothing to worry about, these people are sub-human. This sort of cowardice is what we can expect from our enemies. Do you think a German soldier, knowing that he was going to die anyway, would plead for his life in this way?'

Jung thought that he would personally try anything to stay alive, but dared not say this to his commanding officer. 'I don't think so Sir.'
'Then do not let it trouble you further. You have become a very good soldier and I am very proud of your achievements. You have already shown great bravery in saving the life of one of your comrades. Do not let the last words of a cowardly enemy worry you. He was scum, an enemy of our great nation, you should be proud that you have witnessed

this behaviour first hand. I am impressed that you have a heart, and a conscience, but do not allow your natural compassion for your fellow countrymen extend to these bastards who would see us all dead.'

'Thank you Sir,' responded Jung, who now began to feel as though a weight had been lifted from his shoulders. Wagner, who was sitting next to Jung in the lorry, gave his shoulder a squeeze, and simply said, 'The Gruppenfuhrer is absolutely right. We are proud Germans, and the other peoples of this world are lesser beings than us. Think of it as putting an animal out of its misery. It shows just how compassionate we are.'

The lorry bumped on and was soon passing through the town of Freiburg im Breisgau. They were quickly out on the open road again and after about an hour, during which time most of the group had some sleep, they arrived at a small town called Oberentzen.

'We are now in the Alsace region of France,' Zimmermann called out to his team, who quickly awoke. Most of them had not even realised that they had crossed the border into France. The Gruppenfuhrer had simply stood up and given a half salute at the border post, and the German guards had stood abruptly to attention, with snapped salutes, and opened the barrier. They were not going to ask this very senior officer for papers.

'So, Gentlemen. We will soon be at a military airfield, where our air transport is waiting for us. Please make sure that your fingernails are clean and that your hair is combed. Also please smarten up your uniforms as best you can. We don't want these Luftwaffe boys thinking that we are anything but the cream of The Fuhrer's fighting machine.'

The lorry swung south, down a small country lane, and after about 15 minutes, it turned into a driveway with a red and white painted barrier across it. 'Welcome, Gruppenfuhrer. We have been expecting you and your team,' said a smartly dressed airman, in charge of the barrier.

'If any of your men need to use the latrines, they are over there next to the control tower. After that your plane is ready to leave when you are.'

'Thank you, yes. I believe that we could all do with a quick freshen up before we take off,' replied the Gruppenfuhrer, politely. The lorry rumbled into the large field, in the direction of a clump of grey concrete buildings situated at the far end, centred with a small, windowed tower. This would, for some of the group, be their first flight.

As the lorry pulled up alongside the airfield buildings, Fuchs leapt from the rear of the lorry and ran directly to the latrine block, leaving his kitbag and rifle for Klein to carry. The others winked at each other, because they knew that Fuch's was literally shitting himself at the thought of getting into an aeroplane. This hard man, this killer, was finally shown to be frightened of something.

The others entered the block and soon came running out again. 'My God,' said Schultz. 'It smells like a rat has crawled up his arse and died.' Klein took a deep breath and went in for a piss, hoping he could finish peeing before he needed to breathe again.

Eventually Fuchs came out, looking very white. The others copied Klein's trick and held their breath while they pissed. Not one of the team stayed in the block for longer than a minute and a half.

Once all of the men had been into the latrine block, Zimmermann entered and appeared to be totally unaffected by the stench that was still trapped in the air inside. Once he had finished, he ordered all of the men to go back and wash their hands and faces, and nobody protested.

Suddenly the group were aware of the raucous sound of a triple engine 'plane, coughing into life. They had not noticed it, parked behind the buildings and it was now rumbling across the grass in their direction. 'Have you bought a shit bucket with you?' Schultz taunted Fuchs. 'You can sit out on the wing, if we have to put up with that stink again.'

The Gruppenfuhrer did not mind a certain amount of camaraderie between the men, but he understood how Fuchs must be feeling. 'Leave the poor bugger alone now, not everybody is so good with the flying,' he warned.

'It's not the flying I am frightened of, it's the crashing,' whispered Schultz to Neumann, who also found Fuch's fear a little amusing.

The three engines were whining right in front of them now, and the 'plane swung sideways on to the group. The airman who had come to greet them just after the latrine session politely informed the group that this was Adolf Hitler's private aircraft, a de-commissioned Junkers JU-52 Bomber.

The Luftwaffe man approached the 'plane and opened the fuselage door. He then swung down a set of steps, and politely waved the men aboard.

'Turn left for your seats, gentlemen, you may put your equipment in the area to the right of the door. They all clambered in and were quite surprised to see the level of luxury on board. There were deep leather seats which were certainly not the norm with this type of 'plane. Still, they reasoned that if the Fuhrer himself was using this as his personal air transport, then it would have to have been modified to suit his needs.

They dumped their kit in the open space towards the rear of the aircraft and then moved forward to the seating area. There were two rows of twin seats each side and there were six windows either side of the cabin, so everybody could see out. 'I will sit with you,' said Zimmermann to Fuchs, who looked as if he were going to vomit. 'You sit in the window seat and you will very soon relax, once you find how exhilarating it is.'

As they were all settling in, a man in immaculate Luftwaffe uniform approached from the cockpit area. 'Gentlemen, welcome aboard our special aircraft. My name is Oberstleutnant Braun and I am the co-pilot of this aircraft. My colleague at the controls, is Lieutenant General Hans Baur. We are both highly qualified pilots, and in fact Hans Baur is the Fuhrer's personal pilot.

'Is anybody here nervous about flying?' The officer asked cordially. 'We have a fine soldier here who has not flown before,' responded the Gruppenfuhrer, 'but I know that he will feel more comfortable with two such experienced men at the controls. If you are good enough for the Fuhrer, you are certainly good enough for us, don't you agree Fuchs?'

'Thank you Gruppenfuhrer, replied the Oberstleutnant, politely. Now, gentlemen if you would excuse me, we have to take off shortly, and we should get you to the West coast of France within two hours. Please buckle up your seat belts for the take off, and once we are airborne, I will come back to make sure everybody is comfortable.

The co-pilot disappeared behind a curtain at the front of the aircraft and the 'plane started to move across the bumpy field. The cabin fell silent as the aircraft jolted along the grass for what seemed an eternity. Suddenly the aircraft swung hard right in a hundred and eighty degree turn and then stopped. For a moment, Fuchs thought it had broken down and that mercifully they would have to go by road after all.

The slow tick-over of the three engines, increased suddenly to a screaming crescendo, then the aircraft lurched forward at an alarming rate. The aircraft was bumping quickly now along the grass runway, with ever increasing speed. Suddenly the whole thing soared upwards and away into the air. The Gruppenfuhrer put his arm on Fuch's shoulder, 'You see there is nothing to worry about. Look out the window and you will have the most wonderful moving picture of the countryside. You can take comfort in the fact that Germany now owns the whole of France, and that every piece of land that we fly over belongs to us!'

Fuchs was still very afraid, but he could see what the Gruppenfuhrer was doing, and he tried to believe that maybe they would eventually arrive at their destination, unscathed. He appreciated his officer's efforts to keep him calm, and his respect for the man had grown immensely. He had seen him comfort Jung, when he was spooked by the death of the Polish soldier. All this, and yet he was still a feared officer with a reputation for harsh treatment of his troops.

During the flight, all of the men stayed awake, excited now at the prospect of the mission and also fascinated by the French landscape sliding by beneath them. They chatted the whole time, and occasionally Schultz would make a joke, or sing one of his impromptu songs. Their commanding officer was happy to see them all relaxed, because he knew that soon, they would be totally focussed on the mission.

The co-pilot appeared from behind the cockpit curtain after a while, and told the group that they could undo their seat belts for now. He also showed them a small locker where there were a couple of bottles of Schnapps, with some small glasses. 'This is the Fuhrer's favourite, but we have plenty of it back at base, so you are welcome to help yourselves.'

The group looked at Zimmermann for approval, and he just waved his arms and said, 'We have plenty of time to sleep it off before we reach our final destination.' All the men took a glass, and Wagner took one over to the Gruppenfuhrer, who spent a very long time breathing on it and then furiously rubbing it with his handkerchief, before finally holding it up to be filled by the climber.

After about an hour and a half, Zimmermann called to everyone to look out of the windows. Beneath them was Paris, and although they were flying at a height of around 3,000 metres, they could clearly see the river Seine snaking through the town, and also the Eiffel Tower. 'When our mission is over Gentlemen, we will have some fun in that city.'

Even Fuchs felt a little more relaxed, although he was beginning to dread the landing. Somehow it did not seem possible to him that an aircraft

could collide with the runway at great speed and stop safely. He turned to his commanding officer, who again sensed his fear. 'How many times have these type of aircraft crashed while landing, Sir?'
'It is better to ask how many crashes has our very experienced pilot had.' Replied Zimmermann, kindly. 'I can tell you that he has executed thousands of take offs and landings, many times with the Fuhrer on board, and he has never had a problem.'

'I apologise for being so stupid, Sir. I promise you that I will have no fears when it comes to combat with the enemy.'
'I know that already Fuchs, otherwise you would not be on this mission. I have absolute confidence in your abilities.'

A few minutes later, the affable co-pilot re-appeared from behind the cockpit curtain. 'So, Gentlemen. In about fifteen minutes we will be landing in another military airfield, at Picquigny. I have been in touch with the airfield, and they have confirmed that there is transport waiting to take you to your final destination.'

'I hope that you have all enjoyed this flight, and now I must ask you to buckle your seat belts again, and return the bottle and glasses to the locker. Please excuse me once again, I have to assist with the landing.'

The cabin area began to fall silent, as the aircraft could be felt descending rapidly. Fuchs was shaken visibly when the undercarriage bumped down, and again, Zimmermann reassured him. 'Relax, that is just the wheels locking into position for landing.' The trees were getting closer now, and as the aircraft turned to make its final approach, the English Channel became visible through the right hand windows.

Zimmermann again engaged Fuchs in conversation, telling him that there would be just a slight bump when the wheels hit the ground, but then they would be safely down. He watched as the fields grew ever closer and the trees were now visible alongside the aircraft. The aircraft touched down lightly with no bouncing around, and was very soon racing across the grass runway and eventually cruising to a halt. The others noticed that Fuchs was as white as a sheet. To them, it was quite amusing because they had never seen him scared before.
Finally two men appeared from behind the cockpit curtain, the affable and polite co-pilot Braun, along with the stern faced Hans Baur, who growled, 'I apologise for the poor landing, Gentlemen. I am only glad that the Fuhrer is not on board this day, he is very critical of my flying skills. In my defence, I can say that this landing strip is merely a

converted field, which still has many bumps in it.' He then gave a half smile, and wished everybody a safe journey on from the airfield. None of the men had absolutely any idea what the man was talking about, and came to the conclusion that he was having a joke with them. Zimmermann later informed the men that Hans Baur was great friends with the Fuhrer, and even the most perfect of landings would be criticised as a matter of course. It was the Fuhrer's way of letting you know that he liked you.

The co-pilot opened the door and fitted the steps to the side of the aircraft. One by one the men collected their kit from the rear portion of the aircraft and then climbed down the steps to the grass.

Another army lorry rumbled up to within a few metres of the group, and once again they were loading their kit into the back of it. Zimmermann thanked the pilot and co-pilot, salutes were exchanged, and he climbed in with the rest of the men. 'So now Gentlemen. We are almost at our final destination on French soil. In less than an hour, we will be at the port of St. Valery Sur Somme. We then meet up with our friends from the Kriegsmarine.'

A more serious mood began to fall over the group. The Gruppenfuhrer too, assumed a slightly colder stance as they drove towards the coast. 'Attention, Gentlemen. We have one last opportunity to discuss the mission without any unwanted ears overhearing. Even when we are aboard the submarine, the Commander only knows that we are going to try to knock out the decoding apparatus, on the cliff top. He will submerge again once we are unloaded, and will await our signal to tell him to leave us and return to base, or otherwise to shell the house because we have not been able to get close enough.'

He continued, 'He knows that we will not be returning as we have another mission to accomplish, but that is all. When we get to St. Valery Sur Somme,' at this point Zimmermann consulted his wristwatch, 'at about 1600 hours, we will collect all of the kit for the mission, from The Hotel du Port on the harbour front, which the Waffen SS have commandeered. We will have very little time to clean up and eat, before we have to set sail. The submarine, once underway, makes about 7 knots, which means our passage time will be about 9 hours. It is essential that we set sail at the latest 1700 hours.

As soon as the lorry rumbled up to the Hotel, two well built Kriegsmarine officers approached the rear, and quickly introduced themselves.

Leutnants Zur See, Erich Perschel, and Heinz Jacobs helped the team to unload their equipment and carry it into the building. They were all ushered into a large dining room to the rear of the large building.

A bearded Kriegsmarine officer stood at a large table at the end of the room and as soon as the last man had entered, his voice boomed out. 'Good evening men. My name is Korvettenkapitan Schaeffer, and I am the Commander of your 'under sea transport' to the coast of Great Britain. All of your equipment has been loaded onto my boat already, because we are very short of time. Everything is exactly as you have personally requested through your commanding officer.'

The Gruppenfuhrer moved forward through the men and called back to the Commander. 'Thank you, Korvettenkapitan; I am Zimmermann, in charge of this mission. And yes we are very short of time, now.'

'You will be in charge of this mission once you leave my submarine, but for now Gruppenfuhrer, I am in control. Please sit down all of you and pay attention. I have asked for some food to be brought in here for you, as there will be no opportunity to eat on my boat. You may eat while I am talking. We will sail in just under 45 minutes, so I will be brief.'

'Once aboard, you will be quite cramped, because I am carrying a full crew of 44 men. Your equipment has been stored in and around the torpedo tubes and you will have to make yourselves comfortable as best you can. Should we come under surveillance from the enemy during the trip, I will demand absolute silence. Not even a whisper will be allowed. Does everybody understand?'

'I have already briefed my men as to the required level of discipline whilst aboard your boat, so I believe that you need not repeat this now,' Responded Zimmermann, slightly annoyed at the arrogance of the submarine commander. 'That's as may be Gruppenfuhrer, but again I remind you that I have managed to avoid my boat being captured or sunk, since I took command and I am not prepared to risk her, or the lives of any of my crew, for a bunch of unruly soldiers, who don't play the game by the rules.'

Zimmermann exploded. 'Enough, Schaeffer. We are all here on the direct orders of the Fuhrer. You are simply providing a means to an end for our mission. Should I telephone the Fuhrer directly now and tell him we require a replacement commander for our boat to take us to England, or do we agree that you will take us there without any further lectures?'

As for unruly soldiers, we have had a very long day, and have already seen combat much earlier, probably while you were still asleep. These men have been hand picked by me, and Herr Himmler, and they are the most disciplined force in the whole of the Waffen SS. They appear a little dishevelled now because we have not stopped travelling, since running through the Black Forest, long before dawn this morning.'

The Korvettenkapitan was about to reply, but saw the steely look in the Gruppenfuhrer's eyes, and thought better of it. 'Yes Gruppenfuhrer Zimmermann, looks can be deceptive. You will forgive me it is just that in the Kriegsmarine, we are taught to be smart at all times.' The commander realised that this man in front of him was no ordinary soldier, and believed that he probably did have the ear of the Fuhrer. He decided that he had said enough and called to his men to bring in the food.

The team were extremely impressed with their commanding officer's handling of this awkward, pompous, probably queer, submariner. 'Probably the wrong time of the month for the bearded fairy,' volunteered Schultz, to the rest of the team. 'I bet they all avoid him in the showers, especially when he drops the soap.'

A food trolley was wheeled in and the men were told to simply help themselves. There was coffee, some cold meat and fresh bread. It was gone in a flash, and the men all wondered what the next course would be. Another trolley arrived loaded with slices of fruit cake, which disappeared just as quickly. That was it, their meal was finished.

The pompous submarine commander addressed them again, but in slightly less authoritative tones. 'Men, we now have ten minutes left for you to visit the wash rooms, before we have to leave.' They made their way out of the room and along a short corridor to the very plush looking wash rooms. 'Please do your best to tidy up, Gentlemen. I don't want that bastard thinking that he has got the upper hand,' growled Zimmermann to his team.

They quickly used the toilets, and scrubbed their hands and faces. They used the nail brushes provided, assisting each other with cleaning various dirt stains from their uniforms, and within seven or eight minutes, they looked very smart again. Zimmermann was impressed with their ingenuity, and praised the team for their efforts. As a final gesture, they used the towels provided, to clean their dusty boots, and they once more looked like the smart fighting unit that they actually were. They marched out of the wash rooms, and back to the dining room, where the Kriegsmarine officers were waiting.

The Gruppenfuhrer led them in and barked the command, 'HALT,' as they got to the centre of the room. The submarine commander's jaw dropped when he saw the transformation in the team. They stood completely still and stared straight ahead without any visible movement. Zimmermann now barked, 'AT EASE.' and as one the team's left feet hit the floor, again standing completely still in an astride stance.

'I am impressed, men. You look so different, now,' squirmed Schaeffer. He felt that he should try to make amends for his earlier indiscretion. This man Zimmermann looked dangerous, and he had no wish to be reported to the Fuhrer, or perhaps worse, to Herr Himmler.
They were ruthless men, and the German army, above all other services, always seemed to have the admiration and sympathy of Adolf Hitler.

'So, Gentlemen. Please now collect all personal weapons, like knives and pistols from your kit, and leave everything else, including rifles, here. We have everything we need for our little holiday, already packed in the submarine. This was supervised by our colleagues in the Waffen SS

The group collected their weapons as instructed, and again formed up to march from the hotel to the quay. The Korvettenkapitan marched ahead with his two officers and he was embarrassingly aware of the disciplined marching skills of the group of soldiers behind. The whole scene took on an air of comedy, as the two services tried to compete with each other, goose stepping exaggeratedly the short distance to the quayside.

It was high tide and the river was swollen and running fast, just a couple of metres below the top of the timber boarding that formed the walls of the quay. The group stopped by a wooden ladder that stood up from the boarding.

At this point, the Korvettenkapitan stared at the middle of the river, and whistled. Immediately a periscope appeared from the fast running water, swiftly followed by the conning tower. The whole shape of the boat was now visible and finally the stern deck gun broke through. In no time at all, the boat seemed to drift effortlessly towards the side of the quay.

The team watched as the large vessel, bearing the markings V11 C on the bow, seemed to hold station alongside them, despite the fast moving current. The Korvettenkapitan made one last snipe at them by boasting,

'Now that is discipline, men. It takes years of training before you can attain that level of control. The ever jocular Schultz, muttered under his breath that the Gruppenfuhrer was demonstrating more control, by not actually shooting this arrogant bastard of a seaman. He also whispered to the group, 'How the fuck did he do that whistling trick, to make the bastard thing appear?' Nobody had a clue how he did it, the periscope had been completely submerged. The conning tower hatch suddenly opened, and another bearded seaman indicated to the group to climb down the ladder and get in. The submarine commander now stood back with his two officers, to allow the group to climb aboard.

Each was given instructions on where to hold on, and how to avoid sliding off the bowed surface while attempting to reach the short steel ladder on the side of the tower. The whole process was completed very quickly, without incident. Most of the group felt that there was a tinge of disappointment in the eyes of the Korvettenkapitan that nobody had fallen off the sides of the vessel.

'I am so glad that you all managed to get aboard without getting your feet wet,' he almost sneered. 'Most soldiers are a little inept when it comes to seamanship.'
'My men are trained for all situations, and they are not 'most soldiers,' they are 'my' soldiers. This is merely one small accomplishment for them in what has already been a very long day,' the Gruppenfuhrer fired back.

The inside of the submarine was cool, dark and claustrophobic, and the men, including Zimmermann were told to doss down, around the massive bundle of kit that was stacked in the torpedo room. The group immediately set about checking the large rucksacks that were stacked with their individual specialised equipment. Zimmermann told them that each bag was numbered personally for them. 'My bag is 1, you are 2,' he told Neumann, and so on until each had been allocated a bag. They then opened their own bags and started to check every single item that was packed within.

After about an hour, Zimmermann asked them if they were all happy with their kit. 'For my part,' said Jung, 'The radio set and the quality and quantity of spares is faultless. Also the tools and meters are better than I have been used to working with in the army.'
'My equipment too, said Wagner. 'I am used to top quality climbing equipment and this is all Swiss, the absolute best.'
One by one the others confirmed that they were totally happy with everything, and after what appeared to be quite a short time, one of the

Leutnants slithered along the narrow corridor and asked if they would like some coffee. 'We are already nearly two hours into our journey, and well out in the English Channel,' he volunteered cheerily.

They sat and drank strong black coffee from large white enamelled mugs, while the Gruppenfuhrer again addressed then in hushed tones.
When we surface, it will still be very dark, and the Kriegsmarine guys have been practicing getting the inflatable boats out, and blowing them up as quickly as possible with portable electric pumps. We should be on the water inside of three minutes once the hatch is opened.'

'Once again a reminder that we must not talk at all, any sound could be heard from the top of the cliffs, even at the distance the submarine will have to be from the shore. Once we have beached, Wagner and I will go straight to the base of the cliff and prepare his climbing equipment. As soon as the boats are deflated and packed away, the rest of you will join us.

'Wagner, you are in charge the minute we hit the beach, and we will just follow you up the cliff using your moves.'
'Yes Sir. I will signal you up one at a time, as agreed,' replied Wagner.
'Once I have reached the top, I will make secure the rope, and wait for the killing team to arrive.'

A couple of other minor points were discussed, and instinctively the team began to spread out on the vibrating floor of the submarine, and to a man, were asleep within three or four minutes. The u-boat ploughed on and the crew who were on high alert status, were well aware that it was a particularly quiet night for any kind of shipping, even fishing vessels, in the English Channel.

'Gruppenfuhrer, we are now twenty minutes from the drop off point' spoke the voice of Korvettenkapitan Schaeffer, in hushed tones.
Instantly the team were awake and quickly standing, stretching their arms and legs and breathing deeply. One by one, they made a visit to the submarine's ablutions, most of the men taking the last nervous opportunity to have a shit and a piss before leaving the safety of the craft. Finally, hands and faces were blacked with Erdal, Germany's finest boot polish. 'Ladies, whilst putting on your make-up, please be careful not to mess up your collars and cuffs, we need to look smart again later,' whispered Zimmermann, with a wry smile.

Chapter 6

'Let's scrounge another roll up', said Corporal Ron Jenkins, to his mate, Sergeant Joe Parsons, who he was on night guard duty with, this evening. The two had been stationed together at Pett Level for the last few months, and had formed a very close friendship.

On the occasional nights that they were not on duty, it was their habit to commandeer an army jeep, and make their way to the pier ballroom in Hastings. They had got 'lucky' with a couple of Pett village girls at a dance there and often these girls would walk to the top of Chick hill for a clandestine meeting with the pair. Christine and Joanne were both nurses and worked the same shifts at the general hospital in Hastings. This was unknown to the men's commanding officer, Lieutenant Colonel Burgess.

Discipline was fairly relaxed at this strategic gun emplacement, with some three hundred men stationed there. However, there had been an air of heightened alertness over the last few weeks, due to rumours that Hitler was about to invade Britain. In fact recently, a rumour had circulated that the RAF had defeated a sea-borne attack and some 10,000 German soldiers had been drowned mid channel. Neither of these men believed that this had happened, but they were nevertheless, like most of their fellow soldiers, always on high alert whilst on duty.

It had been a quiet night, with very little activity out in the channel, over which they had a very commanding view. The brick built pill box was a two storey structure, built at the very top of this small inland cliff. They were standing at the observation slit, alongside a powerful pair of binoculars mounted on a steel tripod. The sergeant handed his mate his 'Golden Virginia' tobacco tin and asked him how his guts were doing.

Poor old Ron had eaten something which had violently disagreed with him and he had visited the 'shit pole' three times within the last two hours. 'If it carries on like this, I'll go and see the fuckin' medic tomorrow', he grimaced to his mate, 'I'm in fuckin' agony.

Suddenly, the two were aware of a siren going off in the direction of Fairlight, close to the cliff-top. 'Wonder what the fuck that is then, mate?' exclaimed Joe. 'No bastard will tell us what's going on at that house up there, but Burgess tells me we have had to provide an additional six men at all times, for guard duties there. They were aware of dogs barking in the distance, and suddenly a high powered spotlight was sweeping across the foreshore, from the same location.

Joe got back on the binoculars, and swept the visible area of channel in that direction. Shortly the field telephone rang on the small wooden table in the far corner of their look-out post.

'Lieutenant Colonel Burgess here, Sergeant. Everything's all ok. Just had a call from the house on the cliff, and it seems a bloody badger chewed through their alarm cable. All quiet otherwise up there?'
'Yes sir, no problems, until now it's been a quiet night.'

'Only that silly old bastard Burgess, mate,' said Joe to Ron. 'It seems that a wild animal has chewed through the alarm system up the road, and that's what all the fuss is about. I'd still like to know why that house needs six guards with dogs, and why the whole place is alarmed up.

'Christine was sayin,' that someone saw that Alan Turing bloke, you know the one from Hastings who is a wizard at de-coding stuff, being driven into the driveway a couple of weeks ago, in the back of a big black Humber six cylinder job. Whatever it is they are up to, it must be bloody important. Oh Christ, my guts are hurting again.'

'You was alright earlier, when you was givin' Christine a good seein' to in the field' laughed Joe. They had met Christine and Joanne earlier on that afternoon when they had gone out on 'food patrol', which usually involved trying to grab a couple of chickens from a local farm, and stealing a few vegetables out of the fields. Nobody ever questioned why these two always seemed to be the least successful at this type of sortie, and they continued to go out in the jeep together on many occasions. The Sergeant seemed to have a lot of sway with the camp commander.

Each time, they would have a pre-arranged meeting place with the girls, who sometimes bought a picnic with them. There would be very little time for messing about, they would drive to the nearest woods or open fields and get straight down to it. None of the four were bashful, so it was a 'touch of the all togethers,' as Ron said, as they stripped off, and as Joe delicately put it, 'shagged the arses off the girls'.

On one occasion, an elderly woman walking with a farm dog had almost tripped over the cavorting couples, and she had instantly recognised one of the girls. 'You should be ashamed of yourself, Joanne Davis. Your husband was only called up six weeks ago, you little strumpet!'
'We're just enjoying ourselves, you old witch. You should try it sometime, if you can find a man who's not too fussy, or a bit short sighted. You might even find that you like it, although I doubt it.

I don't suppose you've ever had a man anywhere near you.'

The old woman scurried away, muttering to her dog as she went. The four carried on as if nothing had happened, with Joanne screaming out, 'faster, faster, Joe,' as their session began to reach a climax. Christine just sighed, and said 'Ron, you really touched me deeply.' Eventually when they were getting dressed again, Joe asked whether Joanne was worried that the old woman would somehow get word to her husband. 'Andy's from up north, so he doesn't have any family down here, and hardly knows anyone in this area, and in any case realistically, he's not likely to be coming home.' 'Poor bastard', thought Joe.

Christine's father was a local fisherman and the girls had bought some crab and prawns with them along with some fresh bread, which they had all tucked into after their sex session. It tasted ok to all of them but it seemed that Ron was the unlucky one who had eaten something 'bad'.

Ron opened the tobacco tin and took out the packet of 'Red Rizla' papers, then skilfully rolled a thin cigarette, which his mate lit for him with his Ronson lighter. 'Maybe this will settle my guts', he said, despondently.

While he smoked the roll up, Joe got back on the binoculars and scanned Rye Bay once more. The night was very black and the sea was quite calm, with no visible shipping activity. He stepped away from the tripod and addressed his mate again.

I was just wonderin' Ron. You know the girls aren't at all bashful, and we've both seen everything they've got to offer. Well it's only lust as far as I'm concerned, and I think it's the same with you, ain't it?
'Course it is mate, I've got my Mary at home haven't I?
'Then why don't we suggest to them that we do a swap around next time we meet them and you can shag Joanne and I'll have Christine?'
'Two for the price of one, sounds good to me mate, and I've got to be honest, I really do fancy Joanne as well.'

'The good thing is with them, they don't seem to be at all bothered about us not using french letters, maybe it's because they are nurses, and just know how to stop themselves from getting pregnant,' observed Joe.

'I wondered about that too, mate. 'Spose you must be right, they would know what to do, wouldn't they? We've got ourselves a deal then, but how are we going to put it to the girls?'
'That's easy,' replied Joe. 'I'll just say when we meet up that you

happened to mention to me that you liked the way Joanne had done her hair, when we last got together. And that I then said, 'steady on Mate, you'll be asking to shag her next!' I can then say, that I said I didn't really mind, because I really like Christine's smile, and if he wants to shag Joanne, I wouldn't feel at all bad about takin' care of Christine either.'

'We will just let the conversation flow from there, but my guess is that they will be as 'up for it' as we are.'

'I'll look forward to that then', retorted Ron, who then suddenly grabbed his guts and shouted, 'fuck it, I have got to go to the shit pole again.' Joe watched as his unfortunate mate struggled to get down the iron ladder set in the corner of the room. This took you to the ground floor section of the pill-box and the steel exit door was right alongside it.

The company latrines were quite a way from the pill-box, being in the second of the row of cottages to the east of the gun emplacement. If any sentry on guard duty wanted a piss, he could just walk to the edge of the group of buildings and do it on the grass. If one was desperate for a shit, the practice was to go to the 'shit pole'. This was a three foot section of scaffold pole with a steel loop welded to it, set in concrete at the edge of the cliff, and leaning outwards at a slight angle. It was one of four, set into the ground in a square formation, to support the strainer wires for the wireless mast.

The 'shitter' would stand behind the pole and drop his trousers and underpants, then grasp the pole tightly with both hands and lean his arse out over the cliff and drop his guts down the cliff face. It wasn't quite so dangerous as it sounds because about five feet below, there was a fairly wide ledge, so the worst case scenario, if you did manage to let go of the pole, would be that you would land in your own shit, plus anybody else's who happened to have been recently.

After the ledge, there was a steep drop to the bushes below, which were now mainly covered by water, but there was (unsurprisingly) a good deal of vegetation growing around the ledge, so there would have been plenty of shrubs to grab hold of to stop one from hurtling towards certain injury.

Ron's forehead was turning hot and cold, as he almost fell out of the pill-box door and turned right up the bank and scrabbled the few yards along the edge of the cliff. He struggled with his fly buttons and with the other hand, slid his braces from his shoulders.

Chapter 7

The sea was quite calm and the inflation of the rubber boats seemed to take very little time at all. The submarine commander had grudgingly told Zimmermann, 'Good luck, Gruppenfuhrer, I will await your instructions.' He also made sure his Kriegsmarine crew assisted with getting the boats inflated, and passing all their kit to the Waffen SS squad, once they had slithered into the boats from the hull of the submarine.

Within a few strokes of the paddles towards the shore, they noticed the huge black sea monster slowly slipping below the water, until only the periscope was visible. Once they had put a distance of a few hundred metres between them and the u-boat, they could no longer even pick out the periscope.

The seven silently and smoothly paddled on. The black cliff-line looked very menacing in the darkness but the men in both boats were adrenaline charged to the limit and they were now completely focussed on the job that they had come to do. While they were out on the water, they all knew that they were at their most vulnerable, and they worked hard at getting the boats as fast and as quietly as they could into the relative safety of the shoreline. The sea was very calm. They homed in on the tall chimney of the house that they were going to attack. It stood out above the cliff-top, and seemed to be more prominent than any other feature, for at least a kilometre either side.

Not a word was spoken as they silently pulled the boats up the shingle beach and unloaded them. The boats each had a large threaded rubber bung inside, which meant that after three or four turns of the bung, the craft could be deflated in seconds and quickly rolled up. They were both stowed into their respective bags, and the team moved forward.

Wagner was already at the base of the cliff with Zimmermann at his side. Silently he laid his large rucksack onto the shingle, while the others pressed themselves against the base of the cliff and waited. They all had a piss, which was a symptom of nerves, because they had all been able to use the submarine's facilities, less than half an hour earlier.

Quickly, Wagner assembled the required equipment, and within two minutes, he was away up the cliff face. His progress seemed slow at times, with the watchers below wondering how he could possibly move any further upwards on a sheer section. A minute or so later, he was some ten metres above this point and again feeling for the correct path to move upwards again. He was avoiding fixing pitons by the normal method, instead choosing a heavy rubber mallet to drive them in. The effect was that an occasional dull thud could be heard, but nothing that would have alerted guards to the fact that there was an enemy climber on the cliff face. In fact, the noise was remarkably similar to the occasional lazy thump of a wave into one of the many crevices in rocks along the base of the cliff.

At one point, the team from below, could have sworn that Wagner was neither suspended, nor making contact with the cliff face either, but he suddenly moved upwards again, and very soon was virtually at the cliff top. Then he was gone. A few seconds passed and a couple of small stones landed on the shingle just in front of the team, and this was the signal to go. Fuchs was next up.

For a stocky man, he conducted himself well, and it seemed in a very short time, he was also disappearing over the cliff top, albeit he did not have to create the path, just follow Wagner's rope. Next up was Klein. Zimmermann had chosen these two to be first because any killing would need to be silent, and these two were the specialists in this field.

Klein seemed to be even faster up the rope than Fuchs, and very quickly he had joined the other two at the top of the cliff, in deep undergrowth, consisting of thick bracken, gorse and rough grass. Very quickly, Neumann, Schultz, Jung and finally Zimmermann, were at the cliff top too. Once assembled, the whole team started to crawl forward, with Fuchs and Klein leading the way on their bellies. Silently they were cutting a discreet tunnel below the brambles with the Swiss pruning shears bought for this single purpose.

Suddenly, Fuchs stopped as he was about to cut the next part of the pathway through. The pruning shears had enclosed around a very hard piece of vegetation and on feeling it, he realised that he was trying to cut barbed wire. He whispered to Klein, who took the pruning shears back and passed forward the wire cutters, again Swiss. Almost without pause, Fuchs carried on, and was making good progress for what would seem to have been the last two or three metres before reaching the cliff path, just above them now. The pathway would be the last barrier between them and the rear garden of the house.

He could sense the team behind him and knew that his skills were vital for this part of the operation. There may be guards on the footpath, (they already knew that it was guarded at both ends), or in the garden of the house itself, but he would be first out of the undergrowth, and the first to have to deal with any killing that needed to be done. He made his next precision cut in the barbed wire. Everything had been done in such a way that when they left the house, they could literally slide backwards through the tunnel they had made and bend the barbed wire back into place, and soldering the cuts with a special cold solder that Jung the radio man had bought, leaving the enemy wondering who the hell, and how the hell, they had been attacked.

As Fuchs snipped the wire, he felt a painful electric shock through his right hand, shooting up his arm and jolting his elbow, and simultaneously a loud siren started up from the area of the house.

'Abort,' was the whispered command from Zimmermann, who was last in the crawling line. 'No time to cover up, it could compromise the rest of the mission'. With that the whole team started to slither backwards through the tunnel that they had just cut, with Fuchs disobeying the 'cover up' order by coolly putting the cold solder around the last cut in the barbed wire. Finally, he smeared mud over the join. As he did so, he felt something extra stuck along the back of the wire, in the form of a, cotton covered electric cable. 'So this is what the bastards have done,' he thought. Instinctively, he used the pliers to tear the cable away from the back of the barbed wire, on both sides. This may give the impression that an animal had bitten through it from the other side. He then manoeuvred backwards at the best speed he could muster, doing his best to throw grass and bracken across the tunnel as temporary cover, as he reversed.

The whole team were at the bottom of the cliff within a minute while Wagner, who had waited at the top for Fuchs, gradually reversed his clime.

One by one, he removed the pitons and dropped more rope behind him, until he too was with the rest of the men. The equipment was re-packed in seconds and Zimmermann indicated to them to push eastwards along the beach. They were aware of dogs barking from the area of the house and the alarm siren was still wailing.

They had put a few hundred metres between them and the climbing site, when they were aware of a huge spotlight being shone from above, down onto the beach. Luckily for them, the operational angle, presumably from the cliff path, would not allow the light to show the base of the cliff, but bathed the foreshore with light at a distance of roughly 30 metres from the point where they had been. The beam swept mechanically, left and right, but nothing but beach could be seen by the operators.

The team pressed on again, not speaking. They soon reached the barbed wire coils that protected the small sandy beach at the area known as 'Cliff End'. There was also a curved line of concrete anti-tank traps coming off at an angle from the cliff face. These were round with a coned top and each gave the impression of a large concrete candle. The actual size of each was over one metre in diameter, and three lines of these went on as far as they could see in the darkness, and they knew from the aerial photos they had studied, that these covered the entire length of Rye bay.

They saw the small brick built pill-box positioned in the sand, just above the high water line, and Zimmermann took the decision not to attack it. He whispered, 'let's try and get around the back of it away from the observation slit, and see whether or not it is manned. We don't want to be attracting any more attention right now.

'With respect Sir, any sentry should have been out checking, with the racket that the alarm siren is making', volunteered Schultz.
'True, but we must be very careful, just the same.'

The whole squad climbed silently across the barbed wire rolls, using a much practiced technique of compressing the coil into a square section with four rifle butts, and throwing a thick, rough mat across the lowered structure and simply diving over it. As soon as the first was over, he would take over one of the rifle butts to allow the others to follow, and so on. Once they were all across, the rough mat would be torn off, and the rifle butts used to reshape the coiled wire.

The two 'silent' killers, Klein and Fuchs, were at the entrance to the pill-box, as the others stood back. The two quite quickly rejoined the group, and Klein whispered that they could hear loud snoring coming from within. This was the break that they needed, and as they quietly made their way further eastwards across this sandy section of beach, they heard the frantic ringing of a field telephone coming from within the pill-box.

By now, they had reached the cover of the bushes at the end of the Royal Military Canal, and watched, half amused, as the lone soldier stumbled from his guard post and pointed his rifle aimlessly in every direction, and then re-entered the pill-box, presumably to report that all was quiet.

'What about the submarine, sir?' enquired Jung, who was charged with making this crucial contact.

'Thank you Jung, but we will finish our little exploratory visit to the Toot Rock emplacement first,' whispered Zimmermann. 'Once the submarine emerges and opens fire, all hell will be let loose, so we have to be well clear by then. 'It will not do that arrogant shit of a seaman any harm to be kept waiting, he dare not move until we make contact. How the hell did he ever get to be in charge of a submarine, anyway? I am sure he is the type of man who prefers little boys to ladies.' The team smiled.

The squad now focussed on the next part of the mission. They were all a little despondent at this first 'failure' in terms of the overall mission, but there was nothing more that they could have done.

Secretly, Fuchs realised that had he been more careful, he may have felt the electric cable glued to the backside of the last section of barbed wire that he had cut through. Probably this was just a basic electric fence cable linked to an alarm which would trigger should the circuit be broken. He hoped the Gruppenfuhrer would not realise that this was an avoidable error caused by him.

Meanwhile, Zimmermann now was leading the team away towards the canal and they moved slowly forward, crouching low. They were aware that there may be guards at this end of the towpath, and again had made the decision only to attack if they were compromised. Zimmermann already knew that once the submarine started to shell Tongs House, the local guards might think that as the land mission had failed, the raiders had made it back to the u-boat, before launching this secondary attack.

As the squad reached what should have been the road, they were confronted with a large mud bank, some two metres high, again with coils of barbed wire on top. Water came right up to this mud bank, and stretched to the East as far as they could see, in the very dark night conditions. The Market Stores was the first 'saved' building, immediately to the side of this bank. Just in front of the shop, stood two sentries, both chatting and smoking. There were several British army vehicles parked on waste ground opposite the little shop.

This came as a total shock because although they knew that the area had been flooded, the latest aerial photos did not show the water coming across the level this far. They stopped momentarily, and at that moment, Neumann caught Zimmermann's sleeve, as he pointed in the direction of the new cliff line in front of them. They were all breathing as low and as quietly as they could, considering the effort that it had taken to carry all the heavy equipment.

A short distance away now, was their second target. It looked very foreboding. Standing defiantly, right at the front edge of this small inland cliff, was the large pill-box, with the ugly observation slit, just beneath its thick concrete roof. The whole structure had an air of invincibility about it, as it looked out proudly across the channel. It now became apparent that Toot Rock was in fact an island, completely surrounded by water.

'We'll have to re-inflate the boats,' whispered Zimmermann. One by one, they reversed back over the small sandy hump that led back to the beach. The boats were quickly unpacked and the rubber bungs which were held inside the hulls with stainless steel cables were screwed back in. The inflation pumps were similar to a motor tyre pump, but the barrel of each was huge. Steadily and quietly, Jung and Schultz worked the pumps with their feet, and in three minutes, the boats were again ready for action.

There was still a reasonable amount of cover between their position and Toot Rock, because many trees and bushes were still much higher than the water level, but this situation was certainly more difficult than they had anticipated.

Zimmermann whispered, 'We will follow the line of bushes running parallel to the sea wall and then cut in to the cliff face just at the foot of the pill box. Hopefully the bastards up there will be pre-occupied still with the goings on at the cliff house, and looking out to sea, observing the channel.'

As luck would have it, the two sentries had decided to take a stroll along the road in the direction of Chick hill, so the team were able to slide the boats into the water and silently paddle away. The Gruppenfuhrer was in the lead boat, along with Fuchs and Klein, while Wagner, Neumann, Jung and Schultz followed. The paddles were wooden but with large rubber blades and they moved through the water quietly and easily. There was a ghostly feel to the whole thing, because across to their left was a row of abandoned houses, with water reaching up to their first floor windows. Jung wondered whether these buildings would ever again become homes.

Just below the pill-box, they paused momentarily, looking up the rock face towards the observation slit. They could hear men's voices, coming from above, and although muffled by the enclosure, it was seemingly a conversation between two men. They could also smell tobacco smoke.

They moved into position a few metres further along the escarpment, and again, Zimmermann took the lead. They left all their heavy equipment in the boats, as this was only an observation sortie. The boats were secured to some bushes growing out of the cliff face and again they set off. They felt their way delicately up the slope, gently pushing aside any vegetation, until they found themselves on a grassy ledge about two metres from the top. As the Gruppenfuhrer crawled up into position, he slid his hand through some rather sticky mud, but the smell that followed instantly told him that he had put his hand in shit. He managed to get onto his feet into a crouched position and shuffled across to the side of the cliff, now just below the top.

The next one up was Jung, and Zimmermann was able to warn him with hand signals, that there was shit on the ground. It seemed to be everywhere. The seven were once again all assembled together, all the rest having avoided actually touching the shit, although they had all trodden in it. Just as they were about to scramble up the last section and look around, they heard the slamming of a steel door. They all tensed as they heard muffled footsteps stumbling towards their position.

Klein pushed up next to the Gruppenfuhrer, his long knife glinting in his hand. They all pressed themselves tightly to the side of the cliff face. Suddenly, a man's face was visible from above, but they were immediately aware that he had swung round, grabbing a steel pole that jutted out above them. Everything happened so quickly then, that they held their breath for several seconds afterwards to try to take in what had just occurred.

Corporal Ron Jenkins had only just made it to the shit pole in time. His trousers and underpants around his ankles, he swung out and let everything go, he would worry about finding his hanky to wipe his arse once he had emptied his guts down the cliff. Below him, the proud and cleanliness obsessed Gruppenfuhrer, already suffering from a shit covered hand, had just received an offering of hot, wet, shit from above. It had totally covered his military cap, and was running down his face.

Klein knew that he had no choice. The man may have been pre-occupied when he arrived, but once he had finished his ablutions, he would surely see the group of them just below him. He could not reach the man to pull

77

him down to execute a strangle hold and stabbing through the heart, so all he could do was to stand up and ram his knife upwards.

Ron felt relieved, maybe this would be the last time he needed to shit, as he felt much better now. Just as he felt that he would pull back and sort out the mess, he felt a searing pain in his backside. It seemed to come from deep inside him and he wondered what kind of food poisoning could do this to a man. For two seconds, he hung on, believing the pain would subside, but suddenly the strength left his arms, his head fell backwards, and his eyes watched the sky black out.

He fell on top of the men below, but rolled right over them and straight down the steep drop into the water and wild bushes below. The odd thing was, he didn't utter a sound. The team gathered their thoughts for a few seconds before Zimmermann finally whispered, 'let's do the quick check here and get away, before this soldier is missed'. Within a few seconds they were up on the top of the cliff and looking around.

They were free to walk around this grassy area, and noted the radio mast. To the east was a hatchway into the ground which they knew was billeting for a few men, as well as shell storage facilities. Seaward from here, and to the left, a huge camouflage net concealed one of the Bofors guns. This was actually set into the side of the cliff, and reached from the underground chambers. Again they were able to hear the sound of men talking and laughing.

Further down the escarpment, and to the east, was a row of buildings, the first of which seemed to be the ammunition dump as it was clearly of military construction, with very thick walls. Another smaller gun which they were not previously aware of was positioned in front of this. The officers and more senior ranks would be billeted in the cottages further down. On the other side to the cliff face was a steep grassy slope, and as they looked down they could see several guards patrolling. A pair stopped to talk as they passed. It seemed that these guards had some protection in the form of dug-outs, set along their patrol path.

The team moved back closer to the cliff side, and saw the other Bofors gun similarly camouflaged, just the other side of the massive pill-box.

'Enough', whispered Zimmermann, who had done his best to use the clean grass to get the worst of the shit from his face and hands. As they climbed back over the cliff edge, the Gruppenfuhrer slipped slightly and lost his footing on the ledge, and for good measure, sat down squarely onto the pile of shit that had been deposited there.

None of the team dared to comment. Even Schultz felt that any attempt at humour would be inappropriate. They got to the bottom of the cliff and back into the boats in silence. They now set off in the direction of the woodlands that had been designated as their hiding place for the next few days. It was not difficult to avoid being seen by the guards, as they crossed the water towards the hills behind. They had paddled swiftly back behind the abandoned houses, in the direction of the newly built bank, which had been constructed in a rough line, which they quietly followed, to the base of Chick hill.

As soon as they reached the base of the hill overlooking Pett Level, Zimmermann ordered Jung to signal the u-boat. It had been agreed that a one word signal would be used, which the decipherers would not be able to make any sense of. The code words were quite simply, 'Goodbye' for get going, and 'Hello' which was the instruction to fire at the house.

Jung took moments to send the signal meanwhile the same procedure for deflating and re-packing the two boats was carried out. Within a minute, they heard close firing out to sea, and realised that the u-boat was now doing the job that it had stayed for. The 88mm cannon on the front deck of the boat would be more than capable of destroying an un-fortified house. They heard round after round of the shells thumping into the cliff face, or whistling overhead where they had flown too high. There was no doubt that these all too clever British bastards would be destroyed in the inescapable fire storm.

Zimmermann was very annoyed with himself, although he said nothing. Secretly, he was thinking that they had fucked up on both parts of the mission so far. He was concerned that the dead soldier would be found by the latest, a few hours time, and then the British would realise that a task force had stayed behind after all.

This, coupled with the fact that he stunk like a sewer, had not put him in the best frame of mind. He checked his watch and was suddenly aware, that they faced a punishing run across country, to reach the safety of their woodland retreat, before first light. He would show these bastards what he was made of, and regain some self respect. 'Follow me Gentlemen, we must hurry now.' He set off at a cruel pace, and the team followed him, inhaling the stench of him with every breath.

Chapter 8

Sergeant Joe Parsons was becoming concerned about his mate. He had been gone for twenty minutes or so, and whilst it was acceptable to the senior officers that a man could pop out for a piss, it was not acceptable that only one man stayed on sentry duty for more than five minutes.

Joe made the decision to call Lieutenant Colonel Burgess, to see whether Ron had been taken to the sick bay. Then he hesitated, because if that had been the case, a replacement sentry would automatically have been sent up to the box, straight away. 'What a fuckin' dilemma,' he thought. He went to the west side of the pill-box, and called down to one of the guys on the Bofors gun, just below him.

'Do us a favour, Mick. Ron has got a real guts problem and he went to the shit pole about twenty minutes ago and hasn't come back. Could you have a quick look before I call Burgess?'

'No problem, Joe. Give us a minute,' was the friendly reply. Joe paced up and down, occasionally glancing out to sea, but now really worried that something bad may have befallen his mate.

Shortly, Mick scaled the steel ladder to the top floor of the pill-box, and said, 'Sorry mate, there's no sign of him'. I've been to the shit pole and there's no doubt someone has done a rare old crap down there recently. It stinks to high heaven, but there is no sign of Ron anywhere.'

'What the fuck should I do, Mick? I daren't tell Burgess how long he's been gone, but I have got to fortify the guard now.'
'Just tell him that he's been gone about five minutes, and you need a replacement, as he isn't at all well and needs to go to the sick bay.'
'What if he's already gone to the sick bay? The bastard will know that I'm lyin' then.'
'I know, I can quickly run down to the sick bay to see if he's there and then come back and tell you,' suggested Mick.
'Thanks mate, I owe you one.'

Mick shinned down the steel ladder, and sprinted across the ground towards the ammunition dump. The next building along housed the camp kitchen on the ground floor, and the sick bay upstairs. It was one of a group of private houses that had been commandeered by the military, and the army had pretty well wrecked it. He entered the front door and saw

80

the camp cook asleep on the sofa, in the corner of what would have been the sitting room. He quietly crossed the floor and went up the narrow staircase, which he thought was never going to be ideal for stretcher cases.

He entered the room to the left at the top of the stairs, and saw the medic, asleep on a bed in the corner. 'Sorry to wake you up Jack, but have you seen a guy with bad guts in here this evening?'
'Eh?' responded the startled medic, as he struggled to pull himself out of his sleep.
'Corporal Ron Jenkins has got a case of food poisoning, we think.'

'The only patient that I have got here at the moment is the poor bastard with the bullet wound in his leg, next door. He'll be off to hospital tomorrow. It looks like it's going septic. A bit ironic that it happened on the firing ranges at Lydd. Complete accident, a ricochet.'

'Thanks mate, sorry to have disturbed you.' With that, Mick quietly went down the stairs and out of the building. 'Nothing for it,' he thought. 'I will just have to let Burgess know. At least Joe won't get it in the neck, because the Lieutenant Colonel won't know how long he's been gone.

He made his way down to the officer's house, another commandeered property at the bottom end of the small lane. A guard stood at the doorway and immediately issued the challenge, 'Halt, who goes there?'
'Private Mick Meadows, 231 797. I urgently need to speak to Lieutenant Colonel Burgess about a missing soldier.'
'He won't like being woken up about something trivial,' said the guard, also with the rank of private.
'This isn't fuckin' trivial, you stupid bastard. He's one of the pill-box sentries, and he's gone, retorted Mick. 'The Lieutenant Colonel will have to allocate another sentry immediately.'
'That's different then, why didn't you say that in the first place?' responded the awkward, 'jobsworth' private.

The Lieutenant Colonel appeared inside two minutes, still slipping his military tunic over his shoulders. As soon as he enquired of Mick why he had been awakened, all hell broke loose. The heavy sound of a cannon, firing close by could be heard, followed by the 'thump, thump' of shells hitting their target.

Meanwhile, in the pill-box, Joe had done another quick scan of Rye Bay through the binoculars, when suddenly he saw a large vessel, perhaps half a mile to the west and about a mile and a half off shore. 'But that's impossible,' he thought. 'I only looked across there thirty seconds ago, and it wasn't there then. There's no way it could have moved in that fast. Even a destroyer would have been visible for a few minutes before it could get to that position.'

The truth suddenly dawned on Joe. This had to be a submarine. But was it hostile, or one of ours? In a flash, Joe's question was answered, as the vessel opened fire towards the cliff top.

He immediately got on the field telephone, first to Lieutenant Colonel Burgess, whose phone was eventually answered by another officer, clearly woken from his sleep. Burgess was already sprinting up the little lane that led to the emplacement at the top of the hill. For a portly man, he was quite a fast runner, and the private Mick, had trouble keeping up. As soon as the two reached the top of the escarpment, they were able to see the u-boat, firing in the direction of the 'protected house' as the camp commander called it. Burgess was the only officer, who knew exactly what the importance of the house on the cliff top was.

Burgess reached the first Bofors gun manned by the Canadians and shouted 'open fire on that bloody u-boat.' He then sprinted to the other, 'British' gun, the other side of the pill-box, but they had already started firing at the sub, upon the instruction of Sergeant Joe Parsons. The flood lights were on and both guns had a clear line of fire to the vessel. It was estimated that the u-boat had fired some fifty or more rounds, before the water around it became a maelstrom of return fire. It slipped back into the dark waters of the English Channel. Later, the Canadian gun team claimed a hit, but the Brits had total confidence in their own accuracy.

The Lieutenant Colonel then visited Joe, upstairs in the pill-box and grabbed the phone from him. He was eventually patched through to the Admiralty, who diligently took the report of the enemy craft, and the co-ordinates, told him they would send a craft to investigate, and then bid him a polite 'Goodnight'.

'So, now tell me about your missing sentry,' said Burgess, in a fairly unsympathetic tone. 'My Corporal has not felt at all well all afternoon, Sir. He came on duty just the same Sir, I know this man personally, and he is not a shirker, Sir.'
'Get to the point Sergeant,' retorted Burgess, a little irritated.

'Well Sir, he had a badly upset stomach, and he had to go and relieve

himself, if you know what I mean. He was gone nearly five minutes when I decided to call you.'
'Why did you send private Meadows down for me then? At that point, Mick Meadows climbed up the steel ladder and explained that he had to go to the sick bay for some aspirin for a headache, and volunteered to let the Lieutenant Colonel know personally.

'I would also like to volunteer to join Sergeant Parsons as his second in command on sentry duty for the rest of the night, Sir.'
'Very well, I will arrange for another man to be sent up to assist the gun crew, as your replacement,' said Burgess, who then climbed back down the steel ladder. As his head was just about to disappear, he called across, 'It will be getting light in a couple of hours, so I will organise a search party then for Corporal Jenkins.

'Thank you Sir,' said Joe, and as soon as the camp commander had slammed the steel door downstairs, he winked at Mick and said, 'Thank you private Meadows, you are a gem! I won't forget your help, son.'

As soon as dawn broke, the Lieutenant Colonel got up a search party of a dozen men, and they spread out around the entire camp to look for the missing man. 'Keep me posted, Sergeant Bridger, meanwhile I will be in my office reporting the incident to HQ.

The vegetation was thickest in the water in the area just below the shit pole, and one of the search party, private John Barton, felt this would be the best place to start looking. It was possible, he mused, that if someone was feeling really sick, he might have had trouble holding on to the pole.

Suddenly Barton felt very sick too. Directly below him, was the dead Corporal Jenkins, trousers around his ankles, and completely impaled upon a broken wooden stump, part of a dead bush. He was sitting bolt upright, some four or five feet out of the water, and staring up at the sky.

Before he looked away, he noticed that the stump beneath the Corporal's arse had turned completely black with the man's blood. His head went hot and cold as he turned to run back towards the officer's house. He got just to the other side of the radio mast area before he collapsed face down into the grass.

His mate, Private George Watson, saw him go down and ran across to help him. Within a few seconds, the whole of the search party had gathered around young Barton, and it wasn't long before he came to.

'Found him,' he gasped, 'He's dead, it's horrible.'
'Ok, son,' said a sympathetic Sergeant Evans. 'I'll go and take a look.'
Even the battle weary Sergeant Evans had never seen anything quite so horrific, as he looked over the edge. The man had obviously let go of the shit pole, for whatever reason, and plummeted straight to his death.

Burgess was summoned and he requested that the local GP come out to the scene, as the medic here would not be able to write a death certificate. Meanwhile equipment was obtained from the workshops and six of the party got into the large rowing boat that was used to ferry the men to dry land. Once they had reached the horrific scene, Sergeant Evans ordered them to carefully saw through the broken stump, in order to get the Corporal's body down. The Sergeant supervised the work, and eventually the team were able to lift the body down into the boat, with the tree stump still firmly imbedded in his rectum.

They ferried the corpse back around the escarpment and then carefully stretchered it up the steep slope to the emplacement. The Lieutenant Colonel had been on the field telephone to all the guards and had warned them that a quite unconventional doctor would soon be arriving, and to let him through without delay. A little while later, the sound of squealing tyres could be heard coming from Pett Village. The 1938 open topped Alvis raced down Chick hill and screeched to a halt at the start of 'the level' as the locals called it, by the Market Stores, which was the start of the new bank section. Dr Adrian Hart jumped out with his medical bag.

One of two guards let him through a rough gate in the barbed wire rolls and the rowing boat was waiting for him. As he approached, the doctor called out cheerily to the two crew members, 'I was wondering how the fuck I was going to get across, thank you lads, this has got to be better than swimming.'

He was swiftly rowed across the couple of hundred yards of water between the bank and Toot Rock and was led up the steep bank at the back of the emplacement, by a young corporal who was rather too full of his own importance. 'This secret path leads to the top, where everything you will see is classified, as top secret.'
'Really,' replied Adrian, 'and there was me thinking that this was Toot Rock, where I had my first bit of tit, and many a shag, long before the army got its fucking grubby mitts on it.' The soldier thought it better not to respond, this was obviously one of those stupid locals, who understood nothing about security.

The Corporal's body was laid out under a blanket in the open section of grass just behind the radio mast. Burgess met Adrian Hart and introductions were not necessary. They both enjoyed a tipple, and the officer and his wife were billeted in the house, next door to the Harts.

'How did it happen then Arthur?' enquired the doctor.
'He had a bit of an upset stomach yesterday but logged on for sentry duties anyway. His fellow guard said that he felt ill again after having been to the lavatory a couple of times earlier in the evening. Apparently, the men use this over here as a latrine if they are desperate, and this is what he did.'
The Lieutenant Colonel walked over to the shit pole with 'The Doc', and they both looked down. The state of the ground on the ledge below was disgusting. 'There are a lot of boot prints down there,' observed the doctor, and Burgess just shrugged his shoulders and said, 'I expect the men did a quick search last night when he first disappeared.'

They then walked back to the body, and the army medic pulled back the grey blanket, to reveal the bloody corpse. 'Jesus Christ,' said Adrian. 'He couldn't have landed more accurately on that stump if he'd tried.'
The doctor started to press and feel the abdominal area and said, 'The stump has gone right up here', pointing to the belly button. He carefully examined the rest of the body, and could find no other signs of injury.

'What the fuck would have made him let go of the pole? Asked the doctor, and as if to answer his own question he walked back to the pole to see whether there was any sign of oil or grease that could have bought about the demise of this poor, unfortunate soldier. The pole was dry.

He came back to the body and again addressed the officer. 'Where is the other guard who was on duty with him?'
'I'm afraid we've had to bundle him off to the sick bay. As soon as he heard that his mate had been found dead, he went to pieces, so the medic here has given him a mild sedative. He is probably asleep at the moment.'
'Well I would like to talk to him anyway, perhaps I can come with you and you can convince him that I need to check him over as well.'

'No problem,' said Burgess. 'Come with me.' The medic replaced the grey army blanket over the body and stood guard over it.
'Wake up, Sergeant. I've bought the Doc to see you.'
'Thank you Sir,' slurred the Sergeant, who was normally completely on

the ball. 'I appreciate you comin' to see me Doc, but there is nothin' you can do for me. My best mate's dead and I feel responsible.'

'Why the fuck is that?' asked Adrian, in his usual tactful bedside manor. 'I should have made him come here to the sick bay last night, and requested a replacement guard from you, Lieutenant Colonel.'
'What symptoms was he displaying? Adrian asked.
'He had to go to the shit pole at least twice, earlier on last night, and he had a break of about two hours and he suddenly had to run off again. He said that his head felt hot and cold at the same time, and that his guts were killin' him. That's all there was to it, until he was gone too long and I had to call you, Lieutenant Colonel.'
'Did he have any hallucinations?' pressed the doctor.
'No Doc, we were havin' a logical conversation at all times. He did his duty up in the box just the same as me.'

'Thank you for your time then Sergeant. I may be speaking out of turn, but the 'Boss man' here may be able to get you a bottle of whisky or two, which could help with your grieving process, and also with sleeping. It's always hard to lose a friend especially in circumstances like this, but this is not your fault. Best thing you can do right now is get back to sleep, and I will tell the medic you are not going to be fit for work for a few days.'
'Thanks for your kind words, Doc. Goodbye.'

The Lieutenant Colonel and Adrian Hart walked back up to the open field of the gun emplacement. Adrian walked back to the medic, and again lifted the grey blanket for another look. Between them, they rolled the body over, and Adrian carefully examined the rectal area, where the small broken stump was embedded. He noted that the entire base of the stump was blackened with dried blood, and wondered how so much haemorrhaging could have occurred from a blunt tree stump.

'Still, that one is for the coroner,' he said to the Lieutenant Colonel. 'I cannot write the death certificate because a post mortem will need to be held to verify the cause of death.'

As Adrian walked down with the Lieutenant Colonel to the rowing boat, he enquired. 'By the way Arthur, what the fuck was all the gunfire, and the sirens going off last night?'

'Bit hush, hush, old Boy.' I will have to go to the 'protected house' to make sure everything is ok there, but my guards have been on the field telephone to tell me that the house is undamaged, despite Jerry shooting a

submarine load of shells directly at it from the sea last night. Truth is, that Alan Turing chap has got a machine there that can decipher all the German u-boat communications. I can tell you because I know it won't go any further. He told me that the Hun always give the game away when they change the codes, because however complex they are when their Enigma machine shuffles them, every bloody communication always finishes with 'Heil Hitler.' They always work back from this and are able to eventually work it out.'
'Stupid bastards,' replied Adrian. 'And you are right. What you have just told me will not go any further.' With that, the Doctor climbed back into the rowing boat and the somewhat unconventional GP asked the two oarsmen to hold station for a moment. 'One more thing Arthur, I will arrange for the collection of the body, and by law, I have to ask the local police to attend.' Lieutenant Colonel Burgess nodded.

Once Adrian had got back to the bank, he thanked the crewmen and climbed back into his beloved Alvis. 'May as well visit that crusty old bastard, Tom Warden with the heart problem, in Fairlight,' he thought. He manoeuvred the long car around narrowly avoiding the parked army trucks, and accelerated away in that direction.

Later that morning, a Hastings based detective arrived at Toot Rock and met with the Lieutenant Colonel. 'Detective Constable Richardson, Hastings police station. I have a report of a rather tragic accident here.' 'Look old boy, this was a very straightforward accident, the only strange thing is the way my man impaled himself on the broken tree stump.'

After some checking at the site of the Corporal's demise, and at the shit pole, followed by a quick look at the body, the young detective made a few scribbled notes. 'Yes, very straightforward but how unfortunate that he didn't just land in the water down there. He might have got away with a broken leg or something. Anyway, I shan't be bothering you any more, I will submit my report and that's the end of it. Of course the coroner will still have to do an autopsy, but that's just a formality.'

Within the hour, an ambulance arrived at the Market Stores to collect the body, which was duly ferried across. Meanwhile, Lieutenant Colonel Burgess poured himself a very large whisky, and prepared to get on the telephone to Corporal Jenkins' wife, Mary.

That afternoon, Sergeant Joe Parsons, who had by now discharged himself from the sick-bay, took Private Meadows to meet Christine and Joanne at the recreation ground at the top of Chick hill. 'Tragedy, girls,' said Joe. 'Poor old Ron has been seconded to drivin' duties for a General, based in the North of England. He won't be coming back, so he sends his love and apologies, plus this bottle of whisky for us to share, and asked me to introduce Mick here to you Christine, so you wouldn't be lonely.'

'Ooh hallo, you look nice, it's a shame about Ron though,' exclaimed Christine. 'Still, you look like you could be a good stand in for him.'

I'll do my best Darlin'. Ron was sayin' that you girls like a touch of the 'all togethers.' I am happy with that if you are, and in fact if one of you don't fancy me, I don't mind goin' with the other one instead.'

'Not backward in coming forward, your mate, is he,' laughed Joanne to Joe. 'Still, I don't mind either way, no offence Joe, but variety is the spice of life, as they say.'

'That's settled then, laughed Joe.' He walked to the side of Christine and took her hand. Meanwhile, Mick was quickly at the side of Joanne and the two were soon chatting, as if they had known each other for ever.
'Usual spot is it then girls?' enquired Joe.
'Nice,' responded Christine. 'By the way, did either you or Ron get a dodgy tummy the other day? Joanne and I did, we put it down to the crab, or prawns, that we brought along. My Dad says sometimes you can get a bad one, but you wouldn't know while you're eating it.'

'No problems darlin', we've all got cast iron guts, eatin' that army food every day.' Joe smiled wistfully, but at the same time he knew that it was that bad crab or prawn that had, in a roundabout way, killed his best mate. 'Maybe we could stick with the cheese sandwiches for a while though, it might be a bit safer, eh?'

They reached the 'usual spot', in the sheltered corner of a Pett field, just behind the church. The pathway that ran alongside it was very rarely walked by anybody. The old lady and dog had been a 'one off'. They had never been disturbed before. Soon the four were laughing and joking, and drinking 'army' whisky direct from the bottle. Before long they were cavorting naked, in the warm, autumn sunshine. Both men, and both girls, were enjoying the excitement and the pleasures of a new lover. Life was good again for Sergeant Joe Parsons, but he made up his mind to write a letter of condolence to Mary, Ron's wife.

Chapter 9

Zimmermann was leading his men at a manic pace. They would all have much preferred that he was at the rear of the squad, because the stink of shit coming from him was appalling. They were all forced to run into it behind him, and breathing heavily, as they were, it was sickening at times.

At one point, the Gruppenfuhrer stopped and checked his compass, which had a luminous pointer and graduations. He then checked his watch, and immediately pushed the squad onwards. He called back at one point, 'we are desperately close to sunrise now, and still some way from the woodlands.' At one point, they had cut too close to some farm buildings and a farm dog started barking for all it was worth. Luckily there was no human intervention and they pressed on.

After about an hour and a half of gruelling cross country running, they eventually arrived panting heavily, at the edge of Beckley Woods. 'Two minutes breather, men,' announced Zimmermann, who was not surprised that the men all chose to sit a good distance from him, among the first copse of trees. 'I know that I stink, but I can do nothing until we make camp.'

They soon pressed on again along a country path that was heavily wooded either side. By now it was completely light, but they knew that it would be unlikely that they would meet somebody walking in the woods this early. Still they were fully alert to any possibilities. They had not come this far to be compromised now.

Eventually as they were heading in a northerly direction through the woods, Zimmermann identified the spot that he thought would do for them. The aerial photographs that they had seen did seem to show this area of trees as one of the most thickly populated in the entire woodland. He checked his compass and was now able to see the map, which he had been carrying for the entirety of the run. Once again they followed the Gruppenfuhrer, this time deep into the pine trees, which were very closely planted, and immediately they were plunged into a half light as they pushed through. Their large rucksacks banged against every other tree trunk, until Zimmermann whispered, 'Halt.'
They had arrived at a small clearing with a couple of larger tree stumps, 'probably oak', thought Zimmermann. He dropped the heavy load from his shoulders and sat down on the larger stump. The rest of the squad set

about unpacking and preparing for a meal. At this point, the Gruppenfuhrer stood up and made a whispered apology to the team.

'Men, these are the sort of things that can happen on a mission, but I am good to my word. When I come back, I will smell like a tart's handkerchief.' With that, he picked up a spare uniform and military shirt, which had been tightly rolled together in his rucksack, plus some underpants and a towel along with a large bar of green soap, and a fingernail brush. 'Well done, Gentlemen. That was a very hard run.'

With that, he was gone. The men got busy opening rations and preparing a meal of tinned beef, carrots and potatoes with powdered orange juice to drink. On this mission, there would be no hot food. It would be a giveaway, especially if someone walking in the woods should catch the aroma of cooking. They also wiped the black from their faces and hands.

Some three quarters of an hour later, the Gruppenfuhrer returned, and true to his word, he looked and smelt as if he had just come out of the shower. 'I have visited the Eggshole Brook, just south of here, and I believe the locals will change the name to Shitshole Brook soon,' he whispered. He carried with him the dripping wet, but now clean uniform which he carefully laid across the branches of a pine tree, to dry.

None of the men had eaten, it was protocol to let the officer start and they would follow. As soon as Zimmermann started, they followed and within minutes, a fairly substantial, if somewhat basic meal was consumed.

'So Gentlemen, just think where we were only 24 hours ago.' Again Zimmermann spoke in hushed tones. Some of the men reflected upon the distances that they had covered, and the action that they had already been involved in, and it was very hard to comprehend all the events that had happened since yesterday morning.

'Now Gentlemen, we will sleep for as long as we like, because not until tonight at midnight, will we head back to Pett Level and set the explosives against the anti-tank traps further along the road from Toot Rock. Before we do that, we need to just now take stock of our situation.'

'There will be no doubt that the British will assume that the men who killed the soldier at Toot Rock were the same who set the alarm off at the house on the cliff. They may think that we made it back somehow to the submarine, but it is most likely that they will know that we have gone to ground somewhere. What we must hope is that their search pattern will be limited to the sort of distance that their soldiers would be capable of covering, fully laden with kit. Remember Gentlemen, there is no-one who can compete with the German soldier, and this will always be our advantage.'

'From our observations at Toot Rock, we now know that the secret weapon of the British soldier is his arsehole.' It was now clear to the men that the Gruppenfuhrer had recovered his sense of humour. 'Seriously though Gentlemen, we know that the enemy will now be on a greatly heightened alert status, and everything we undertake from now on will be exceptionally hazardous.

He spread the map of Pett Level onto the large tree stump and pointed at strategic areas. 'We now know that the majority of the guards are at the water level, maybe eight along here at the base of the emplacement, and two at the end of the banking here. Also at the far end, where the roadway runs up to the private houses from the beach, there is this other pill box, just above the water line which can easily be taken out. Once our fellow soldiers have joined us, there will be sufficient numbers to simultaneously deal with all of these targets. I don't believe that we have any threat from the sentries at the cliff top house because they will not be able to desert their posts. That is assuming that the u-boat did not totally destroy it. That, we will check tonight.'

'We must however deal with the pill box on the beach, even though the sentry there will probably be sleeping again. Also we must now assume that there will be guards on the cliff edge at Toot Rock. I therefore propose that we will utilise our sniper friends here, Neumann and Schultz, with Jung and Wagner alongside you to take them down from below. We will use our silent killing skills in the shape of Klein and Fuchs on the ground at the rear of the emplacement. I will be assisting you both with this work.'

'Our comrades from the Waffen SS who will be arriving in the next few days, will be charged with taking out the two Bofors guns, each manned by six men, here and here. Also we are now aware of the additional lighter gun at the armoury. They will also make sure that the men in the main pill-box are neutralised, and they will start the killing by silently attacking the 'civilian' blocks down here, where we expect there will be many men sleeping. This is something that we Germans can never understand. You have nearly three hundred soldiers and yet at night, which is the most vulnerable time, only about ten percent of them are on active duty. It is true that there will probably be a good number holed up in the underground tunnels towards the eastern Bofors emplacement, but a few grenades should quickly wipe them out.

'Any questions so far, Gentlemen?'
'Who will be in command of the larger team who are coming over soon?' asked Wagner.
'There is no dispute, here. I shall be in total command of the entire operation, including when the invasion forces land also, except I will have joint command over them with Von Rundstedt. We have worked together before and this will not be a problem. We both have our different skills.'

'These men are already fully briefed, but each one of you men will be ranked above them, as my personal elite force of six. They will however, take my orders and execute them to the letter, and I will need to know if anyone of them does not perform. We will as a small team, have in my opinion, the most interesting part of the mission to undertake.'

'Jung meanwhile, will be communicating directly with the main invasion task force, in the form of Von Rundstedt, who should be around the middle of the Channel when we attack the emplacement.'

'Once the Toot Rock situation is dealt with, the invasion force will be storming through the anti-tank traps and heading East and West along the road that we know to be just below the water line, running parallel to the sea wall. Once they have reached Pett to the west, and Winchelsea to the East, they will form a pincer movement meeting up initially at Icklesham and then heading inland on a pre-planned route which we believe will give us the least resistance on our journey to London. At the moment, that route must remain top secret. They will also mine the road at the bottom of Chick hill and at the far end of the beach, by the Bridge Inn, to ensure no British mechanised harassment from behind. Further road demolition will take place as required, on our little trip.'

'We will as a group set off to meet their commander, Von Rundstedt, at Icklesham. We will use one of the British army trucks parked at the Market Stores. Jung, you will drive us. We will stay together as a team at all times.'

'Jung, I would like you to send a scrambled message now to High Command, for the attention of Von Rundstedt, Army Group A,…… Then we will sleep.'

The whispered sound of Zimmermann's message along with the tapping of Jung's Morse code seemed to drone into and penetrate the brains of the whole team, but it was quickly done. The message ended as always, 'Heil Hitler.' 'Message dated 12th September 1940.'

'One last thing men, when we position the explosives tonight, we will not need to take any other equipment other than the boats and our weapons.'

Within a few minutes the whole team except Schultz, who had elected to take first guard duty, were sleeping like babies. Some time later on in the morning the sound of gunfire awakened the men. There was an aerial battle raging in the sky, and at one point an aeroplane was heard to scream downwards out of the sky. It hit the ground with a huge explosion and the ground around them shook. It seemed as though it was only a few hundred metres from their position.

'Let's hope that it was one of theirs and not one of our brave Luftwaffe boys,' volunteered Zimmermann, almost philosophically. Our boys have been softening up this area for months now, as well as providing us with the information and maps essential to our mission. Bombs were heard dropping in the distance but it was impossible to tell how far away the attack was from here.

Some time later, the drone of returning bombers could be heard, almost immediately overhead, and then the different sound of the Bofors guns, opening up from the Pett Level battery. Another loud explosion skywards, and again the whine of a crippled aircraft as it started its final dive, this time seeming to crash into the sea. 'That would almost certainly have been one of ours', said Zimmermann dryly. 'We will make sure that we provide a very special ending for the gunners down the road, when we make our attack. Those guns will very soon now be out of action, permanently'.

The men resumed their sleep with Neumann taking over on watch, and Schultz huddling down to a now undisturbed nine hours. The watch changed silently every one and a half hours, with no further interruptions to the team's rest.

Gradually the men stretched, and bearing in mind how their commanding officer had dealt with his dirty state much earlier on in the day, they had privately agreed to make themselves look as clean and as smart as they could. The first pair to go was Neumann and Wagner. They left the camp and were gone some twenty minutes or so, before returning to allow the next shift, of Jung and Schultz to clean up. Finally it was the turn of Fuchs and Klein. They had found Eggshole Brook quite easily and still had a little bit of light to complete their ablutions. The first pair dug a deep shit hole in the soft woodland floor, with their field shovels, and the last pair filled it back in and then kicked earth and leaves over the area.

Once they were all back at camp, Zimmermann asked the question, 'No signs have been left, Gentlemen?'
He knew in advance that the men were never careless in this respect, but liked to keep them on their toes. 'I shall be going down now and I don't wish to find a single indication that you have been to the brook'.
'No problem, Sir', was the response from Klein. The men trained constantly for survival in enemy territory and they were always taught to bury everything, deep enough for an animal not to easily uncover it.

As darkness began to fall, they agreed as a team that the safest place to hide the rest of their equipment would be up a tree. This way, even if a courting couple should venture deep enough into this part of the woodlands, nothing would be visible on the ground. Once again, the team consumed a large meal. They had ample rations for six more days, after which they would be able to help themselves to whatever they wanted as the invasion force advanced.

Zimmermann went through tonight's arrangements again, in minute detail. Once finished, he ordered Wagner to shin up a slightly larger pine tree, a few metres into the more densely wooded area, not far from the small clearing they had been occupying. When he was about five metres high he dropped down a rope and one by one, the large kitbags were hauled upwards into the tree and individually tied to the branches. They all blacked up again. 'Now we go Gentlemen', whispered Zimmermann.

The team gradually back tracked over the route that they had taken much earlier on this morning, and were relieved to know that they were not now under any pressure to beat the daylight. At Billingham Farm, just north of Udimore, (the place where they had heard the dog barking), they elected to take a route a few hundred metres to the east, to avoid the same thing happening again. It was amazing how the whole team managed to communicate with a few 'silent' words and a few hand gestures, and they all fully understood what was happening. This time they skirted around a large pond and then traversed to the east of Spout Wood.

The rest of the trek went by without incident, and very soon they were

standing at the point above Pett Level, where Jung had sent the radio message to the u-boat. From where they stood, they could make out a few features on the cliff-top, silhouetted by the sea behind. Zimmermann was disappointed to see that the large chimney of the house that the u-boat had shelled was still prominent on the horizon. 'It looks as though that pompous Kriegsmarine fairy, is not such a good shot despite all of his posturing and 'holier than thou' attitude. Not to worry, in a couple more days, it will be totally irrelevant, because we will be in charge.
It would have been good to know that the next few vital messages could not possibly have been intercepted though'.

This time, the team took a very different route to the one they had taken on what was now yesterday. They had reached an area to the South East of Icklesham, known as Wickham Cliff. The Gruppenfuhrer checked his watch and it was now nearly 1am. 'When we get down the hill, we will again inflate the boats and utilise them fully, because the land is not only totally flooded as you can see, right up to the sea wall, but it could also be mined.'

Schultz joked quietly to Fuchs, 'You had better not fall out of the boat because your cock dragging in the water is likely to set off a land mine' Fuchs retorted smiling, 'If I fall in then I will be sure to float on my back.' The ever ingenious and quick witted Schultz responded, 'If that is the case, Zimmermann might look across to you and think the British have a miniature submarine in the water with its periscope up. If we are ordered to sink you, could I please have your watch?
'Bastard, you are just jealous of my manhood', responded Fuchs amused.

Quickly the two boats were again inflated and the team were soon quietly moving across the expanse of water from the rear line of hills overlooking Pett Level, to the sea wall. They were a lot further away from Toot Rock than the previous night's escapades but no-one took anything for granted.

Good fortune seemed to be with them yet again, because as they were about two minutes into the trip, about forty Luftwaffe night bombers crossed the coast line and headed inland almost directly above them. The two Bofors guns opened up simultaneously, and the men knew that all eyes from the gun emplacement would be on the sky.

Very soon they had finished the short trip and pulled the two boats out of the water and up the sea wall. Just before they had reached the sea wall though, the Gruppenfuhrer had asked the two oarsmen, Neumann and Wagner, to do a sounding, in the area where they thought the road should be. They quickly established, by scraping the blades of the paddles over the submerged tarmac, that the road was in fact still there, and only perhaps half a metre below the surface. The tanks and army vehicles of the invasion force would have no trouble traversing this.

They were now on the beach. This immediately afforded them some cover, because the level of shingle was much lower than the top of the sea wall at this point. 'Right Gentlemen', said the Gruppenfuhrer. 'We will now search for a land mark that we can easily find again when we come to blow the charges. They started to head eastwards behind the sea wall and very soon, Klein noticed something unusual.

'Sir, see the groins there. That one has what looks like a diving platform on it. I have not seen another one so far, but shall I go on for a few more groins to check that this is the only one here?'
'Yes, thank you', replied Zimmermann, and the whole group sat down on the cold shingle and waited. They watched the rugged frame of Klein disappear into the darkness. As they sat there, Zimmermann started to look around and the rest of the team looked at the solid lines of concrete anti-tank traps that stretched out in both directions along the beach, as far as the eye could see. They gave the impression of giant, fat candles on a never ending cake.

Soon Klein returned and said triumphantly, 'It is the only one, Sir'.
'Very good, then we plant the explosives here. I have also noted that there is a manhole cover just on top of the sea wall here as well, directly in line with this groin.

From now on, it was Zimmermann's turn to put his expertise into practice. The whole team had been disappointed when he had dismissed Schmidt, but they all knew that you do not answer back when you are dealing with a man of Zimmermann's calibre. So now, it was his turn to show them what he could do. Secretly they were all impressed by his ability to work with the team and not expect any man to do anything that he wouldn't be prepared to do himself. In this respect, he was at least as good as their old officer.

They took the explosives bag out of one of the rubber boats, and carried it to the first concrete 'candle'. Zimmermann waved to Neumann to dig down alongside the concrete structure until he hit the base. Neumann used his field shovel and worked steadily away, while the rest of the team used their hands and arms to scoop the loosened shingle backwards, away from the excavation. The amount of exposed concrete on each structure above ground was about one and a half metres in height and as Neumann dug down, it became clear that there was almost this much concrete buried below the level of the beach as well.

Eventually, he reached the base of the round structure, and Zimmermann told him to now excavate backwards beneath the concrete itself. Neumann's head was by now level with the shingle on the beach and there was a huge pile of displaced shingle and sand behind him. The only consoling factor was that as he dug deeper, the shingle had given way to more solid sand, which proved to be much easier to shovel. Once he had got below the structure and could get his hand directly underneath it, Zimmermann ordered him to stop. Neumann climbed out of the hole and the Gruppenfuhrer slid into it to replace him. He carefully positioned the dynamite charges, which were covered in a waxed paper to keep them dry. 'Two will blow this bastard sky high', he whispered to the team.

He carefully brought the fuse wire up the side of the structure and held it while the team then back-filled the trench again. The wire was them traversed backwards across the beach from the cardboard roll, and again the team were asked to bury this as it went. This time they only had to make a trench of around half a metre depth. Once they had made it to the sea wall, the trench was in-filled and the cable then carefully dragged through the soft pitch that cemented the blocks of the wall together, in a zigzag pattern until it reached the top. It was then cut and the end pressed hard into the pitch.

To ensure that the end could be easily found again, Zimmermann pushed two shells from the beach, hard into the pitch, either side of the wire, and checked that they were secure. No locals were allowed to use the beach any more, since the declaration of war, and the Toot Rock soldiers would not be likely to venture this far away from their emplacement either.

The whole exercise had taken them best part of thirty minutes, and Zimmermann then ordered them to the next trap. The whole process was repeated, this time with Schultz on the shovel, and the rest of the team moving the displaced shingle backwards furiously. The second charges were laid in about twenty five minutes, despite the fact that the Luftwaffe bombers had returned overhead, this time with British fighters in tow. The whole team had stopped to watch as two of their bombers trailed smoke and eventually plummeted into the Channel. It was impossible to say whether the crews had managed to escape. The whole episode just hardened their resolve, and they worked furiously to finish the job.

'We are half way there Gentlemen', whispered Zimmermann, after they had undermined another trap. 'Then we will have a gap wide enough for our tanks to pass through easily'. They worked flat out on the last three, this time with Wagner and Klein taking first turns on the shovel. The rest of the task was completed in less than an hour and a half. They altered their technique slightly in as much as they changed the main digger after five minutes and let a fresh man get into it. This added an air of competition with each man trying to outwork the others.

Once the work was completed, and the Gruppenfuhrer was finally happy that there was no visible sign of them ever having been there, they repacked the equipment and slid the rubber boats down the bank of the sea wall, and back into the cold black water.

Within twenty minutes the team were setting off from Wickham Cliff to their now familiar camp at Beckley Woods. This time the journey seemed a lot easier, because they were not as a team carrying the same load as the previous night. Secondly they were not under the same time pressure to beat the dawn. Nevertheless the Gruppenfuhrer still maintained a good pace, he could not afford for his men to become complacent, however he knew that they would appreciate the fact that he was leading them at a slightly slower tempo.

The whole team felt much happier as they crossed fields, streams, fences and lanes to return to the camp. Tonight had been a tangible success for them all, and no-one doubted that when they returned to detonate the charges, the six anti-tank traps would be blown sky high. This would be the gateway for their countrymen to enter enemy soil, and they would have created it. Even Fuchs felt that he had impressed his commanding officer and that he could have a real chance once they were back in the Fatherland, of having his prison sentence reduced or even quashed.

He would make sure that when the opportunity came again to further his reputation as a faithful and loyal servant of the Fuhrer, he would take it. The others had their own thoughts as they headed back to their base in the woods. This time, they were fully settled in their camp before the first light of day began to show.

As soon as they arrived at the clearing they immediately retrieved the kit that they had secured up the pine tree last night, and laid it upon the ground next to them. It was time for food again, and within a very short space of time they were dining on a meal of tinned meat, tinned vegetables and cold black coffee.

After the meal, Zimmermann quietly thanked them for their hard work and then announced to Jung, 'Please send the following message to Von Rundstedt, Army Group A. (Codename VR) 'Send more to the party tonight. Time arrival for 2am Saturday 14th September, at agreed spot, we love the night life. We will make area welcoming and be ready to take them directly to our club, ready for your directions for main party. Again Jung worked skilfully at the Morse key with the scrambled message, and as always, ended with 'Heil Hitler'.

Within minutes, a scrambled response came back. 'To Gruppenfuhrer Zimmermann. (Codename WZ) Second wave will arrive at 2am tomorrow 14th September at agreed meeting place. Confirm that big dinner party is Monday 16th September. Wear smart clothing.' 'Heil Hitler'.

Soon the team were sleeping again. They were not tired by their efforts but they were always capable of sleeping. They never knew when they may have to go two or three days without sleep, so it was never a problem for them. This time it was Jung who took first watch.

While he sat on an oak stump looking over the rest of the team, his mind went back to the Polish soldier and his last dying words, 'Prussian Year', or whatever translation that Zimmermann had given to it. He was now comforted by the words that his commanding officer had spoken to him, and although he was the least professional of his team as far as soldiering was concerned, he felt proud that he was an important part of this unit, and knew that he had contributed to the success of this mission.

More importantly, he hadn't let anyone down, and that was a great confidence booster for him personally. When he got back to the Fatherland, he could hold his head up high. He could tell any children that he may have, once he had met a wife, that he played an important part in bringing the war to a close. And here he was in enemy territory, guarding one of the highest ranking officers in the third Reich, along with the most deadly team of professional soldiers, all sleeping soundly.

Another wave of bombers flew overhead, this time it seemed that the British fighter aircraft had met them head on. A terrific battle went on right above them and again several planes could be heard crashing into the ground. Again the Bofors guns opened up at Pett Level, and for half an hour the sound of aircraft diving and weaving through the skies, along with continuous gunfire, filled the air. On this occasion, all the men slept through the noise without stirring.

Jung reflected on the fact that if someone approached them on foot, then even the sound of a small twig cracking would have the whole squad wide awake with arms at the ready, yet they could condition themselves to sleep through an air raid. Oddly, despite being in a dangerous situation on enemy soil, he felt no sense of danger. Such was the confidence that he had in his fellow soldiers. He knew also that he had their respect too, not the least for his extensive expertise with all things radio.

Chapter 10

Doctor Adrian Hart had endured a very busy day indeed. He had to deal with an extraordinary number of patients, as well as a couple of home visits on his journey back from the surgery. Helen had presented him with a large glass of red wine as soon as he came through the door, and told him she had walked Rufus already, so he could now completely relax, and tell her about his stressful day.

'That old bastard in Fairlight, Tom Warden,' started Adrian. 'He knows he's got a dodgy ticker and shouldn't be eating and drinking the amount that he does, or smoking, so I got the district nurse to go and weigh him today and he's put on half a stone in the last two weeks. I gave him one hell of a bollocking, especially as I could smell fish and chips in his bedroom. He and his fucking daft wife assured me that he has been eating only fruit and salads. Also I could see the ashtray hidden under the bed and could smell smoke in his hair when I have told him that he must stop smoking or die. Same response, so I told him he had better call a mortician next time, rather than a doctor, because he would be of more use to him. I won't call on him again, I have literally told him to find another doctor, who will put up with his crap.'

'I suppose you just can't help some people,' said Helen, sympathetically. 'Look, dinner's all ready, so why don't you tell me the rest while we eat. It's your favourite, lamb chops. I popped in to see Mr. Harris, the butcher whose wife you managed to help out a couple of weeks ago. He insisted that I have these 'on the house', no ration book or anything.'

Half way through the meal, the intrusive sound of the telephone ringing, disturbed their conversation and instinctively, Helen went to answer it. Very often, she could head off an 'emergency', or at least pretend that Adrian would be home in another half an hour or so, in order for him to be able to finish his meal in peace.

'Sorry Love, it's a real emergency, according to that man from the joint technical board. Doctor Gordon, I think he said.'

Adrian Hart, who under any other circumstances would have told Helen to say that he would call back in half an hour, leapt to his feet and ran outside to the hallway to grab the telephone.

'Hope I'm not disturbing anything,' came the smooth tones of Major Gordon Roberts, 'but something's come up, and we need to have a meeting with the rest of the team tonight. Can you suggest anywhere where we can talk, without being disturbed?'

'How about the rear bar of the Two Sawyers?' suggested Adrian, 'I know the landlord, Derek. I can convince him that it's a medical chat, not for general consumption, and he will close off that section of the bar. Also we can get a drink, which by the sound of things, we are going to need.'

'Jolly good, see you there in twenty minutes then?'

'Can we make it thirty?' responded Adrian, and put the phone down.

He went back to his meal and the company of his wife, immediately having to explain that he would have to 'pop out', after all.

The short walk from their cottage, to the Two Sawyers, in Pett Village, was reflection time for Adrian. He soon dismissed the stresses and strains of his working day, when he considered that this special operations thing was probably his most vital role, both in his lifetime, and in the history of this great country. 'What could it be that had 'come up', as the Major had put it', he mused, as he strode purposefully towards his village pub. Once again, his resolve strengthened, as he said to himself, '*My* village pub.'

The whole concept of losing this lifestyle that was so essentially British, to people up and down this great country of ours, was not something he was even prepared to consider. He would not let his country down, and he knew that the men in his team could be relied on totally as well.

With that, he was sweeping through the side door of the Two Sawyers, and immediately saw Major Roberts, with George Dobson, Harry East and Ted White, already standing at the main bar, each with a pint of the local brew in their hands.

'Let me get you one in,' offered the Major, and Adrian gratefully accepted a pint of beer as well. As soon as Derek the landlord delivered his pint, Adrian asked, 'Will it be possible to use the back bar for a private meeting for an hour or so, Derek? It's just boring medical stuff, which the regulars won't want to hear, but it's vital to us chaps. There will be a couple more of us coming along in a moment.'

Derek nodded, and instructed his barmaid Sarah, to keep anybody else out of the rear part of the premises. He was well used to the Doc's unusual and eccentric episodes, and he also knew that there would be some money spent tonight, this always was the case when Adrian was here with friends. At that moment, Badger Higgins and Bill Jacobs came through the door together, and the Major duly obliged with another couple of pints. 'As we are all here, let's go through to the back where we can discuss things,' he suggested affably.

They were now all seated around a long oak table, and Derek called over to Adrian, 'Just shout through when you gentlemen need top ups.' The ever obliging landlord did think to himself that with the exception of the chap who had bought the first round, none of these gentlemen looked like they had much to do with the medical profession, but then again it was none of his business, as long as they kept drinking and caused no trouble.

'Thank you for coming Gentlemen,' said the Major, in lowered tones. 'I have to tell you that it looks as though our little party is going to be happening very soon. I don't wish to over dramatise the situation, but our latest intelligence reports have confirmed several things. Firstly, aerial reconnaissance as well as reports from our chums in the French resistance, confirm that there has been a massive build up of German troops and shipping, all around the Northern French coast, in the last two weeks. There also appear to be hundreds of steel barges, which we believe will be towed behind their ships and will carry the troops with their vehicles and equipment.'

'Now, let's deal with this first. Our propaganda boys have delivered a real coup in as much as two nights ago a massive batch of leaflets was dropped over Berlin. I have one here. This will be broadcast soon, by the BBC. The Major pulled a leaflet from his inside pocket, which he passed around the table. It was amusing to say the least, and all the team knew that previous propaganda had indicated that the Brits had a system which would set light to the English Channel. The translated document read.....

'We English, as you know, are notoriously bad at languages, and so it will be best, meine Herren Engellandfahrer, if you learn a few useful English phrases before visiting us.

For your first lesson we will take:
"Die Kanaluberfahrt....the Channel crossing, the Chan-nel cros-sing."
Now just repeat after me:
"Das Boot Sinkt....the boat is sinking, the boat is sin-king;
"Das Wasser ist kalt....the water is cold. Sehr kalt....very cold."
Now I will give you a verb that should come in useful. Again please repeat after me:
"Ich brenne....I burn;
"Du brennst....you burn;
"Er brennt....he burns;

"Wir brennen....we burn;
"Ihr brennt....you are burning;
"Yes meine Herren, in English, a rather practical language, we use the same word 'You' for both the singular and plural:
"Ihr brennt....you are burning;
"Sie brennen....they burn."
"And if I may be allowed to suggest a phrase: "Der SS-Sturmfuhrer brennt auch ganz schon....The SS Captain is also burning quite nicely, the SS Captain is al-so bur-ning quite nice-ly!"

They had all read the leaflet, but Adrian was the first to say, 'Yes, it is amusing, but it's not likely to stop the fuckers from coming.'
'Quite so, old boy, quite so,' responded the Major, 'But this brings me on to point two.'

'Although they have been pounding our airfields for the last few weeks, they have actually done very little to weaken the RAF, quite the reverse in fact. We are building new 'planes at a faster rate than at any time during the war. We know that one of Adolf's criteria for a successful invasion was the almost total destruction of the RAF. We have fed back propaganda that would suggest that it is on its knees, but in reality, we have enough 'planes to virtually take out an invasion force mid channel, always assuming that the Royal Navy doesn't get there first.'

'The plan is in place to achieve this, so in this respect, the propaganda leaflets are accurate. If we can instil a level of fear and trepidation, into the heart of the enemy, before they even set off, so much the better.'

The Major continued, 'The main point is chaps, that assuming we are correct and they are just about to set sail for these shores, then hopefully they will never make it this far. Our role will only come into effect if they are successful, and this is why I have called you together this evening.'

'Our signals chaps at Crowborough, have been picking up some interesting transmissions recently from this area. They are all scrambled but we do know that the day after tomorrow's date is mentioned, and we also know that there is probably a traitor in our community, perhaps a German sympathiser, feeding the bastards information. Alan Turing has been working on these messages, but they are not a straightforward code, they are using some pre-agreed terminology and then coding it, to throw us off the scent. Hence we can only make an intelligent guess as to what they mean. Also we have had to move Alan to a safe house where he has no proper equipment as yet, following the shelling of Tongs House the other night. You probably weren't aware that he was working from there.

'Now Chaps, back to our job. Hang on. Shall I get another round in?' Adrian went up to the bar and shouted for Derek that they were ready for a top up, and the glasses were soon re-filled, and they were once again, 'all ears' listening to the Major.

'You will need to be in the bunker by midnight tomorrow, and stay there for at least the next two days, either until we issue the 'all clear', or until Jerry has passed over your little piece of this green and pleasant land, at which point you will then do what you have been trained to do.'

'I feel that it is only fair gentlemen, to warn you that statistically your life expectancy, once the Krauts have passed by, is calculated to be less than two weeks. All I can say is that if anybody wants out, you will not be blamed, and we will put a replacement into the team.'

At this point, Adrian stood up and re-called Derek. 'Have you got any decent whisky, mate?' he enquired.
'I have some Bells, is that any good?'
'Great, have you got enough for a double for each of us?' replied Adrian.

Very quickly, they were again seated and this time it was Adrian's turn to speak. In lowered tones, he addressed the whole table. 'I don't know about all of you chaps, but I know one thing. I would sooner be dead than be ruled by the Nazis. I am not a hero, I think that I am actually a bit of a coward, but what future could we look forward to if we hadn't done our best to protect this wonderful country of ours? Having said that, I will just re-iterate what the Major said. If anybody wants out, you will not be blamed, simply get up and leave now, there will be no recriminations.'

Not only did nobody move, but each and every one voiced that they were definitely not going to leave, some endorsing Adrian's words about self doubt. Ted White also spoke. 'I was called up as a young man, during the 1914- 1918 war, and I want to talk to you all about 'cowardice'. There is nothing wrong with having a natural fear of danger. It is our basic survival instinct. There were many times in the trenches when all of us young soldiers would discuss our feelings, and there weren't many who didn't admit that they were shitting themselves each time we went into action, including me. Some even did shit themselves, literally. The 'hard men,' who said they were afraid of nothing, were nearly always the first to crack.'

Ted continued, 'I have seen many a 'hard man' with just a small wound, crying like a baby, and yet other men who could put up with the most atrocious of injuries and not complain at all. None of us are cowards, but there may be times when we doubt ourselves. The best thing in any fighting unit is the knowledge that you can count on your comrades, come what may.'

'Gentlemen, you can count on me, as an old soldier, and I feel pretty sure that I can count on you too. Having said that, you may yet see this old bastard shit himself one more time, but I will still be there with you.'

'Well said, Ted' responded the Major. 'Gentlemen, there is not much more to be said, other than I will organise an army lorry to collect all of you tomorrow evening, at 10.30pm. I will not be there, because I have my own special orders from Mr. Churchill, but you can rest assured that I will be able to monitor your progress and maybe offer some assistance, if needed. It is best that you meet away from prying eyes, so I have arranged for the first small lay-by just along Watermill lane, to be the meet up point. Your driver, by the way, is one of us, so he will drop you as close to the bunker as possible.'

The Major drained his glass, stood up, and quietly said, 'Good luck, chaps. I have every confidence in you all, and we will very soon be enjoying another drink in here once the immediate threat has been eliminated.' With that, he was gone. The team sat around the table a little awkwardly once he had gone, but very quickly, Adrian called for Derek once more and asked him to bring the rest of the bottle. 'Put it on my tab, mate,' he said with a twinkle in his eye. It was not unusual for 'The Doc's' monthly tab to exceed twenty pounds, but he was always good for the money and he also knew that Derek would not try to have one over on him.

'Well chaps,' said Adrian, who, like the others, already had a story prepared for his forthcoming quick disappearance. 'I suggest we drink up and go home to our wives, for one more decent night's sleep in a comfortable bed, before we await the arrival of our overseas cousins, beneath our beloved Sussex soil.'

'I am so sorry, Darling,' began Adrian, but he had already caught the resigned look in his loving wife's eyes. 'The Joint Technical Board has been working on something for months now that will cut down on permanent injuries to our wounded troops. Problem is that as a GP member of the team, I have to make myself available at short notice.'

'I will be required to treat some chaps that have been sent home from the front, who otherwise may not have much hope. It shouldn't be for much more than a couple of weeks, though. I will be replaced by another GP in about a fortnight's time. Why don't you visit your Mother in Tunbridge Wells for a couple of weeks? I will sort out a locum to take over my duties, and cancel any appointments tomorrow, and the time will pass very quickly.'

Helen and Adrian made love that night, and Helen couldn't help noticing how tender and loving Adrian appeared to be. 'Well, if that's the effect going away has on you, maybe you should go away more often,' declared Helen, who was only too aware how distracted her husband could be at times, especially after a stressful day.

They fell asleep in each other's arms, with Adrian declaring his undying love for his wife just before they finally dropped off.

By the time Adrian had seen his appointed patients the next day, and sorted out his replacement for the next couple of weeks, it was mid afternoon. His wife had dropped by at the surgery, with Rufus their dog, on her way to Hastings railway station, to say one last goodbye. This suited him well, because he needed to sort out his uniform and full kit, ready for life underground, without having to invent any more lies. For a short time, he wondered about the others in the team, and what stories they would have had to invent, in order to justify their time away.

The telephone rang a little later, and it was Patrick O'Donnell, the Hastings coroner. 'Hello Adrian. I have just completed my examination of that poor bastard soldier from Toot Rock. You were spot on with the diagnosis. The chunk of tree up his arse was what killed him. It must have rammed up him at such a speed, it tore his rectum to pieces. Did you say that he had fallen from the top of the Rock?'

'Yes Paddy, something like a drop of twenty or thirty feet.' He replied. 'Well just the trauma of the incident would have been enough to kill him, but he lost an awful lot of blood as well,' said the coroner.
'Okay, Paddy. Thank you for keeping me informed. Do you need a reason for him falling in the first place?'
The coroner responded, 'didn't he suffer a bout of 'the trots' during the afternoon and evening? His body was very dehydrated.'

'Yes Paddy, and my suggestion would be that he was simply overcome with weakness, having emptied his guts, and was just unable to hold on to the pole they use when they are desperate for a crap.'

'Really appreciate your input, Adrian. Let's get together for a beer again soon. Does your local landlord still do a lock in?
'He does when you and I are drinking together,' laughed Adrian, and the two agreed that they would find the time in the next few weeks. They said their goodbyes and Adrian continued with his final pieces of admin.

'Reality check', suddenly he thought about the practicalities of life underground and called out to his nurse, Maureen. 'Do me a favour, would you Maureen? I need a couple of bottles of whisky to take with me, it will be used to help treat the poor soldier's wounds,' he said with a twinkle in his eye. Maureen knew Adrian only too well and privately thought that the only wounds that the whisky would be used for treating would be deep inside the doctor's throat. Still, Adrian was a good and compassionate, if sometimes eccentric, and extremely infuriating boss, but she wouldn't have things any other way.

The last patient was dealt with, and a very stuffy character, Dr. Atkinson the locum, had come by to meet Maureen and familiarise himself with the surgery. Adrian placed the two recently procured whisky bottles into his medical bag, slipped off his stethoscope, and handed his surgery keys to Maureen. Dr. Adrian Hart was finally free to serve his country.

At least, this was how he felt, and yet somehow he mused, the reality was very different. Life would carry on as normal, for his patients, for his nurse, for the locum, but meanwhile in a sort of parallel universe he may be involved in a desperate battle to save this country. 'Of course,' he reasoned to himself, 'if this were the case, then everybody will be aware that we have been invaded, because the police and the home guard will be desperately trying to move and protect the civilian population, so nothing could possibly be secret anymore.'

With these thoughts running around his brain, Adrian headed back to Pett Village in the Alvis, which he had been driving with the hood down, during the last few days of good weather. 'Better put the top back up when I park her up tonight,' he thought. Suddenly a cold chill ran down his spine as the dreadful thought crossed his mind, 'This might be the last time I drive her, ever.'

He was soon indoors, and all of his kit was packed by 7.30pm. 'Three hours to kill,' he thought as he checked his watch yet again. He had not eaten anything and had already drunk two or three large brandies, so he took the decision to walk to the Two Sawyers and get a decent cooked meal, before the next few days at least, of enforced cold food.

'Hello Doc,' called a couple of locals, as he entered the main bar. 'Good evening Adrian' welcomed Derek, who soon had a bottle of red wine uncorked at the bar. 'I can do you sausage egg and chips, the sausages aren't too bad, or I have some local scallops, which the cook is wrapping in bacon, and serving with mashed potatoes.'

'The scallops, sound great,' responded Adrian, who began chatting with a couple of locals about keeping a small fishing boat on the beach, 'when this bloody war is over.' Adrian had always loved the sea, and had a special liking for all types of seafood, so this idea had always appealed to him. The three were agreed that they would jointly purchase and operate, a small motor driven craft, and obtain some decent nets and lines, with the view to obtaining free rations of all things currently living and thriving in the English Channel.

The meal was quite superb, especially washed down with the half decent bottle of red wine that Derek had been able to supply. Times were very hard when it came to any kind of foodstuffs, and although Adrian was not on the breadline financially, he was well aware of the shortages that he and his fellow countrymen, were undergoing. Also he was not a wine 'snob'. He was fully aware that the elite would not consider drinking anything other than white wine, with a fish dish. The fact was, that none of the locals here would have been any the wiser, and secondly, he preferred, the more rounded, oaky flavour of red wine. Some was better than others of course, such were the fortunes of war, but once this war came to an end, we would be able to resume our direct trade links with France, who no doubt produced the finest red wines. 'God knows where most of it is coming from at the moment,' he thought. 'Maybe it's better not to know.'

A couple of pints of the locally brewed bitter, enjoyed with a few more locals who had by now come into the bar, and Adrian stood up to leave. He had been watching the time carefully and it was now just coming up to 10pm. By the time he strolled home and collected his kit, it would be time to walk along to Watermill lane. If anyone should see him in his military gear they would just assume that it was a 'Home Guard' thing.

The rest of the team were already at the appointed meeting place, and had all been quietly discussing their forthcoming role underground and how they would all get on together. Effectively, Adrian was their Sergeant, although this was more an unofficial title bestowed on him by Major Roberts. Army tradition would not allow for the official appointment of someone with just about one week's military training, directly into any rank.

At no time however, did this team follow typical military protocol, nor did Adrian ever take an overbearing tone with any of the team. There was simply no need. They had all volunteered for these duties, and they were all there for each other. The truth was that all the men had the utmost respect for 'The Doc', and although he often gave them cause for amusement, and could be the subject of the occasional joke, he was an intelligent and totally committed member of the team. They all agreed as well that he was a 'bloody good doctor'.

Before he arrived a couple of other members had mentioned that they had packed some booze as well. Badger Higgins had got himself a couple of bottles of Irish whisky, courtesy of some local Gipsies. He had exchanged a deer that he had 'come across' on a local gentleman's estate, for them. The Gipsy community used a blend of chopped up venison, blood soaked sawdust, and dripping fat and offal, to produce a fairly credible venison sausage, which local housewives and butchers would always pay good money for. A large deer could produce up to 200 sausages, depending on how much sawdust was added to the mix, so the whisky exchange was a bargain as far as they were concerned.

Next one to confess to having packed some 'medicinal supplies', was, Ted White. The old first world war soldier, suffered a lot of pain in his feet, having lost some toes to trench foot, and found that a drop of 'mother's ruin' in the form of Gordon's gin, gave him a more restful night's sleep.

The other three team members, Harry East, George Dobson and Bill Jacobs were more the 'cup of tea, last thing at night' types, but having said this, Harry had slipped a half bottle of Brandy into his bag, knowing that there would be no hot drinks, in the bunker.

'Attention, my lovely boys', said Adrian as he arrived alongside them. 'Evening Doc,' was the general response to this. They chatted quietly for a short while and right on time, the transport arrived at 10.30 to take them to Beckley Woods. The team quickly and quietly climbed aboard the back of the truck and were very surprised to see another dozen or so men already sitting on the seating rails that ran along either side of the lorry. The men were at first reticent to talk to each other, not knowing whether the others were 'in' on the special operations thing.

'Good evening Gentlemen', the voice came from deep inside the canvass covered truck. 'Captain John Clifford, World War One veteran. Sorry chaps, I should have mentioned to start with, that we are all in the same boat, here. I know that you Pett boys are going to be dropped off at Beckley Woods. Then we are off to Brede High Wood, and finally Vinehall Forest, which is where my team here are headed. We all apparently have what Major Roberts described as the 'finest bunkers in England'. Let's hope the bugger is right. Who knows whether we will see each other again soon, but if we do, let's hope we run into one another while we are sticking some dynamite up the enemy's arse'.

'Here here, was the mumbled response around the truck. It seemed like only a few minutes and the truck had slowed at a bend in Horseshoe Lane, and the driver's navigator came round to the back of the truck and said 'This is the nearest piece of road to TQ 865222'. Adrian's team were swiftly up and out with all their kit. 'Good luck', the collective farewell came from within the truck, and Adrian called back, 'Good luck to you all as well.'

The short trek cross country, was an interesting one because they had not approached the bunker from this direction before. Luckily, Badger seemed to know exactly where they were at any time, and within about twenty minutes of steady walking, the team had arrived at the large oak stump, that signified home. On route, Adrian had stopped for a piss on a couple of occasions, and the team had duly waited for him to catch up. Other than this the trek had been uneventful and quiet. They had not needed to use their standard issue Ever-Ready torches, as it was quite a clear night with a bright half-moon planted in the sky. Only when they had reached the more densely wooded area, had they used one torch, to assist with their passage into the area of the bunker.

Now they were there, they knew what had to be done. The large black key had appeared from Adrian's trouser pocket, inserted into position, and the heavy oak stump was tilted back on its steel hinges and the team one by one, entered the hole via the steel ladder. Last man in, was Bill Jacobs, arguably the strongest man of the group, who had no difficulty in pulling the hinged stump back from its open position, with the attached chain, whilst taking the weight of it upon his shoulders, until he had taken a couple of steps down into the bunker. The stump settled back down onto the forest floor

Once inside, Adrian suggested that they all familiarise themselves with their equipment and the explosives available to them. Ted White got on the radio to report that the group had 'gone to ground'. He did not know who he was communicating with, just working a frequency that he had been given, clearly someone who was co-ordinating these small units. His call sign was 'Pett Crew', and his radio counterpart was 'Battle Station'. The communications were loud and clear.

The men spread out and all agreed which bunk would suit them best, and began to make themselves comfortable. They chatted together for a short while, but very soon, the excitement of the day, coupled with their efforts in getting here, took their toll. Within twenty minutes, the entire team were sleeping like babies, although one of those babies, Harry East, had a real grown up problem. He snored very loudly indeed. Although they had heard him at Coleshill, they had been at bit more spread out there, and it hadn't seemed to be quite such a problem. A few of the men were woken by him but managed to find some way of covering their ears, and eventually they all dropped off again.

There were six bunks and there would be one man awake for the entire time in the bunker. Badger Higgins agreed to take first watch, and after a period of two hours, the watch would rotate, as would the bedding arrangements.

Pett Level Beach, Circa 1950, Showing the Author Aged 4, by the Anti Tank Traps and the Old Pillbox.

Pett Level Cliffs, which the Germans Scaled in 1940.

Remains of the Beach Pillbox.

The Only Complete Anti Tank Trap Remaining.

The Pillbox, Near the Officer's House.

The Officer's House Today.

Rye Road, where the Boy and his Dog were found.

Preserved Special Operations bunker, in Southern England.

Ziggy, John, 'Badger' Higgins' Dog.

The Station at Doleham Halt, Today.

The Cottages at Doleham, Today.

The German Soldiers' Unmarked Grave.

The Two Sawyers Inn, Today.

Tongs House, Today.

The Barrack Room Roof, Looking West.

The Barrack Room, Today.

The Underground Shell Storage Facility.

Sleep Well, Tommy but Stay Ready.

The Old Entrance to the Underground Fortifications.

The Second Bofors Gun Site.

The Row of Cottages, Commandeered by the Military.

The Rough Scrubland, Below the Observation Post.

Today's view From the Observation Post.

The Machine Gun Stand, in the Observation Post.

The Officer's bunker, today.

The barrack room, looking out.

Chapter 11

Gruppenfuhrer Zimmermann and his team had slept, washed, and eaten and now it was time for them to head back to Pett Level beach to meet their new comrades from the Waffen SS. This was the next major step with the invasion plans, although each team member now felt very confident. They had by now, been on enemy soil for three days, and had marched across England's fields and streams and along its lanes, completely unchallenged. It made very little difference in their minds whether there would be seven men marching, or forty. They were all trained to be totally discreet whilst operating on enemy soil.

The time was just approaching 22.00 hours and this time the Gruppenfuhrer ordered his men to bring every piece of equipment with them. 'We would hope to be able to get back here,' he told his team, 'but in case we are compromised as a larger force, then we will need to be flexible. Either way, we cannot afford to abandon any piece of equipment. We all know that everything that we are carrying is vital to our success.' Once again the boot polish was used to 'black up'.

The team were fully loaded and once again marching in the direction of Pett level. The journey was fairly un-eventful, other than they were travelling at a time when some local people were likely to be still out and about. At one point, a military vehicle rumbled up the hill towards them and they simply melted into the surrounding woodlands, each side of the lane. It droned past, its side lights shrouded, casting a strange yellow glow towards the ground around its front wings. 'If that is a British army military patrol, then we really do not have anything to worry about,' whispered Zimmermann, to his team, as they once again progressed towards the coastline.

The team had reached the top of Chick hill, without any further incident. They stood just inside the front garden of a house, whose lights had long since been switched off. They progressed to the bottom of the hill where they turned left at 'Miss Broad's Tea Rooms'. They were now on high alert, because they knew that the two guards from the other night, would probably be at their posts, and must not be alerted in any way. Sure enough, as they walked the short distance towards the beach, the two sentries could be seen, standing in front of the Market Stores, smoking and chatting, much as before.

The team were lying flat against the wall of a cottage on the opposite side of the road to the Market Stores, and at a timely moment, when both sentries had their backs to the team, Wagner picked up a stone and threw it over the roof of the little shop, a split second later, a splash was heard, as the missile hit the water beyond the new defence wall. Both sentries slid their rifles from their shoulders, and climbed to the top of the wall to get a better view. Slowly they both edged along the wall to the side of the Market Stores, their rifles pointing directly in front of them. A torch was seen to be shining across the water, where several ripples were still shimmering across this watery expanse.

Simultaneously the team of seven men slid behind the several parked army vehicles, and within seconds, they had gained the sanctity of the beach once more.

'Must have been a duck, mate,' said Private Earnest Goodwin to his good mate, Private Henry Duffey. The pair had been friends since their days at junior school, and as luck would have it, they had ended up being called up together, and finally ended up here together on guard duty. They both felt relieved that they were still on British soil as well as being in one of the best defended areas on the South coast of England. 'Yes mate, you're probably right, they do make a bit of a splash when they dive down.'

The time was now just after 0100 hours and the team had positioned themselves at the foot of the cliff, for the arrival of the second wave of Waffen SS soldiers. This time, they were a little further away from the point where they had scaled the cliff, staying within two or three hundred metres of the small beach at Cliff End. Once again, the beach pill-box had presented them with no problems, just as before, the sound of heavy snoring had come from within.

Zimmermann held the Zeiss binoculars up to his eyes and scoured the horizon, but there was nothing to be seen, as yet. He sat with his back to the cliff, the same as the rest of his team, although the tide was a lot further up the beach compared to when they had landed. At about 0140 he whispered to the team seated either side of him, and pointed out to sea. What a discreet disembarkation this had been, as the only things visible were half a dozen or so, inflatable boats, looking like tiny black dots on the horizon. There was no sign of the craft that had delivered the men.

Steadily, the tiny flotilla came closer and closer to where the team waited, and almost exactly at 0200hours the first of these was being pulled ashore. The agreed signal was a stone, thrown in the direction of the first crew. Very smoothly, and very quickly, the rest of the men had beached, deflated their boats, and stowed them, and were listening to the Gruppenfuhrer's instructions. Soon the much larger team were heading back over the barbed wire coils and past the heavily sleeping sentry, once more.

Once again, a degree of luck presented itself once they reached the point where the two guards normally stood at the Market Stores. There was no sign of either of them, so the team were very soon heading up Chick hill and away towards their woodland hide. The team felt that they must show their strength, and superiority, in leading their new colleagues across country to Beckley Woods. In total, there had been eight inflatables, delivered by two submarines. Each boat carried the maximum load of four persons. Hence, there were now a total of 39 men.

The Gruppenfuhrer knew the rest of the team, but not quite as well as he had got to know the smaller unit, so he felt that he must impress upon these new men that he could lead from the front and perform as well as any of them. Once again, he maintained a punishing pace, and long before the first vestiges of dawn, they were all settled down back at their base area. To allow for the larger sized unit, four men from the new team were put on first watch duties, with the agreement that they would change the guard after one and a half hours.

All was quiet for the rest of the night. Both German and British teams had spent a night within a few feet of each other and yet neither was aware of it at this stage. Adrian's team were approximately fifteen feet below the German troops' position, but were sleeping like babies.

They had awoken at around 06.30hours and had easily established a 'morning' routine. Drinks had been prepared and tins had been opened, the latrine had been well and truly 'christened'. Their task was quite simply to wait. They had checked the actions of the 'Russian' guns and had loaded and un-loaded them. The actions had been oiled, and the barrels cleaned. The radio communications had been checked, but there was nothing new to report from, or to, 'Battle Station'.

At about 1100hours Adrian decided to gently 'up periscope' and have a tentative look around up top. 'Jesus Christ', whispered Adrian, 'I don't fucking believe this.' The others of the team were immediately attentive. 'Fucking Krauts , must be two or three dozen of the bastards, they are up there now.'
Badger whispered, 'you don't suppose this is a test, do you? Let me have a look Doc.' Badger slipped through the half cupboard to the latrine area,

and took over Adrian's position at the periscope. 'They are definitely Krauts, there's no way any kind of test like this would have been thrown at us, with them wearing full German uniform and everything. We could only reasonably be expected to try to kill them.'

'Easier said than done, with the team all trapped down here,' mused Adrian. 'What the fuck are they doing here though?' Each man manoeuvred into position to use the periscope and each agreed that this was 'for real'. Ted spotted the radio man, Jung with his set spread out on a blanket in the foreground, and leather head phones on his ears and realised that he would not be able to alert 'Battle Station'. All the time the Germans were using their radio, there was a risk that another local signal could be picked up, and the game could very much be up.

The decision was taken by Adrian, to lower the periscope, and thus lower the risk of it being detected. They would take another look at around 20.00 hours. Meanwhile they must maintain radio silence. These men could not be an invasion force, because communications first thing would have confirmed a landing, and pre-warned them that a force was moving inland. More likely this was a commando style force and they were here to make a raid on a specific target locally.

As soon as they were able to watch them again, they would keep the periscope up until they moved off, probably tonight, and then they would have the element of complete surprise, as well as some back up provided by 'Battle Station' as soon as they were able to re-establish contact.

Up top, the Germans had been discussing and planning the attack on Toot Rock and the Gruppenfuhrer had organised the men into small units, each tasked with a specific duty once the assault began. 'Is everybody clear?' he asked, as he pawed over the local map. Before anyone could answer, a child's voice called out.

'You're Germans, you lot.' The astonished team looked up to see a small boy, aged perhaps nine or ten, with a cocker spaniel type dog straining at the end of a lead. Clearly the dog had smelled something and had pulled its owner from the woodland path, straight into their lair. 'Fuck it,' said Zimmermann, who realised that they were now completely compromised. 'Grab him, Fuchs, and Jung take the dog's lead.'

The young lad looked shaken as the reality of his situation unfolded. They obviously were German soldiers. He had just heard them speaking 'foreign'. Now they had captured him and Rogue, he was in big trouble because his Mother had warned him not to go too far into the woods. 'You never know what kind of people you might bump into, if you stray too deep into them woods,' she had told him. 'Rogue doesn't mind where you take him for his walks as long as he gets plenty of exercise.'

Meanwhile Zimmermann was talking quietly to his close team. 'We can't let him go, but if we kill him, this place will be swarming with people trying to find him within a few hours. Fuck it, fuck it, fuck it.' Klein, for once was the man with a solution, albeit one with a selfish motive. Wagner and Neumann did not like this suggestion at all, but realistically they didn't have any other option. Schultz felt a little uneasy too, but also realised that they had no other options.

Zimmermann reached into his kit bag, and pulled out a small bar of German chocolate. As he approached the boy, he instructed the team in German what had to be done. Klein took over from Fuchs and put his hands on the boy's shoulders, Jung moved away with the dog. 'You are a very clever young man, said the Gruppenfuhrer in very good English, as he approached the cowering lad. 'You have worked out that we are German soldiers, but I bet you haven't worked out what we are doing here?' He spoke with as friendly a voice as he could muster.

'Some sort of commando raid, I s'pose, said the lad. The Gruppenfuhrer looked hard at the boy, and replied, 'Yes, sort of, but not one where we want to kill people. We are here to try to make contact with Winston Churchill to see if we can make peace between England and Germany. That would mean the end of the war for all of us. Do you know where Winston Churchill lives?'

By now Zimmermann was kneeling immediately in front of the lad and broke open the 'Hachez' chocolate bar. He put one piece in his mouth and offered the other half to the boy. 'As proof of our friendship, I would like you to have this half,' said the Gruppenfuhrer. 'I am Wolfgang Zimmermann, what is your name?' The boy was not sure, but he felt that it would be better to take the chocolate than run the risk of upsetting this strange looking man. He slipped the piece into his mouth and started to chew it. 'My name is George Sinden,' he replied, thinking that he would look for a chance to run, if the opportunity arose.

In a split second Klein had lifted the boy from behind, his arms wrapped around his shoulders, and a sickening 'snap' was heard as the little lad's neck was broken. His lifeless corpse was dropped to the ground like a broken toy. 'Now the dog,' the Gruppenfuhrer ordered, and almost instantly Schultz had appeared with a large thick pine log, which he smashed down with great force across the unfortunate animal's back, killing it instantly. 'Now smash the boy's body with the log, right across his back,' was the final command from Zimmermann. A sickening thud followed, as Schultz smashed the log down for the second time, clearly splitting the boy's ribcage from behind.

The whole team of nearly forty soldiers could hardly believe what they had just witnessed, and stood there in the woodland, in shocked silence. The Gruppenfuhrer very quickly took control of this situation. He stood forward and addressed the whole team.

'Gentlemen, sometimes in war, we have to do some very unpleasant things, and there is no possible way that we could have allowed this stupid boy and his dog to have compromised our mission. We could not keep him prisoner, there would have been a civilian search party. We could not let him escape, as there would have been a military search party. Klein here, and Fuchs, will carry the boy and the dog to the closest main road, and arrange the bodies to look like a motoring accident.' The team studied the local map and Klein and Fuchs decided to head for the Rye road, the A268.

'On this one occasion only, I am prepared to let you go with overalls covering your uniforms. We cannot risk either of you being spotted wearing military attire during the day. People would instantly put two and two together and make five.' Zimmermann would never have normally made this concession, as they were invading soldiers, on enemy territory. The uniform would normally have been their protection, because enemies the world over, do not treat with much compassion, troops who have tried to integrate as locals. Spies are shot, everywhere, full stop. Also, in the Gruppenfuhrer's mind, it was deemed to be un-professional soldiering.

Already the two bodies had been stuffed into a large kitbag, which was bundled onto the back of Klein, who set off straight away in the direction of the main road, with Fuchs as back up. The rest of the party fell into a strange silence as they watched the two depart, looking like a typical pair of local workmen.

As the two made their way through the Northern part of the woodlands, they spoke very little, but occasionally they would switch the heavy kitbag from one to the other. After 35 minutes of fast moving, following the direction of Bixley lane while still keeping within the shelter of the woodland area known as Flatroper's Wood. They reached a small farm settlement that appeared to be deserted, and Klein ventured into one of the broken down barns that stood on the land. He started to rummage around, picking things up and putting them down again.

He quickly emerged with a triumphant look on his face, as he clutched a car bumper, together with an Automobile Association badge. 'Brilliant,' said Fuchs. They pushed on and were very quickly within earshot of the main A268 road. The woodland ran right up to the road, so at no time were they compromised.

They waited by the hedgerow and listened. There was no sound of any approaching vehicles or persons. It was only about mid-day as they scaled the style separating the woodland from the road. The two bodies were shaken out of the kitbag and the boy was laid face down half way across the road with the loop of the dog's lead thrust into his right hand. The dog was laid ahead of the lad, at full stretch of the lead, as if the animal had pulled his master into the road. The bumper and the AA badge were thrown into the road just behind them. The pair studied their work and the picture looked completely authentic.

Anybody arriving at this scene would see this as a 'hit and run' accident. Within the space of a few minutes the two were once again deep into the woodlands and running back to join the rest of the squad. When they returned, they still felt that there was some coldness towards them especially from the new arrivals, but this was not their problem. They had simply obeyed orders, even though Klein would have been the first to admit, that he had felt excited by the task of snapping the boy's neck.

The Gruppenfuhrer questioned them when they got back, as to the positioning of the bodies in the road, and whether the whole scenario looked realistic. He thought that the AA badge and the bumper were excellent additions that should keep the local police busy for some time. More important, was the fact that there would be nothing to link the 'accident' with his team of soldiers hidden deep in these woods.

'Attention Gentlemen,' called the Gruppenfuhrer quietly. The men moved in closer to hear his words. 'We all know that what has happened here has been unpleasant, but we also know that our mission cannot be allowed to fail. I have to make decisions that will ensure the success of our invading forces, arriving here tomorrow. Nothing can change this and nothing can be allowed to compromise this. Tomorrow will be your turn to change the course of this war and your own destiny. I hope you do not have to

individually make such a demanding decision, but if you are faced with it, may God give you the strength to carry it through.'
'May I suggest now that we now get as much rest as we can, we have all got a very heavy day tomorrow.' The guards were appointed and the usual one and a half hour duty rota was agreed. Very soon the whole area fell completely silent.

Below ground, the special operations team were eating a lunch consisting of corned beef and dry bread. Luckily, they had not witnessed the horrific killing of the boy and his dog. Had they done so, it may have been impossible to contain their anger, and they would have almost certainly put themselves into a situation of grave danger.

Chapter 12

There was a nervous knock at the door of Dot Sinden's cottage, on the outskirts of Peasmarsh village. 'I'll give George a right telling off,' she thought, as she went to open the door. 'Little bugger has been gone with 'Rogue' for nearly two hours now, and his lunch has gone cold,' she mused as her hand pulled the door open.

She was shocked to see two police officers, with very grim expressions, standing there. 'Mrs Sinden?' enquired the older of the two.
'Yes dear,' she replied, 'whatever is the matter?'
'May we come in?' The two officers entered the small cottage and once again the older of the two spoke. 'My name is Sergeant Watkins, and this is Constable Robinson of the Rye constabulary. Do you have a son, named George?'
'What on earth has the little bugger been up to?'
'Sit down please, Mrs. Sinden. Robbie here will make us a cup of tea if you will let him.'

Now, the poor lady began to feel very uncomfortable indeed. 'Oh Gord, what are you going to tell me?'
'There's been an accident on the top road, and a local gentleman said that he recognised the lad and his dog, and gave us his name and address.'
'There's no time for tea then, I'll have to get to the hospital,'
'Of course you will have to formally identify your son, but I am afraid to say, that both the boy and his dog have been killed by a car, that failed to stop. It doesn't look like your boy did anything wrong, as we believe the car must have been speeding, or possibly the driver was intoxicated'

The terrible reality suddenly hit Dot Sinden, and she burst into tears. 'What on earth are you telling me? My little boy's not dead, he can't be. He's only nine years old.'
'We have a car to take you to Rye hospital, where we must ask you to identify the lad. I am very much afraid that this probably is your son, because he had a small black and white spaniel with him.'

'Rogue, is he dead as well? How can this be happening to me?'
'I am so sorry Mrs. Sinden. It appears that the car hit them at speed as they were crossing the top road. We have taken the dog to the police station and wrapped him in a blanket. You might want him back to lay him to rest in the garden. As for George, there will have to be an autopsy to verify the cause of death. Meanwhile, we have started enquiries to find the driver and vehicle that did this. Have you got a neighbour or relative

nearby who would be willing to come with you?' enquired the kindly policeman. The younger officer shuffled about nervously, not knowing where to look or what to do.

'Grace Murray. She lives next door. She is my friend. But don't go shocking her, let me go and tell her.' With that, Dot went to the hall and in almost a matter of fact way, put on her coat and scarf, and went next door, to inform her friend.

Within a couple of minutes, the Wolseley police car was driving in the direction of Rye hospital, with the two ladies in the back, hugging each other, and sobbing. The two officers in the front did not speak during the short trip, although they both seemed quite relieved that Mrs. Sinden had a friend to accompany her.

They drove around to the rear of the hospital and pulled up at a blue and white enamel sign, bearing the word, 'Mortuary'. The younger officer stayed by the car, while the other three persons walked to the door and the Sergeant pushed the electric bell. A sad faced, white haired gentleman in a white coat opened the door, and bade the three to enter. He took them to a white marble table which had the shape of a small person beneath a white sheet. As soon as Dot saw the boots sticking out from beneath the sheet, she knew that this was her son.

'I am sorry that I haven't had the chance to clean him up, ladies. He was only bought in about twenty minutes ago.' He pulled back the top of the sheet to reveal the very white and still face of Dot's son. Dot immediately exclaimed, 'you stupid boy, what were you doing on the main road?

She asked the question of her unhearing son, almost as if she expected him to answer. She leant forward to kiss his face and called out, 'What's this, he's got chocolate in his mouth. He didn't have any money for chocolate. It's Saturday and I don't give him his pocket money until Monday morning. Sixpence is what I always give him.' I told him I would put it up to a shilling once he is ten. Mind you he would have to do some more jobs around the garden to earn it. Who's going to help me now? His father was taken two years ago, God bless him. He died of pneumonia, only 42. What am I going to do,' she wept.

'I take it then that this unfortunate lad is your boy then?' The comment seemed completely unnecessary, but police protocol had to be followed. 'What happens now then?' enquired the poor bereaved woman. The officer explained that an autopsy would have to take place in order to officially confirm the cause of death, and then the lad's body would be released for burial. The process normally took about two weeks. She might want to make an arrangement with a local funeral company.

'As soon as we have caught the perpetrator of this terrible crime, because that is what it is, we will let you know, Mrs. Sinden. Now, my colleague and I are going to drive you home to Peasmarsh, and your friend here can take care of you.' The officer had dismissed the importance of the comment about the chocolate as he knew that small boys often succumbed to a bit of shoplifting or sometimes traded different things with their friends. It was just what boys did. He had a son of about the same age, so his heart went out to Dot Sinden. He couldn't really imagine what she must be going through. He would have a couple of pints tonight in The Pipemaker's Arms in Rye, before he went home. He was then off duty until Tuesday morning.

Meanwhile the crime investigation unit were studying the car parts found at the scene of the accident and desperately trying to identify them. The long process would begin of identifying and visiting all registered vehicle owners in the area, once the car make and model were established. When Sergeant Watkins and Constable Robinson got back to the police station they had a lengthy report to fill out. They worked until about 4pm when their report was finally written up and sketches of the body positions in the road were recorded, along with the visible injuries to the victims.

The station Inspector then came to the office, and suggested that the two of them 'call it a day'. 'If any new information comes to light, I will telephone you at home, otherwise I will see you both on Tuesday morning. Go and get a few pints down you.' The Inspector knew how stressful a death could be, especially that of a young person, and he was happy with the performance of both these officers.

On Monday morning, the Inspector had received some very odd news. He called Sergeant Watkins at home. 'Sorry to trouble you on your day off Sid,' he began. 'The thing is, the boffins have worked out that the bumper belongs to a 1932 Lanchester, model 15/18. This is the weird bit though. It's a rear bumper. The other odd thing is that there were no fixings ripped off during the accident. It's just like it fell off the car. The one bit of good news is that there are only seventeen registered in the whole of Sussex and Kent. The London boys will have about thirty to check out, but hopefully it will prove to be a local car and we will have the culprit in custody by Wednesday night. It won't bring young George Sinden back, but at least his mother will feel a bit better knowing that we've arrested the bastard.'

Police officers across the two Counties were calling on owner's addresses by eleven o'clock that morning. There was no doubt in Inspector Arthur Dunlop's mind that the culprit would be local, and that he would be in custody by this evening.

Meanwhile, Sergeant Watkins stayed at home. He knew that once the owner of the vehicle was found, he would be needed to go in and interview him. Better then, that he stayed in by the telephone. In actual fact, he wouldn't have it any other way, nor would his constable, Mike Robinson, who had already told him that it would be alright to knock for him on the way in. If they had to go in to the Station, they would be very happy to do so because they could then both go and tell Dot Sinden that they had caught and charged her son's killer.

Chapter 13

Adrian and the special operations team felt trapped. They were aware that there were about thirty or forty German soldiers camped just above them, but knew that they could not make a move until the enemy moved off. What was totally frustrating was not being able to know when that was likely to be. 'As soon as they make their move, the sooner we can jump the bastards,' said the Doc, in hushed tones, to the rest of the team.

'Might be better to link up with a couple of the other units,' suggested Ted. 'We are well outnumbered, and they are all very well armed by the look of things.' A couple of the others nodded in agreement. 'I can get on the radio as soon as they move. They won't be able to make any communications while they are marching, so there is no chance they will be aware of the threat to them.'

'Why don't we gently put up the periscope and see what the bastards are up to now?' suggested Adrian. 'At least we can get a feel for what they are doing and when they are likely to be moving. It's now just after 4 pm and they will probably at least be preparing to do something quite soon.' 'Good idea Doc, but very gently.' whispered Harry, 'We don't want to be discovered now. We have the upper hand, even if we are below them at the moment. The point is that we know that they are here, but they don't know that we are, so let's keep it that way.'

'May I suggest that we leave it for two more hours, until around 6 pm,' said Badger. 'My thinking is that as this is not an invasion force, they will not think about moving until nightfall. Let's face it they won't get very far in full German Military kit during daylight hours, even in this sleepy neck of the woods.'
'Badger's right, they won't move until its dark.' said Bill.
George simply said 'Yep, that makes sense to me.'

Adrian, who by nature could sometimes be somewhat impatient, had to see the logic in the other team member's thoughts and after a little time, he said, 'Okay lets rest for another couple of hours and we will push the periscope up then and have a nose around. Are we all agreed, chaps?'
'The whole team nodded, or quietly said, 'Yes Doc.'

The next two hours went painfully slowly for all of them. They couldn't talk openly, because they were well aware that any noise could travel, perhaps even up the periscope tube itself, and as Harry had earlier pointed out, right now, this team had the advantage. Meanwhile Adrian was putting together, in his head, the plan for following and subsequently attacking the Troops above them. They would allow the Germans to clear this camp area, and immediately, Ted would put in a call to 'Battle Station,' to advise them of the new developments. It had always been agreed that 'Battle Station' would not attempt to call them, for fear of compromising their position, so there was no chance of getting reinforcements until the Germans moved. Ted would then close the bunker down, while the rest of the team would be following the German troops one at a time, at staggered distances, so as not to lose them, but also so as not to leave anybody behind.

Badger could do very realistic 'owl calls', so he would be closest to the enemy, while the rest of the team homed in on him. In reality, the whole operation should not take more than five or ten minutes, by which time the whole team should be just about 50 yards behind the Germans. There was just over half a moon tonight, so they should not have too much difficulty in keeping the enemy in sight. This 'tracking' procedure had been practiced many times during the week away at Coleshill, and the team had become very skilled at it. They were always ordered to track some very experienced soldiers, and bearing in mind that these soldiers knew they were going to be followed, they had scored some excellent ratings for their stealth and agility.

The biggest danger was always that if the enemy got a hint that they were being followed, they could leave a couple of soldiers behind, well hidden, until the followers passed by, and then the tables were turned, and the following troops would then themselves, be trapped.

All of these thoughts passed through Adrian's head as he lay on his bunk. He also thought about feeding his men well, before they left the bunker. He could have no way of knowing how long this mission would last, once they had left the safety of the bunker, or how far the Germans were prepared to march to achieve their objective. He felt that the target would probably be quite local, and also that the Germans could not have landed too far from here. There was only so much ground that could be covered under the blanket of night, and they would then presumably have to move off again to another hideout. He suddenly thought about the dead soldier at Toot Rock. It had all appeared to be cut and dried at the time, but could there have been outside forces involved? Also, there was the incident at Tongs House. Both of these events happened on the same night two nights ago. The more Adrian thought about it, the more certain he became that Toot Rock must be the target. There was no other military or civilian target in this area. 'Why though?' he questioned. 'Of course, the bastard

Krauts above us can only have one reason for attacking it. They have to try to neutralise it in order to allow troop landings ay Pett Level.

'It has to be Toot Rock,' he suddenly exclaimed, and the rest of the team were instantly focussed on him. 'Think about it guys,' said their leader, suddenly aware that he was speaking in louder tones than he should be. The team gathered around his bunk, and he continued in a quieter voice. 'There was all that shit that happened there two nights ago, and suddenly this lot up top are hiding here.'

'Why would they target Toot Rock, though?' asked Badger.
'Good point, but just think about it,' responded Adrian. 'There must be forty odd soldiers above us right now, and that is not a small force. Their target has to be something major, and something local. We know from The Major, that there is no secret manufacturing for the war effort going on around here, or anything the size of Toot Rock, until you get close to Dover. The closest, secret facility is too far away, at Three Cups Corner.

'There are about three hundred soldiers stationed at Toot Rock, so the only reason that I can think of, is that the Krauts want to land an invasion force on 'The Level'. In order to do this, they must wipe out these troops, and more importantly, the guns, that cover the whole of the beach and under-cliff.'

'Hold on a minute, though, Doc,' ventured Bill. 'What would be the point of them attempting to bring troops in at Pett Level? They know that the whole of the Level is flooded, and also there are deep trenches cut into it, so no tanks could get very far. We also know that the road across the level has been sabotaged at both ends with very deep excavations to stop any vehicular movement.'

'You are absolutely right, Bill,' replied Adrian, 'but you have to remember that all of the 'below water' stuff may not have been noted by the Germans, bearing in mind that the trenches were all dug out in one afternoon, and the sea wall was breached as soon as the diggers had disappeared, covering all the excavations with millions of gallons of water. *We* know that it is virtually impenetrable, but *they* might well think that once they have got over the sea wall, they have got an easy ride inland, or along the roadway.'

'It all makes sense, Doc.' Said Harry East, and the others agreed.
'Okay,' said Adrian. 'We are pretty sure that this is their target, so we had better formulate a plan to eliminate them. Once we start trailing them, we

will take with us the two flame throwers, which George and Bill will carry, as well as operate. Also a rifle each, with three hundred rounds of ammunition. We will also take a dozen hand grenades each, which we will carry in the small haversacks.'

'If we can meet up with the teams either side of us, so much the better, but if the reach Toot Rock before we have any back up, then we may have to tackle the job alone. One thing though, thinking about it, and that is, once Ted has informed 'Battle Station', they should be able to get some regular troops involved, to help at Toot Rock, plus they will be able to warn the chaps there that an attack is imminent. Those Nazi bastards will have quite a warm reception, not to mention any other fuckers that might be mid channel. Let's hope that 'Battle Station' has a hot line to the Royal Navy and the RAF.'

Every member of the team was now buzzing with anticipation. Food tins were opened and a larger than normal meal was consumed. The time was just after 1800 hours when they finished and had tidied up after themselves. The agreed weaponry had already been sorted, and was stored at the base of the steel ladder, ready for their exit. Adrian walked through the small half cupboard to the latrine area, and very gently and slowly pushed the well oiled action of the periscope to the 'up' position.

Above ground, the German troops were sitting around eating. It appeared to Adrian that the food rations of the Krauts were no better than the supplies that *they* were saddled with. Tin cans were being opened, and food was being forked directly out of them. Tin mugs were being offered up to German mouths, and there was no sign of a cooking stove, so he could only assume that they were eating and drinking everything cold, in exactly the same fashion as his own team.

He watched for ten minutes or more, occasionally feeding bits of information back to the team. He became aware of a tall soldier, standing only a few feet away from his vision, but with his back turned to the periscope lens. By his bearing, he could tell that this was the commander of the group, and it was pretty obvious that he was lecturing his men. At one stage, a map was held up by another member of the team, standing next to the leader, but Adrian could only see the blank, reverse side of this. 'They are planning to do it tonight, by the look of things,' he softly relayed to the rest of his own team. 'Their chief is pointing to a map, I can only see the reverse side, but what wouldn't I give to see the front of it, just to confirm our suspicions. I propose that I lower the periscope now, but we have a look every twenty minutes from now on.'

The whole team were ready to go. At last, this was their chance to do what they had all signed the official secrets act for. They were going to take on the enemy, but on their own home soil. Not one of the team seemed worried that they would be taking on a superior force. Not one of the team seemed worried that these German soldiers were probably highly trained commando style fighters. They, themselves, were strong and fit, and each member of the squad was very able to put into practice, the dirty tricks that they had been taught at Coleshill.

Also, it seemed that the entire team already felt a superior strength to the opposition. This was *their* country. This was *their* home that they were defending. They all felt that there was no possibility of them being beaten on their own territory. They were all aware that France and Holland and Belgium, etc. had been over-run by the Nazis, but this was England. The Brits just don't give up that easily. Plus, they all knew that the English Channel had provided, and would continue to provide, a barrier that could destroy most of a potential invasion force.

The periscope was raised once more and the scene had not changed very much. The troops were still sitting around, but by now there was no more sign of food or drink. Some of them were cleaning their weapons, and one man was throwing his knife at a tree. 'Fuck that,' said Adrian, 'one of these bastards is throwing a knife at a tree from about twenty feet away, and he hasn't missed it once.'

'I shouldn't worry about him too much Doc,' said Badger. 'The tree hasn't got much chance of ducking and diving, like we have. Also he won't be quite so accurate once he has had a grenade or two up his arse. And if we get the opportunity to use the flame throwers, he might find it very tricky to throw at all when all he has left is burnt stumps for arms.'

'Well said,' agreed Bill, who, as well as George, had had a lot of practice using the flame thrower, at training camp. They had been taught the ideal height to hit the enemy with the flame. 'Keep it low, heat always rises, and if their bollocks are on fire, they won't be too keen to retaliate,' had said their instructor. 'Also, if their bollocks are on fire, their faces will follow, in seconds.' The one thing that they had to remember was that once ignited, the flame projection must happen within a split second, otherwise they would simply be lighting up their own position for the enemy. On the other hand, once hit with the flame, the enemy are never able to fire back, as the heat is all engulfing, and they are instantly forced to turn their backs. This leaves them open to grenade or rifle attack, although very few actually survive the terrible burning ordeal, anyway.

Adrian gently pulled the periscope back down, and in exactly twenty minutes, it was pushed upwards once more. This time, there was more activity. It seemed that some of the soldiers were leaving the camp, carrying their wash kit. 'Maybe they want clean underwear and fingernails, before they end up on the mortician's slab,' he joked.

The periscope was raised and lowered a few more times, and each time there was evidence of further activity. The light levels were beginning to fade by about eight thirty that evening and it also appeared that there was a bit of drizzle in the air. The entire German team seemed to have disappeared at some stage and then returned again some fifteen minutes later. Clearly, their ablutions were high on the agenda, thought Adrian, who passed his observations back to the team.

Finally, due to the fading light conditions, it was agreed that it would be safe to leave the periscope up, and Adrian handed over watch duty to Harry. He had been watching the movements up top, eventually reporting that a small, neat looking guy had been on the radio for quite some time when suddenly he exclaimed, 'They are getting ready to go.'
'Right,' said Adrian, 'we had all better black up now as well.' A 'Cherry Blossom' tin did the rounds, and with that, Ted squeezed into his radio position, in front of Harry, and awaited further instructions from his boss.

'They have blacked up and are moving off, and the tall bastard with the scar, is leading them back out through the trees,' reported Harry. 'All of them have left, and if I am correct, I counted 39 in total.'

Adrian was fired up. 'Go Ted, go Badger,' he said excitedly. Within seconds, the hatch was being opened, and Badger was gone, carrying all of his personal equipment. Meanwhile Harry had climbed to the top of the steel ladder, again carrying all of his agreed equipment, and waiting for Adrian's instruction to move. A few seconds passed, while Adrian listened to Ted's efforts to make contact, and finally he called out, 'Harry, go.' The sound of Harry climbing out of the bunker seemed to reverberate throughout the whole of the small space occupied by the team. Once again, the next man, George, moved into position at the top of the ladder, awaiting further instructions. His co flame thrower, Bill, was already fully kitted up at the base of the steel structure. The sound of muffled communications came to the ears of the remaining squad.

'Battle Station, Battle Station, this is Pett Crew, over,' called out the determined voice of Ted White. 'This is Pett Crew, Pett Crew, come in Battle Station, over. Still there was radio silence from the other end.

After a few more seconds, Adrian, who had been studying his wristwatch intently, ordered George to move out and his fire raising colleague, Bill, took his place at the top of the Ladder. By now, Adrian was beginning to feel very uncomfortable. 'The best laid plans,' he complained to Ted. 'If the bastards at 'Battle Station' don't answer soon, we will have to go.'
'It could be they only have one operator, and he has gone for a piss,' suggested Ted White, who was well aware of the urgency of the situation.

There was a sudden crackling in his headphones, and Ted heard the response, 'Pett Crew, Pett Crew, this is Battle Station, over.'
'Good evening Battle Station,' replied the level and unruffled voice of Ted White. 'We have been in the bunker for two days now and we have had 39 German soldiers living above us for most of that time. They have just moved out and we are following them, but we will require back up.'

'All understood, Pett Crew. Do you know their intentions?'
'As far as we can see, their target is Toot Rock. We believe from their actions that they are going to attack the position to allow an invasion force to come ashore at Pett Level, tonight or early tomorrow morning.'
'What weaponry are they carrying?' asked the radio operator at Battle.
'They are heavily armed, and they have sophisticated radio equipment. They have been communicating within the last half hour or so, so maybe Crowborough have picked up something?'

'All copied, Pett Crew, wait one,' was the response from 'Battle Station'. Ted, like Adrian, was impatient to join the rest of the team, but he knew that he must hold station until a further response came from their radio contact. It seemed like an age to both of them, before any further communication occurred, but this time, a familiar voice came over the headphones. 'Pett Crew, Pett Crew, this is Battle Station, over.

Meanwhile, Adrian had issued the last order to the one remaining man on the ladder. 'Go Bill, we will be with you soonest,' he directed the instruction to the base of the steel ladder that was just visible in the failing battery lit area. Now Adrian directed his whole attention to Ted's conversation. 'Good evening, Major,' he heard Ted say. 'Yes, all fully understood, will pass this on, thank you, and out.'
'Was that Major Roberts?' Adrian enquired of Ted.
'Yes, he has asked us to follow as closely as possible but not to engage.'

'Well, what the fuck are we supposed to do?' asked Adrian, passionately. 'He says that he will have back up with us before we reach Toot Rock, and our task will be simply to observe the Krauts, and be in a position to accurately pin-point them, once they have arrived there.'

Adrian seemed disappointed, but knew that the Major's orders must be obeyed. They could not, as a small unit, compromise the 'bigger picture'. 'Come on then Ted. Grab the portable set, and let's go.' Within a few seconds, the remaining two members of the squad, were lowering the tree stump and locking it back into position in the ground. All the lighting had been switched off, and they knew that if they had to return, the battery system may have recovered enough for them to effect a full battery change, without losing power altogether.

The two quickly found their way out of the more dense area of woodland, in the same direction that the Germans had taken earlier, and were very soon aware of an owl, hooting in the distance. 'That's Badger, alright,' whispered Ted. The pair quickened their pace, and despite Ted's slight disability, they were covering the ground at a reasonable speed, despite the quite heavy load that they were both carrying. They were breathing quite deeply, but this was not a reflection on their level of fitness, it was more the fact that they had been imprisoned in the bunker for two days, and this was their first piece of real activity.

After three minutes, they came upon Bill, who quietly asked them to follow him. A few more minutes and they came to the spot where George was crouched down on the pathway. Another owl hoot went up, and they knew they were heading in the right direction. Several minutes later, and they had met up with Harry. It was only at this point, that Adrian realised that he may have miscalculated the time it could take to catch up with the enemy. They would all be moving as quickly as his team, and already had a good head start. Although Badger would be in touch with their position, the rest of them would struggle to make up the distance.

He thought it best to push as hard as they could during this first half hour, and hope that maybe the Germans would encounter an obstacle that would slow them, or perhaps have to make a detour, which would require a stop for map reading.

Badger was not overdoing it as far as the owl calls were concerned, he didn't want the Germans to suspect anything. He knew that the team would be able to follow the direction of the sound and that he need only give them an update every ten minutes or so. It had also occurred to him that his team may struggle to keep up, because the Germans had set off at a cracking pace, despite the huge amount of equipment they appeared to be carrying. Badger was very fit, he covered the ground with ease, but he was well aware, that some of the team may find the going a little heavy. The one bit of comfort that he felt was that so far, Adrian's prediction seemed to be correct. Everything suggested that they were heading in the direction of Pett Level.

He kept back to a distance of about sixty yards, and was easily able to track their movements. Occasionally he would hear a twig snap, or simply the rustling of many boots across the by now, quite wet ground. Badger knew that the rain would help his team. The sound of falling rain helped to mask other sounds, especially in open countryside. At one point, he caught sight of the entire group of German soldiers, running low across an open meadow. He held back at this point, because he could not risk entering this open space until they had well cleared it.

Some three minutes behind him, the others were blowing hard, but still moving well. Once again, they heard the owl call, and once again they realised that they were probably not much closer to Badger, than they had been at the start. Adrian spurred his team on. Although he enjoyed a good drink, and probably drank far too much generally, his overall fitness level was quite good, and he was determined that as a team, they were not going to fail.

'Come on lads, Badger sounds a bit closer,' he encouraged them. They all knew that this was the Doc's way of spurring them on, and they all put even more effort into their run, although they all realised that the Germans were going to be just as fast, if not faster, than them.

Badger was able to make his move again, and he covered the open meadow, crouching low, as the enemy had done. He hit the next smallish piece of woodland, and stopped as soon as he had got inside the cover of the first few trees. He let his breathing settle, and then he listened. Very shortly, he could make out the sound of low voices, not very far in front of him, possibly only fifty yards dead ahead. He turned his back on the sound, stood behind a tree, and let another owl call out into the air, directing it skywards.

The others heard it and were encouraged. They soon reached the top of the open stretch of ground that the others had already traversed. Adrian warned them to be extra careful, and they proceeded in single file, until they reached the cover of the next group of trees. Immediately they became aware of Badger, standing directly in front of them, and holding his finger to his mouth, in a hushing action. The other hand, was pointing, towards the centre of the wood. They were all very excited now. Somehow this felt just like the exercises that they had undertaken at Coleshill. They knew that the group that they were following was very close indeed, and they would need to be patient and let them make their next move. Once the leading team were on the move again, their own movements would drown out the sound of anyone following. The big advantage that they had over the Germans was, oddly enough, numbers. Forty men, however quiet, would always make more noise than six.

Meanwhile the Gruppenfuhrer had stopped his team so that Jung could make radio contact with German High Command. He quietly addressed his team as the response came through. 'Gentlemen, we are on the verge of making history. The first ships of our heroic invasion forces are preparing to set sail in five hours time. We have to time everything to perfection from now on. We must not attack the emplacement and guns, or blow the anti-tank traps too early, or we will give the enemy a chance to send reinforcements. We will have radio contact again, once we are in the agreed positions. Then we will make the fine tunings of our mission.'

Soon the Germans were marching again, this time at a slightly steadier pace. They knew that they were early, but at the same time they preferred to get the danger of the cross country march out of the way. They only wanted to get into their attack positions, ready for the start of the mission.

At one point, they had to cross the B2089 between Cock Marling and Udimore. This was something they had accomplished several times now, in both directions, but had never before encountered any traffic. They were all surprised to see dozens of military vehicles heading in the direction of Rye. As soon as the last of the vehicles passed, the Gruppenfuhrer raised his arm to beckon his team on, and instantly dropped it again as he heard another vehicle coming. A further group of army trucks rumbled past, and finally the area fell silent. They crossed the road swiftly and silently and were soon moving into the cover of the countryside beyond.

Their followers were some two hundred yards behind them at this point, because the ground was much more open now. Adrian whispered to the others that maybe the Major had, as promised, managed to arrange some back up. If these trucks were anything to do with it, then there would be substantial help for them at Toot Rock. Encouraged by this thought and also the fact that they had been pursuing their prey for nearly two hours now, without any indication that the enemy was aware of them whatsoever, they started to feel even more confident.

The rain was teaming down now, and although they had military capes, they were pretty well wet through. For a while, they thought of their own predicament, and then reflected on the German soldiers' situation. They would also be wet through, but soon they would be facing the might of the British army. As a team, they knew that it was better not to take any prisoners, simply eliminate the threat, and that was exactly what they intended to do.

After another hour, Adrian's men were really keyed up, as they were getting very close to what they now knew to be the target area. They watched as the forty or so Germans reached the area known as Wickham Cliff, and then seemed to settle down into the woodland that ran down to the water's edge. They had pulled several large waterproof sheets over them, and had simply disappeared from view.

'You don't suppose this is some sort of trick, do you?' enquired Harry. 'Anything's possible with these bastards,' replied Adrian, 'but I don't think so. My guess is that they are now just waiting for a command, before they make their move.' It was now just after 23.30 hours, and the special operations team had worked their way to the east of the Germans, and were now sheltering in the wooded foot of this steep escarpment.

Adrian was able to give his team a 'pep talk'. The noise of the rainfall obliterated any other sounds, and the distance between them and the Germans was about two hundred and fifty yards. 'Well chaps, we have to *assume* that we do not have any back up. There may well be some, but I can't see how they will be able to link up with us. Meanwhile, we have to think about the troop movements that we saw earlier. I have not been aware of this amount of local military, for a long time. Maybe these vehicles were carrying soldiers as back up for Toot Rock.'

'A quick question, Doc.' Said Badger. 'These guys are not carrying anything as heavy as mortars, so they won't be able to attack the rock unless they swim, or are using inflatable boats. There are three hundred odd troops stationed there anyway, so why would they think they would stand a chance?'

'A very good point, Badger,' said Adrian. 'I believe that the answer is quite simply, surprise. Let's face it. If we hadn't been in the bunker, then no bastard would have been aware of them anyway. They may even have already been on the rock, as there were a couple of incidents two nights ago, and the more I think about it, the more certain I am that these fuckers were involved.'

The others were listening intently, as the Doc continued, 'They could easily slip in under the pill box coming from different directions, and they probably would not be spotted. Let's face it, the guys in the observation post are looking out to sea, and not at the water immediately surrounding them. This rain as well will make it even more difficult. Things will be very different now though. The Major will have warned the commanding officer, who I know quite well, Lieutenant Colonel Arthur Burgess. Bit of a bumbling old bugger, but he has some three hundred odd troops with him, British and Canadian, including some battle scarred officers. You can bet your life they will all be on duty, and wide awake, tonight.'

'Okay, Doc. That all makes sense, but what is our role going to be?' asked George. He was a very powerful man, and he had a strong desire to take on the enemy close up. His closest ally was his good friend, Bill, who also had a desire to 'mix it' with the Krauts. Both of these men were chosen as the strongest pair of the group, to be the flame thrower operators. The flame thrower was a heavy piece of kit, in its own right, without the two gallons of fuel that was carried in its tank.

'We must wait until we see exactly what these bastards are going to do,' was Adrian's response. 'We cannot attack them now, because although we have the element of surprise, realistically we would not stand a great chance against a squad of some forty or so of them. If they decide to split up, then we would stand a better chance of taking them out in smaller chunks. Also we don't know whether the Major has arranged a team to come and help us. My only fear with that is, I really don't know how they would find us.'

So the decision to wait was taken. Adrian offered all of his men a large swig from his whisky bottle, as a little bit of a warmer. He knew that the alcohol would in fact thin their blood and cool them down, but it was a gesture of togetherness. He also knew that once the adrenalin was running through their veins, they would have no problem with cold. Ted had been listening in on the portable, but as yet, there were no communications to monitor. 'Why don't you head a little further to the east, to avoid being heard and see if you can get an update from 'Battle Station', whispered Adrian. 'You can give them this position for us and the Krauts, now. Keep it short and sweet, in case the Krauts pick it up.

Chapter 14

A mere couple of hundred yards or so to the west, the Gruppenfuhrer was again addressing his team. 'I will take one inflatable, with Neumann, Wagner and Jung, to the sea wall directly opposite, and we will blow the anti tank traps to smithereens. We will not undertake this action until we hear that your attack has commenced at Toot Rock, otherwise we may not be able to cross the water again safely to join the rest of you. One solitary small boat is pretty much like the sitting duck, as they say.'

'Fuchs, Schultz and Klein, will each lead an attack on the target, followed by the rest of the team assembled. All of the remaining inflatable boats will be utilised, and we are already agreed which side you will launch your attack from. You three must now decide which direction you prefer to take, and then decide which men you want in your team. In total you will be attacking with nine boats, so I suggest that you use the minimum spread technique.

They had already agreed their positioning, their objectives and technique. Every man in the team was completely comfortable with the job that he now had to do. The Gruppenfuhrer was impressed with the way that his close team had taken to commanding the larger, lower ranking group. They spoke quickly and quietly, and as it was agreed that the approach would be made from the eastern end, they would launch towards the area of the emplacement from further along the cliff line that they were now sitting on. Schultz, Fuchs and Klein would take the first boat, and beach at the bottom of the roadway, that runs up the rock. They would wait for the 'attack' time, concealed in the bushes at the base of the rock. Then, Fuchs and Klein would silently kill the pill box guards at the lower end of Toot Rock. The officer's shelter would also need to be checked.

Then, by blocks of houses, they would move up the group of coastguard cottages, taking out any opposition as they went. The ability to achieve this part of the mission as quickly as possible would be paramount. The sound of gunfire, and grenades exploding, would provide the signal for Zimmermann and the explosives team to blow the concrete anti tank traps. Meanwhile, Schultz would lead four men to the lower guard positions on the rear side of Toot Rock, and as silently as possible, take out the sentries positioned there.

The main attack on the guns and ammunition stores would be the hardest part of the operation. By now, the Gruppenfuhrer and his team would have completed their task and they would now make their way back in their single boat, to the end of the roadway, to rejoin their colleagues. They should be arriving at a scene of destruction, and desolation. There should be no viable opposition and they should be able to immediately get on with the task of permanently disabling the three guns. The Gruppenfuhrer had decided on the best method of tackling this. They would pack high explosives down tight into the barrels and then stuff them with earth and rocks, rammed down hard.

The large group had completely forgotten the fact that they were cold and wet. The sound of the rain hitting the waterproof sheets that they were crouched beneath, huddled in a large circle, suddenly seemed to get louder. Zimmermann checked his watch, and once again, ordered Jung to send a coded communication. After what seemed like an eternity, during which time Schultz quietly kept the group amused, with various jokes and stories, the time eventually came to make their move. The Gruppenfuhrer did not mind Schultz, keeping the team entertained. He felt that it would keep their spirits up, and distract them from the long wait. Schultz was a very able sergeant, and Zimmermann had complete confidence in him.

Zimmermann stood up, and the rest of the team followed. 'So Gentlemen, it is now time. Once again, I remind you that it is us, in this small group, who will determine the outcome of this war. Although we will certainly be again called upon for our expertise, and assistance, once we have considerable numbers of troops ashore, our main purpose will have been achieved, here in this next few hours. Let us now make history. Good luck. God speed to you all, we will meet up again very shortly.'

With that, the larger body of men packed away the waterproof sheets and set off to the location where they would launch their inflatable armada. Immediately, the explosive team's boat was unpacked and Neumann, with the help of Wagner, took turns to inflate it. Within a couple of minutes, they were sliding the small craft into the black waters of the enormous lake that was Pett Level. It was now a quarter past midnight.

They were once again very aware, that this part of the mission would be their most vulnerable time. The small boat slid silently through the water, and soon they had covered about half the distance towards the sea wall. The rain, it seemed, was falling harder than ever now, and the four found it hard to see the gun emplacement in the distance, half a mile to their right hand side. 'The good thing, Gentlemen, is that if we cannot see them, it will be even harder for them to see us,' whispered Zimmermann. Within a few more minutes, the team were hauling the craft up the slope of the sea wall, and over the top to the relative safety of the beach. They wasted no time. The groin with the 'diving board' was quickly located, just three groins further along to the west. Zimmermann and Jung focussed their attentions on finding the buried cables that they had previously pressed into the soft black tar. It was fortunate that this material had been used to fill the gaps between the concrete sections. It provided a perfect concealment for the wire, as well as keeping it perfectly dry. Neumann and Wagner busied themselves with preparing the detonators.

Shortly the cables for all six concrete traps were located, and a jointing box with a long length of cable wound tightly around a wooden reel, was securely attached to each. The cables were played out from the wooden reels as the whole team made its way eastwards. They moved slowly towards the cover of a couple of concrete traps that were to be preserved, at which point, the detonation devices were securely attached to the cable ends. The remaining, unused kit was now packed back into the boat, and the team settled down once again, to await their signal to detonate.

The group was seated in two halves, facing each other, with their backs firmly planted against the concrete walls of two traps. They were, according to Zimmermann, now situated at a 'safe distance', from the explosion zone. They had utilised the waterproof sheets again, as the rain was probably now, at its heaviest for the whole night. 'There will not be any problems with radio equipment getting wet, I hope?' questioned Zimmermann of Jung.

'Everything should work alright, Gruppenfuhrer. I have the radio well wrapped up,' replied Jung, 'although I may have to continue to operate it under cover. If anything gets wet, it can generally be dried out again. The only real problem would be if anything short circuits. This should not happen, unless the set ends up under water.'
'In that case, we shall make sure to keep our little boat afloat for the next few excursions that we need to make,' responded Zimmermann.

Their leader looked across to the pair sitting opposite, and asked Wagner whether he felt nervous. Wagner had, like Jung, been drafted in for his skills, and not primarily his soldiering abilities. However, he had conducted himself very well in the field so far, and had not demonstrated any fear, or revulsion, at whatever task had been thrown at the team.

'I do not feel nervous, but I am very excited at the prospect of completing our mission, Gruppenfuhrer,' he replied honestly. 'I suppose, in some respects, action in battle could be compared to tackling an unknown and dangerous mountain. You must have respect for the foe, but at the same time, you know that you have the skills and determination to successfully tackle the challenge. This, coupled with a team of comrades, who you know will not let you down, is what makes you come out on top.'

Zimmermann looked philosophical, as he contemplated his response. 'That is a very interesting analogy, comparing the field of battle to the climbing of a mountain. When you think about it further, there will be times when you need to progress very slowly, perhaps an inch at a time, in either scenario. Each situation could result in instant death, should you put a hand or a foot wrong. There will perhaps also be times when you think that you will shit your pants. Yet when you succeed, and complete your objective, it is the most wonderful feeling in the world. We will, as a team, very soon enjoy that feeling. First though, Gentlemen, we have a couple more tasks to complete.'

'And how are you feeling, Neumann? Are you excited and ready for the next part of our mission?'
'Yes Gruppenfuhrer. But I hope that I will be able to put my sniping skills to good use once we arrive at the escarpment.'
The leader once again considered his response. 'I asked you to stay with our small team, because you may be required to take out any hostile elements, as we approach Toot Rock. There is no guaranteed easy ride, so although we would hope that all resistance is neutralised by the time we arrive, we are still vulnerable until we have beached, and spread out on dry land. As we come into firing range, you will be required to cover the landing point, and take out any resistance, if it happens.'

'Once we are safely ashore, your skills will really come into play. By then, the remaining living British troops will be tucked away in the gun emplacements, and underground, as well as up in the pill box. We will utilise the larger team to attack with grenades at close quarters, and then we will watch the bastards run like rabbits from a burrow. You will be able to pick them off from a safe distance. We cannot chance that any of them should be able to go to ground whilst still armed. We need to keep every one of our team alive, so your role will be absolutely vital. Does this make you feel better?'

'Thank you, Gruppenfuhrer, yes. I will not let you or our team down.'
'I already know this, Neumann. You are a good soldier.'

'And, finally my technical man, Jung,' said the Gruppenfuhrer, as he turned towards the young soldier, sitting alongside him. Zimmermann was well aware that out of the whole team, Jung was perhaps the most inexperienced in the field of battle. He had though, been very impressed with the way Jung had handled himself, particularly on the exercise in Bavaria. He was a sensitive man, and had been upset by some events. However, when he had to use his skills, he always remained calm, and seemingly completely focussed. Whatever was happening around him, he appeared to be able to blank it out, and get on with the task in hand.

'Yes, thank you Gruppenfuhrer. I have to admit to being scared most of the time, but when I was on guard duty a couple of nights ago, a strange feeling of calm enveloped me. I looked down at the whole of our small team, including you, and you all slept like babies. I felt completely safe though, knowing that if anything happened, I probably would not have needed to wake anybody, you would have just all been there straight away. The most vicious and noisy dog fights went on for a long time, sometimes directly overhead of our position, but nobody stirred. I knew though, that if a small twig had been broken on the ground, anywhere near our camp, you would have all been wide awake. I think that what I am trying to say, sir, is that I would have been completely out of my depth in the situations we have been in, except for the team around me. I trust all of you implicitly, and I also give you my word that I too, will not let you down.'

'Very interesting,' smiled the Gruppenfuhrer. 'Do you know that I was genuinely, not aware of any aircraft activity. I very much doubt whether the rest of the team were either. Your theory is probably quite correct, in as much as we can subliminally blank out sounds that present us with no immediate danger. I would like to do a study of this phenomenon after the war. What if you could program tired men to actually not need guards at all? Thank you for bringing this to my attention, it provides an interesting discussion, don't you think?'

The team of four continued to quietly discuss all aspects of soldiering, and also to reflect upon the path that their mission had taken, so far. The time passed quickly and the Gruppenfuhrer regularly checked his watch. The talks kept the team relaxed, which was what Zimmermann had hoped to achieve, just prior to the major operation they were about to embark upon. The attack on Toot Rock was scheduled to begin at 0.300 hours, and as that time approached, the team became more keyed up again.

Jung asked the Gruppenfuhrer, whether he had ever experienced fear during a conflict situation. 'I don't mean to be insolent Sir, but we are all

human beings and we all have feelings, so I wondered whether you personally have ever felt very afraid in the course of a battle.'
'You know what, Jung? We were, crawling along the ground once, And we were pulling ourselves along, just by using our forearms. We were crawling through thick brambles. We had chosen this route because the enemy would think that the terrain would have been impassable. Suddenly, I have to tell you, I am nearly wetting my pants. My expensive watch has gone from my wrist. I tell you it took an eternity to find it, hanging from a bramble, with the fine leather strap broken.' The Gruppenfuhrer had been watching the expectant faces of the three men as he told his tale. He suddenly smiled broadly, and his features looked quite human in the very poor light conditions that they had become used to. He finished, 'I am always now very careful to make sure that my watch stays securely with me'.

At this point, the Gruppenfuhrer checked his watch again, and almost as if on cue, gunfire and loud explosions broke out from the direction of Toot Rock. The rain had eased slightly and it was possible to see flashes from gun muzzles and grenades, in the distance. 'It's time to make our own bang, now,' exclaimed Zimmermann. The four huddled down behind the cover of their concrete traps, and they were ready. Almost as a treat, he invited the two least experienced soldiers, Jung and Wagner to detonate the explosive charges. Each of them was handed three detonators and the Gruppenfuhrer counted backwards from three. At the count of zero, the two men simultaneously hit the plungers and they all instantly felt a wall of wind hit them.

The sound of the explosions happened a split second later, and as they lay low, they felt a shower of stones and sand, engulf them. A couple of larger sections of rock and concrete landed close to their position and one heavy piece hit the front of the trap that Neumann and Wagner were sheltering behind, with terrific force. Suddenly all was silent, apart from the ringing in their ears.
'You know, Gentlemen, I had forgotten to warn you about the blast wall of pressure. It is very impressive, yes?' It had felt as though a strange force had gone by them, and this feeling was new, to all except the Gruppenfuhrer.

'I don't think I will ever hear properly again,' said Wagner. 'My ears are hurting with the noise.'
'Don't worry,' replied Zimmermann, 'The feeling will settle after about half an hour. Meanwhile Gentlemen, look at what we have achieved.'

The whole team had been so shocked at the violence of the close explosion, that not one of them had looked across, to see the damage. The four of them were amazed at the craters that had appeared, where the six concrete traps had been. There was now a gap some thirty feet wide between the remaining undamaged traps, and as a bonus, a section of the sea wall had been blown away at the top. 'Excellent work, Gentlemen, now we can execute the next part of our mission.'

They quickly slid the inflatable boat back down the sea wall and pushed it into the water. Very soon, they were paddling out towards the middle of the lake, before bearing left in the direction of Toot Rock's 'blind side'. Zimmermann whispered to Jung, 'As soon as we have landed at Toot Rock, and we have established that we are secure, I will ask you to radio to German High Command that the first boatload ashore will have to level out the crater that we have made in the beach. We don't want our own actions to hinder the advance of our trucks and tanks.'

'Yes, Gruppenfuhrer, and now the messaging will be much quicker, because the enemy are aware that we are here anyway, so not so much need to scramble ordinary communications,' replied Jung.
'Good point, but we must not become complacent,' was the response. 'We must always consider the impact of information flowing freely backwards and forwards, and whether the enemy may be able to benefit from it, militarily. Please always discuss with me first, the way that we handle any communications. We will need to grade each topic, before we allow it to be transmitted.'

After ten more minutes, Neumann was lying down at the front of the boat, with his rifle resting across the rubber bow, and pointing towards the landing area. His eyes scoured the bushes growing out of the water's edge, where they were hoping to land. The rain was still falling, but not quite so heavily. It was more of a light drizzle, but it still affected his vision, to some extent. His senses were keyed up, his finger rested lightly on the trigger of his Mauser K98 rifle, the stock of which was pulled tightly into his shoulder. The team had been aware for some time that the sound of gunfire had ceased, soon after they had re-entered the water. They had been preoccupied with their own mission, so had not registered that the battle had stopped quite suddenly. A deathly hush filled the air.

'It sounds as if our boys have taken full control,' whispered Zimmermann. He started another sentence but the sudden 'Shhhhhh,' from Neumann, pulled him up short. The three behind him were huddled as low as possible in the cramped area, but still able to see almost as much as Neumann, who by now, was pointing his rifle slightly to the right. They were all aware of a slow moving shape, first pushing through the bushes, and then moving into the water, towards them. The shape was that of a man, crouching forward, whilst at the same time attempting to keep his hands raised in the air.

Chapter 15

Major Gordon Roberts had sprung into action. The moment that 'Battle Station' had contacted him and patched him through to the Pett Crew's bunker, he knew what needed to be done.

'Put me through to the prime minister,' he barked into the telephone receiver. 'It's Major Roberts.' The poor operator at number 10, Downing Street was quite used to this type of call, but nevertheless, the correct protocol had to be observed. 'For security purposes, I will need your code name, sir,' he stated dispassionately.
'Code name, 'Wimbledon Common,' said the Major. There were a couple of clicks on the line, and quite soon, the familiar, gruff voice of Winston Churchill, came on the line.

'Gordon, what can I do for you?' asked the prime minister.
'Good evening, Mr. Churchill, Sir. I am sorry to disturb you, I will be brief. I have some very serious news, but we may be able to deal with this issue, just in time. Simultaneously, we may be able to permanently embarrass Adolf Hitler.'
'The latter seems to me, to be the more rewarding, however you had better impart the information contained in the former, in order that I may facilitate a considered assessment,' said the prime minister. With that, Major Roberts quickly and precisely recounted the events leading up to the radio call from the Pett Crew.

The prime minister coughed, and then continued, 'This corresponds with the latest intelligence, delivered to me earlier, courtesy of the RAF. I have received reports of German troops starting to board the enormous barges that have been building up on the northern coast of France for the last few weeks. We were anticipating a launch within the next few days, but now it looks as if we could be expecting guests tonight.'

'Problem is, Gordon, we don't really want them to go to the trouble of coming all that way, only to be turned away at the door. We have every airfield in the south, on red alert. We have decided that it will be better to stem the flow at its origin. We will commence flying, at a safe height, along the French coast at regular intervals. When we receive reports that the first of the barge ships is leaving harbour, we will make our move. We have predetermined all of the locations. We will then, once they are at a safe distance from the French coast, dissuade them from proceeding.'

'We are not flying across the channel in the normal, direct route. We will deliver a constant stream of bombs, from west to east. Many of these planes will be dropping incendiary devices. To the enemy, it will quite simply appear as though a never ending attack is occurring. They will experience the wrath, and the fervent heat, of Hades. There are enough planes prepared and ready armed for this, that they will have time to return to base, refuel and re-arm, and rejoin the party, for the next round.'

'We will reverse operations, and attack from east to west, just when we consider that they might have calculated our range. Even if we lose fifty percent of these aircraft, it will be a small price to pay. And if we do, the enemy will still not be aware, because the ferocity of the assault will continue to be relentless.'

The gruff tones of the prime minister continued. 'Finally, we have a further prestidigitation concealed up our British sleeve. The backroom boys have come up with a signal jamming device that will interfere with all radio messages from enemy shipping. This is already in position, overlooking the Channel, at the RAF station, on the Firehills at Fairlight. The device produces an unbearable tintinnabulation that will virtually deafen anybody monitoring, or attempting to facilitate communications. They will not be able to communicate with their command base, or even with accompanying ships, to let them know what is happening. The advantage of this is that they will just disappear beneath the waves, and the adversary will not be capable of assessing, or comprehending his losses.'

'I am impressed, Prime Minister.' Gordon interjected. 'Does this mean that it is unlikely that anything will reach our shores?'
'It is almost certain, Gordon. We also have a few local, Royal Navy craft available to mop up if necessary, should the Hun get too close for comfort. However, we do expect a few German corpses to be washed up on our beaches over the next few days. I hope that some of these will be quite well incinerated, because it will perpetuate the myth that we have the ability to ignite the Channel into a blazing inferno. We have done our best to implant seeds of doubt into the German psyche. We will of course take great pleasure, in returning any burned bodies, to their fatherland, for the *personal* attention of Herr Hitler.'

'I may be able to help with that one,' responded the Major. 'Our special ops chaps are in possession of a couple of flame throwers. They will be right on the tail of the Germans, as they approach Toot Rock, and the chaps in charge of the equipment, are more than capable, prepared and indeed willing, to light their fuses and send them directly to Hell. 'There

are other special ops teams in the area, who will be heading for Pett Level shortly, but I need some help from you to organise some further back up, once my boys have achieved the objective. I hope they won't be needed.'
'Quite so, Gordon,' replied the prime minister. 'You may leave this one to me. I have direct contact with Brigadier Anderson, who already has some three thousand troops in the Newhaven area, in anticipation of this day. They will be mobilised within the hour. Better keep your radio man a little further back from the Hun, we wouldn't want anything to go wrong now. I have had one more thought, Gordon. That is, once this threat has been dealt with, and we have given the Hun a bloody nose, we will need to facilitate a massive 'cover up' operation. The locals, indeed the rest of our nation, must never, ever, become aware of the threat that we will have repelled.'

Mr. Churchill continued, 'You know how these things can be blown out of proportion, and the recognition that German troops were actually able to land upon British soil, must never be leaked. Do whatever it takes, whatever the cost, and however elaborate the deception. I know that I can count on you. You know the area intimately, so you are best placed to action this. Give it some thought.'

'Should you encounter any opposition, or petty local bureaucracy, then General Anderson will be able to smooth the waters for you. One thing though. Your men have all signed the official secrets act. I cannot let Brigadier Anderson's men get involved in the first part of this, because his soldiers could spread the story like wildfire. They can only be situated away from the initial action, and you must facilitate a complete clean up operation, to take place as soon as it is completed. The only reason that I will order Anderson to the area, is as a final backstop, should anything go wrong. His troops will be informed that this is just another night time manoeuvre. Please make your chaps aware that the main army force is 'in the dark' on this one.'

'I appreciate the trust you have placed in me, Mr. Churchill, and I shall not let you, or this great nation of ours, down.'
'I already know that, Gordon. And that is why you are one of the key members of my 'special club'. Goodbye for now then and good luck. We will share some champagne and finest French brandy with Anderson and our wives, later this week. I will be watching your movements with avid interest.'
'Goodbye, Sir. And thank you.'

Major Gordon Roberts suddenly experienced an almost surreal sensation in his brain. He had just been speaking, almost informally with the greatest prime minister that this country had ever produced. The content of the discussion concerned the greatest threat that this country had faced in modern times. Yet it all seemed so matter of fact. He was charged with assisting with the elimination of German troops that had been somehow able to land on British soil. Many men working for him were ready to give their lives if necessary, to ensure the security of their country, and they now also would have the back up of the British army.

It was a strange feeling, but he reasoned that should an invasion force be able to get here, the task would be a hundred times more dangerous. He hoped that the prime minister's plans would work as well as he clearly expected them to. In theory, if there was an endless supply of bombs and aircraft, then ultimately the German craft would not be able to survive the incessant pummelling. It had to work.

As for the scenario at Toot Rock, he just needed to alert Lieutenant Colonel Burgess. The rest would be up to him, but he had some three hundred troops at his disposal, which would certainly be sufficient to combat the threat from the forty odd Germans that the Pett Crew had reported. One worry had however, entered his head. The worry was that there was a possibility there were more units of a similar size in the area, all waiting to converge on Pett Level. He shook himself out of this thought process and got back on the telephone. He was working from his small office in the back bedroom of his house, at Broad Oak, Brede.

'Toot Rock Command,' spoke the familiar voice of, Lieutenant Colonel, Arthur Burgess. 'Major Roberts here, Sir. I have just come off the telephone to Winston Churchill. We have an imminent problem.'
'Are you pulling my leg, old boy?' responded his fellow officer.
'I wish I was sir, this is red alert stuff. It's all about to kick off. I have it on very high authority that an invasion force is about to set sail, with Pett Level and other desolate coastal areas being the main targets. That however will not be our priority. The immediate threat is a troop of German soldiers who are heading in your direction as we speak. As far as we can tell there are about forty of the bastards. They will have to attack by boat, unless they can swim with all of their equipment. In theory, they should be sitting ducks.'

'Their mission will be to neutralise your lot and scupper the guns, so that the arriving visitors have an easy ride. Brigadier Anderson is mobilised and heading here with about three thousand men, from the Newhaven area, but I don't know how long it will take them to get here. I suggest you double the guard and get every single man to action stations. Sorry Sir, I am not trying to tell you how to defend your own fortress, but to my mind, it would be easier to kill the enemy in the water.'

'I couldn't agree more, Major. Do you have any idea how long we have got to prepare?'

'A few hours Sir, possibly four or five, but you will need to get a strategic defence plan into place immediately. We are only aware of one group of soldiers, but it is just possible that there are more. You know that I have some special troops attached to me?'

'I had an idea that you were up to something a bit hush hush', replied the base commander, 'but I hadn't got a clue what it was. Are these troops local to us right now?'

'My men are following the Germans as we speak. If they have the opportunity to deal with them before they get here, then they will. The problem is that they are woefully outnumbered, so I have asked them to hold off, until I can get some reinforcements to them. A Brigadier Anderson has some three thousand troops in the Newhaven area, in readiness for a situation such as this, so they will soon be on their way to the top end of Pett Level. Anderson has been advised of the situation, his men have not. They must not be made aware that there are already enemy soldiers on British soil. They will only need to get involved, should things go horribly wrong. Your men will have to be sworn to silence.'

'I have radio communications with my own team, but they can't do too much while they are tracking the Hun. Anyway, I must go now, I have to do some stalking of my own. I wish you luck, oh and by the way, the prime minister has asked us to provide a few burnt bodies. If some of the enemy are drowned on the way, maybe your men could retrieve some and we can doctor them up later. He wants the RAF to deliver them back to Berlin to perpetuate the story of an inflammable English Channel.'

'I'll see what we can do for him. Do you suppose there might be a medal in it for us, if we manage to oblige?'

'I couldn't say, Lieutenant Colonel. It certainly won't hinder our chances, of that I am very sure. Anyway Sir, I must go. Brigadier Anderson will also make contact, very soon. Good luck then, and give the bastards hell.'

'Thanks, I intend to. See you soon.'

As soon as Major Roberts had completed his call, he got back on to his communications centre and asked to be patched through to Brigadier Anderson.

The communication was poor, the sound of moving vehicles and engines, as well as wiper blades, swishing to and fro, echoed noisily in the background. Brigadier Anderson knew the Pett Level area quite well, so it made things easier, when discussing the best route to take, to get into position. 'We will head for the high ground, above Pett Level. We will come up the A21, from Hastings, then along the B2089 and head down to Winchelsea. We will then turn back along Wickham Rock lane and head off the road, and through the fields, to get there. Over'

'Absolutely spot on Sir, I will now give you the co-ordinates for the windmill just north of Wickham Cliff, a location that will give you, but not your men, the most commanding view. You can camp them down at the base of the mill, and surrounding farmland, and I will come back up to meet you. I can then take you to the expected conflict area to observe the proceedings. What is your approximate eta over?'
'We should be there by approx. 24.00 hours, if we are able to keep up this pace. Over.'
'All understood, Brigadier. I will make contact with you later. Meanwhile I will be monitoring the situation personally. Out.'

At this stage, Major Roberts made one more call to the operator at 'Battle Station'. He immediately ordered the release from their bunkers of the other local special ops teams. Tell them to approach Wickham Cliff from the east, as the Krauts will head to the western side, to start their little escapade'. He also told him to let 'Pett Crew' know, that they could expect some additional back up. 'Please reiterate to them, that there is no need to go it alone, they will have a few more of my men with them, long before they need to get stuck in.'
'All understood, Major. I will now instruct the other local special ops teams to leave their bunkers, and head for the eastern end of Wickham Cliff, with all speed.'

Chapter 16

Lieutenant Colonel Arthur Burgess assembled his team, on the ground floor of the officer's house. 'Men, we have as a team, the most terrible, and imminent threat to our security, and we have very little time to deal with it. These orders have come directly from the prime minister. There is a force of about 40 German soldiers, heading on foot towards us as I speak, to attempt to take out the Bofors guns, and of course, us. This is in readiness for a large invasion force, possibly already on its way across the channel. We have all signed the official secrets act, but most of the troops stationed here, have not. It is imperative that the following events remain top secret, but we have to involve our men, in order to defend ourselves. Have you any suggestions boys?'

'The best suggestion that I can come up with Sir,' spoke a young Major, 'would be to assemble all of them in the lower barrack room and basically tell them that if they ever leak a word about tonight's events, they will be shot for treason.' He considered further, and continued, 'Do you have a blank copy of the document that we have all signed, sir?'
'Indeed I do Major Jennings. However, I am not sure that we would be able to churn out three hundred copies of it, given the fact that the Hun could be crossing the water to our little island fortress, in a couple of hours or so. Also I am not sure of the legality of an enforced signing.'

Major Jennings, who had previously worked in law, came up with the following suggestion. 'If we can get a document typed up, which states that they have signed the official secrets act voluntarily, and without coercion, and dated with today's date, you will have acted within the law, and it should stand up in a military court.'
'Splendid, splendid, but we don't have the *time* to do it tonight!'

'Right, Sir. When we have dealt with the threat, we must get them to sign in retrospect. Meanwhile, we must tell them, that anybody who is *not* prepared to sign tomorrow, will leave this emplacement tonight, and be taken to join another unit. The statement, made by you, as camp commander, must be recorded in writing, and I will be happy to oblige. Anybody remaining at Toot Rock, will by his own actions, have agreed to these terms. I personally believe that not one man will refuse to sign, and that every man will want to stay with his unit. Quite honestly, Sir, we will be totally buggered if they want out anyway.' All of the remaining officers agreed that this would be the correct course of action, and

151

then another major spoke out. 'Sir, may we discuss how we are going to repel the threat?'

'Certainly we can Major Barlow. My initial thought was that we should destroy them in the water, which on a clear night would be very straightforward. The problem that we have is that visibility is piss poor tonight, with the heavy rain forecast to continue well into the early hours. When we finally do see them, they may have a small chance of returning fire successfully, and gaining a foothold onto the Rock. Also chaps, we will not know whether we have been able to see all of them or not, so some could escape and regroup. The reason I mention this is that we are only aware of around 40 soldiers, but it could *just* be possible that there are more teams of a similar size in the area.'

'Gentlemen, I believe that the best form of defence would be to allow them *all* to land, which will make them feel as if they have got away with it. Then we go for the kill. We can prepare several ambushes for them, at the most vulnerable points. Chaps, if you were the enemy, which direction would *you* choose to attack from?

The question was answered simultaneously by several of the assembled group. The overwhelming response was, 'from the bottom of the lane.' It was agreed that this would be the most difficult area to monitor, because of the thick bushes growing around the water line. There were also some small trees, growing out of the water, again obstructing visibility. On this night, it would be very difficult to spot a small boat, or even several, until they were virtually ashore. It was also known that there were few fortified buildings at this end of the emplacement, other than the lower pill box, and the officer's bunker, so a surprise attack would be likely to meet with less resistance.

The assembled officers quickly agreed their defence plan. Among the troops stationed here were some 120 Canadian soldiers, seconded to the British Army. Lieutenant Colonel Burgess was in overall command of the emplacement, and a Canadian officer, Captain Johnson, was in command of this section of men. 'I would like to volunteer my men to defend the bottom end of the little street,' he said. I believe that the guys in the pill box should leave it, because they would be a sitting target. It would not take much to rig up booby traps in there. The Krauts will have to enter them to neutralise the threat from our boys, and once they have set off the fireworks, we will know they are coming.'

The group of officers listened intently to Captain Johnson. There had always been friendly rivalry between the 'Brits' and the Canadians, but it was warm hearted, and nobody had ever come to blows. They were after all, working for a common cause. The British officers had great respect for this man. He was not boastful, just completely practical in his assessment of the situation. 'Nobody should remain in the civilian houses. Let the enemy waste their ammo and grenades attacking empty properties, including this one. It can be patched up again later. I suggest that my men line the grass banks to the northern side of the street, heavily camouflaged in the long grass down there. The Krauts, especially when they realise that the houses are all empty, will be expecting us to be holed up in the fortified buildings up top. When they reach about half way up, the ground drops away more steeply towards the water, and this will provide an ideal defence bank for my guys to lay up behind.'

'What sort of spread will you give them?' questioned Burgess.
'I guess that around 50 yards either side of cottage number nine, should be enough to wipe out a body of forty men. We should leave the lights on, both up and downstairs in that one house, which will affect the enemy's vision, once they get close to it. If they should even think to look in our direction, it will appear blacker still. While they are focussed on the first 'live' house, we will attack them with grenades, and then immediately open fire. Every other man will be ready with the pin pulled on a 'pineapple', slightly further down the bank, so they can stand up to throw. The rest will be lying down behind the top of the bank with assault rifles cocked at the ready. As soon as the grenades are thrown, the back line will shoulder their rifles, and join in the turkey shoot.'

'The plan is excellent, Captain. There is however, one floor in your assessment, and that is that some of them may choose to go behind the cottages and across the back gardens. We could lessen this threat by piling coils of barbed wire high and wide, from behind the lower bunker, to this, the Officer's House. Once they have set the alarm off they will not want to hang around, cutting through a ton of barbed wire that could possibly be booby trapped. They will take the fastest route, and that will be straight up the lane. I do believe however, that we should also provide a small diversion, to direct their attention away from the sides of the lane. Maybe, all it would take would be a sergeant barking loud orders from the area of the first gun, to give the impression that we are preparing to defend that higher ground. I don't believe we should fire down at them from that point, because that may scatter them into the very area that your chaps are hiding in.'

'Gotcha, Lieutenant Colonel. That Sergeant Campbell has got the loudest drill routine that I have ever heard. If he barks the order to 'hold your fire' just after twenty or so men have loudly cocked their rifles, it should set the scene a treat. Either way, if we are not able to take the whole troop out, the guys up top will be ready for the second front.'

'Are we all agreed on that one then Gentlemen?' asked Burgess urgently. The assembled team all nodded their approval. 'Now we need to plan the escarpment face protection, just in case the Krauts decide that it would be better to try a little climb before we give them a hiding. I honestly believe this route would be much less likely, but we have to defend all sides. May I suggest that you, Major Barlow, take 50 men armed with grenades, and pistols, and stretch out along the top edge of our little cliff. Inside the observation post we will post a further six men armed with Bren guns. No bastard will be able to get past that lot. While I am addressing the men, each group commander will go to the armoury and with the help of a fellow officer, grab the necessary munitions, as required, for each area of defence, and barrow them to their appointed zones. Those officers remaining will get ready to temporarily take over watch duties.'

'Finally chaps, we have the northern slopes, which should in theory be the easiest to defend. We will withdraw the sentries patrolling the waters edge, and have 80 troops watching and waiting to fire down from the top. It is a wide expanse of land, and the only real problem is likely to be visibility. Major Wicks, I would like you to take command of this section. I suggest you set up a couple of machine guns, within sandbags, that will be able to strafe the whole area. The rest of your men should be armed with Bren guns. Let them take a sandbag each, to shield them. There will not be much chance of the enemy getting very far up the northern slope. 'Very happy to, Sir,' was the smooth response of this well spoken officer.

'Finally. Major Pettitt, and Major Martin. You are charged with the protection of the two Bofors guns at all costs. You will take the Canadian side, Major Pettitt. The Brit gun will be your responsibility, Major Martin. I don't need to impress upon you both the importance of keeping these guns in action. However, if it comes to the point where you have to defend them, then I am afraid the rest of us will already be history. You may both use whatever methods and weaponry you like, to operate what would effectively be the last ditch defence, but I would suggest that you give some thought to using the remaining men on the rock, to hide in the shell storage facility behind each gun. Once the enemy is focussed on debilitating our weapons, your men can attack from either side. It is a risky strategy, because if they are doing their job properly, they should have already checked out the passageways. Let's hope for all of us, that it doesn't come to that.' Both men nodded.

'Right then, chaps. Get every man to come to the lower barrack room, including the sentries, once they have done a final scan. Those of you who are not directly commanding a unit will take over their posts for the next ten minutes, while I present this 'secrets act thing' to them. With nearly three hundred men, I will have to do this in three shifts. I will start with your men, Captain Johnson. Fuck knows what we will do if anybody does want out, but like you, Major Jennings, I don't believe anybody will. Once the men return to their areas of duty, it is up to you to take your own troops to your designated defence zones, and brief them. Major Jennings. Let's go into my office and quickly concoct something that will suffice for tonight, then we will join the men in the barrack room.' With that the remaining group of officers swiftly left the house and sprinted up the small lane to go about their allotted tasks.

Ten minutes later, Lieutenant Colonel Burgess and Major Jennings entered the large barrack room that was now heaving with bodies. A larger crowd of men were gathered outside, on the grass, and even on the thick concrete roof of the barrack room itself. The rain was pouring down, and most of the troops were soaked through. 'I will be very brief, men. The Major handed the recently typed document to his commanding officer, who read from it as follows:

'This is an emergency and I am asking all of you to respond to it. Simply put, you will be asked to witness tonight, something that must remain top secret, forever. I and my fellow officers, have already signed 'The Official Secrets Act,' therefore we are already committed.'

'What I need, is your personal agreement that you will sign an official document tomorrow, individually swearing your lifetime silence regarding any events that you may witness here over the next few hours.'

'It is the duty of the British Army to inform you, that any breach of this agreement, could result in you being tried for treason, and ultimately shot as a traitor. As a result of the severe penalties that could be imposed, I am prepared, as your commanding officer, to allow any one of you, who may be unhappy about this agreement, to leave Toot Rock immediately. Should you take the decision to leave, I must ask that you move outside now, and wait under the radio mast. You will then immediately be permanently transferred, and transported to another unit.
If you decide to stay, it will be taken as a sign that you are prepared to make a legally binding agreement with the British Army, King and Government. The agreement will be deemed to have been signed

voluntarily and without coercion. The correct documentation will be administered tomorrow.

This document has been read out by me, Lieutenant Colonel Arthur William Burgess, overall commander of the Toot Rock Battery, and witnessed by Major David Frederick Jennings, on the 15th day of September, in the year of our Lord, 1940.

The officer finished reading the document and not a man had spoken. He addressed the assembled group of about 100 men clearly, and his voice echoed around the thick concrete walls of the barrack room. 'Well men, does anyone want to leave? Do you have any questions?'

One soldier at the front, requested, 'Permission to speak, Sir?'
'Granted,' replied the officer.
'This is an extremely irregular request to make, to a group of ordinary soldiers, isn't it, Sir? Most of us in this room are Canadian, and I am not sure quite how far we come under the rule of English law.
'I agree with you entirely, Private. However these are very irregular times, and sometimes in war, we have to make the rules up as we go along. All I can say is that if you do decide to stay, you will then *fully* understand why this has to be done. Does this answer your question, or help with your decision, Private?'
'Not entirely, Sir. But I am a soldier. Canadian or otherwise, I am here with the men that I trust the most in my life, and I don't actually want to be anywhere else. On this basis, I am happy to stay, and sign your document tomorrow. I can keep my mouth shut, if it is for the good of us all, and for the safety of my fellow countrymen.'

An exclamation of muttered, 'Here, here's,' went around the room, and then the entire assembled mass called out, indicating that they were staying too. 'Thank you men, I appreciate your understanding.' Burgess was relieved that the Canadians were in, because he felt the British guys would be even more committed. 'Please vacate the ops room as swiftly as possible and allow the next lot to come in. We don't have a lot of time.'

The mass exodus, followed by the refilling of the room took only a few minutes, and the process was repeated. At the end of the reading there was pretty much the same response from the second group, and again for the third. Not one man wanted to go. Burgess knew in his heart that it was more a matter of his men not wanting to leave their units, rather than wanting to agree to keep tight lipped for ever, that had motivated them to agree. Also there was an element of the 'power of the masses' that had come into play. He as an officer had witnessed this phenomenon many times. Nobody wanted to be the odd one out, so they stuck together.

As soon as the first group had left the ops room, Captain Johnson was onto them and quickly giving a brief explanation of what needed to be done. 'Now you know why this has to be kept secret,' he told his team. His men were very fired up at the prospect of doing battle with German troops. He had to remind them that the ideal scenario would be 'the quick knock out', and nothing too prolonged. 'I need every one of you to survive this skirmish. We don't know what further threats we will have to deal with in the near future.'

The next hour was spent checking and setting up equipment, booby trapping the lower pill box and bunker, and agreeing the ideal point of ambush. This happened to be about half way up the row of coastguard cottages, where the ground in front of them dropped away quite steeply across the lane.

Chapter 17

'Fucking Hell,' whispered Neumann. 'It's Klein, and he looks badly hurt.' As the injured man waded deeper into the water, it became obvious that he had been wounded in the throat. Zimmermann's heart sank. 'What the hell does this mean?' he questioned. The other two quickly paddled across to Klein, who collapsed over the side of the small craft, and fell into the rear floor space among the explosives and other equipment. The Gruppenfuhrer ordered them to pull back to a safe distance and immediately started to check the severity of the injuries to his trusted man. 'What happened,' he asked quietly. Klein's eyes said it all. He tried to speak, but it was almost intelligible. It seemed he had been hit in the throat by shrapnel. There was a gaping, bloody hole in his larynx area.

The Gruppenfuhrer put his ear down to Klein's mouth, and he could then make out the strained whispers that were coming from him. 'Fuchs went first into the pillbox, and I was right behind him. The guards were not there, but before we could back out, there was an explosion. Fuchs took the full blast, he was killed instantly. I took this one to my throat, and I have lost some blood, but I am alright. I lay down in the bushes outside the pillbox. The rest of them had already started up the path. It was simply a massacre. As they reached the first lighted house, they were attacked from all angles, first, many hand grenades, instantly followed by rapid gunfire. There may have been as many as a hundred guns, as well as more grenades landing among them. I don't think that any one of them had the chance to return fire. They went down very fast.'

Klein stopped to gather his thoughts, and breathed deeply. Zimmermann held his water canteen to Klein's lips, and gently told him to take his time. Klein started again, 'I do not believe that any of our boys survived, they were completely surprised. As I crawled deeper into the bushes, I could see the Brits checking all of the bodies, and putting an extra bullet through each of their brains. They were ready, and very well armed, we must have totally underestimated their power, and ruthlessness.'

'And what about Schultz and the rest of the men?' asked the Gruppenfuhrer kindly. 'All dead, killed elsewhere and then their bodies dumped with the main crew's corpses,' whispered Klein.

'They must have been warned, but how the hell can this be?' asked the Gruppenfuhrer. 'Right now, though, we must think of us. There is not any point in us attempting to even get near to the guns. The enemy are obviously on high alert, and we are now just four able men. We must regroup and work out our next move. Klein gurgled that he would still be able to help. He was feeling better now he was back in the company of his fellow soldiers. 'That is very admirable, Klein, but for now, we will head back to the cover of the rear cliff line and clean up your wound. Then we will work on a new strategy.' The Gruppenfuhrer was trying to put a brave face on things, but knew in his heart that things had now changed dramatically.

He ordered, Wagner and Jung to paddle back towards the area that they had left, earlier on that night. He thought about the invasion force which would by now be less than an hour and a half away. 'As soon as we land, we must get a message to German High Command, to warn them that the Bofors guns are still active. They will have to attack Toot Rock from the air, to protect our boys coming in. At least we have achieved the gateway for them to enter, so come what may, our men will be landing and coming ashore, very soon. We have to work out how best to support their actions.' The five were now less than five or six minutes from the rear cliff line, and once again, Neumann took up his position, as a precautionary measure, to ensure a safe landing and concealment.

Zimmermann's brain was buzzing. He could only think that from the moment they had killed the soldier at Toot Rock, the Brits had gone on to high alert status. The problem with this theory was that they had been able, to travel unchallenged back and forth, from their hide, to Pett Level. They had crossed lanes, streams, woodlands, fields, fences, main roads, side roads, a railway line, a river, and farmyards, to the point where they knew the route blindfold. The only military activity of any kind that they had witnessed was tonight, when the train of army trucks had rumbled along the road, near Udimore. They were heading away from the area. That would have been at around 23.00 hours, so even if they had turned back, they would have been able to attack his men before they left.

If the Brits knew they were here, every road would have been blocked and the countryside would have been awash with troops, night and day. There was no chance that the British would have taken the risk of waiting, when they didn't know where or when his team would strike. Also if a large force was there tonight, they would have taken them out in the water, as they paddled off. They were at their most vulnerable then. 'Do you think they could have deciphered our radio communications?' he asked Jung. 'It is possible, Gruppenfuhrer,' the young radio operator replied, 'but it is more likely that they have triangulated the area of the coded signals, and put two and two together.'

'I believe you are correct,' replied Zimmermann.
'This would make much more sense. But for now, we must again be silent. We are very close to land again.' The five readied themselves for beaching and deflating the boat. They could then safely go to ground and plan their next move.

Klein pushed himself up slightly at the back of the inflatable boat, and made himself more comfortable on the relatively soft rubber stern. The others meanwhile, sat bolt upright, surveying the approaching shoreline intently. He felt better now that he was back with the remainder of his old team. He could hardly believe that his best friend Fuchs was dead. Schultz too was gone, along with all the others. 'How could this have happened? Surely, if Zimmermann had been with them, this could not have been possible.' Suddenly he realised, that although he had only been under the Gruppenfuhrer's command for a few days, this unconventional officer had inspired total confidence in the whole team, including him. Klein then made the decision that he would stay with his commanding officer, come what may, from now on.

He started to drift off, as his subconscious brain imagined that the Gruppenfuhrer could *think* his way around any problem. Klein realised that his own personal actions had only ever been based on an immediate physical response to whatever situation arose. He also knew that this was not always the correct path, but no other solution had ever been shown to him. When Zimmermann joined them, he had started to think differently. Yes, this senior officer could be as violent and ruthless as the rest of them, but not without considering the options as well as the consequences. He made up his mind that he would follow this man, protect him, and make sure that no harm befell him, or the remaining members of the team.

His body jerked awake at the subconscious thought of this. He wasn't going to be able to protect anybody if he was asleep. He would be the one that they could all rely on if it came to any more fighting. He stared at the backs of the three men directly in front of him, and could see the head of Neumann, at the front of the boat. He felt stronger, now. He began silently to deep breath. He would will himself back to full strength, despite the throat wound. He knew that his vocal chords were probably destroyed, judging by the hole in his throat, but he hadn't sustained any further injury other than to his eardrums, which he suffered when he followed Fuchs into the booby trapped bunker. His ears were still ringing very loudly, but he knew that this would subside after a period of time. They were now just a few metres from dry land. All appeared quiet.

Chapter 18

The rain was pouring down, as the team of thirty five German soldiers, silently paddled their small boats into the thick bushes masking the water's edge. They made little noise, as they gained a foothold onto the lower ground of the Toot Rock coastal battery. The boats as always, were deflated, and stowed beneath a very thick bush. As an additional precaution, brush and some small rocks were spread on top of them.

Schultz, Klein and Fuchs had been allocated shared command for this part of the mission. The team that had joined them consisted of privates and lance corporals. With Schultz holding the higher rank of Unterscharfuhrer, (Sergeant) he was in overall charge. In readiness for this mission, and in recognition of their hard work and commitment, Klein and Fuchs had been promoted to the rank of Rottenfuhrer, (Corporal) courtesy of their previous mission commander, Generalleutnant Peschel.

Schultz quietly ordered the men to settle down in an area of dense brush situated to the north of the pillbox that would ultimately be their first target. The waiting would not be pleasant, they could not sit down, nor could they stand. Some sat on their haunches in an attempt to keep dry, while others lay down on the waterproof sheets that they carried in their kit. It wasn't ideal, but then they were in a battlefield situation. Nobody ever told them that it was a soldier's right to be comfortable in the field.

They all observed the small line of similar looking cottages that ran up the left hand side of the lane from the larger house at the foot of the hill. They could see that half way up the lane, there were lights on in one house, and similarly, a couple of others were lit, further up. The larger house, as well as the first group of six or seven cottages, was in complete darkness. Schultz instructed the team as to how they would make the attack. 'We must not assume that the first houses are empty, simply because they are unlit. Troops could almost certainly be sleeping there and perhaps one is a hospital sick bay. If they are full of sleepers, then at least they will be soft targets. We will need to make certain that there will be no resistance from these, as we move up to our main objective. The success of our mission will depend on speed and surprise.

Both Klein and Fuchs were very impressed, and totally surprised that the normally jocular Schultz was proving to be a good leader of men. Gone was the banter that he had shared with them, while they were waiting to go, on the other side of the lake. His voice was quietly controlled.

Every one of the men listened intently as he spoke. 'Please bear in mind, that as a team, our only task will be to eliminate all opposition. Once the Gruppenfuhrer has completed the destruction of the anti tank traps, his team will join us to complete the mission. They will then be free to place the explosive charges into the three guns that we know are active here.'

'Once we have neutralised these houses, where we believe that the majority of the troops will be sleeping, we can expect much more solid resistance from the fortified area. By the time we get up there, it will be obvious to the gun crews and observation post guards that they are under attack. They are certain to have a 'lock down' procedure, which we will work out how to overcome, once we are knocking at their door. There is a very large barrack room, which is connected via underground tunnels to the rest of the fortifications. What we do know is that there are air vents coming up through the ground, which will provide us with a perfect posting box for our grenades. This should take care of another batch. Then we will have to be patient, perhaps provoking the enemy into making a mistake, whilst looking for our way in. Are there any questions, men?' Schultz enquired quietly.

A whispered response came from a private that Schultz only knew by sight. 'May I ask Sergeant, what happens if we meet a welcoming committee that we have not anticipated, once we have dealt with the main threat in these houses? I am talking about the possibility of a protection squad spread out to defend the remaining troops at the top.'
'That is a good question, private. I will be taking a team to the northern water's edge to destroy the guards there. We will set off half an hour before the main party will start. Once we have dealt with this threat, we will be able to cover the area that any such team could be operating from.

When the rest of you have dealt with the threat from the houses, you will have to spread out, so that you are not presenting a single, narrow target to the enemy. You will storm the top of the hill with a fanning action, firing ahead constantly, and curling round to regroup for the final attack on the fortified positions. You all know how to react, should you come under fire, and you *must* assume that this will be the case.'
'Thank you, Sergeant,' responded the SS private.
'Is there anything else?' asked Schultz. The rest of the team were silent.

'I would like a volunteer to go over and check the barbed wire, running up to the walls of the first house. We really need to cover the backs of these houses, in case armed men are escaping at the rear while we are attacking the fronts.'

'I would like to volunteer to do this,' responded another SS private. 'Thank you, private. Do not attempt to cut through, or disturb anything at this stage, just observe and report back, I will make the decision.' The soldier was gone for a few minutes before he returned, with his whispered report. 'The barbed wire is the thickest that I have ever seen, Sir. It is some five rolls across at the base, as well as three high and three wide, at the top. We could cut through it, but there are electric cables running through the coils at each level. My opinion is that it is alarmed, as well as electrified.'

'Thank you, private,' replied Schultz. 'I believe then that we will need to go through each house and check that no enemy troops are able to escape at the rear. In order to minimise the length of time we spend clearing the houses and moving up, we will operate in the following manner. We will cover the first eight houses with three men to each. This will get us half way up the lane. Three of you will be ready at each door, as Klein and Fuchs deal with the scenario at the pillbox. The moment that they arrive at the first house after their hopefully silent attack, this will be your signal to simultaneously enter the houses. The first man of each trio will be ready, with pistol drawn. He will either open the door, or if it is locked, he will shoot the lock to allow entry. The two behind will storm the ground floor and proceed upstairs, while the pistol man will go directly to the rear door of the house to check that nobody has escaped.'

'The team allocated to the first house, will be backed up by the remaining four 'spare' men, who will follow them in and immediately exit via the rear door, in order to cover the backs of the rest of the houses, as we move up. Frontal attack teams, please be aware, that when you are checking the rear exit for escaped soldiers, our team of four will be covering the outside. We do not want to end up shooting each other.'

'As soon as the first eight houses are cleared, we will move up again, but only six houses this time. Meanwhile the three teams closest to the first lighted house will triple up and attack this together. It is fair to assume that the enemy are awake there, and that they should be well prepared for an attack by then. It is of course possible, that the lights will be off by the agreed assault time, but we have to plan on the basis of what we see now. As Fuchs and Klein will not be directly involved in the house attacks, they will move to a position outside the front of this house. They will hide down the slope opposite, covering the doors and windows, just in case the enemy decide to counter attack.'

'Finally, you will all storm the last few houses, where we know that the enemy will be wide awake by now, lights or no lights. Are there any further questions now, men?'

'How many minutes do you anticipate it will take before we reach the top of the lane, Unterscharfuhrer?' asked a young private.

'A good question, private. It really depends on the amount of resistance that you encounter, as you enter each house. Let us assume that the first eight houses put up little resistance, you should be in and out of them within around forty seconds. By the time you have reached the top of the lane, you should have only been engaged for about two minutes or less. With a little bit of luck, we will be jointly attacking the fortified section before they have had time to react to what is going on.'

'Thank you, sir,' replied the young soldier. 'And may I ask how we are going to get past the fortifications?'

'We will be saving as many grenades as possible, for this part of the mission. I suggest that you will probably need two grenades for each house, to stun the ground floor area as we enter, then we will let loose with the machine guns. The second grenade will be used for the top floor. There are thirty five of us in total, and we are each carrying six grenades. I am no mathematician but I believe that this will leave us with over one hundred and sixty grenades for the main attack. Please all of you be aware however, that if you need to utilise more grenades during the house attacks, then do so. We do not want any of the enemy troops left with the ability to follow us up there.'

'May I ask if there are any further questions?' Another private, whispered, 'Please Sir, how will we destroy the guns?'

'This will be up to the Gruppenfuhrer's team, private. As soon as they rejoin us from their own mission, to open a tank sized hole in the anti tank traps. When they rejoin us, their plan is to stuff the gun barrels with dynamite, followed by debris, well compressed on top of the explosive. Once detonated, it is expected that the barrels will be blown to pieces. Either that, or Rye bay will be the most lethal area for shipping, in the world. I sincerely hope that the invasion force does not arrive a little too early, just in case.' The whole team quietly recognised the Sergeant's humour. 'Thank you, Sir,' replied the smiling private, 'what time are we scheduled to start?'

'Exactly 0.300hours, so we still have a little more time to kill.'

From this moment on, the team made themselves as comfortable as possible, given the saturated ground that they were forced to lie on. They relaxed in silence, each man dealing with his own thoughts, fears and doubts. After what seemed like an eternity, their popular leader quietly announced that it was 'thirty minutes to go.' From this moment, the men started to stretch their arms and legs, and silently deep breathe. The majority went to the bushes for a piss, and waterproof sheets were once again stowed in their kitbags. Weapons were quietly checked, and grenades were removed from the kitbag's side pockets, and positioned within easy reach, in buttoned military tunic pockets.

Schultz, the well known comedian of the group, especially to the smaller, 'first' team, was at this moment, very sombre. He quietly addressed the team of soldiers, who were by now, very keyed up and ready to go. 'I can only say to you now, that I expect us *all* to come through this next stage. If anybody does not, then it will not be for the lack of planning, training, commitment, and resolve. I hope to see all of you at the top of the hill.' He double checked the time against Fuch's watch. With that, he was gone, with his designated small team of four, to take out the guards at the northern water's edge.

The five of them quickly moved up the right hand side of the lane, and were quickly out of sight. Meanwhile, Fuchs and Klein counted down the minutes before they made their first move. Twenty minutes had passed, and no sound of conflict had come from the area where Schultz's small team had headed, so the assumption was that they had successfully dealt with the guards, in the silent manner that was anticipated. The rain had now become heavier again, but this could only play to the team's advantage.

Klein and Fuchs had prepared their favourite 'close up' weapons, in the form of knives, coshes, cheesewires and of course, their Mauser K98k's. To the rest of the team, it seemed that the pair had taken on a strange air. They appeared to be behaving almost like excited schoolboys. At the stroke of 0.300 hours, Fuchs said, 'We are now just going to kill the first of the Tommy Bastards,' then we will meet you again at the start of the run of houses. Please give us a few moments, to slice up the meat, boys.'

With that, the men charged with the clearance of the houses, moved silently into position at each of the first eight doors. They would wait, just until Klein and Fuchs re-appeared, and the simultaneous attacks would commence.

Fuchs could feel Klein's warm breath on the back of his neck. They had accomplished similar manoeuvres, many times before, and they felt very comfortable, almost moving and thinking as one man. They approached the darkened pill box from the blind side, and stopped to listen intently at the door. It was not unusual, to hear the sound of snoring coming from within. If this happened, they would never assume that there were no guards on duty, just that there was at least one of them sleeping. They continued to listen intently, but no sounds came from within. They knew that there must be guards, so they had to think that they were either, very awake and focussed on their field of vision, therefore not talking to each other, or else they were sleeping very silently. It was not important, they were soon about to be very unpleasantly surprised.

The two men did not need to communicate with each other at any level. They both instinctively knew what their next move would be. They slowly and silently entered the dark concrete doorway to the inner sanctum of the pillbox. Both held a double edged dagger in their right hand, and a short wooden cosh in the left. They stood now in the darkness of the cold concrete enclosure, with their backs against the rear wall. They could now see the observation slits, showing just slightly lighter than the inside of the box. Rain water was dripping from the front of them, but there was no sign of the backs, or heads of any guards. They waited, as their eyes acclimatised to the pitch black of the building. It was just possible that a couple of guards could be sleeping on the floor in front of them.

Two minutes on, and the pair were certain that they were the only people currently inhabiting the concrete box. Fuchs tentatively moved towards the front wall of the structure. He wanted to look out across the murky vista to see if there was any sign of life outside. It just might be possible that the two guards had gone for a piss together, just before they had arrived at the door. If they had, then it would make the job easier, because they would be re-entering from the relative light, into total darkness.

Klein watched the dark shape of his partner, as it was suddenly silhouetted with a brilliant orange light. The noise was completely deafening, as he watched Fuch's head burst apart in front of him. He was aware of a searing pain directly in his throat. He was aware of falling to the ground, half conscious. He was aware of not being able to see or hear anything. Just an excruciatingly painful loud ringing in his head, that was so overpowering, it even drowned out any thoughts of self preservation.

'Fuchs, are you okay?' he finally managed to whisper. His voice came out somewhere a long way in front of him, and he couldn't seem to make any normal vocal noises. He lay gasping on the cold dank floor for another ten, or twenty seconds, before he was able to move at all. First he managed to get up on to his knees, then he stumbled forward, sticking his left hand into the sharp, wet fragments of Fuch's skull, soaked in blood and oozing a slimy discharge. He knew already that his mate must be dead. He had seen his head explode in front of him. He had taken the full blast of the explosion. His brain was now struggling to come to terms with what had happened. Somewhere in the back of his head he was aware of the sound of explosions, and gunfire. He knew that he must get out, and warn the rest of them that the pillbox had been booby trapped.

He managed to lean up against the cold wall, and eventually he was on his feet, and staggering towards the entrance. He stopped to support himself at the doorway, and then the stark reality of the situation hit him. The team would have heard the sound of the explosion, perhaps at first thinking that he or Fuchs had set it off. When they did not re-appear, they would have known that the pair had walked into a booby trap. They were continuing with the attack anyway, and they now knew that the Brits were expecting them.

Klein knew that the only thing he could do, would be to get across to where the boats were stacked, and wait until it was all over. It was still raining quite heavily, his throat hurt like hell, and was still bleeding. The noise inside his head was almost unbearable and he wondered whether it would ever go away. He would get under his waterproof sheet and unfold a boat to lie on. He staggered across the lane to their earlier waiting area, and was again aware of gunfire. He squinted in the direction of the cottages, and saw some of the men running out of the lower cottages and moving away, up the slope. The sound of grenades exploding in the upper floors, and window glass shattering out onto the road, was followed by more men appearing from the further cottages.

He watched, transfixed, as the body of men assembled outside the house with its lights still on. He now realised that this had to be a trap, and he called out to them to back off down the hill. Sadly, no sound came out of his mouth. At this moment, he also realised that he had committed the ultimate sin. He had lost all of his weapons in the blast, they were all still back in the pillbox. If he could reach his gun, he may still be able to warn them. He turned to head back, but stumbled and fell. He was lying flat on his stomach, facing up the hill to where his mates were gathered. The area by the front wall of the house lit up, as a huge volley of grenades landed amongst his comrades. Every one just dropped to the ground helplessly. The explosions had not died down when the rapid sound of gunfire took over, and the now still bodies of his comrades, were forced into a kind of weird death dance, of flailing limbs, and jumping torsos. Heads shook violently, arms shot into the air. Legs kicked disjointedly, and then all was still, once more.

Klein now felt very alone. He had never really felt fear before, but he was now resigned to the fact that he was soon going to die.
He still couldn't move very well, in fact he was almost transfixed, as he kept looking up the little lane. Surely his mates would get up and fight back in a moment. A dark mass of movement arose from the sloping ground to the right hand side of the lane, and quickly Klein realised what was about to happen. All professional soldiers would do this. They could not take the risk that one or two, of the enemy soldiers could be playing dead. The mass of men walked through the fallen troops, and swiftly and clinically put a bullet into the brain of each one as they lay there.

'What the fuck can I do now?' thought Klein. It first occurred to him that he could retrieve his Mauser, and with the benefit of surprise, he could take out a good number of the ambush team up the hill. He managed to crawl to the side of the lane, and was soon out of the direct line of vision. He managed to stand and he was a little stronger now. He drew a deep breath and walked unsteadily back towards the pill box. He was very aware that there may have been more than one booby trapped device, so decided to just find his machine gun and knife. He now remembered that the shoulder strap of the firearm had slipped off behind him, as he was knocked back by the blast. He felt sure that this area would be safe, because he had staggered around it when he first managed to stand.

He entered the dark foreboding structure and kept his body tight to the back wall. He got down onto his knees when he reached the centre of the wall and started to gently feel around on the smelly damp floor. As his eyes re-acclimatised to the light conditions, he could just make out the fallen shape of Fuchs. He moved slowly towards the far wall and suddenly his left knee came down on something hard. It was a machine gun, he couldn't tell whether it was his or Fuch's but it didn't matter. He could not feel either of their knives on the floor, and decided it would be better to get out before anything else happened. The thought occurred to him that he should say goodbye to his best mate. This would be the last time he would see him.

He knew that Fuch's head had been blown apart, but he still felt it appropriate to speak to him. His husky, whispered voice came out in front of him. 'Goodbye, my old friend. You took the blast for me, and I would have done the same for you. Thank you for your friendship.' The noise of the expulsion of a long, low fart came from the corpse of his dead friend, tailing off finally, and leaving the most awful stench in the cold air of the pillbox. 'Bastard,' croaked Klein. 'I was trying to be serious for a minute.' With that, Klein was back outside, and regrouping his thoughts. He had planned to get back up the slope and attack the men who had killed all of his comrades. He knew that he would die in the onslaught, but his best mate was now gone and there was little hope of him getting off this island alive.

He then had a moment of clarity, suddenly remembering that the Gruppenfuhrer's team would be making their way across the lake, and would have to be warned. Also he considered the four men who had gone to the rear of the row of cottages. They must still be alive. Also there was Schultz and his four man team. He had heard nothing from their direction, so perhaps they had managed to kill the guards silently, and were preparing to attack the fortified area of the battery alone. Maybe however, they were waiting for the Gruppenfuhrer to arrive, to fortify the team, before continuing with the assault. These thoughts all flashed through Klein's brain. He took the decision to lay low, back in the bushes and wait for the explosives team to arrive.

Klein had finally managed to get settled. He had found the strength to partially inflate one of the rubber boats, which he was now using as a bed. He had pulled the waterproof sheet out yet again, and laid it over the top of himself. He was wet, he was in a great deal of pain, both from his throat and his ears, but he had made himself as comfortable as he could, under the circumstances. His head poked out from beneath the blanket, and his eyes were scanning the vast expanse of water to the side of him. He had not been aware of any explosions coming from the sea wall area, but then he was still profoundly deaf at the moment. Even the grenade attacks followed by the vicious bursts of gunfire, had seemed very distant to him.

He could turn his head carefully and still found that he had a reasonable view, through the thick brush. He could still see a fair number of enemy soldiers, standing guard over the bodies of his fallen comrades. In the distance, in the direction of the fortifications, came the sound of more gunfire. It appeared that there was a return of fire with what sounded like fixed machine guns. The sound rattled on for several minutes before total silence, apart from the terrible ringing in his ears. It took over his brain and dominated his thinking once again. Before he could consider what may have been the outcome of this exchange, more local explosions happened, this time from behind the lighted house.

He knew that this probably heralded the end of the road for the rest of his comrades, and as if to provide confirmation, the front door opened, throwing a shaft of light across the lane. Men carrying bulky loads slung over their shoulders, came through, one at a time, and out into the middle of the massacre scene. They released their loads into the pile of bodies, and at this point, Klein realised they were simply dropping more corpses into the pile. Four bodies were dumped unceremoniously on top of the existing pile, and once again the enemy took the precaution of putting a gun to each of the four 'new' heads.

'If Schultz's team have survived, then there are now only ten of us left alive,' thought Klein. 'Maybe the Gruppenfuhrer will have a solution to the problem when he gets here, but I think it will be now very hard for ten men to take on three hundred.' He also considered the fact that this was not a soft enemy that they were facing here. These were ruthless bastards who were quite prepared to carry out soldiering in the same way that he had always been taught. 'We don't take prisoners,' he thought, 'and neither do they.'

It was not long before another scene unfolded before his eyes. The rain had slowed considerably now, and he was able to make out more detail from the happenings at the lighted house. A trolley, probably one used for ammunition, was being trundled down the lane from the top end. It was not difficult to see, as it got nearer to the lighted area, men's arms and legs, swinging out over the sides of it. It was being pushed by four men, one on each corner. As they reached the pile of bodies, a similar scene unfolded. One by one, five bodies were pulled from the trolley, and dropped into the middle of the existing mass. Once again, the men standing guard over the growing group of corpses, lowered pistols to the heads of each of the new arrivals, and discharged a bullet into their already dead brains.

'There is no chance for us now. They have all had it, even my other mate, Schultz. I am the only bastard left, and I am completely fucked up.' Klein realised that he must stop the Gruppenfuhrer and the others from walking into the same trap. He looked at his watch and tried to calculate how much longer it would take the final boat to get to the landing point. He took the decision to get into the water and wait for them to arrive. He could make no noise to warn them, and was worried that they may assume from the gunfire and explosions, that they had been successful in their mission, and call out to him. 'Please let them make no noise, when they see me,' he thought.

He did not have to wait long, which was a blessing. The weight of the heavy machine gun, which he had now realised, belonged to Fuchs, was beginning to wear him down. It was slung behind his back as he did not wish to appear to be an aggressor as the team finally spotted him. He carefully moved out of the cover of the bushes and reeds as he saw the small craft approaching. His hands were held as high as he could manage, but the effort of moving, had weakened him once again. He saw the gunman laying in the bow of the boat, and the other three men crouched down behind him. He now knew that it was them. He moved out slowly, clearing the last of the weeds, by now he was up to his thighs in the cold water. He heard low whispers coming from the boat, and the next moment, he was being hauled over the side. He lay in the bottom of the boat, surrounded by explosives and kit. For now, he knew that he was safe again.

Chapter 19

Adrian's team had watched helplessly as the first of the inflatable boats paddled out across Pett Level, in the direction of the sea wall. They could do nothing. Shortly, they witnessed another nine boats paddle out and away in a dog leg manoeuvre taking them first to the centre of the lake and then turning in towards Toot Rock itself. Visibility was very poor, and at this stage, they lost sight of the entire flotilla.

The team were very frustrated at not being able to get involved, but realistically they knew that they would not stand much chance on their own. Some back up was supposed to be coming, and hopefully Lieutenant Colonel Burgess would be well prepared to deal with the attack team headed towards Toot Rock. Finally, Ted came back to the group, saying that at least two more special ops teams would be with them very shortly. The signal was to be a reciprocated owl call. Clearly someone else shared Badger's bird cry skills. It was not long before the distant sound of an owl reached the team's ears, and immediately Badger responded with a long warbled call. Meanwhile Ted was instructed to radio Toot Rock to pre-warn them of timings and numbers.

A couple of minutes later and the owl sounds were much closer. Adrian had instructed his team to hide, and they were huddled down in some thick bushes. 'You never know,' he told his team. 'The fucking Krauts could have latched on to this one.'

The sound of light footsteps could now be heard quite close by, and then a familiar voice softly spoke out. 'Are you there Doc?' It was the voice of Major Gordon Roberts. Adrian whispered a short response, 'Here Major.' With that, a group of men appeared in the clearing just in front of the cover that they had made for themselves. Introductions were swiftly done, as well as they could be in pitch dark conditions. The eleven men that the Major had brought with him were in fact, the two teams that they had shared a ride with the other evening, on route to their respective bunkers.

Adrian quickly brought the Major up to speed, with the night's activities so far. The Major then explained that there would be a huge number of troops arriving in the area of the windmill, with an eta of about half an hour. He would go back up to meet their commanding officer, Brigadier Anderson, who was the only man with knowledge of this local threat. 'The only reason that these troops will get involved is if our own situation gets out of hand, or if an invasion force actually does appear. Other than that, it has been explained to them that there are special exercises going on here tonight. It is just coincidence for them that this is their stop off point, on the way to a barracks in Deal. Their commanding officer, Brigadier Anderson, has explained that as these south coast regions are prime 'invasion territory', we need to show the enemy that there are substantial troop movements all the way along the channel coastline.'

'Okay boys, what's the plan?' asked the Major. Adrian was the first to speak. 'We can only attempt to calculate what will happen from now on, Major. Then we must be ready to react to any situation as it arises. If the Toot Rock team do their job well, then we should not really expect too many of the attack team to return. It's the one single boat that went straight across the lake towards the sea wall that worries me. None of us have been able to fathom out what their purpose is.'

Tricky, that one. Unless they are part of a signals team, to welcome their chums ashore.' The Major considered further. 'You don't suppose that they have the equipment to blow a hole in the wall, do you?'
All of the larger team of men considered this, and one of the Vinehall Forest team spoke out. 'The problem that I have with that one is that they would need several hours to undermine the concrete traps, in order to get enough explosive underneath them to create a large enough gap for the enemy to drive through. If there were only four of them and one of them was the boss, I honestly don't think they would have the time.'

'A very good point, Sidney. The only thing is, it now seems that these bastards have been around for a couple of days, so it just might be possible that they have been across there already and done all of the preparation work.' The whole team considered this. The leader of the Brede High Wood team, Sergeant John Wilson, asked whether they could lay their hands on a small boat so that they could get across the lake and prevent the Germans from carrying out their mission.

The Major discussed this for a moment, with Captain John Clifford, the WW1 veteran, and team leader of the Vinehall Forest crew. Finally, the Major spoke again to the whole team. 'Even if we could get our hands on a boat, we would be putting ourselves at risk, coming across an expanse of water towards them. They are in a higher position, and would almost certainly spot us coming in, even in these shitty conditions. In the water, we would be like sitting ducks. What the Captain and I think might be better, is that if *they* return here, then we will turn the heat on *them*. We should start to prepare an attack scenario for them, and any others that might survive the onslaught at the Rock.

The following few minutes were spent in open discussion, in which Virtually every man had a say. Some contributions were small, but very useful. The Major brought up the subject of the two flame throwers that George and Bill, from the Pett crew, were carrying. He also mentioned the 'need' for some badly burned German bodies. 'I suggest that we get ourselves over to the point where the first boat was launched, and see what opportunities we may have. They walked along the sloping banks, until they found trodden down reeds at the water's edge, with clear footprints leading down to it. 'This was definitely the spot,' said Badger.

'We will need some sort of shield, said the Major. The flame throwers will glow momentarily before you pump the flame out forwards, and they are also relatively short range, so they will need to be camouflaged until the very last moment.'

'Why don't we just shoot the bastards when they are further out, and then retrieve the boat and burn them on the bank here?' The question came from another member of the Broad Oak team. 'No can do, old boy.' was the Major's sharp response. 'The problem is that we want to give a true impression that these men have actually been burnt to death. Any bullet holes would make it look like a put up job. We can throw in a few extra bodies with other injuries, which we can then torch. There are bound to be a good few casualties from Toot Rock a little later on.' Hopefully, all Krauts,' he added as an after thought.

The Major checked his watch and stated that he needed to head back up the hill to meet the Brigadier at the windmill. 'Oh, by the way boys. When the top brass is around, we had better stick to military titles. We wouldn't want him thinking that we are an unruly bunch.' They all smiled. It was always the Major's way to be very relaxed in front of his men, and they with him. They had all 'volunteered' and they were all determined to succeed one hundred percent. No enlisted soldier could have been more committed than these men, and the Major knew it.

While the Major was gone, the whole team set about preparing the ground for the possible attack scenario should the Germans return. Three fairly large fallen tree trunks were carried out of the top woodlands and down the bank to an approximate height of four feet above water level. Two were laid onto the wet grass bank side by side, and the third sat on top, in the gap between them. These would form a bullet proof barrier, behind which the two flame thrower operators could prime up, and subsequently flare out, as the boat approached the shore. The idea for the tree trunks was copied twice more, thirty yards either side of the main barrier, in order to provide covering fire, if absolutely necessary. The training officers at Coleshill had told them that it was extremely rare to receive any return of fire. An enemy hit by a jet of pure heat, would always be forced to turn away. The benefits of using these weapons at night, was that the target was immediately picked out, and could be followed if it moved.

As soon as this preparation work was completed, the Major reappeared with a tall man, who he formally introduced as Brigadier Anderson. The whole team stood to attention and saluted. None of them were sure whether the senior officer had noticed, in the pitch dark. 'No need for that sort of stuff in the battle field, chaps,' was the officer's response. Quickly, Major Roberts introduced each of the team leaders to the Brigadier. 'It looks as though you chaps have the whole thing covered admirably,' he commented.

'I don't think that I can advise you further, it looks like you have done a spiffing job, here. Hopefully with what our prime minister has planned, my lot should not be needed at all. I shall only call them, should things go horribly wrong at Toot Rock over there, or if we do actually start to see enemy shipping on the horizon. If everything is taken care of, we will be on our way in the morning, probably much to the relief of that bloody rude farmer up top there. The bugger didn't seem too keen on the idea of three thousand men camping in his fields overnight. Damned fool actually had the gall to approach us with a loaded shotgun, asking us what the bloody hell we thought we were doing on his land.'

Adrian smiled, he knew the gentleman in question. He was an irascible old bastard, named Frank Dayrell, and this would have done his already high blood pressure no good at all.

'With you being a medical man, I suppose you don't really approve of a chap having a little tipple now and again? The Brigadier said to Adrian. Adrian picked up the man's thread and quickly responded, 'Let's put it this way, Brigadier. If you are offering, then this is one man who will not be refusing.'
'I rather hoped you would say that, because I have just topped up, with a few bottles from the Newhaven army store, of a half decent whisky. When we get to Deal tomorrow, I will no doubt be able to top up again.'
'In that case, how could we refuse?' replied Adrian.

I will give one of your chaps a signed note, requesting a couple of bottles,

And maybe he would be good enough to pop up to the mill, and ask the guards for Captain Cannon. He will hand over the goods, and we can stay warm while we wait for something to happen. Badger stepped forward and volunteered to make the short trip, as he was probably the swiftest over the ground. Meanwhile, Adrian produced his bottle which had a few slugs left in it, and it did the rounds until it was empty.

The Brigadier also suggested that Badger ask Captain Cannon for a large flysheet and ropes, so that the whole group could rig up a waterproof shelter among the trees. 'May as well be comfortable while we are waiting for a bit of action,' he quipped. Badger was away and sprinting up the hill, he didn't mind running the errand, but he didn't want to miss out on any action either. He wasn't gone long. As soon as he returned, the team, who had already cleared a suitably sized plot among the trees, quickly set about securing the flysheet to the surrounding trunks. Some of the others had already brought in some more fallen pieces of trunk, to make a rustic seating arrangement, beneath the waterproof sheet.

A guard was posted, to stand on the bank, just clear of the trees, and it was agreed that the guard would change every ten minutes. Harry East took first watch, and he also agreed to change the guard, after each short session on duty. The whole group, sat around chatting quite informally, well aware that they could not do anything, until the enemy made their move. The whisky was being appreciated by the entire team. Captain Cannon had also managed to provide a canvass bag, with enough small tot glasses for them all. As well as these, he had put in several packets of 'McVities, rich tea biscuits. The whole thing felt quite civilised.

They had been sitting around for nearly two hours, with the Brigadier telling tales of military encounters past, together with experiences of different women from various parts of the world. 'It's not true what they say about the Chinese girls, by the way,' Exclaimed the Brigadier, 'although, as a medical man, I shouldn't have to tell you that, Adrian.' Suddenly the sound of a muffled explosion came from the direction of Toot Rock. They all came out of the woodland, and onto the bank. The guard had seen nothing. The rain was coming down hard, and visibility was very poor at that moment. They could just make out a few twinkling lights on the rock but nothing else.

Suddenly a great flash came from the direction of the sea wall, and a split second later, an almighty tremor shook the ground. They heard the whistling of flying debris, followed by the crash of it being scattered back over the ground. With that, it was once more, completely silent.

The whole team stood, watched and listened intently, but all was still. At last something was happening. They didn't have too long to wait until the next piece of action started. Grenades were exploding, one after the other, followed by short bursts of gunfire. About a minute had passed, and it went quiet for a short time. Then a series of almost simultaneous explosions rocked the ground again. The noise was immense. They saw some flashes of light this time, coming from the area of the rock. The unmistakable sound of rapid gunfire ensued, and once again all was quiet. Another minute passed and the sound of single gunshots rang out at two second intervals. Again, silence. The frustrating thing was that nobody had any idea what was actually happening. Yes, they recognised the sound of grenades exploding, and the sound of rifle fire, but there was no way of knowing whether it came from the Krauts or the Brits.

A few more minutes had passed and the sound of rapid gunfire started up again. This time, it sounded more like a battle. There would be an opening salvo from one or two guns, followed by the sharp rattle of opposing fire from a heavy machine gun. The battle lasted for several minutes, before gradually the firing diminished, and once more complete silence ensued. The silence was broken again by what appeared to be more grenades exploding, only this time just a few. Things once again went quiet. The team discussed what they thought could have happened.

The Brigadier suggested that the first muffled explosion had probably been the signal for the big bang that came from the sea wall. After that, it was difficult to calculate what had happened. The speed of the events made it very difficult to work out what was happening, but he suggested that the single shots, coming at regular two second intervals, were almost certainly 'dispatching' head shots. 'It is something that we have always trained to do, but you can bet your life that the Hun will be no different.'

'As a young soldier, I mistakenly spared the life of an enemy rifleman who lay on the ground badly wounded. I pointed my pistol at his face and he looked so pathetic. He looked into my eyes and managed to say in English, 'Please.' I threw his rifle well away from him and left him to die. A minute or so later, a fellow soldier had fallen right next to him, and the bastard that I had spared picked up his dead mate's rifle and started shooting again. A good friend of mine was killed as a result of my own foolish compassion. I learnt a lifetime lesson that compassion must never exist on the battlefield.'

The whole group were impressed with the Brigadier's honesty. They all took the point, and fully understood the reason for his 'confession'.

The group had fallen quiet, and once again the sound of four, distant single gunshots rang out. 'Sounds like more headshots,' said the Brigadier. It's just hell not knowing which side is on the receiving end. The final sounds came after another three or four minutes when once again the single shots rang out. This time there were five.

They all stayed on the bank, listening and watching, but nothing else happened. About fifteen minutes passed, and the Major suggested that if the team at the sea wall had left soon after the loud explosion, they would be at least, at half distance across the lake by now. The decision was jointly taken, to move into position now, just in case the Krauts were coming back. Bill Jacobs and George Dobson, carried their heavy equipment down to their log defences, and lay the machines, behind the makeshift barriers, and set about preparing them to fire.

Meanwhile a couple of men from the Vinehall Forest team, who were good marksmen, settled down behind one of the other defence barriers. This left two places behind the last of the three defences. 'If nobody minds, I think that Harry East and I should take that position,' said Adrian. The pair had scored the highest marks during target practice sessions at Coleshill. 'That's fine with me,' said the Major. 'I suggest that the rest of us lay back at the base of the woodland and spread out wider still. The Krauts will not stand much of a chance with the different levels and spread that we have prepared for them. Please though, all of you remember, not to get trigger happy, we really only want to burn them. Only fire on them, if they manage to return fire or if for some reason, the flame throwers do not work. Is that clear, everyone?'

As one, the group replied, 'Yes Sir.' With that they all settled down into their agreed positions, including the Brigadier, who seemed as keen to get involved as the rest of them. He lay flat out on the woodland floor with his head and shoulders just poking out of the very wet ferns that bordered its edges. The Major took up position next to him. 'He whispered directly into the Brigadier's ear, 'We had better get this right, we have got an invitation to Winston's place later this week. He has some cognac and champagne that he wants to share with us and our wives. Only if the invasion force doesn't get here of course. He and for that matter we, will be a little bit busy if that should happen.'

'Better make sure that this lot is quelled, then. Ted White was listening on the headphones of the portable Bush set, and suddenly exclaimed, 'That was the operator at 'Battle Station', to say that the men at Toot Rock have killed thirty four Germans, and as far as they can see, that is

all of them. That seems to leave one unaccounted for, because there were thirty nine to start with, and only four went across to the sea wall.'
'Get back on to Battle Station to relay that message back to Toot Rock,' suggested the Major. 'We can't have even one man left alive there. He could still be capable of wreaking havoc, especially if the men there have let their guard down now,' A few seconds later, Ted reported that he had re-contacted 'Battle Station', who promised to pass the message back to the rock immediately.

'Better switch off for a while now Ted, we don't want a communication coming through just as we spot the German boys about to dock. It might just frighten them off,' the Major advised. The whole area now fell silent, and an air of heightened tension was apparent in everyone. They waited and waited, but no sign of the small boat.

Perhaps a further twenty minutes had passed, when a slight rippling sound came from the lake. Everyone froze. There was nothing visible as yet, but the sound became more pronounced, and yet it was still only a gentle swishing sound of water. Then, out of the murky darkness came a black shape, which looked somehow like a tiny steamer with three funnels and a pointed bow. As it drew closer to the bank, it was clear that the funnels were in fact, men. They were sitting bolt upright, and the two on either side, were slowly and quietly paddling the craft towards the shore. The other man was sitting right behind them in the centre of the boat. A forth man, whose head was just visible, was lying flat, pressed into the bow with a rifle pointed directly towards the shore.

As the Major and the Brigadier observed this from their higher position, they were also suddenly aware of a slight glow, coming from behind the middle defence logs. Neither said a word, but they both knew that the two flamethrower's had been fired up.

'Steady boys,' whispered Zimmermann, who suddenly felt a cold chill, running down his spine. The young boy, George, stood in front of their boat. He was looking down at the Gruppenfuhrer, and offering him a piece of chocolate. 'Take this Wolfgang.' Zimmermann was now completely transfixed as the boy's arm stretched out towards him, and became a blazing inferno. The heat was all engulfing. There was no air, no escape. The Gruppenfuhrer was vaguely aware of screams coming from the others, and then the young George Sinden took his hand and said, 'Come with me, Wolfgang.'

At the back of the boat, Klein saw the fireball hit the other four men, and the orange flames coming from all of them. He pushed himself backwards, taking a deep breath as he did so. It was a relief to be in the cold water. The others had shielded him and had paid the price. He hid behind the stern of the small rubber craft, but was aware now that the boat too had started to burn. The smell was unbearable and the smoke was choking, he turned away, facing outwards to the lake, and realised that he had just one chance. He took a deep breath, and dived under the surface. As he swam away, below the dark waters, he realised that the hole in his throat was letting in water which was running straight down to his stomach. He could do nothing about it. He had to carry on. He managed to swim for about forty seconds and came to the surface. He was aware that although he was gasping for air, he must breathe quietly. His first breath was inhaled through his teeth, as well as the wound in his throat.

The heat from the burning boat was still intense on the back of his head, but he had to turn round to see what had happened. Bursts from two flamethrowers were still firing sporadically at the boat, which was now sinking. He could see the shape of his comrades, still burning. Neumann was still laying in the bow, but now slumped forward. His back was smouldering. The other three all lay across the sides of the small craft, with arms outstretched into the water, as if they had tried in vain to get out. Their corpses were still well ablaze.

Klein felt no emotion. His only thought now was survival. He dived under for one last marathon effort, which would take him further away from the inferno that had destroyed the last of his comrades. With Zimmermann gone, he had to look after himself. He must survive. He was the only one left. Again he suffered the involuntary ingestion of water, but this time, it was not such a shock. He was swimming hard, further out into the lake, and when his lungs were bursting, he finally surfaced. This time the view of the burning craft was quite misty. The rain was falling harder again and visibility was poor. He could hear shouts from the bank, and the sound of people getting into the water. He knew that he could now no longer be seen.

The British special ops boys were rejoicing. They had managed to eliminate the entire boat crew without a single shot being fired from either side. Just as the Coleshill officers had predicted, the heat had instantly overcome the enemy, leaving them powerless to respond. 'Fuck me,' said Badger, who was one of the first to get to the boat. There are sticks of dynamite in the bottom of this thing and one of them is smoking.'

'Sling them into the water, NOW' shouted the Major. Badger did not need to be told twice. He leant over the side of the now black and crinkled craft and grabbed handfuls of explosives, throwing them as far out into the lake as he could. There were some tools, but nothing left inside that could be described as hazardous. A huge explosion occurred below the surface, and a plume of water shot out of the lake and high into the air. 'Fucking Hellfire,' said the Major. 'That was a bit too close for comfort. Badger calmly guided the remains of the boat and its crew towards the bank, and other members of the team attempted to lift the still smoking bodies from it. The corpses were far too hot to handle. The decision was made to tip them into the water and then drag them up the bank. Each of the enemy bodies was pulled into the water and pushed down. As each went under, steam was seen to be expelled from their heads and torsos. In turn, they were unceremoniously dragged ashore and up the bank, clear of the water's edge. The four bodies lay side by side.

One of the men couldn't help remarking that he could smell something similar to roast pork. Others had noticed it too. 'All I can say boys, is bloody well done, no pun intended. I am afraid though that these buggers are needed for a bit of a propaganda coup. It wouldn't do for you to start biting chunks out of them. We need complete corpses, not half eaten ones, to send back to Adolf. Mind you, if he thinks that Britain is a nation of cannibals, we shouldn't have any further problems from him in the future.' The Brigadier's speech was so level and matter of fact. With the exception of a few, most of the men had never witnessed anything as horrific as the scene that had just unfolded. Under any other circumstances, most people would have thrown up, and felt complete revulsion. This team of men could only feel relief and joy that they had killed these enemies of their nation.

'Back to reality chaps. I will get back to camp now, and my lot will be gone by about 08.30. I will hang around with my driver, in case you need any assistance with the cover up, tomorrow, but it seems to me that you have got everything well under control. Once again, may I congratulate you and your team Major. You have all done a terrific job here tonight, and I am fairly sure that the Lieutenant Colonel will not have too many problems with the one remaining Kraut. By the way, keep the rest of the whisky and also the flysheet. You might be able to cut it up and use it as temporary body bags.' With that, the Brigadier was striding away, back up the hill in the direction of the windmill.

The Major then took control, once more. 'Chaps, can we get all the logs back up into the woodlands, we don't want any locals putting two and two together. The men set about carrying the defence barriers back into the woods and dropping them at random. Four more were charged with cutting the flysheet into four strips, while two others, gently rolled the German bodies into the canvass material, wrapping them tightly and tying them with the guy ropes, cut to length. Even wrapped, the four bundles still smelled of roast pork. Makeshift stretchers of small woodland trees were quickly cut to size and tied together, and it was agreed that the teams would take turns of just two minutes each to carry the four Germans back to Toot Rock. The WW1 veterans were excused this particular chore.

Finally there was the issue of the enemy weapons, and the boat itself. It was decided that the boat should be cut up and disposed of elsewhere. Nearly all of the team used their commando style daggers to slice up the sticky and acrid, burnt remains. Each man tucked a small piece of it into his kitbag. The German weaponry was collected up too. With that, they were ready to go. 'We will head round to the gate, and get ourselves some sleep for the rest of the night at Toot Rock. Ted, would you mind radioing one more time to 'Battle Station', and they will fix it so that the boat is there to meet us. Within a minute, Ted was stashing the small portable back into his kitbag, and they were on their way. There was almost a feeling of anticlimax as they made their way back to the rock.

They made quite good time, considering the additional burden, and by about 04.45 they were assembled at the gate just east of the Market Stores. The two guards held the gate open and two soldiers in the large rowing boat, assisted with loading their kit and the bodies on board. In total, they had to make three trips, but as the last team arrived at the base of the rock, the enemy bodies, plus all of their kit had already been carried up to the outside of the large barrack room. The team were welcomed by the camp commander, who introduced himself as Lieutenant Colonel Burgess. 'No need for formalities chaps. We've got some hot cocoa on the go, and for those who need it, some damned good army whisky.'

With that, he ordered his men to take the corpses down to the officer's bunker, where all of the other German bodies had now been stored. True to his word, as the team all settled down in the comparative comfort of the barrack room, mugs of steaming cocoa were brought in on tin trays, and two bottles of 'Famous Grouse' were left on a wooden table in the centre of the large concrete room. The men already had the army whisky tots in their pockets from the earlier session. Some chose to fill these up, while others just poured shots directly into their cocoa.

The Lieutenant Colonel came into the barrack room to address the entire special ops team. 'Well bugger me, it's you, Doc! I never knew that you were involved in all this hush, hush stuff, Adrian.' The Officer watched the men as they began to wipe the boot polish from their faces, with the help of flannels, soap and bowls that he had thoughtfully provided for them, along with army towels. 'Truthfully, I had absolutely no idea that you were involved with the military.'
'I am glad you said that, Sir. The truth is that all of these men, like us, have signed the 'Official Secrets Act,' responded Major Gordon Roberts. 'Everything is on a 'need to know' basis.'

'Well, men. I think that I had better bring you up to speed with what has happened here.' The Lieutenant Colonel then went on to explain in great detail, the events that had unfolded during the long night. 'Pretty much everything went according to plan, apart from a party of five Huns, walking right past the Canadians lying down at the side of the lane. Captain Johnson did well to restrain his men at that point, having realised that this was a small splinter group. He knew that they would inevitably be dealt with up top, by the chaps lead by Major Wicks.'

'One thing did go a little wrong though. We felt that if we rolled enough barbed wire around the bottom end of the rear gardens, we would dissuade the enemy from using that route. Problem was that although we had locked all of the back doors of the cottages and removed the keys, they shot through the lock of number one, and sent four men through the gardens to cover the rears. It wasn't a problem at that stage, because we had in fact evacuated every single house, and consolidated the rest of our chaps in the fortified zones here. It was only after a body count was done, that we realised that we were four men short. We hadn't taken out the other five at this stage, but nevertheless we had them under scrutiny.'

'Captain Johnson again came up trumps, because he realised that the only place they could be, was behind the cottages. He sent a team to follow up the same route they had taken, and they spotted them crouched in the back garden of number nine. The rhubarb there should be pretty good, come next spring, I can tell you. It took the buggers completely by surprise. They were looking up the terrace, having assumed that there was nothing happening in the cleared houses behind them. I can tell you, that if these men were Adolf's crack troops, then they are not quite as good as they would like us, and the rest of the world to think they are.'

The officer was in full flow now, and continued, 'The one that got away, is a bit of a puzzle. We know from the numbers that two men entered the lower pillbox. Also there were some weapons found that indicated that the chap with his skull blown open, was not acting alone. We have searched the entire emplacement thoroughly, and have even used a couple of the dogs that normally guard Tongs House. He isn't here. He may have tried to swim away, but it seems that he too was wounded quite badly, we found a separate pool of blood from that of the corpse that was there.'

The Major then volunteered, 'There were certainly only four of them in the boat that we ambushed, so perhaps he has drowned. Nevertheless, we had better keep an eye out, in case he comes out of the woodwork somewhere. Did he still have his gun?'
'Rather afraid that he did, it wasn't left behind at the pillbox, but come first light, we will do another sweep. Meanwhile I have already dispatched two teams to go in opposite directions right around the lake, just in case he should turn up. My guess would be that if he hasn't drowned, he will know that the rest of his team are dead, and give himself up. In order to keep the story as we would wish, we will let it be known that there is the possibility of an enemy paratrooper in the area.'

The Major again spoke. 'I don't think that there is much point in us trying to get any sleep tonight, perhaps it would be better if we get the plan in place for the cover up.'
'Couldn't agree more, Major,' responded the Lieutenant Colonel. I just wasn't sure how tired you chaps are feeling.'
'We will sleep in our own beds tomorrow night. Sorry that's tonight now, isn't it? We should all be able to get away early, once we have agreed the cover up process, so I don't think I am speaking out of turn, if I say that we will all contribute to the strategy, and formulate it now. Is that alright with the rest of you chaps?' He had turned towards the three small teams, and as one, they nodded their agreement.
'Badger stated, 'I don't know about the rest of you, but I feel more wide awake than I ever have in my life.' Many of the men agreed with him.

'That's good then,' said Burgess. I will get one of my chaps to bring in the blackboard, and we can all agree what needs to be done. Meanwhile, I have a little problem which I would like your advice on. In the circumstances of tonight's events, I had to take the decision to ask every one of my men, to also sign the Official Secrets Act, tomorrow morning. We gave them the opportunity to leave last night, if they weren't happy, and I read out the statement with major Jennings as my witness. We are not entirely sure of the legality of this situation.'
Adrian spoke first. 'I am not a legal man, but firstly, may I ask did anyone opt to leave?'

'Not one man wanted to go,' replied Burgess.
'Well to my mind, they have agreed to the terms and conditions, simply by staying put,' said Adrian.
'This is what Jennings said, when we got their agreement, but I just wonder whether they might have the 'peer pressure' get out clause.

'I don't think this would be a defence in a court of law, if they were ever to breach the act,' chipped in Badger, who had probably had more skirmishes with the law than the rest of the team put together. The basic facts are that they were *individually* given the opportunity to leave if they objected to the signing, and yet as individuals, they had *personally* decided to stay.'

'A very good point,' stated the Lieutenant Colonel. 'I will get Major Jennings to organise the mass signings later today, once the documents have been prepared.
Once again, the good doctor spoke out. 'It might be worth asking Brigadier Anderson to look in, in the morning. He may be able to inspire the men further, regarding the need for absolute secrecy, and perhaps also the possible consequences of letting things out of the bag. He has already said that he will stay around when his men head off to Deal, in case we need any help with the cover up operation.'
'Thanks Doc, I will do just that. If the radio chaps can get some direct communications with him, then we should invite him for breakfast.'

'Right then, chaps. The cover up, what topics do we need to cover?'
As the teams threw their suggestions at him, the officer wrote neatly with a stick of white chalk, onto the blackboard that had been placed on an easel in the back corner of the room. The list appeared as follows:

Visible Damage for Immediate Repairs.

1. *Sea Wall and Tank Traps. Damage to be covered with tarpaulins and repaired soonest.*
2. *Front Windows of Cottages.*
3. *Shrapnel damage to front walls of number nine.*

Local Population Calming.

1. *Police car with loudspeakers to cover local villages.*
2. *Message to be composed by us, and read out by Major Wicks.*
3. *Local paper to be contacted regarding 'Unusually noisy manoeuvres at Pett Level.' With an apology from the army.*

4. *Soldiers to enter local inns and shops talking 'loosely' about the very loud exercises that they were involved in. These men to be carefully selected for this propaganda role. Scripts to be prepared.*
5. *Local defence volunteers and police to be warned of possibility of an enemy airman, forced to bail out, who could be armed. Also we will redouble our search efforts come daylight.*

<u>Longer Term Damages.</u>

1. *Rear, sea facing windows of cottages.*
2. *Internal damages to all affected dwellings.*

<u>Clear Up.</u>

1. *Disposal, of all enemy corpses, with selected ones to be used as propaganda, as per the prime minister's request. Go through pockets to try to establish rank. Look for possessions and i.d.*
2. *Disposal of rubber boats and equipment, including enemy arms.*

'Anything else, Gentlemen?' asked Burgess. The men sat quietly thinking for a while, but no-one came forward with anything else. He then called in his two most trusted Majors, Wicks and Jennings, to sit at the front of the briefing, alongside Major Roberts. Pens and paper were duly brought in by a private. 'We need now to compile a list of individual duties from the agreed agenda, and how we are to achieve them.'

A lively discussion opened up once more, and various duties were assigned to the Majors and to the camp commander. These duties were allocated as follows:

<u>Lieutenant Colonel Burgess.</u>

Order soldiers along the sea wall now, before completely light. They are to take long tarpaulins, if necessary laced together. These to be stretched from the first undamaged anti tank trap to the next sound one, the other side of the damaged area. Plus they are to inspect and cover any damage to the wall itself. The Royal Engineers to be ordered by Brigadier Anderson, to replace all missing or damaged traps, by later today.

At first light, send a team of forty men, to search for missing enemy soldier. Utilise all of the enemy inflatables to cover the expanse of water, starting from the bottom of the lane. Instruct the team that drowned men, are very often almost invisible, if lying face down in the water. Dispatch another sixty troops with dogs, to assist the land teams already searching.

Order the internal repair teams to deal with windows and shrapnel damage. Window repairs to be completed by this evening. It is noted that George Dobson is a builder and could assist with wall repairs required to conceal any shrapnel damage.

Slightly longer term, commission internal damage repairs to affected properties. George Dobson can again help. George will inspect later.

Arrange the very discreet burial, of all 'unwanted corpses'. This is to be done somewhere in the grounds of the battery. The trench digging team will be utilised for this task. Canvass shelters to be erected to conceal activity. Graves are to be dug to a depth of eight feet. Unmarked, but we must record the exact spot. Camp bulldozer to cover up after.

Major Roberts.

Senior police contact to arrange delivery of car and driver to be at the Market Stores by 0.800 hours. Also advise him of missing 'Airman'.

The commander of the local defence volunteers to be made aware of the possibility of 'missing airman' being at large.

Contact the prime minister to arrange collection of 'selected' corpses. The process of selecting appropriately damaged bodies will be undertaken by Major Roberts and assisted by Major Wicks.

Major Wicks.

Assist Major Jennings with the writing of the 'apology' script for broadcasting around the villages. Also assist with the composition of the article to be printed in the Hastings Observer, later this week. Finally, to prepare a dialogue for the agreed, 'selected' soldiers to spread around local shops and businesses. Joint decision as to which men are used.

At 0.800 hours, 14.00 hours and 19.00 hours, tour local area,, broadcasting the apology. If required, stop to reassure locals.

Major Jennings.

Prepare all documents as listed above, with the help of Major Wicks, until he has to leave for the broadcasting mission. Initial composition must be the 'apology, broadcast', as it will be required first.

Prepare, 'The Official Secrets Act' documents, and bring in all troops, during the course of the day, to sign. Lieutenant Colonel Burgess to supply the register of all troops stationed here. No exceptions will be allowed.

With these preparations completed, it was getting light, and the various, agreed tasks were starting to be implemented. The three 'public', statements were jointly scripted by Majors Wicks and Jennings. As soon as these were completed, and typed up, it was time for Major Dennis Wicks, to be ferried across to his 'chauffeured' police car. Much earlier, at the break of day, sixty men had been sent to look for the one, unaccounted for German. Dennis had just had time to visit the toilet block, and freshen himself up. He was beginning to feel just a little bit tired by now.

Chapter 20

Klein swam slowly, using an underwater, dog paddle movement. He was still taking water through his throat wound, but he was able to breathe okay. He decided that he should make for the other side of the inlet that separated Wickham Cliff from the next line of inland hills, to the south of Ashes Farm. Suddenly an explosion in the water rocked his body again.

He made the decision to let his trusted Mauser go, and had slipped the strap from his shoulder, and let the weapon drop to the bottom of the lake. This was a decision that was not taken lightly. As a soldier, this was completely against his training, and his nature. The reality was that with the weight of his heavy army boots, plus the weapon, he would not have been able to stay afloat, especially given his reduced strength.

He paddled on for about fifteen minutes and eventually he was hauling himself up the bank and out of the water. He was a tough man, both mentally and physically, but he was starting to shiver uncontrollably. He knew that he must find some warmth and dry out soon, or he would be finished. This must now be his overriding objective. He walked through some trees and could see the outline of the farmhouse, a few hundred metres away. There were no lights showing as yet, although he knew that it would not be long until dawn.

He kept trudging in the direction of the farmhouse, but by now the shuddering had become completely uncontrollable. At one stage, he even called out, 'Why me, why am I the only one left.' At this point, he realised that he was beginning to lose control, and his inner strength, took over for a short time. 'Why the fuck did I ditch my rifle?' he asked himself. He could have stormed this farmhouse, quickly killed the occupants and got himself warm and dry. He could probably have found something to eat, and in the space of an hour, he would have been ready to press on. These negative thoughts were suddenly replaced with a realisation that he still had his cheesewire, tied around the buttons of his military blouse. He only needed to find the strength to use it, and all of his needs could be accomplished.

Soon, he was at the back door of the house, and turning the door handle. It was not locked. He slipped inside, but he found it impossible to keep quiet. The uncontrollable trembling had completely overtaken him and he was now unable to stop the noise of his misery, shuddering out from his lips. His hands fumbled with the buttons that held the cheesewire into position. Where normally he would have been able to achieve this manoeuvre easily with one hand, both trembling hands fumbled for a minute or more, to free the weapon.

Whether his noise had woken the occupants, or whether as farm people, they would normally rise at this hour, he did not know. What he did know, was that a toilet had been flushed upstairs, and now somebody was coming down the staircase, right now. He moved to a position behind the kitchen door, and slipped the cheesewire handles around the knuckles of each hand. He was still shuddering, but he managed to gain some control for a split second.

A tall man shuffled through the door, in his slippers, and turned on the electric light. He did not see or hear anything. There was a sudden, burning pain around his throat and he could no longer breathe. He felt the pressure of his assailant's knee, pushing relentlessly into his spine He was an elderly man, and he was very quickly unconscious. The pressure was kept on, even as the man slipped to the stone floor, and was not released for another minute.

Klein felt much better. He could now see some chance for him to achieve his immediate objectives. He quietly climbed the stairs of the farmhouse, and entered a bedroom. It was empty. He tried a second room and this too was unoccupied. A bathroom door was ajar, and he could hear the sound of the cistern refilling itself with water. The final door was closed, and he grasped the handle and turned it slowly. As the door was pushed open, it creaked loudly. He let himself into the room, which was still in darkness. As he felt the wall for the light switch, a woman's voice said. 'You were quick, my lovely. I hope you've boiled the kettle properly.' Klein did not have the faintest idea what the woman had said, he only knew from her tone, that she thought she was addressing her husband.

The light bathed the room, and Klein saw an old woman lying on the large oak framed double bed. Her grey hair hung around her shoulders, which were still lying back on the large feather pillows. As he approached her, she reached across to the bedside cabinet, for a pair of glasses. She, like her husband, did not know what had happened. This time, the cheesewire was looped around the woman's neck, and pressure applied from the front. Klein simply lay on top of her and pulled. She stared at him throughout the whole ordeal, with an almost forgiving look in her eyes, which remained open, once she had died.

The short bursts of action, had temporarily halted Klein's shivering, but now, he was again aware of the urgent need to get warm. He double checked the rest of the house, in case there were any further occupants, but it appeared that it was just this old couple. In his twisted mind, Klein had done these two a favour. They were old, tired and weary, and he had not made them suffer for very long. These two would never have been able to cope with his countrymen running their country from now on. They were much better off dead. Also, he felt that he had done them the special kindness of allowing them both to die at once, without either one of them having to endure the grieving process, or feel the loss of the other. If there was an after life, they were entering it together. If not, they were simply back in their bed, asleep for ever more.

He was now standing in another bedroom and going through a wooden wardrobe, which seemed to be full of men's clothing. He stripped off and fetched a towel from the bathroom. He was soon dry, but still the terrible trembling engulfed his whole being. He decided to dress with anything that fitted him for the moment, and get warm again first. He could then look at the possibility of a hot bath, depending on what the plumbing arrangements were in this house. Once he was fully clothed, he went back to the kitchen and lit the gas upon the large 'Radiation' stove, and filled the blackened kettle, with water from the tap.

While the kettle was starting to heat up, he lifted the old man's body from the floor and onto his shoulder. He carried him back upstairs, and into the bedroom. He slipped the body of the farmer, down onto the bed next to his dead wife, and finally he arranged the pair together, under the large eiderdown. He was pleased with his work. The two looked so peaceful together.

Back in the kitchen, he started to open cupboards and looked into the pantry. He found some cups and he found some tea in an old tin caddy. 'Don't these British bastards drink coffee?' he asked himself. Nevertheless, he managed to find some fresh bread and also a good quantity of butter. There was a lump of hard, yellow cheese in the pantry, and Klein sat at the table eating a breakfast that would have been 'fit for the Fuhrer'.

By now, it was daylight. He must formulate a plan, and get himself cleaned up, and dressed properly. He was already much warmer, partly from the heat of the stove, and partly from the food and hot tea that he had consumed. He was still shivering, but it was not quite as pronounced now. He could also stop it momentarily, which told him that he was getting it back under control. He decided to pour himself another cup of this 'English; tea. He poured the last of a bottle of milk into the large, white cup, and then topped it up from the old cracked teapot that he had made the original brew in. He sat back into the comfortable, armed pine chair that stood at the end of the table, and sipped the hot liquid.

'Got one for me then Thomas?' The man had burst through the back door, and totally taken Klein by surprise. It was the habit of Private, Albert Clarke, of the Home Guard, to drop in at the end of a night's watch duty. Thomas and Lillian Robertson were old friends, and he was always welcome. As a lad, he had helped out on their farm for many years. He was wearing his home guard uniform and had a 'B.S.A.' rifle slung across his shoulder.

Klein reacted swiftly to the armed man. The hot tea was thrown straight into the man's eyes. At the same moment, he leapt from the pine chair, still holding one arm and swinging it round into the side of the man's head. The soldier did not go down, despite the ferocity of the blow. He now started to defend himself. He swung a couple of heavy punches in Klein's direction and managed to land one on his chin. Klein counter punched with a fist into the man's throat. For his trouble, he received a healthy kick straight into his bollocks. Klein was weakened again and realised he would need to stop the man quickly before he could use his weapon. He had to ignore the pain that had gripped his nether regions, and moved in again. The soldier was young and strong, and soon Klein was reeling back again, this time he had been kneed to the abdomen.

As he fell back into the kitchen, he stumbled into the table, where the breadknife was still lying. He grabbed the handle, and thrust forward again. The soldier had slipped the rifle from his shoulder, and was raising the weapon to fire. Klein slashed the serrated blade down across the left side of his adversary's face, whilst pushing alongside the rifle, which he grasped tightly with his left hand. There was no noise from either man, just the sound of the scuffle. The soldier was not done yet. Klein was too close. He could not use his rifle. He viciously butted his forehead straight into the eyes of Klein. Klein was showered with the man's blood, which sprayed from his face as it jolted forward.

Again Klein was staggered backwards, tripping, and dropping the breadknife, which rattled onto the hard kitchen floor. He could not allow any distance to develop between him and his enemy. One second would be enough for the man to point his gun and shoot. He piled in again, this time prodding the fingers of his right hand into the soldier's eyes. This time the man yelled with pain. Pushing home his advantage, Klein snatched the barrel of the rifle, but the soldier was not about to release his grip. He held on hard with his right hand, and jabbed the point of his left elbow into the side of Klein's temple. While they were still up close, the soldier got in another powerful knee to Klein's abdomen. He had the advantage of additional height, and Klein was hunched forward and not too tall. For a while the two grappled clumsily, moving to and fro, locked in a deadly battle that could only end in the death of one of them.

Klein however, was the professional soldier, skilled in all aspects of 'close up' killing. The home guard, was young and strong, but with the exception of a few bar brawls, his experience had not been as vicious, or comprehensive, as that instilled into the troops of the Waffen SS. Klein began to think about how he could break the deadlock. He decided to allow the younger man to push him backwards, in the hope that he could get to the point where the knife fell, and somehow snatch it from the floor. The strategy worked well. Soon Klein was standing right over the blade. He held on tightly to the rifle still, and dropped to the floor grabbing the knife up again into his right hand. The soldier bore down on him, not allowing him to get up again.

This time, Klein thrust the blade upwards straight into the soldier's crotch. The blade broke as it was plunged hard at the man's groin area, and the now lethally sharp end was deflected straight into the side of his thigh. Again the younger man screamed. Immediately, a fountain of blood spurted from the top of the soldier's leg. Klein was still on his knees, and started to twist the broken blade inside the man's thigh, also using a sawing action. Finally, he could feel the physical strength draining from his enemy, and almost resignedly, the younger man slipped to his knees, and was now staring into the eyes of the German. His grip on his rifle had relaxed, and eventually Klein was able to slip behind the unfortunate home guard and strangle him, simply by pulling the rifle hard against his throat.

He achieved this by slipping his arms underneath the stock to the left, and the barrel to the right, and then locking his hands behind the man's neck. He just pulled and leant backwards. This was a classic strangle hold, and almost impossible to escape from. Klein's right knee between the man's shoulder blades made sure that there was no chance of this happening. The move was held on for two minutes. Klein knew that it was also a classic escape trick to play dead, at which point the aggressor may be fooled into releasing the hold. There was no chance that he would fall for this old trick.

Klein sat down on the floor of the kitchen, nursing his aching bollocks.

His solar plexus had taken a battering too, and the bridge of his nose was throbbing badly. For a while though, he had forgotten the pain in his throat, which oddly seemed to make him feel a bit better. He sat there, with his back resting against the back door of the farmhouse, and the dead soldier lying right in front of him. He did not move for some twenty minutes. He was much warmer now. He began to formulate a plan. The soldier's tunic top was undamaged, and his shirt too. There was some blood, but it should wash out. The trousers were ruined though. There was a huge rip where the knife had gone into his thigh, as well as a very large blood stain.

Klein got to his feet, and tried to lift the soldier, but was too weak. He resorted to dragging the body across the room, and eventually up the stairs and into the farmer's bedroom. He now removed the man's tunic top and shirt. He could not explain why, but he then put the man's body into the bed with the other two corpses. He laid him next to the woman and pulled the covers up to his chin. He looked back at the three heads and felt that he had done the right thing. The woman now had a man to protect her on either side.

He returned to the kitchen, and found the necessary bits to achieve his disguise. He boiled up the refilled kettle and also found a couple of steel pans which he put onto the hob as well. Once boiled, he emptied the contents into the large porcelain sink, and topped up with cold water, from the tap. The temperature was very warm and he once again stripped off. He was able to stand in the sink and have a complete wash down. He had found the farmer's razor upstairs in the bathroom, and was soon looking quite smart again. He was also a lot warmer.

He decided that it would be safer to stay here until nightfall, so he put on the clothes taken from the wardrobe earlier, and washed his own trousers, as well as the blood spattered jacket and shirt of the dead soldier. He had found a bar of 'Sunlight' soap and a scrubbing brush, behind the curtain underneath the sink. He washed these items in cold water, because he had been taught that hot water would set the stains, and cold would eventually remove them. It was another rainy day, so he knew that he couldn't put anything outside to dry. A strange contraption of ropes, hung across the kitchen ceiling, with one rope tied down to an anchor point on the wall. He assumed that this device must be some kind of indoor clothes line.

Having completed his ablutions, he turned his attention to his boots. He also managed to find some boot brushes, and black polish, so he put his still wet boots into the oven, which he managed to light eventually with some difficulty. After 'cooking' for half an hour, as well as stinking the whole kitchen area out, they were ready for some attention. The warm, dry leather absorbed plenty of black polish. He then went to work. It took a long time, but he had plenty of that. Twenty minutes later, he could have passed any parade ground inspection.

At this stage, he was in a quandary. He knew that his now dead commanding officer would never have sanctioned any one of his troops, to dress in anything other than German army uniform. It immediately classified them as spies. However, Zimmermann had made exceptions, in exceptional circumstances. When he and Fuchs delivered the boy to the main road, he had allowed them to dress as locals, for that one small part of the mission. He had only agreed to this on the basis that if they had been seen during daylight hours, the entire mission would have been compromised.

'Well,' he considered. 'My mission is to join up with my fellow countrymen. The only way that I can avoid being noticed is to look like one of the locals again. I, Rottenfuhrer Klein of the Waffen SS am commanding officer of this unit, and I make the decisions from now on.' With that, he felt better. Like most soldiers, he needed to act upon orders, and those 'orders' had now been issued. Confident that the invasion would still go ahead, his plan was to get away from the Pett Level area and meet up with the advancing troops, who would at some stage have to use the A259. Disguised as a British soldier, and with an obvious wound, he could simply smile and gesture to his throat. He would not need any further explanations.

He would, this evening head out to the other side of Icklesham, where he could hide up, until his comrades arrived. The clothes would take quite some time to dry. Meanwhile, he would prepare some food and drink for the wait. The pantry held some very unfamiliar items. Nevertheless, after opening some tins and discarding the contents, he managed to find a tin of spam. He sniffed at the contents of a small brown jar, marked Bovril. He liked the smell. He ended up making six very rough sandwiches with thickly buttered bread, wide slices of Spam, and thickly spread Bovril on top. He wrapped these in a newspaper that was lying on a dresser unit.

He was still in a lot of pain from the blows he had received to the testicles and his solar plexus. His throat hurt, but at least eating hadn't caused him any further discomfort. The pain would ease in time. He felt that the best thing he could do now, would be to get some sleep. He bolted the back door from the inside, and drew the curtains at the kitchen window.

Anybody calling now would just think that the occupants had gone out for the day. He found a bottle of Guinness in the back of the pantry, and decided he must try this strange looking beer. He searched the kitchen drawers for a bottle opener, and then carried the beer upstairs. He settled down in the bedroom where the wardrobe had been raided, put the bottle to his lips, and drank the dark liquid down. It was very different to the beer back home in Germany, but he quite liked the taste.

Within a few minutes, he was asleep on top of the bed, and stayed that way for the next nine hours. He awoke with a very dry mouth indeed. It was now late afternoon and rain was still pouring down the window panes of the room. He carefully pulled the curtains aside, to check outside, to see whether there was any sign of activity, but all was quiet. The next thing was a visit to the bathroom. He used one of the toothbrushes, and toothpaste from a tube, marked 'Pepsodent'. He then emptied his bowels, something that was not too pleasant an experience after the large volume of lake water that he had involuntarily consumed. He used a very strange feeling toilet paper, named 'Izal'. He felt as though he had been using sand paper on his now quite tender bottom. Finally he combed his hair, looking at his reflection in the old bevel edged mirror.

Klein knew that he was not a handsome man. He was very proud of his looks though. He preferred to think of himself as rugged. He knew that some of his comrades thought of him as ugly, but his mother had always told him, that somewhere out there, there would be a woman who would love him for what he was, not what he looked like. When he finally got back to Germany, he would once again, find Ingrid. They would settle down together, and raise a few, pure Aryan children. He continued with this train of thought for a few more moments, and then returned his mind to the task in hand.

He now went downstairs, and checked the freshly washed clothing. It was all dry, although the military tunic appeared to be particularly creased. He would have to try to give at least this one garment, a bit of a press. After scrabbling around in the under sink space, he found a black metal, smoothing iron. He again relit the gas on the top of the stove and started to look for an ironing board. He found the wooden framed item in a cupboard under the stairs, along with a scorched white pressing cloth. After he had heated the smoothing iron on the stove top, and dampened the white cloth, he set about pressing the British army jacket. It took him less than fifteen minutes, frequently returning the iron to the gas, to reheat it. Once done, he decided that he would also press the shirt, and finally his own trousers. These were always his favourite item to press. He loved to get the creases completely straight. Many of his comrades had asked his advice when it came to smartening up their military uniforms. There was, in his mind, only way to press military trousers. That was to heavily dampen the crease lines, and start at the bottom of the legs, and work upwards. The seams must always be straightened on each leg, so that they lay exactly on top of each other. He never failed to get excellent results. Soon, Rottenfuhrer Klein was standing in his freshly cleaned and pressed uniform, and wearing boots that you could see your face in. He decided that he would wait until it was just starting to get dark, before setting off. He now inspected the home guard's rifle. There was a bullet in the breach, but there was nothing else. He wondered whether the man had any more ammunition.

He once again entered the farmer's bedroom, and noticed that nothing had changed. The three looked so peaceful, lying in the big double bed. They might just as well have been asleep. He pulled back the eiderdown on the soldier's side and looked at his white vested top. With the exception of the bread knife wound to his cheek, and the now blackened mark across his throat, he looked good. He was a good looking young man, of fine physique.

Klein respected him because he had put up a good fight. The outcome was always going to be the same, but at least the man had shown some spirit. He had also hurt Klein, before finally succumbing to the superior fighting skills that the German possessed. Klein ran his hand into the young home guard's pockets. He was aware that the man's legs were now very cold and stiff. He found a box of Bryant and May matches, along with a half used packet of Players Weights cigarettes, and finally three more live bullets.

'So', thought Klein, 'I now have four bullets to take on the might of the British army. This should be plenty,' He took the trouble to carefully pull the eiderdown up under the chin of the young man, and then said his goodbyes to the three corpses. He had done the right thing. He was after all, deep down, a decent sort of man. He had only done what he had to do to defend himself. Yes, he got a little bit of pleasure from the killing of the old couple, but not as much as he had done from defeating the strong young soldier. It was always these combat situations, where he obtained the maximum satisfaction. He began to fantasise about Ingrid once again.

Klein returned to the kitchen, and picked up the soldier's small haversack, that was still lying on the floor. It contained a small flask, and a pair of leather gloves. There was also a black rubber, 'Ever Ready' torch. There was too, a small, first aid kit. He felt that he could utilise all of these items. He started by boiling the kettle on the stove. He made tea in the old porcelain teapot, and let it brew. He poured a small amount of milk into the flask and then filled it to the brim with the freshly brewed hot liquid. He screwed the lid down hard, and returned the flask to the canvass haversack. He tried on the gloves. They were a near perfect fit. He checked the torch and it was working fine, showing a bright light. Again he was forced to think about his deceased commanding officer's opinion on these things. He simply would not allow torches to be used. This was because any glint of light had the potential to be seen from a long distance. Multiply this by forty and you have a veritable powerhouse of glitter. This though was different. He could use this prudently, and if approached in the dark, he could shine it towards the person challenging, and take the focus away from his own face.

Finally, he took out a gauze pad and a cotton bandage, from the first aid kit. The hole in his throat had congealed by now, but he knew the importance of keeping the wound clean. It would speed the healing process, and would look a little less obtrusive if he were to be challenged. He took the newspaper wrapped sandwiches from the pantry, and stuffed them into the small haversack.

It was time to go. He unbolted the back door and walked across the fields to the North West. He had no intention of deliberately using the roads and lanes, but if he was forced to, he was sure that he would be able to get away with it. The first hurdle that he encountered was Pett lane. All was quiet, and he slipped across the muddy road and back into the fields. It had finally stopped raining but everything was still very wet. He trudged on and after another fifteen minutes he was crossing Watermill lane. He had seen nobody and heard no sounds. He was now on the outskirts of Icklesham village. He had targeted a point to the west of the village, where he would be able to watch the main road, and hide out until the troops arrived. This was Broad Street Wood. He knew the area, because as a team, they had traversed this territory several times on their way to and from Pett Level.

He had arrived at the spot on the main road, where he would have to cross over to reach his new woodland hide. He could not have known, but a couple of hundred yards up the road, back towards the village was a home guard team, of a dozen soldiers. They were patrolling the village, and were on a state of high vigilance. They had been told about the possibility of an armed German airman, and were not about to let anything untoward happen on their watch. Klein had watched and waited for several minutes.

There was no sound of approaching traffic, no sounds of people talking, and no lights. The people of these villages and towns strictly observed the black out regulations. Unfortunately for Klein, the moment that he chose to sprint across the road, was the moment that the Home Guard team had finished their 'pee and fag break', taken just off the road, on the edge of a field. They had started to march again in a westerly direction. Klein had only just bolted out when he heard the shouted, 'Halt, who goes there?'

There was nothing for it now but to keep on running. The home guard team were all fairly fit men, and given Klein's injuries, he wasn't as quick over the ground as he normally would be. He managed to get along a short track towards the wooded area, but the dozen men had gained on him in that time. Again he heard a shout. 'This time it was, 'stop or we will fire.' Klein hadn't got the faintest idea what had been shouted, but he soon got the idea, when a salvo of gunfire opened up from something like, only fifty yards behind him. He kept running, as he knew that once he had reached the protection of the trees, he would have more chance of taking a couple of these men out. Once again, he was brought down to earth with a bang. This was a British gun that he was carrying. He had exactly four bullets. He was hardly in a position to return fire.

A few trees loomed up ahead of him, and he made an instant decision. He would stop behind the first tree and use all the ammunition that he had. This would at least pin his pursuers down and spread them out, for a short time. He would ditch the rifle and the haversack and then focus on escaping through the rest of the trees. This might buy him half a minute, before the following team had spread and moved in, in a pincer movement. The action worked well. He through himself to the ground as soon as he got into the cover of the first few trees and the rifle was up to his shoulder. He reached into his pocket and found the three spare bullets. He had played with the gun a little, to get the feel of it, back at the farmhouse, so he knew that it was a single shot operation. He saw the movement of bodies, still quite tightly grouped, and took aim. He fired the first shot and watched the group spread, and drop to the ground. As rapidly as he could, he reloaded and fired the remaining bullets in their general direction.

With that, he was gone. He slithered over the ground, in an effort to remain unseen for as long as possible. Once he had passed a few more trees and the wood thickened slightly, he was up and running. He heard more shouts, but at least from a slightly further distance again now. The gunfire started again. He was pitching forward, through the trees and occasionally a bullet would smack into a trunk quite close to him. He found some additional strength, and as luck would have it, he did not trip. The nights of covering large distances with no lights at all had helped greatly in this respect. Also, all of that had been done with a heavy load.

Klein was dodging left and right as he continued to run, smashing into branches and rustling through heavy bracken. Still he remained upright. Although he didn't feel that the soldiers following him were gaining on him, he had to do something to lose them. They were not about to give up the chase, and an occasional bullet still whistled past him. He started to drop downhill and could see the gleaming surface of a pond not too far ahead. His left shoulder was suddenly hit with what felt like a sledgehammer. It was burning as if a red hot poker had been stabbed into his flesh. The bullet had entered his upper back to the left of his spine and Klein knew straight away that he had taken one. He did not slow, he was running like a machine now, suddenly he pitched to the right, changing the predictable element of his run. He reached the edge of the pond, which happened at this spot, to be shielded by a thicker clump of trees, as well as being edged by a steeper section of bank here. There were also many reeds in this part of the pond.

He knew that hiding under the water was his only chance. He was also aware that any ripples left in the water, after he had submerged, would be an instant pointer to where he was hidden. The training that he had done with the Waffen SS had covered this aspect of concealment many times. He had no breathing tube, and no time to find one. He lay with his back on the ground, with his feet already in the water. As he gently slid his body forwards, into the cold waters of the pond, he grabbed at a handful of long grass and reeds, which he stuffed into his mouth. He clenched his teeth and opened his lips to breathe. Finally he felt the cold mud of the bank sliding behind his neck. Now his face was lying level with the surface of the water. He instinctively wrapped his ankles around the base of the reeds, in order to anchor himself and prevent his body from floating up. Similarly he reached out and down with his arms, and grabbed the base of the reeds.

The mouthful of grass, would from above, simply look like a clump of something growing through the reeds. He was aware of noises coming from his left. He heard the sounds, but could not translate. 'Where the fuck is he?' he heard. 'Search this pond thoroughly. He can't be anywhere else. You six, get back to the edge of the wood, to make sure he hasn't concealed himself in the bracken. Spread out, he can't be more than fifty yards back, we saw him run out of the trees.'
Meanwhile, Klein had managed to pull his breathing back to normal.

The other men started to walk around the perimeter of the pond. They stared into the reedy shallows, as they slowly made their way from one side to the other. A torch was flashed around by one of the men. They were determined to find the fugitive. Klein was aware of what was happening, but from now on, he could only rely upon the ingenuity of his original reactions.

The rest of the men had returned by now and joined in the search, almost duplicating the area already covered by their comrades. Klein could do nothing more. A group of the home guard soldiers came round to the exact spot where he lay. He could see upwards through the water that a couple of them had stopped right above him. He continued to shallow breathe, although now even more controlled. He was aware of some low talk, and he was also aware of a simultaneous movement by both of these men. The next moment, he was aware of warm water, pouring all around his face. He realised instantly that these men were having a piss, literally into his face. He did nothing. The men eventually refastened their fly buttons and moved away. The torch was switched on again just two yards from where he lay. He thought about Zimmermann and the 'shit' incident on Toot Rock. He had got off lightly by comparison. At least his neck and face felt a little warmer.

He watched as the British team reassembled only a few yards away from his submerged position. He heard a few more sentences that he was unable to understand, and then was aware of all the men lifting their rifles to their shoulders, and discharging then into the lake. Generally speaking, most of the shots hit the water towards the centre of the pond, but they had covered a wide spread area, nevertheless. The Home Guards hung around for a few more moments and then departed. They walked back in the direction they had come from, with reloaded rifles pointing ahead of them, just in case.

Klein was beginning to feel cold again. He rolled over and silently began to haul himself back out onto the bank. He was cold, but he was also a natural survivor. He knew that he must get moving rapidly in order to bring his body temperature back to normal. He now had no possessions or kit of any sort to carry. He again started to run in the direction north of the pond. He was sure that the British team would not have given up that easily, and felt that for now, he should get well clear of the area. He kept running and this time, the only pain he was aware of was the bullet wound to his shoulder. 'Maybe,' he thought, 'if I can keep getting wounded a little lower each time, eventually the pain will disappear from out of my left toe.'

The thought of this situation amused him, despite the terrible injuries that had already been inflicted upon him. He was still pushing quite hard and covering the ground reasonably quickly. He was also still very cold but knew that he could warm up while he was putting a sensible bit of distance between him and his would be captors. He could return to an area further up the road early tomorrow morning. In the scheme of things, he would ultimately meet up with his fellow countrymen. They would then take care of his wounds.

He was approaching the railway line and had the idea that he could cover a large distance in a short time, if he ran along this for a while. It would throw the Tommy bastards off the scent as well. He climbed over the railway fence and dropped down the bank towards the tracks. This was a single track railway that he had crossed many times before. 'Never alone though,' he suddenly thought. He hit the track running and soon took on a loping pace that saw him covering the ground quite quickly, considering he was literally hopping from one sleeper to the next. He ran for twenty minutes or so, by which time, his shoulder was starting to seize up, and although he was slightly warmer, he was in a great deal of general discomfort and pain.

He now realised that he was approaching a station. It was looming up on the right hand side, and there was a road bridge across the track, dead ahead. He climbed up onto the platform, and continued to run up the ramp that led out to the road. He reached the small country lane which was in fact quite a steep hill. He looked down the hill to the right and could see no signs of life. To the left, he could make out a terrace of a dozen or so cottages, situated on the right hand side of the hill, only a hundred metres up from the station bridge. It was now about nine o'clock in the evening. Klein had estimated that it must be 21.00 hours or thereabouts, and this suited his plan perfectly.

He untied the by now, very dirty bandage from his throat. This exposed once again, the still raw wound. He was beginning to shake slightly. Although the evening was not quite as cold as the previous ones, he was still in a much weakened state, and he had once again been subjected to a long time, submerged in cold water, as well as having sustained another serious wound. As he made his way up the hill, he took the decision to knock on the first door where there appeared to be any sign of life. It seemed as though nobody in England used lights in their houses, but it may be that they were observing blackout precautions, the same as they did in the fatherland. He would simply point at his wounded throat and shoulder and silently refuse any help from outside sources. Once inside, he would be able to assess the situation and work out, whether he needed to kill the occupants, or whether he may be able to fool them into believing that he was a wounded British Soldier. His mind was beginning to play tricks with him. He had a light headed feeling, almost the same as when he had gone out on nights in his home town of Munich, and drunk too much beer.

He started to sway from side to side and staggered towards the front door of one of the middle cottages. He knew very little English, but he was aware what the word, 'Help' meant. He leant against the door and noticed a small brass knocker, shaped like a dog. He tapped on the door lightly. He did not want to make any neighbours aware that this house had a visitor.

Inside, Faye Hawkins had dozed off on the settee. She had been listening to the BBC news and had meant to go to bed immediately it ended, but tiredness had got the better of her. She had fallen into a sound sleep. In the background, Benny Goodman's band music was playing softly. In her dreams, she was walking along with Peter, hand in hand on a Sussex country lane. They looked at each other and smiled. Peter then stared into her eyes, and said, 'Please don't ever love anyone else.'

Faye was then aware of a tapping sound coming from beyond her dreams, and roused to the sound of another light knock at her front door. 'Who the blazes can this be at this time of night?' she thought to herself. She quickly stood up and went to the door. The living room light was still on, and the sight that confronted her as she pulled the door open was pitiful. It was a soldier with a nasty wound to his throat, and also she could see as he staggered forward into the house, a large blood stain across his left shoulder. 'Oh you poor boy,' she said to Klein. 'What on earth has happened to you?' At this point Klein looked into her eyes and whispered, 'Help'.

Faye quickly assessed the situation. This poor man was clearly badly hurt. He needed to get to hospital as fast as possible. She helped him across to the settee, which was still warm from her own body lying on it. She said, 'I don't have a telephone here, but Mr Morris up the road does, and he won't mind me borrowing it to call for an ambulance.' Let me get my coat on, and we'll soon have you comfortable in hospital.' She went across to the coat stand which was placed near to the front door, and Klein watched as she took her red coat from the peg. He now understood what she had said to him. He looked at her and shook his head violently. He forced himself up from the settee and took the coat from her, as gently as he could, and returned it to the stand. He then returned to the settee. 'You must let me help you, said Faye.' The soldier looked at her pleadingly, and pointed to his throat wound, pointed at Faye, and then back to his throat. 'I'm not a nurse, my love. I can wash your wounds and dress them, but you really need to get to hospital, very soon. She came back to him and touched his neck lightly. She lifted his head so that he stared up to the light in the middle of the room. She now realised that his clothes were wet through and he was again shaking quite violently.

She couldn't begin to think how the soldier's injuries had occurred, but her own husband was a soldier, and if he ever needed help, then she hoped that someone would go to his aid. She said, 'I will get some scissors and a bandage, and some warm water.' Klein did not know once again what she had said, but felt that she was going to help him. She pointed to the next room and then went into the kitchen, and started to gather the necessary bits. Klein listened intently for any sign that she might try to leave the house via the back door, but was satisfied that she was indeed, sorting things out. He also heard her fill the kettle, and heard the striking of a match, as she lit the gas on the stove.

Faye returned to the room and thought about the soaking wet clothes that he was wearing. Again she spoke, 'I am going to find some of Peter's clothes for you,' and started up the staircase. At first Klein was nervous, but then he thought that she couldn't escape from an upstairs window, and that she seemed, to be wanting to help him. She returned downstairs with a large bath towel, and various pieces of her husband's clothing. She put them onto the arm of the settee, and patted the pile, whilst looking into Klein's eyes. She then returned to the kitchen.

Klein was quickly stripped off, and dried. He started to put on the selection of clothes that she had left for him. When she returned to the room she was carrying a bowl which she placed down onto the table which stood alongside the settee. She went back to the kitchen and brought back a strange looking bottle, which held a light brown liquid. The bottle was marked 'Dettol'. Klein thought it was probably whisky. She also had a white flannel, which she dropped into the bowl of hot water. He had not finished dressing. In fact the process of taking off his wet boots and clothes, followed by towelling himself dry, had tired him greatly. Again he felt quite light headed. He had managed to get underpants and a vest and trousers on and then was forced to lie down again on the settee.

Faye looked across, and began to feel desperately sorry for this man. She had noticed that he was quite ugly, but that wasn't his fault. In any case, she wasn't looking for a lover, she just noticed, that was all. Also, she thought that the pain that he must be in would be horrendous. This alone would not show someone in their best light. She went over to him, now clutching a small, wooden first aid box. She sat on the floor in front of him and lifted his ankles, one at a time, in order to slip Peter's socks onto his bare feet. The man looked at her gratefully. She grasped his hands and helped him to sit up. She made him lean forward, so that she could check his shoulder wound.

She opened the bottle of Dettol, and it quickly became obvious to Klein, that this was a disinfectant, and not the whisky that he had expected. Faye carefully dabbed away with the wetted flannel, to his blood stained shoulder, and at one point, the soldier gasped quietly with pain. She apologised for hurting him, and carried on. She quickly realised that this was a gunshot wound. The round hole in his shoulder was clearly visible in the centre of a large mauve bruise. She applied a large gauze pad directly over the area, and tied this down with a long bandage which she cut from a roll. She had attended first aid classes when she was younger and she knew that she must wrap the bandage around his chest and over his shoulder to stop it from slipping.

She now carefully pushed him back onto the settee and once again gently lifted his chin, to inspect the very angry wound to his throat. He looked straight into her eyes and whispered, 'Ingrid'. His eyes had become sleepy looking. 'No dear, my name is Faye,' she replied. It suddenly struck Faye that although the name had been whispered, there was something strange about the soldier's pronunciation of the word. The 'R' did not sound quite right. 'You *are* English, aren't you?' she queried. The soldier continued to stare back at her, and again whispered, 'Ingrid'. This time she was even more certain that there was something adrift. The soldier's eyes were fixed on hers and she started to feel more than a little uncomfortable.

Klein suddenly grabbed her shoulders and pulled her towards him. 'Ingrid, Ingrid, meine liebe. He wrapped his arms around her and tried to kiss her. She started to pull away from him, but the man had suddenly found new strength. She now knew for certain that he was a foreigner. He started to rub her breasts with one hand, while the other arm remained wrapped tightly around her waist. She could not move. 'Wir werden Liebe nun,' was the whispered sound from the soldier's mouth. Faye was terrified now. 'What if this man is a German?' she thought. She had only one option left, and that was to scream at the top of her voice.

The elderly widower, who lived next door on one side, was particularly deaf. She knew that the also elderly couple, who lived on the other side, had gone out for the evening. She filled her lungs with air and let out a high pitched scream, which she maintained for as long as she could, before Klein's hands were around her throat, and she screamed no more. She was now, back in the country lane with Peter, once more. She stared back into his eyes and said, 'No, I won't ever love anyone else'.

There was no stopping Klein. He was now just like a wild animal. He had not realised that the woman was dead. He just thought that she had become submissive, and was now ready for sex. He was almost delirious, but at the same time, he was completely aroused. He had to make love to 'his Ingrid'. He seemed unaware that his woman was totally unresponsive. He kissed her and told her that he loved her. He spoke loving words to her the whole time that he was raping her. He eventually fell asleep with his arms wrapped around her naked, dead body.

Chapter 21

Major Wicks was very surprised to see an attractive blonde girl at the wheel of the police car. It was duly waiting for him as he came off the ferry boat by the Market Stores. The Wolseley saloon had been adapted to carry a large loudspeaker on its roof. Inside, there was a square microphone clipped to the dashboard in front of the passenger seat. A large rotary switch, bearing the legend, 'ON' and 'OFF' was next to it.

'Well, it seems that my day is getting better by the minute,' said the smooth talking officer. 'Dennis Wicks, army major, how do you do?' He extended his hand towards his beautiful driver for the day. She took his hand and replied, 'My name is Cherry Watson. I am very pleased to meet you. I believe that I will be taking care of you for the day.'
'I sincerely hope so,' replied the young major, with a twinkle in his eye. Dennis had his script in his hands and together they agreed the format for the mobile broadcast. Basically, Cherry would drive very slowly through the local villages, while Dennis repeatedly read from the script that he had prepared earlier, with the help of Major Jennings. The whole process was to be repeated twice more, later on in the day.

'Fairlight first, my beautiful young driver, if you please.' Cherry slowly drove off and then selected second gear, which she continued to drive in for the entire journey, keeping a very low throttle setting. Dennis fiddled with the switch to the microphone, which he then pretended to switch on. Within the confines of the car, he appeared to make the following announcement. 'I, Major Dennis Wicks, do honestly declare that I am sitting next to the sexiest driver in the entire police force of Great Britain. I may not be able to control myself, if her skirt rises up any higher over her lovely thighs, while she is driving.' Cherry's reaction was firstly one of disbelief. Her mouth had dropped open slightly, as she heard him 'broadcast' this message. Then when she realised that he had been playing a joke on her, she smiled and said, 'Well Major, just how much further up my thighs does my skirt have to ride, before you lose control?'

Major Wicks retorted, 'I believe that I have already come to that point.'
'Well, if you have *already come* to that point, then I can assume that I can feel safe for the rest of our time together.'
'That just depends on how safe you want to feel.'
'I want to feel, *alright*.' The inflection that she put on the single word, said it all to the young major.
'We must see how much time we have left between our broadcasting rounds, and then we can see how we *feel about* each other.'

Their vocal repartee was making Dennis smile. They were clearly 'birds of a feather', and he was already looking forward to getting to grips with this fascinating and beautiful, young woman. With that, the major thought that he had better get on with the immediate task in hand.

'Good morning. This is a message on behalf of the British army. The commanding officer at the Toot Rock coastal battery wishes to apologise for the noisy manoeuvres that occurred last night. These exercises were an essential part of our training, and will not be repeated. There is no need to be alarmed, and once again we apologise for any loss of sleep they may have caused.'

Fairlight, Ore, Guestling, Icklesham, Winchelsea and finally Pett Village all received the message loud and clear. The 0.800 hours round had been completed by just after 10.00 hours. 'The problem that we appear to have now, Miss Watson, is that we have nearly four hours to kill.'
'What are you suggesting?' asked the blonde driver, with a cheeky smile.
'I don't know about you, but I was part of the exercises that we are now apologising for, and I am very tired. I do know a place where we could get our heads down for a while.'
'That sounds lovely, I like to get my head down now and then, especially when I am supposed to be on duty.' At this point, they had reached the top end of Chick hill. 'Turn round here,' said Dennis. He pointed to the bus turning point, and the young driver skilfully drove beyond it, reversed back into it, and then drove off back in the direction of the centre of the village.

They pulled up outside the Two Sawyers, and Dennis rapped upon the door of the inn, while Cherry carefully checked every door of the police vehicle, making sure that it was secure. Derek, the long suffering landlord, opened the door and the young major smiled a knowing smile at him. 'Any chance of a bottle of fizz and a room, for a few hours?' asked the Major. The landlord looked back to see the beautiful blonde woman in police uniform, walking up the pathway, and immediately agreed to Dennis's request.

Derek handed Dennis the key to room number 4, and said he would bring the bottle and a couple of glasses up shortly. The landlord watched as the two disappeared up the dark staircase, and couldn't help noticing the beautiful pair of legs that the lady was sporting. 'Lucky bastard', he thought, as he went to the cellar to find some champagne. Two minutes later, he was tapping on the door of number 4, drinks tray balanced on the other hand. The young major opened the door, wearing just his khaki army shorts. He took the tray from Derek, before the landlord could look any further into the room. The two clinked glasses together, and after a few sips, they jumped on each other. The enjoyment of the sex act was only superseded by the dreamlike sleep that the Major enjoyed afterwards. Just before he dropped off, he apologised to Cherry, and assured her that there would be better to come. 'I'm not complaining, Major. Let's look at it as though that was starters, and the main course is still to come.'

The pair slept like babies for three hours, when Dennis awoke feeling much refreshed. Cherry still lay sleeping and he couldn't help staring at her beautiful face and body. It was almost as though she had caught his thought train, because she quickly opened her eyes, and smiled at him. 'I can see that you are still eager,' she whispered to him. After finishing a whole glass of champagne each, they started again. The large 'Smiths' alarm clock on the bedside cabinet gave the time as 1.30 pm. We have got to be back on the road again soon, said Dennis. 'Well, we had better make best use of the time we have got left,' replied Cherry.

At just before 14.00 hours the pair were back in the police car, but not before Dennis had assured the landlord that they would be back in a couple of hours for the second part of their little adventure. 'Don't bother to make the bed, Derek. We have a small job to do and then we'll be back again by around four pm.

The whole journey through the villages was once again completed, without incident. They were soon back in room number 4, where they finished the now less than fizzy drink. Neither seemed at all bothered that they had already put in two 'performances'. This time the lovemaking was much more prolonged, with both of them taking time to explore the other's likes and fantasies to the full.

Eventually, Cherry suggested they try to get another nap in before their final session on the road, scheduled to start in another two hours. This they did, and the alarm clock was set for 6.30 pm. They were able to freshen up, before the last round of work for this day. At about 20.45, the major climbed out of the passenger seat of the Wolseley saloon, having spent the last ten minutes locked in a passionate embrace with his new lover. They agreed that they would meet up again soon, and exchanged their work telephone numbers.

'Looks like you've done okay for yourself today, Major.' said one of the friendly guards on the gate, who had noticed the goings on in the police car. 'Yes, it's been very hard, all day' he replied, with a smile on his face. The ferry took him back to the rock, and soon he was able to meet with his fellow officers, at the big house. It was strange to look around the living room of the house. It had been cleaned up a little, since the Germans had attacked it the previous night. There were burn marks on the wallpaper and some chunks of ceiling plaster missing. At one point, along the window wall, there was a horizontal line of bullet scars.

'Had a good day, old boy?' asked Major Jennings. 'You look absolutely shagged out. I bet you can't wait to get a meal and some beer. It's on its way. I thought I would wait for you, so we could eat together. Major Roberts will join us as well, if you don't mind.'
'That was very good of you old chap, and you are right, I am completely shagged out. It was a long day. I did manage to get my head down, in between stints though.'

While the two shared a glass of whisky, Major Jennings recounted the course of events from his day. The mass signing had worked out okay, albeit that it was broken into several segments, as the searching troops arrived back at the rock. There were no problems from any one of the troops stationed here, they all signed without argument. That process took until about midday. I was then free to telephone the local rag, with the statement that we prepared earlier. Christ that seems like two days ago.'

'After lunch, I interviewed a few likely candidates for the 'round the village' chat. I have picked out a dozen men for the task. In fact, it has already started to be fed out to the local populous. The chaps went out to the Post office, the Market Stores, 'Auntie' Broad's tea rooms, and the Two Sawyers. Hardly anything is better than word of mouth, to create the picture that you need to paint.'

At that point, Major Roberts entered the room and took over the dialect. 'We had the engineers out by 14.00 hours, and by 16.00 hours you wouldn't know that there had been a huge explosion out on the sea wall. They have done a tremendous job. At the same time, all of the front windows, have been repaired and in fact most of the seaward ones as well. The remainder will be finished by mid morning tomorrow. As for the damaged brickwork at number nine, George Dobson has been on the 'phone and has managed to find some matching bricks, at a yard near Norwich. They will be collected by one of our drivers, tomorrow. He left here at around 15.00 hours today, and will be on their doorstep as they open up tomorrow morning. We have put some boards against the damaged wall in order to conceal the damage, and meanwhile, George has chopped out the broken bricks in readiness for the replacements tomorrow.'

'We erected a marquee at the rear of the barrack room and we had a team of fifty men, pull back a vast mound of earth from the edge of the hill. We collected thirty four bodies for burial, and dropped them into the pit. The vast pile of earth and stones was then piled back on top of them, and the camp parson said a few words.'

'This just left the badly burnt four. We searched their pockets and it would appear from the uniform of one, that he held the rank of Major General. 'Gruppenfuhrer', they call it. We also found a couple of interesting items.' With that, Major Roberts pulled an English half-penny coin from his shirt pocket and passed it to the other two. 'We found this in his trouser pocket, and could not quite work out why he would have been carrying it.'

'Also, there was a letter found in his tunic pocket that would appear to have been hand written by Adolf Hitler. It was badly scorched around the edges. I'm afraid that I can't show you this, as Mr. Churchill requested that I send it to him. We sent it with a dispatch rider to London, this morning. The PM has organised for the burnt bodies to be collected, tomorrow morning, by of all things, a London bus. We will ferry them out to one of our trucks, and meet the bus at Winchelsea. There is a lay-by with no houses close to it, where we should be able to transfer the bodies out of the way of prying eyes. They are all well wrapped up by the way. We didn't think the driver would be able to make it back up Chick hill and could even struggle going up Battery hill, so we have to take the risk of making the transfer.'

'I haven't the faintest idea why they are sending a London bus, but there will be a couple of RAF chaps, one driving and one presumably to make sure that no bugger tries to board the bus on it's way back to RAF Northolt. I believe they are going to drop the bodies, with parachutes attached, from a Lancaster bomber, right over Berlin. There will be a personal message from Mr. Churchill to Adolf Hitler, attached to the body of the Gruppenfuhrer.'

The other two officers seemed intrigued by the Major's words. They discussed the various aspects of his revelations, and Major Wicks asked, 'How come you have the Prime Minister's ear then, Gordon?'

'That's quite a long story, Dennis. Let's just say that I was able to help him out once, long before this war, and he has been grateful ever since.'
'Now I'm even more intrigued,' retorted the well spoken Major Wicks. 'You've got to tell us more.'

At that moment, Lieutenant Colonel Burgess entered the room, and took over the discussion. 'The best news that I have received, is that hardly any invasion craft got further than six miles into the channel. Oddly enough, the RAF sunk five of them, all ablaze as they went down, including the troop barges that they were towing behind them. None of the others had left port at that stage. We cannot yet work out why these stray five were left to go it alone. The last reports were that all enemy troops had disembarked from the barges at every mother port.'

'That is great news, Sir,' said Major Jennings. 'What about RAF casualties, though?'
'Bloody marvellous news there too, chaps. One 'spitfire got shot up quite badly, but the pilot managed to get back to Blighty, before he had to jump out, somewhere north of Folkestone. The rest of them sustained a few scratches and bullet holes, but they will all fly again.'

'The Prime Minister is compiling a letter to Adolf Hitler, with a paragraph devoted to advising him on best practice for invasion tactics. I'd like to be a fly on the wall, when he reads that one. There could be a few Nazi words spoken, if you'll pardon the pun.'
'I wouldn't want to pardon the Hun, Sir,' joked Major Wicks.

'Now gentlemen, Is there anything else that we have missed, or have we covered off everything that we are aware of that needed to be actioned?'
'Just the missing Kraut, Sir. Has anybody spotted him yet?'
'Rather embarrassing, that one, I'm afraid. No sign of the bugger at all.'
Two minutes later, a corporal ran into the room and declared that the local Home Guard had chased and shot at a man only a few minutes ago.
'I will put the call through to you here, Sir.'

Burgess grabbed the phone, and listened intently. 'Where exactly did he disappear, then?' he demanded. He sounded annoyed. 'I will get some troops up there to assist with the search. I assume that someone is still guarding the pond? My men will be there in fifteen minutes.'

'Fucking Home Guard have lost the bastard, I'm afraid, chaps. The odd thing is that he returned fire, three or four times, and then ditched the rifle. It turns out that it was a BSA the same as our units have been issued with. I hope one of those buggers hasn't lost their rifle, or they will be well in the shit.'

'Are all of our chaps accounted for?' asked Major Roberts. 'I had better get on to the area commander and ask him to do a check on his men. You have to bear in mind Sir that the Home Guard are not professionals, so if they have shot at him and he has got away, it isn't really that surprising. The important thing is that we get out there and find the bastard before he does any damage.'

'I couldn't agree more. I will ask Captain Johnson to take all of his men up to Icklesham and they can fan out from the area that the Kraut was last seen. We will drop more men at the furthest possible points for a running man to reach and they can act as backstops for the search.'

The Canadian officer was summoned, and quickly briefed. It was decided to take three of the trucks, one for each compass point except south. A first search team of thirty men would be dropped at Icklesham. Then the trucks would head north, east and west, for a distance of three miles. The remaining troops would then fan out as far as possible, making sure to cover rivers, railways and country paths, which a man on the run would be most likely to use. The ordnance survey maps were laid out across the table and agreed drop off points established. The Captain left the room to assemble and brief his men. Very soon, one hundred and twenty armed men were ferried across the lake to the Market Stores. Army trucks were started and driven away, one by one up Chick hill.

The retired army captain, who met Captain Johnson, was very succinct. 'The man was spotted, as he crossed Rye road. We had all stopped for a pee break, and just resumed our patrol, when we saw him, only two hundred yards in front. We challenged him and he bolted, straight across the orchard into the woodland. We fired on him, he fired back. We hit the ground and spread apart. By the time we had advanced to his position, he had moved on again, gaining some ground. He left this rifle behind and it looks like one of ours. He was last seen approaching this pond. We searched it thoroughly and for good measure, shot the fuck out of the middle of it. Nothing surfaced, so we assumed he had somehow got further. Sorry Captain Johnson, we did our best.'

'That's okay, my English pal. You couldn't have done any more. Where do you and your boys think that he may have headed?'
'Bloody hard to tell, old man,' replied the veteran soldier. 'The younger members of our platoon, ran for ten minutes along the most obvious

escape runs, knowing full well they were not going to be picked off with a rifle. They assumed that the man would have just wanted to put some distance between us and him so they stuck to open tracks. No sign of the bastard at all. Where do we go from here?
'The men that I have with me will start a forward search, while the rest of them in the trucks will put in some distance, in the hopes of providing a safety net, which he will not be able to avoid.'

The Canadians started to spread out, covering the ground quickly, and were soon gone from view. After a period of three and a half hours, the chasers had once again met up with the catchers, but with no result. The 'ring of steel' then slowly closed back in around the start point. Captain Johnson called in to the base, at Toot Rock. 'I'm sorry, Lieutenant Colonel, but we just can't figure out where the blazes he has gone. We could sure use those dogs from up at Tongs House.'

'Have you got anything from the Kraut that we could use as scent for the hounds, though?' enquired Burgess.
'We have the rifle, and the Home Guard guys found a small haversack, with some sandwiches and stuff inside.'
'Good enough, I will arrange for a pair of dogs and handlers to be up there in half an hour.'

After a number of false starts, involving the perimeter of the pond, the dogs finally picked up a trail. They ran around in all directions but ultimately they kept returning to a straight path, through the woodlands, wetlands and open fields. After about an hour, they had reached the railway fence. At this point, one of the handlers noticed a small piece of fabric, attached to the barbed wire that ran along the top of the fence. He also saw that the barbed wire had been pressed downwards at that spot.

The twenty soldiers charged with following the dog handlers soon cut through the diamond mesh fence, and it was not long before both animals were heading along the track in a westerly direction. Again, progress was slow, with the dogs frequently stopping. Then once again their noses were pressed to the stone filled ground around the railway sleepers, and they were once more onto the scent.

The first signs of daylight were beginning to show, as the troops approached Doleham Halt station. Again there was much confusion with the two Alsatians. One carried on along the track sniffing his way under the road bridge, while the other had jumped up onto the platform, and started to work his way up the ramp towards the road. Eventually the first dog retraced his tracks and jumped up onto the platform at exactly the same spot as the other one. Soon they were sniffing closely together and running around across the road bridge.

Captain Johnson looked up the hill and saw a terrace of cottages, running up the right hand side. A vehicle approached, and soon the men realised that it was actually a police car. The two police officers stopped alongside the team, and both got out of the car. 'I suppose you men are searching for the German airman?' said the sergeant. Captain Johnson responded with 'We sure are officer. Have you got any ideas?'
'Not exactly, but I have to warn you and your men that this is no ordinary ditched pilot. We received a report of a missing home guard, early last night. His wife had become concerned when he didn't return home. She then checked with the brickworks and found out he had not been to work yesterday. It seems he was in the habit of visiting his friends at a farm near Pett, when he clocked off from night patrol. He would drop in for a cup of tea and a chat, early morning. Then he would head straight off to work, at the brickworks.'

'When we got to the farm, everything was in darkness, and eventually we smashed the glass in the back door, and walked in to the scene of a massacre. The home guard as well as the farmer and the farmer's wife, were all dead. The bodies had been arranged in the big double bed of the main bedroom. The old couple had apparently been strangled, and there was evidence of a brutal fight with the home guard. Hard to tell exactly how he died at this stage, but it wasn't pleasant.'

'We have been assigned to join you in the search, because the man is now wanted on suspicion of murder. Is there anything we can do to help you and your men?'
'Well, I guess the more of us there are, the greater the chance of one of us spotting the bastard. It might be just as well that you guys *are* with us, because I don't think we would be able to hold back on an enemy who is prepared to kill old folks.'
'I couldn't agree more, Captain. We, as police officers, are supposed to uphold the law, but I reckon this one might fall down the cell steps a few times, before he stands trial.'

'Well sergeant, it sounds as if the dogs are on to something here, I wonder whether he could have hidden himself away in one of those houses up there.'
'I hope not,' replied the Sergeant. 'I wouldn't like to think what he might

have done to the householders here. He is obviously desperate, and capable of the most horrendous brutality. What I can't understand, is why he chose to do this? If he had just handed himself in, or surrendered when challenged, he would have been fed and watered, and treated fairly. His war would have been over, and he would effectively have been safe. Why would he go on the rampage, knowing there was no way out?'

'Yeah, that's a tricky one, a real bummer. Maybe he thinks he would be shot for dropping bombs over England.' The Captain knew that he could never reveal the real reason behind the missing German's behaviour, and quickly ordered his men to push forward behind the dogs, who were straining hard on their leashes. The two animals were now at the first cottage in the terrace. They pulled onwards, now with more direction and purpose. Their noses were moving fast across the ground in front of the short terrace. They sniffed hard around the gate of one of the middle cottages, and jumped up at the top rail, pushing the gate open with their joint weight. At this point, Captain Johnson ordered six of his men to go around to the rear of the terrace, to cover any attempts to escape. The police sergeant sent his constable with these men

Klein awoke to the sound of thumping on the front door. 'Open up, Mrs. Hawkins, we are concerned about you'. The thick curtains were still drawn across the window, and he quickly put on the clothes that the woman had given him. He now realised what had happened the previous night, and of course, that this woman was not his Ingrid, just a boring English housewife. He went to the kitchen and found a carving knife, which he slipped into his trouser pocket. He went to the back door, and immediately saw a policeman in uniform through the curtains covering the glass window section at the top of the door. Behind him, were five or six, armed soldiers. They had not yet seen him. He knew that finally, the game was up. His brain was once again clear. He felt no pain from his numerous injuries.

He was not going to go without a fight. He quickly severed the gas hose behind the stove, with the carving knife. He found a box of matches on the draining board, and waited as long as he could. The smell of gas had already filled the kitchen area and it was beginning to permeate the living room as well. The men at the front were still hammering at the door, and the ones at the back were now physically trying to break it down. Klein stood at the foot of the stairs, with one foot on the first tread, and matches in hand. He may yet have the opportunity to leap out of a top window, while the men below were distracted by the explosion.

Finally the back door slammed open, and at that moment, Klein struck the match and threw it forwards towards the kitchen. Voomp! The noise was louder than he could have imagined, and immediately his ears started ringing again. He was away up the stairs, and into the back bedroom. He Grabbed at the window handle and shoved the window open. He stood up on the ledge, and looked down to see three men pointing their rifles up at him. At that same moment, he could hear the sound of heavy footsteps coming up the stairs. He dived towards the three, with arms outstretched. Mid flight, a bullet struck him, to the side of his face. The soldiers had quickly spread, to avoid him landing upon them. That bullet was the only one that was needed.

Klein realised in mid flight, that the smaller of these soldiers was the little boy that he had killed, back in the woods. He looked up at the German, and said, 'Come with me Klein, you are in real trouble. The Gruppenfuhrer is furious with you for not wearing your uniform.' These were the last words the German heard. He landed on the ground at an angle, with such force that the impact immediately broke his neck. The three soldiers heard the loud crack. His body was lying on the ground with his backside stuck up in the air. His head was turned to one side as if he were trying to look back at the sky. His legs had somehow become trapped underneath him. It was an almost comical sight.

'I don't fancy takin' advantage of him, do either of you two?' one of the three said. 'I don't think so, Stanley,' replied another. 'His chin looks a bit too stubbly for my liking.'

Chapter 22

The policeman who had entered the house first, staggered back out into the garden. His face was blackened, and he complained that his ears were hurting him, but he appeared luckily not to be too badly hurt. The three soldiers who followed him in were holding their ears as well, but other than that, they seemed okay.

The team at the front door had burst in simultaneously, which effectively saved the house from being blown to pieces. The pressure of the blast was dissipated by the two open doors. The first man in was staggered back by the explosion, but eventually he got to the gas stopcock and turned it off. He saw the naked body of Faye Hawkins on the settee, and the police sergeant picked up the bath towel from the floor and laid it over her.

'What a tragedy,' spoke the officer. 'I knew Mrs. Hawkins, and her husband, Peter. The poor sod was only called up a few months back. Somebody is going to have to break the news to him. I know that he will be devastated. They've only been married a couple of years too.'

Captain Johnson quickly realised that this scenario would also need to be covered up. People were beginning to come out onto the road, attracted by the noise of the explosion, as well as the gunshot. He ran through the house and quietly ordered the three soldiers to bring the German's corpse inside, immediately. He had to take a chance with the two policemen, and hoped that Major Roberts would be able to explain to their commanding officer, why the truth could not be revealed.

He pulled the police sergeant to one side, and said. 'I cannot explain everything right now, but I have to tell you that I have the authority of Winston Churchill, to take control of this situation. Your area commander will confirm that this is so. Please just listen when I talk to these people.'
'But this is a civilian situation,' protested the sergeant.
'Partly it is, I will agree. However there are elements here that cannot be allowed to be revealed, especially the existence of the German. It is fortunate that he is wearing the uniform of the home guard. We may be able to salvage something from this.'

The first of the householders approached the police sergeant, and immediately, the Canadian stepped in. He politely explained that several of the men, including the two police officers, had been temporarily deafened, and were unable to communicate. 'What has happened is a gas explosion that has killed the poor lady who lived here.' He said authoritatively. 'My men and I were on patrol, just passing by, when we saw the two officers investigating the report of a gas leak. We offered our assistance to break into the property.'

'But my wife and I heard a gunshot, just after the sound of the blast,' said an elderly gentleman.' The Captain had to think quickly, and replied, 'Yes, I know, that was one of our boys, sadly he was first through the back door. He was clearly fatally injured, and as he staggered back out, still holding his rifle, he fell, and the weapon discharged itself. He was dead as he hit the ground.'

'Fuck me, I make a bloody good liar,' thought the Captain. The elderly householder went to speak with the other residents who had by now appeared, relaying the Canadian officer's words. Shortly, he returned to the officer, and asked, 'May I ask, Sir. Who reported the gas leak?' Again the Captain thought quickly, and responded, 'apparently, someone out walking their dogs early this morning, smelled gas. They didn't like to knock on the doors here, but reported it to the two policemen who were patrolling on the top road.'

'Just think, two people dead, just because the dog walker felt awkward about knocking on the door,' said the gentleman.
'It probably would have still ended with the same result, because the lady would have had to turn the lights on, to come downstairs, which would have surely ignited the gas.'
'It would have saved your soldier's life though.' The elderly gentleman was pensive. 'Yeah, sadly that may be the case, but the fact that we managed to bust open the front and back doors, managed to dissipate the force of the blast, which could have otherwise resulted in the two cottages either side, taking a hit too.'

Once again, the old man was pensive, and this time he asked, 'Do we know at this stage what caused the gas to ignite.'
'Nosey old bastard,' thought the Captain. This time though, one of his own men helped him out. 'I believe that the trigger for the explosion may have been the radio set, which has blown to pieces. It may have been left switched on last night, and the hot valves may have been enough to do it. As a radio engineer, I know that if a valve goes faulty, or the glass becomes cracked, it could effectively become as lethal as a naked flame.'

'Thank you very much,' replied the old man, who now seemed satisfied with the answers given. Once again, he reported his findings to the rest of the neighbours, who then returned slowly to their homes. Meanwhile, the real 'radio man' had set up communications with Lieutenant General Burgess at Toot Rock. Things there had gone into overdrive. The prime minister was informed of the capture and killing of the last German. He had discussed in detail with Major Roberts, the courses of action to take, and he himself, would speak with the local police commander.

Soon, an ambulance arrived to remove the bodies of Faye Hawkins and Klein. The ambulance was a military one, and the driver knew that the destinations for the two corpses would be very different. He arrived alongside the Market Stores at 07.30 hours and very discreetly, the now well wrapped body of the German, was carried across to the large rowing boat, and ferried back to Toot Rock. The driver then turned around and headed for Hastings general hospital's morgue.

Another two stories were prepared for this week's edition of the local newspaper. The first stated that a civilian woman, as well as a local home guard who attempted to rescue her, had been killed in a gas explosion at Doleham, earlier this week. The home guard was the popular, local young man, Private Albert Clarke. A close friend told the newspaper that Albert was a cheerful and friendly man, who would always lend a hand to anybody in need.

The terrible and tragic death of Mrs. Faye Eileen Hawkins, a young, recently married woman, whose husband was away with the British Army, was a terrible accident. Her husband Peter, had been informed by his commanding officer, and was returning home for the funeral. Her parents were said to be devastated. Her father, Edward was also a member of a local home guard unit, although he had not been on active duty with them for a few weeks.

The second story, also gas related, concerned the tragic deaths of an Icklesham farmer and his wife. Thomas and Lillian Robertson were found gassed at their farmhouse. It is believed that they may have fallen asleep having accidently left one of the gas burners switched on, on their kitchen stove. A spokesman for the South Eastern Gas Board, said, 'These two incidents were absolutely tragic, and although unrelated, they serve as a reminder of the need to use extreme caution, when dealing with town gas. All customers are reminded that it is essential to report any smell of leaking gas immediately, and to ensure that gas appliances are always turned off after use.' A local spokesman said that he believed that Mr. and Mrs. Robertson had no living relatives.

The Rye police had received a report from the coroner, which was extremely disturbing. The boy, and his dog, could not have been hit by a vehicle of any kind. Their rib cages had been smashed both front and back, something that could only happen if they had been crushed against a wall. There was no wall. Both the lad and his dog's neck had been broken. In the opinion of the coroner, this would have been almost impossible as they were clearly different heights. There was evidence of pine sap, impregnated heavily into the fur of the dog, on one side. The boy had similar traces, on his jacket, again on just one side. This side was where the major bruising had occurred.

The evidence gathered at the scene, did not tally either. There were no traces of blood on the road. The bumper was identified as being a 'rear', with no sign of sheared bolts or fixings of any kind. The same went for the AA badge. It would be extremely unlikely that this could have been knocked off of the vehicle, without any fixings still attached to it. The initial conclusions were that the two were killed elsewhere, and dumped on the roadway, with the intention of concealing the true cause of death. 'In short,' said the coroner to the Chief Inspector, 'we are looking at this becoming a murder enquiry.'

Thus, one more story was fed to the local paper, the next day. The Sussex County, Police Chief Superintendant had received a direct instruction 'from the very top'. He immediately made contact with Rye Police's Chief Inspector. 'I know that this is going to be a little difficult to concoct, Rodney. The fact is, we need to do a bit of a cover up regarding the recent car accident that didn't quite add up.'

Later that day, Sergeant Watkins once again appeared at Dot Sinden's home. 'Come in Dear,' said Dot. 'Have you got any news for me? Have you caught my son's killer? Sorry, Sergeant. I am forgetting my manners. I will put the kettle on.' As the two sat in Dot's living room, cups of tea in hand, the unfortunate police sergeant relayed the tale that he had been ordered to tell.

'Yes, Mrs. Sinden, we have found the man responsible for your son's death. His name was Gilbert Jacobson. I say *was,* because he is also now dead.' Dot's mouth fell open, as she gasped in surprise.
'On the day that he ran over your son and his dog, he had been drinking very heavily. His wife had died in London the day before, and he decided to drive to Camber, where he and his wife spent their honeymoon. I am not sure why he did this, maybe he was trying to turn back the clock, and relive some happier memories.'

'We cannot tell whether he knew that he had hit your son, or not. All we do know is that he later drove his car straight off the road and into a tree, in the Orpington area. He was killed outright, and the car was completely wrecked. We have identified the car from the bits that we found in the road, so we are certain that it was him. As this is a clear cut case, his body has been cremated at a London hospital, and his ashes scattered in woodlands, close to his home. The car remains were taken to a local scrap yard, and they will have been melted down today, as we felt it would be disrespectful to allow the scrap yard to sell any parts from it.'

'So he has escaped justice, and I can't even stand at his grave and beg him to tell me why he did it,' wailed Dot.
'I am not so sure about escaping justice, Mrs. Sinden. I am not a very religious man, but if we believe what it tells us in the Bible, he will have to face up to his crime, right now. Your young George, and his dog, will be at the Lord's side, when he hands out the punishment. He will be made to explain directly to your son why he did it. He will also have to witness all of the pain and heartache that his actions have caused. He will feel your pain, too. Take some strength from these thoughts, Mrs Sinden.'

'One more thing, I have got Rogue's body with me in the police car, all nicely wrapped up in a new blanket, and Constable Robinson has a shovel. We will happily bury him in the garden for you, if you would like us to. The lads at the station have clubbed together and had a small memorial plaque made.'

'You are all so kind, I am overwhelmed,' said Dot. 'I will put the kettle on again, but I would just like to touch Rogue once more before you lay him to rest.' With that, the sergeant walked out to the nervously awaiting constable, and asked him to bring the dog and the shovel round the back. Dot chose a 'nice spot', just next to the back fence, close to her rhododendron bush. The constable took off his jacket, rolled up his sleeves and the deep hole was quite swiftly dug out. Dot brought a tray of tea and some biscuits outside, and knelt down beside the body of her son's beloved animal. She touched the woollen material of the blanket, stroking it and speaking softly to the dead animal.

'You can put him down to rest now,' she smiled at the young policeman. Steadily, the earth was piled back in and trodden well down. 'We don't want any badgers coming along and digging him up again, now do we?' commented the kind, but rather thoughtless and inept constable. Dot didn't seem to notice his inappropriate remark. To her the young man was merely stating the obvious, and being practical. Once the two policemen were satisfied that the grave was secure, the younger went back to the car and returned with a large flat stone, which he laid over the top of the freshly dug soil.

Tears welled in Dot Sinden's eyes, as she read the inscription....

> 'Here lies Rogue, faithful and best friend to George Sinden'
> 'They entered the gates of heaven together, on 14th September 1940.'

Dot sniffed back the tears, as she said, 'Thank you and the other policemen, who contributed. I really appreciate what you have all done for me. I hope you will both be able to come to George's funeral as well?'
'We will be there if you would like us to be, but we wouldn't want to intrude,' said the senior man.
'I would be honoured if you can both attend.' The poor woman replied.

The two policemen were soon driving away from the Peasmarsh property. The sergeant was feeling very guilty at having to lie to the honest and innocent lady, who had just lost her beloved son. 'What's it all about then, Sarge?' asked the young constable. The sergeant considered for a moment, before replying. 'It was apparently some big wig, where the revealing of his true identity would have harmed the defence of the South Coast. The Sussex chief has asked me to talk to you about this. He has impressed upon me that this must never go any further. He also said that he has been watching your progress with interest, and will be looking to offer you promotion, some time in the future.'
'You know how these things work, Robbie. Least said, soonest mended.'

Meanwhile, at Toot Rock, news had come in of some suspicious looking bundles washed up on the beach at Winchelsea. This was nothing unusual, with the amount of shipping that was regularly being sunk. Many packages containing food and drink, and sometimes more valuable items, had been picked up by the troops patrolling the beaches, over the last few months. Sometimes they had caught local kids, especially one 'persistent little bugger', as they called him. His name was Lou Parsons, and he lived in a cottage near to the bottom of Chick hill. What he took away from the beach deprived the rest of the men their additional grub. The camp cooks had broken open many sacks of flour that had set as solid as a rock on the outside. Once opened, the outside shell could be cracked, revealing the perfectly preserved powder, within. Tins with their labels washed off presented a more unpredictable outcome.

Soon a team of ten men arrived at the far end of the beach, and were amazed to find the badly burned bodies of nine German soldiers. Although the hands and faces were badly charred, it was still possible to make out the uniforms and insignia, typical of the German army. Very soon, the bodies had been transported by barrow, along the sea wall. Eventually they were ferried back to the rock, where once again, the contents of their pockets, along with any identification tags, were removed.

The corpses were then wrapped in a similar fashion to the other four, and then stored alongside them in the officer's bunker. Mr. Churchill was contacted by Major Roberts, who was delighted to inform him that they now had a collection of thirteen, authentically burned German soldiers. They would be taken up to Winchelsea Town, to meet the London bus in the morning. 'Just as I thought, the tide has rolled them in and you may yet see more,' said the Prime Minister. 'This number will be perfect for my purposes, though. Well done, once again.' In a more sober tone, the wartime leader said, 'Remind me though what the total number of British deaths has been, Gordon.'

'It seems to have been contained at six. One of the corporals, here on the rock, a farmer and his wife, a local home guard, sadly a little boy, oh and his dog, and finally a local housewife.'

'And have you managed to operate the whitewash machine in every case?' enquired Mr. Churchill.
'Absolutely, Prime Minister. Thank you too for getting the police chief involved, he has come up trumps with a couple of very helpful strategies.'
'No problem, Gordon. Is Friday afternoon good for our little get together at number ten? I will keep a copy of my letter to Adolf. I think you may find it somewhat amusing. By the way, I have just received some relatively reliable intelligence. It would appear that as of today, Herr Hitler has called off operation Sealion, in favour of a trip to Russia.'

'That is definitely worth raising a glass to, Prime Minister. We will come up on the train, provided the Krauts haven't bombed the railway line again. We should be there by about 15.00 hours if that fits in with your arrangements, Sir?'
'No, I'd rather you make it 3 o'clock, Gordon. I look forward to seeing you again then.' With this last piece of mischief, the phone line went dead, and Winston Churchill was gone. It never ceased to amaze Major Roberts how the Prime Minister could still find time for a leg pull, even

though he was steering this country through its most perilous time in history.

Early on the following morning, Flying Officer Henry Williams, and Pilot Officer, Leonard Knight arrived at a quiet lay-by on the outskirts of Winchelsea. The somewhat less than inconspicuous, bright red London bus sported a destination board which read, 'Out of Service'. The boarding platform had a waist high thick webbing strap, stretched across the entire opening. Leonard unclipped the strap as soon as the bus had pulled up. The engine was left running.

A minute after the bus arrived, an army truck reversed quietly up to the rear of the vehicle. Pleasantries were exchanged and thirteen soldiers, each with a heavy, blanket bound bundle across their shoulder, stepped carefully down from the army vehicle and boarded the ground floor of the bus. Soon, thirteen German soldier's bodies were laid neatly and evenly along the ground floor of the public service vehicle. The British men re-boarded the army lorry. They watched through the canvass flaps as the pilot officer re-attached the webbing strap across the boarding platform. He was heard to call along the bus, 'Standing room only'. He then pressed the red bell button, and a tinny, 'ding ding' could be heard within the body of the bus. With the signal to go, Flying Officer Williams twisted the pre-selector gear knob and the bright red vehicle set off.

'Bloody odd, that one,' said one of the chosen 'transfer team.'
'Yes, why a bloody London bus?' asked another.
'No doubt there will be some extraordinary reasoning behind it, but it seems like it will stand out like a sore thumb. Maybe they just don't have any spare military trucks at that end,'

Chapter 23

Two days later, on Friday 20th September, The Fuhrer was at his command headquarters in Berlin. He had endured a bad night, having hardly slept at all. The sound of bombs landing and buildings crumbling, and great chunks of masonry crashing to the ground, worried him greatly. Hermann Goering had been summoned to his private bunker to explain himself.

'You assured me that the R.A.F. was finished,' hissed The Fuhrer. 'The success of Operation Sealion depended upon it, and yet it appears that the first few ships of the exploratory fleet were totally destroyed at the start of the week. How can this have happened, when you have told me that most of the southern England airfields are out of service? Thank God that I have now made the decision to bring Churchill to his knees by taking Russia. Once this is accomplished, he will have no choice but to agree to our peace terms. We will control the whole of this continent, and we can then starve Britain to death if needed. We will see how proudly he stands then, my friend.'

Goering shifted awkwardly on the hard wooden seat. He knew that he could not lie to The Fuhrer, but knew also that he must say the *correct* thing. 'I apologise, Herr Hitler. My intelligence, backed by hundreds of photographs, indicated severe damage to all of the runways at Biggin Hill, Hawkinge, Kenley, etc, etc. We did not let one of them off the hook. Many aircraft were destroyed on the ground and also in combat, by my brave pilots of the Luftwaffe. Technically it is not possible for them to send their bombers across here without the fighter cover.'

'Tell me then, Herr Goering. How many of these unprotected enemy bombers were shot down last night?' Goering was now sweating profusely. 'None reported so far, Fuhrer,' he choked out.
'How many did you say?' screamed the Fuhrer, as he thumped his fist onto the desk. Almost in a whisper, Hermann Goering, feared head of the mighty Luftwaffe, said, 'None, Sir.'
'So please inform me now, since the bombing raids started on 26th August, nearly one month ago, how many aircraft in total have your brave Luftwaffe fighter pilots claimed?'
Goering could hardly speak. 'Three, Sir.'

'THREE, THREE, THREE!' The Fuhrer was now standing behind his desk and his dark hair had fallen in front of his brow. Hermann Goering wondered where this would end. 'And just so I can completely

understand the picture that you are painting for me, please remind me what is the number of fighters that your brave Luftwaffe boys have lost during this period.'
'At the last count Fuhrer, it is forty seven. The Luftwaffe boss braced himself for the explosion that he knew would come, but it didn't happen. A frantic knocking at the door diverted Adolf Hitler's attention momentarily. 'Come in then,' screamed the Fuhrer. A nervous army officer entered the room carrying a small leather satchel. 'What the hell is this?' The young officer was used to The Fuhrer's outbursts, but he still shook in his boots, whenever he witnessed them. He saluted and shouted, 'Heil Hitler,' before approaching the leader at his desk.

He was again sitting down, and had pushed his fallen dark locks back into position across the top of his forehead, stuck there with his own sweat. 'Fuhrer, it is my duty to inform you that we found thirteen well wrapped bodies in the neighbouring streets, within a one mile radius, at first light. Each had two parachutes attached to it. We have collected them all and taken them to the barracks. The wrappings have all been removed, and sadly, each one is a badly burned German soldier, in what appears to be SS uniform. One man is very highly ranked; he appears to bear the insignia and badge of a Gruppenfuhrer. This satchel was tied around his torso, and the envelope within is personally addressed to you.'

'Leave these items and go.' The young soldier did not need to be told twice. He again saluted in an exaggerated stance and shouted 'Heil Hitler'. He was then gone.
The Fuhrer's mood had changed completely. Hermann Goering felt somewhat relieved, but also fearful of what mood the latest piece of news would evoke in his leader. 'Jesus Christ, this has got to be my friend, Wolfgang Zimmermann. How could he have screwed up? You know, Hermann that I can blow my top sometimes, but I love all of you like my own family. If one of you is lost, I feel the pain as if you were my own son.'

'What does this mean, and what does this letter say?' The Fuhrer leant across his desk to pick up his steel bladed letter opener. A black Swastika was inlaid into the white ivory handle, which he took hold of, sliding the blade into the corner of the envelope. It was now open, and he pulled a short hand written note from within. He noted the quality of the beige vellum paper, and was struck by the black ink handwriting. He read the contents aloud to his Luftwaffe chief.

As he read, his face at first sad, became a picture of rage and hatred.

Dear Adolf,

We are sending your friends home early, as it does not appear that the English climate is suited to them. It is sometimes very hot here at this time of year, especially on the beaches of the South Coast. As you can see, your troops have been quite badly burned.

Perhaps you might like to send them here again during the winter months, but then again, if they really prefer the colder climate, Russia may be a more favourable option.

You will find that the Russians will be as welcoming as the British, although once your boys have had enough, they will be sent home again.

These holiday excursions are so exhausting, don't you think? Anyway, I can't wait to personally welcome you to 'The Gallows'. It is a pleasant little hotel, where our guests just don't ever seem to be able to leave. You will, I know enjoy your short stay, we have perfected the art of producing boiling water from the English Channel, so nobody need go without a nice hot bath.

With very best wishes, from England. Sorry once again that it proved to be too hot for your boys.

Winston.

Hermann Goering studied the painful expression on his Fuhrer's face. He did not know whether he should speak, or keep quiet. Finally, Adolf Hitler almost whispered, 'Bastard. *He WILL pay for this!* Once we have conquered Russia, I will make it my *personal* quest to put a ring of steel around his stupid, tiny island, and eliminate everyone capable of putting up any resistance. We will take away every man between the ages of fourteen to seventy. I will *personally* pull the lever on the gallows when Churchill comes out to surrender.' Every desirable woman in Britain will become our sex slave. The rest can starve. His fury was suddenly spent.

He continued in normal tones, 'For now though, we have to play down this minor defeat. We will deny that any of our troops were ever on English soil. We will deny that we lost a few ships and a few hundred men in the English Channel. It will never make the history books. I shall not allow it. I will make sure that my friend 'WZ' is honoured, and given

a fitting military burial. Go now Hermann, I must speak with my
Generals.'
'Russia *will* be taken in the next few months. Then I will turn my
attentions to what has now become a *very* personal battle.'

Meanwhile, in Pett and the surrounding villages, life was beginning to
return to the normal wartime routine. Sadly though, Ted White had been
forced to leave the special unit, on medical grounds. Both he and his wife
would never recover from the terrible death of their daughter. Ted knew
exactly how Faye had died, but could never tell his wife. She was under
the impression, like the rest of the locals, that her beautiful daughter had
been killed in a gas explosion. Ted would have to live with this lie for the
rest of his days.

Dot Sinden visits her son's grave every Saturday morning, without fail.
She stays for a few minutes and gives him an update on her week's
events. She keeps the grave spotless, as well as the grave of Rogue,
buried in her back garden.

Peter Hawkins could no longer cope with life. He received a discharge
from the army on medical grounds. He was found hanged in the rear
garden of the marital home at Doleham, two months later. Pinned to a
branch of the tree, at the level of the noose, was his favourite picture of
Faye, wearing a white summer dress and hat.

The rest of the special operations team carried on with their lives as usual.
They occasionally spent a night in their woodland hide, although they had
been informed by Major Roberts, that the chances of a further invasion
attempt were greatly lessened. The Prime Minister's intelligence sources
seemed to think that if Hitler ever managed to conquer Russia, he would
seek to make a peaceful settlement with Britain.

Major Burgess continued to command the coastal defence battery, known
as Toot Rock. Not one of the men stationed there ever uttered a word of
the strange events that befell that particular military site. The two local
nurses, Joanne and Christine, both married to serving soldiers, managed
to fall pregnant at the same time. Shortly afterwards, Burgess transferred
Sergeant Joe Parsons and Private Mick Meadows to other duties. They
were seconded to a base in Scotland, where their expertise on gun

emplacements and observation posts, would be utilised at a newly established coastal battery.

The good Doctor Hart carried on with life as the local GP, still treating patients of all ages, for all types of ailments and inflictions. On one occasion, a young boy was rushed into the surgery with his mother, having suffered severe burns to his right hand and arm. A paraffin stove had been knocked over as the lad was falling, having tripped up on a rug. Adrian was physically sick at the sight and smell of the burnt flesh. He started to shake as well. Maureen, his nurse, apologised to the pair and dealt with the lad as best she could. He and his somewhat bemused mother were then sent by taxi cab, directly to the local hospital. Adrian needed a double whisky, and had to take the rest of the day off. He didn't, indeed couldn't explain his behaviour to Maureen.

Badger still sold black market meat to local butchers and housewives. Harry, George and Bill all kept busy at their various trades, but they all still stayed ready. Britain could not have survived without people of such spirit and determination. Eventually the terror and threat that Nazi Germany posed, was annihilated. This was due to the grit, determination and patriotism of similar people all around Britain, our forces in the theatre of war, as well as the rest of our allies. We owe each and every one of them a huge debt of gratitude. Let us never forget why we are a free nation today.

END